Snowfall's Embrace

& Other Graveyard Sagas
from Beyond the Sister Moons

Nathan Sykes

BLUE FORGE PRESS

Port Orchard ✺ Washington

Blue Forge Press is the print division of the volunteer-run, federal 501(c)3 nonprofit, Blue Legacy (EIN 83-4307421), founded in 1989 and dedicated to supporting artisans marginalized due to race, age, disability, economics or other factors. We strive to empower storytellers from all walks of life with our four divisions: Blue Forge Press, Blue Forge Films, Blue Forge Gaming, and Blue Forge Sound. Find out more at www.BlueForgeGroup.org

Blue Forge Press
7419 Ebbert Drive Southeast
Port Orchard, Washington 98367
blueforgepress@gmail.com
360-550-2071 ph.txt

Table of Contents

Inheritance 7

The Beach 25

Legacy 41

Datgelu 55

Ascension 73

Under the Sister Moons 97

Cargo 121

Reckless Abandoned 151

Consumed 189

Synchronous 211

Tales Around the Hearth 241

The Merkon 275

Snowfall's Embrace 303

An Interview with Nathan Sykes 347

Snowfall's Embrace

& Other Graveyard Sagas from Beyond the Sister Moons

Nathan Sykes

Inheritance

How long had he been in the car, Dakota wondered? The sun was setting and it seemed as if he'd been driving the same stretch of road for days. Nothing but desert surrounded him in every direction, and the excitement that had once energized his trip was tired and defeated. He wasn't even blasting the music anymore. All he wanted at this point was to find a motel, climb under some sheets and let sleep take him far away from the mundane scenery he'd been stuck with ever since he crossed over the Arizona state line.

As the sunlight began to fade, Dakota turned the music back up, reached for his pack of cigarettes, and frowned as he pulled the final smoke out. After a long drawn out sigh, he lit it and brought it to his lips, inhaling deeply and banging his head to a song as he rolled down the windows. Every so often he'd see another car on the road and he welcomed the relief that washed over him because it confirmed that he wasn't out here all on his own; that he didn't cross over into some bizarre twilight zone episode, and everything was going to be okay.

This is exactly what happened as his cherry inched its way closer to the filter, a dread crawling along his spine knowing he'd be out of smokes once it got there, but as he passed the car he saw a lone gas station off the side of the road. Dakota couldn't have been happier at the sight, and though he somehow still had a quarter tank of gas left, he figured he'd kill two birds with one stone. He pulled in and stopped at a pump before hopping out and heading toward the building. An elderly Native American, Navajo if he wasn't mistaken, was sitting in a wooden rocking chair outside the entrance.

"Yá'át'ééh!" the old woman blurted as Dakota made eye contact with her when he reached for the door. Dakota froze in place and they just stared at each other for a moment.

"Hey there," he replied and waved, but the woman just looked him up and down and went right back to rocking and staring off into oblivion. A chill came over him and he rushed inside. As much as he was relieved to see other people he couldn't wait to get back in his car and drive away from the place. Dakota grabbed a water from a reach-in refrigerator and then approached the clerk at the front counter, a middle-aged man who was also Native American.

"Yá'át'ééh!" the man greeted him with his booming voice as Dakota set the water onto the counter.

"Yacht... tay..." He tried to return the greeting. The clerk gave him a stern look and he scanned the water as Dakota pulled out his wallet. A sense of déjà vu came over him then, but he quickly dismissed it. He wanted to get his cigarettes and get back on the road.

"You are Navajo, yes?" the man asked.

Dakota paused and had to think for a moment. "My biological father was..."

"Was? I'm sorry to hear that." The man offered his condolences, though his facial expression remained the same.

"Thanks... but I didn't know him. That's actually why I'm

out here. Old man croaked," Dakota continued awkwardly, confused and uncomfortable, "and gave me a very specific window to come..." He trailed off as he noticed the clerk looking him over as if studying him, intrigued that this stranger to his ways was somehow kin. Dakota could see the wheels turning in the man's head and wanted no part of it. He didn't understand how his biological father knew how to find him, and if he had known how to find him then why he only reached out to him in death? If the Navajo he'd met up to this point was any indication as to what his father had been like in life then he was happy the man hadn't, yet he felt a sting in his ribs whenever he thought about it. A bitterness that nestled snugly within his chest cavity, and it was restless and curious.

"Interesting that it's during the lunar eclipse... will it be just the water?" the clerk asked without breaking eye contact, still watching the boy under his scrutinizing gaze. Dakota had felt like breaking the eye contact himself, quite a few times in fact, but a strange powerless sensation had paralyzed him and he hadn't realized that he had been holding his breath until the clerk had asked the question. Immediately, relief flooded his senses as he felt the paralysis of the man's gaze release him, and he was able to breathe again. He looked over the man's shoulders and pointed to the cigarettes behind the counter.

"N-nah," Dakota stammered, and the man's eyes narrowed slightly as they shifted from the boy's eyes to his outstretched finger. "I'll take a pack of Marlboro 27's, and..." Dakota recoiled his hand and began counting bills as he went through his wallet. "Thirty on..." He leaned far enough from the counter to see which pump he was on. "...the pump."

The clerk said nothing, but he retrieved the smokes and took the cash before proceeding to complete the transaction and handing Dakota his change.

"Thanks…" he said awkwardly before hurrying out to his car.

"Fucking weird…" he muttered to himself as the door closed behind him. He heard the creaking of the rocking chair halt and rolled his eyes, cursing himself under his breath. How could he forget the old lady out front? *Stupid!* He avoided looking her way as he started gassing up, packing the cigarettes as he waited. As soon as he heard the pump click he got out of there as quickly as he could.

The sky was a beautiful splash of reds and oranges now, quickly receding from the coming darkness. He lit a smoke, rolled down the windows and blasted the music as he continued his journey, trying to shake off the uncomfortable feeling that had made its home settling in his gut. A while later he noticed a man hitchhiking along the side of the road, far enough from the gas station that he figured they must've been walking for hours. It would be dark soon enough, and the thought of being stranded out here at night made his body shudder, but neither was he ready for another bizarre encounter. As unsettling as the one at the gas station had been, Dakota was still very tired and he knew if he didn't come across a motel soon he'd have to settle for a nap on the side of the road. The thought wasn't a pleasant one, especially with strangers walking about at night. His curiosity got the better of him though, and he lowered the volume of his music, coming to a stop beside the person.

"Hello?" Dakota asked. The guy stopped walking and approached the passenger door. The sun was nearing the horizon and each passing second robbed the world of some more daylight, but at that particular moment it was directly out that window and Dakota had to squint against the light to address the hitchhiker. The man lowered his face to peer in through the window at his would-be savior, blocking the light and giving the boy's eyes a break, but masking his face in darkness as he did so.

"Hey, thanks, man!" the hitchhiker said appreciatively. Dakota could tell the man was older by his voice, maybe in his forty's or fifty's, and the silhouette of his face gave away a bushy beard. "Is it cool if I jump in?" The man asked. Dakota waved him in.

"I won't be on the road long. As soon as I come across a motel I'm stopping," he told the stranger. It was getting dark out and even after they got back on the road, Dakota couldn't quite see his face.

"That's where I was headed anyway," the man said. "Would've taken me all night, but shouldn't take long in the car. Hey, mind if I smoke in here?" Dakota looked over at him smiling. What a grand idea that was.

"Nah, go for it," Dakota told him as he lit one up himself. "So, you live out here?" Dakota asked.

The man laughed. "You could say that. Seems I'm always coming out here. You?"

It was Dakota's turn to laugh. "No way... I can't wait to get out of here." They smoked their cigarettes in silence after that. Then, after a bit of time passed, the older man spoke up.

"You're going, and I'm coming." He chuckled, almost as if to himself.

"What was that?" Dakota asked, not sure if he'd heard the guy clearly.

"Hey look at that!" he exclaimed, a finger pointing ahead. "And there we have it." Dakota looked and sure enough, there, finally, a motel. He parked the car and the guy hopped out, shut the door and leaned in. "Thanks again. See ya around, kid." He shot a couple finger guns his way, making that clicking sound one does, and then he was gone. Dakota was just relieved to have a bed to sleep in for the night. He lingered in the car to finish his smoke and closed his eyes as he relaxed against the seat. Then he rolled the windows up and walked into the lobby half expecting an awkward or eerie confrontation with someone.

He was fortunate enough to get a room without incident, and he felt really good about helping someone out too, nearly collapsing onto the bed when he shut the door behind him. He couldn't wait to sleep. He pulled his toothbrush and toothpaste from his bag and started brushing his teeth. It wasn't until he went to spit in the sink that he noticed something off in the reflection. Was he really that tired? He'd heard of sleep deprivation causing hallucinations, so he tried to shake it off. He reluctantly looked up at the mirror to see himself staring back, and all seemed normal. He reached up to turn off the faucet and screamed when his reflection grabbed his hand.

The reflection put a finger to its lips as it began to move forward, leaving the confines of the mirror. Dakota tore his hand away and fell backwards onto the floor, watching as the reflection climbed down from the sink counter, moving toward him. He began to hyperventilate as he crawled backwards into the room, his heart pounding in his ears. "No, no, no, no, no, no!" He screamed, but the words echoed in the room as the reflection screamed them as well. "Stop!" They yelled in unison as Dakota's back hit the side of the bed. The reflection kept moving toward him and he had nowhere else to go, his body paralyzed with fear, and tears welling up in the corners of his eyes.

His doppelganger opened his eyes impossibly wide until

the eyes were encompassed by a darkness all around them, seemingly hovering in place. Dakota's heart was now beating so fast it felt like it was going to explode in his chest. Light began shining from behind the floating eyeballs of his reflection as it lowered itself down to his level, its face now just inches from his own. The lights got so bright he couldn't see its eyes anymore. Snot was running from his nose and a couple tears streamed down his cheeks, his quick breaths raspy and shallow as the lights became so bright they were blinding, and he could no longer make out a face.

Horns blared from the oncoming vehicle as it swerved to avoid hitting him. Dakota screamed, locked his fingers around the steering wheel and breathed a sigh of relief as he steadied the car on the road. *What in the actual fuck?* It had taken a moment to calm down, realizing it had just been a dream... a really messed up dream, but the adrenaline was dissipating. He went to light a cigarette with a shaky hand when he realized he was alone in the car. "What the hell?" he said aloud to nobody. Already shaken up, and now thoroughly confused, he pulled over to the side of the road. He gave himself a minute to process everything that just happened until he'd calmed down a bit. When he killed the engine, the silence that greeted him was unnerving. Goosebumps crawled along his limbs as he sat in the driver's seat listening intently. It was as if someone had muted the world.

He opened the door and climbed out of the car. The sound of it shutting behind him did little to put him at ease. His body was still recovering from the shock, but when Dakota stretched his arms high above his head the sensation felt so good he nearly toppled over. He groaned as his limbs reached their limits, then lit a cigarette and leaned against the car. He hung his head back with his eyes closed and took in a deep breath. The crisp night air filled his lungs and after holding it there for a second or two, he exhaled. It helped shake off the twilight zone feeling, and when he finally opened his eyes he was struck by a raw and unhindered view. No city lights polluted the sky. There weren't any lights anywhere except in the heavens. He couldn't believe how beautiful the night sky was out here, away from civilization. The stars were so much brighter than back home and he felt himself relax for the first time.

The immediate awe that had overcome him only multiplied tenfold when he noticed a shooting star, then another, and another. A grin found its way upon his handsome, albeit exhausted face as he took it all in. He scanned the night sky as he brought the cigarette to his lips, but stiffened up when his eyes fell upon the moon. It was completely dark, and he remembered something about there being a lunar eclipse. The image forced his mind to revisit the gas station and the memory seemed the least of all the strange things he'd experienced that day. Shaking the thoughts away, he tried looking at it from a different perspective and found that it was quite fascinating. He shrugged and diverted his attention back to the cosmic wonders splashed across the sky as if it were a tapestry hanging up above, an art gallery made just for him in that moment. He lost track of time and couldn't recall how many cigarettes he'd smoked while stargazing. His eyes fell upon the dark moon once more. Dakota stared at the lunar eclipse curiously. How long was a lunar eclipse supposed to last? He was about to check the time when he picked up on a faint sound coming from somewhere out in the vast darkness surrounding him. He immediately sprung up from the car and threw the smoke at his feet, putting it out.

He strained his ears in a particular direction trying to

make out the sound. After a moment it became loud enough to discern, and it sounded like something was running across the desert sand. It was definitely some sort of creature, and it sounded like it was running straight for his car! A panicked yelp erupted from his mouth as he ran to the car, jumped into the driver's seat, and fumbled in his pockets for the keys but dropped them into the driver's footwell. As he was about to retrieve them, silence once again overcame him. Dakota froze with one hand extended toward his feet. Whatever had been running through the desert had stopped, but it had been somewhere nearby. Cold sweat broke out above his brow and his hand began to tremble as he held his breath and listened intently.

Nothing. Nothing at all. It was too weird to dismiss, but he reached forward and grabbed the keys from the floor and sat up. Once he started the car he checked his rearview mirror out of habit, and behind his car, illuminated in red light was a person. "Are you kidding me!?" Dakota was tired. He was exhausted from the constant adrenaline and frights, and he was beginning to think he was losing his mind. "Who's there?" He screamed out the window. "I will run a mother fucker over! Test me!" He put the car in reverse and checked the rearview mirror again. Nothing. Shoving the shifter back into park Dakota finally lost it. He started screaming and crying, convulsing with rage and frustration, and hitting the steering wheel over and over again.

"You alright, kid?" A man's voice came from outside the driver's side window. Dakota couldn't scream anymore otherwise he would've, didn't stop him from nearly shitting his pants though. He instinctively leaned toward the passenger seat and looked out the window with wild eyes, using his arm to wipe his face. It didn't sound like the guy he'd picked up earlier, if that guy had even been real.

"Who are you? What do you want?" he asked, his hand ready to put the car into drive and get out of there in an instant. When his eyes finally adjusted and he saw who it was his he wished he had run the man over when he had seen him in the brake lights. The man from the gas station! "It's you? From the gas station?" Dakota squealed angrily.

The man bent over enough to look into the car and waved. "I told you it was a lunar eclipse tonight..."

Dakota began screaming at the top of his lungs. He screamed profanities, curses, indecipherable gibberish, and peeled off the side of the road.

"Wait, kid! I'm tryna help!" the man yelled but the boy couldn't hear him.

He was flooring the gas pedal and flying down the empty desert road. He didn't care about his biological father's inheritance anymore. He wasn't even curious anymore. He just wanted to get the hell out of Arizona and back to a city where things made sense. Then he saw the hitchhiker again as his headlights shined over him. The person shrouded by the darkness of night shot a couple finger guns at him. He couldn't hear them obviously, but his brain still registered those clicking sounds all the same. Thoroughly confused, Dakota just kept accelerating, his brain moving even faster than his car. Then he saw the hitchhiker again, sticking his thumb out as they did. He just kept going... then he saw them again, and again... and again! Finger guns! "What's happening!?" he cried out to himself in a state of pure panic.

As he approached a hundred miles per hour, his high beams pouring light upon the street for what seemed like miles, a creature ran into the road. At first glance it looked like a really large coyote, but then it stood on its hind legs and he saw the eyes glow the way animal eyes do when light reflects off of them. Dakota screamed again and he swerved, narrowly missing the huge creature and spinning out of control until the car hit the dirt or sand, and started flipping over and over. A cloud of dust and dirt swarmed around the upside-down car once it settled in place, and Dakota started coughing and groaning. "C'mon Dakota! *Wake up!*" he screamed at himself. "This can't be real..."

Still buckled in and hanging from his seat with his face squished between the airbag and the ceiling, one hand searched for the buckle while the other pushed the airbag away from his face. *CLICK!* Dakota fell from his seat. He started to crawl out of the open window when he glanced into the side view mirror, about to scream at himself to wake up again.

His reflection grinned and screamed at him instead. "*Boo!*"

He didn't know his voice could reach such a high pitch, but he managed to do so as he punched the mirror over and over until his knuckles were bleeding. Then he pulled himself free of the wreckage, trying to wrap his brain around everything happening, and could only hope this was some twisted nightmare. Covered in scrapes and blood, a horrified Dakota realized this was no dream. He began looking around frantically, expecting the hitchhiker to approach him at any moment, or for that creature to attack ferociously, but neither came. Instead, Dakota saw headlights coming down the road. He lunged behind his wrecked car and out of sight.

A truck began its short trek from the road to the site of his crash, but Dakota was paranoid now. As far as he was concerned, anything could happen. He didn't know how to rationalize anything that had happened on his trip so he didn't try. He also knew if he told anyone that they'd think he was crazy... maybe he was crazy? Maybe he's just sitting on the side of the road having a seizure? Part of him hoped that was the case. He hung his head in defeat... what was he supposed to do? He was at the mercy of whoever was driving this truck, and he was too tired and beaten to put up a fight or try to flee.

The truck's headlights lit up the entire area and Dakota sat in the shadow of his car. He heard the door open and close, and footsteps walking toward him. "Kid?" a voice called out. Of course. "Are you alright, kid?"

After a long, resigned sigh, Dakota stood with his hands up. "What do you want?" he asked. "I don't have any money..."

The man from the gas station chuckled. "I'm not tryna rob you, kid. I'm tryna help. I'm sure you've seen some weird things tonight, yeah?" he asked ominously.

Dakota lowered his hands slowly, unsure what to expect. "What's going on?" he asked incredulously.

The man from the gas station looked around nervously. "Get in the truck and I'll explain everything."

Dakota scoffed openly at the request. "You're mad if you think I'm getting in that truck. Tell me now. I don't know you!" The stranger put his hands up to gesture he meant no harm, and his shoulders sagged in defeat.

"Alright, but it's not safe out here." He began walking toward the truck as he went on. "Didn't think it was strange that your old man requested you arrive during the lunar eclipse?"

Dakota grumbled. "He wasn't my old man. I never knew him... and what does the lunar eclipse have to do with anything?" As if the question was an invitation for them to take in the sight, they both looked at the moon, still fully eclipsed. "Is the eclipse supposed to last this long?" Dakota asked ignorantly.

"It hasn't," the man answered without skipping a beat. "It hasn't been eclipsed for very long at all." Dakota's jaw dropped. "It's been eclipsed for at least an hour…"

The man looked at him with pity. "It hasn't though. Listen… Your father…"

Dakota groaned again. "You knew him then?" He interrupted.

"I'm tryna explain, kid. Your father lived out here in the middle of nowhere, all alone. He isolated himself from the world. He was cursed, and now that curse seeks a new host: you. We've gotta try and break it before the end of the eclipse." The man explained. Dakota couldn't believe what he was hearing, but he wasn't foolish enough to scoff at the man or argue anything he was saying…not after all he'd seen and been through since arriving in Arizona.

"Alright… how do you know all this?" Dakota asked him.

"I am Navajo. The whole tribe knows this. It is believed there is nothing to be done about it… so we choose to let it run its course, and we stay out of its way, but your father and I believed there was a way. We have to get to his house, now. We don't have much time!" Dakota had no choice and the man seemed to genuinely want to help, so he got into the truck. They sped off into the darkness of the desert, and Dakota saw the hitchhiker out in the middle of nowhere.

He gasped and pointed. "Did you see that guy?" he shouted. "I keep seeing that guy trying to hitchhike everywhere. He was in a dream of mine too! Who is he?" The driver nodded and looked over at Dakota briefly, eyes wide, then turned his attention back to the driving.

"It's the curse Dakota. Don't pay attention to it!" the man told him.

Dakota looked at him inquisitively. "How do you know my name?" he asked. The man ignored his question as he drove them further into the desert. Dakota saw the hitchhiker again, but this time he started running after the car. Wide eyed, Dakota turned to see the man keeping up with the truck and was about to say something when he drifted further and further back until he couldn't see him anymore.

"Don't look at it!" the man begged as he pulled Dakota around. "Listen!"

It wasn't long before they arrived at a house in the middle of nowhere. It was a small shack nestled up against a giant rock. They got out and Dakota followed the man into the house. Immediately, Dakota noticed the disarray of everything. Things were flung all around like there had been a huge struggle there recently. Candles were lit everywhere, and despite the shack being haphazardly constructed, the air was eerily still inside. Dakota picked up a faced down picture on the floor and flipped it over. The man from the gas station was in the photo with another man, presumably his father. There were other pictures on the walls, and all of them had the two men together throughout the years. "Were you guys related or something?"

The man ignored Dakota as he ventured further into the shack, revealing a hidden door at the back. There was a cave in the huge rock at the back of the makeshift house that led down into the earth. "Down here!" the man said frantically. Dakota took a step, then stopped. "What's down there?" he asked.

"Look, kid, we have to do this soon!" he said, nearing a panic. The door to the shack crashed open. They both turned to see a figure moving toward them.

"Thanks, Uncle," the newcomer said. "You brought him straight to me." Dakota looked to the man from the gas station with accusation written all over his face. "Get him down there so we can get this over with," Dakota heard the man say to his uncle.

"*No!*" Dakota screamed. "What do you want with me?" Dakota's face was getting hot and his heart was thumping against his chest now. How did he end up here?

The uncle began pleading for this to end. "I'm not going to let you do this!" he yelled at the hitchhiker. "Dakota come... *No!*" Dakota turned around to face the intruder just in time to see him swinging a heavy object at his face. Then the world went dark.

He could hear voices, but they were muffled. He tried to open his eyes but they felt droopy. He could see the flickering of flames through his eyelids though, and feel the heat against his skin. He heard shamanic drumming, humming, some rattling, and chanting. His heart began racing again. He opened his mouth to scream but he didn't have the energy necessary for such an attempt. He could hear a struggle as the voices became more and more clear. "Don't do this!" the uncle begged. "We can break the cycle!" Dakota managed to open his eyes now as he groaned from the pain in his head. He tried to move his arms and legs but they were restrained.

The assaulter walked over to Dakota and grabbed his chin in his hand. He turned Dakota toward him so he could see his face for the first time. He must've been in his mid-forties, a bushy beard protruding from his face, a necklace of bones around his neck, long hair to his shoulders, and a crazed look in his wild eyes. Those eyes... he knew those eyes! "Yeah... you see now, don't you?" the man observed.

"But... it's impossible... how?" Dakota asked.

The man shrugged nonchalantly and smirked in Dakota's

face. "I don't know the ins and outs of the curse Dakota..." He paused and scrunched up his face. "Still weird... all I know is, this is the way it has to be."

Dakota was in shock. He still couldn't process what was happening. "But... how are you, you? How are you here?" This had to be a nightmare. There was no other explanation.

The man squeezed Dakota's chin and looked annoyed then. He moved closer to Dakota's face, his face staring back at him... well, an older him. "I don't know! But you're what's going," the man, the older version of himself, emphasized his point by turning away from him and pointing away, before returning his crazed gaze back to his younger self. "...and *I'm* what's coming!" he said as he pointed to himself. "There is nothing you can do to stop it. There is no escaping it. It is inevitable, and now..." He squeezed Dakota's face even tighter, turning it to face the other man. "You're gonna watch this."

The older Dakota released the younger Dakota's face and walked toward their uncle. *His* uncle! He had an uncle... his head was in a fog, trying to keep up with everything. The older him grabbed an ornamental knife as he walked over to their uncle. "This wasn't how it was supposed to be, but here you are uncle. Should've stayed out of it."

Dakota sensed a semblance of regret in his older self's words. He looked from him to his uncle, to the knife and put two and two together. It was a sacrificial dagger. "No!" Dakota tried to scream, but it only came out as a whimper. "Please! Don't do this!" It was too late.

The older Dakota prepared for the killing blow and the tempo of the drums quickened, working toward a crescendo, the rattling and the chanting became louder with every second, and then the older Dakota drove the knife into his uncle's heart.

The drums, the chants, the hums and the rattles all abruptly stopped at once, replaced by a silence accented only by their uncle's pained cries. Dakota watched the killer twist the knife until their uncle's cries of pain were silenced, and his body slack. Then he slid the knife out and took it to the center of the ritual, or shrine, or whatever it was. Dakota wished he had learned of his heritage, of his family and their beliefs long ago, but it was too late.

The older Dakota began speaking in tongues and flicked his uncle's blood on his younger self. Dakota's vision became blurry and the room seemed to swirl and breathe. Inhale. Exhale. Everything was changing. He was changing. He heard the restraints clank against the floor of the cave as he dropped freely to his knees, tears running down his face. He barely registered the smile on his older self's face before he shot him a couple finger guns, making that cringe-worthy clicking sound as he did, then vanished through the only exit.

Dakota let out a feral agonizing scream that reverberated off the walls. He could hear his bones snapping apart and grinding against one another. He could feel his blood boiling beneath the surface, and his limbs twisting this way and that. His face felt like it was going to explode as it seemed to contort and crush itself. He heard his cries change into deep guttural sounds, and he dropped to the floor rolling around as his body turned against him, human teeth dropping into the dirt.

Dakota leaped to his feet and began smashing his face against the stone wall, but nothing would stop the pain. He could hear everything! He could hear rodents and insects clambering around the desert in search of food, the wind sending a nearby tumbleweed rolling away, and the other Dakota's steps becoming fainter and fainter until they were gone. The flickering light of the flames blinded him, and when he lifted his arm to cover his eyes it was no longer his arm, but a long furry limb that ended in claws. He looked around for a mirror, and finding none he lunged for the exit. He moved so quickly he hit the threshold of the opening instead, nearly sending himself staggering back to the floor. He flew up the secret passage and into his late father's hut, found a mirror and what he saw looking back at him was not of this world.

He screamed in horror, but only grunts and growls came out. He'd become a giant beast that somewhat resembled a coyote wearing his eyes! Throwing the mirror against a far wall, it shattered into pieces and he flew from the shack out into the desert, screaming and crying. He tried to speak, to call out for help... but still, the only sounds that came forth were guttural, feral and beastly. He traversed the desert terrain quickly... so fast and effortlessly he almost found a joy in it. Then he heard a car in the distance heading his way. It wasn't until the headlights blinded him that he came to an abrupt stop upon the asphalt and stared in disbelief as his car swerved off the road, flipping over, and over again.

The Beach

For Katie

Bruce and Katherine Swan parked at their favorite beach. They'd been going there on their anniversary every year for the entirety of their forty odd years of marriage. Their relationship was far from perfect, but they loved each other and never gave up on one another. Bruce held his wife as they made their way down to the beach, smiling and reminiscing on their life together.

He had been fresh out of the military and starting a new life. He was new to the company that had hired him, and had felt so utterly alone. The people kept to themselves mostly, giving him a wide berth whenever he roamed from his office. He had suffered from PTSD and was barely sleeping, had no friends, and got anxious around loud noises and large groups of people. He had been lonely and depressed until the day he ran into Katherine.

For whatever reason, he decided to venture to the campus cafeteria that morning before starting on his work for the day. He remembered the noise... it had been so loud and overwhelming that he had nearly turned around and opted out of breakfast, but then he'd heard someone scream his name. "Bruce!" It was a woman's voice, barely audible over the

"

morning buzz and chatter of the lunch room. He hadn't even had the time to process what was happening when arms flung around him in a tight embrace, a face buried in his shoulder.

It was Katherine, an old friend from high school he had lost touch with throughout his service. They had never been more than friends, but some of his fondest memories from school were with the woman. He remembered the warmth and the hope that had swelled within him when he returned the embrace, and from that moment on they had been inseparable. Even now, after all the years of marriage, Bruce still loved Katherine with every fiber of his being. In fact, their love had only ever grown stronger. That's the funny thing about love... the hard times eventually fade away, leaving only the good times to recall when couples were lucky enough to make it that far.

The couple reached the sand and found a nice spot on some driftwood with plenty of time to relax before the sunset. He continued holding her as they gazed out toward the horizon. In her youth she had been the one to keep him warm, but as they got older the ocean breeze learned how to chill her to the bone, and so the roles had been reversed. This was Katherine's favorite place. The beach was one of the first places she'd ever taken Bruce. She told him it was the most magical place in the world, and even though it seemed like an ordinary beach to him in every way, he had never disputed her claim. Perhaps he was just too smitten, but he liked to think he was preserving the child-like spirit that nestled within her, what little was left of it anyway.

They had shared so many stories laying on this beach; so many romantic and intimate memories were attached to the place. They had made love on the beach under the infinite majesty of the unencumbered night sky. They'd made life-long friends out of total strangers walking on these sands. They'd spoken their vows and gotten married there, raised a family and brought their children many times over the years. Music and dancing, bonfires and parties, cuddles, kisses, and the laughter! Bruce opened his bag and pulled a couple beverages out, toasting the love of his life.

"Happy anniversary my love. My heart will always be yours," he told her, his smile wearing the wrinkles of a lifetime of experience. There was no need for her to respond. He knew exactly how she felt, and their embrace tightened as they looked to the horizon, awaiting the unparalleled beauty of the sun setting where the ocean met the sky. He gave her a kiss as it started and they watched the sun slowly slip away from their world, inviting darkness across the land. Bruce sipped on his drink all the while they took it in, basking in the beauty that never left them disappointed... always leaving them in awe and filled with love and wonder.

As the darkness chased the last remaining remnants of another year away, Bruce pulled away from Katherine and looked at his wife as he rested his hands upon her. "You saved me, you know," he told her. "You taught me how to live again. How to enjoy the beauty of life. You woke me up inside... a part of me I didn't even know existed, and I'll love you forever for it." A tear slid down his cheek as he finished his drink and gave her a smile once more. A couple shooting stars whizzed past overhead, and the milky way was now visible. "Why did you have to go? I miss you so much."

Tears welled up in the corners of his eyes as he cradled the jar of Katherine's ashes in his lap. He opened another beer and started washing that one down as well. "I wish I could just talk to you one last time..." He was on the verge of sobbing, but pulled himself together. Katherine had asked for her ashes to be scattered along her beach, but after six years Bruce still couldn't bring himself to fulfill her wishes. Their son had offered to do it for him, and their daughter offered to go with him and help... to be there for him, but he didn't want to put it on them. He promised them both he'd finally do it though, and he unscrewed the lid from the jar.

"I miss you so much!" he cried, heaving as he began stepping toward the water. "I don't want to do this anymore... not without you!" Bruce stepped into the wet sand and kept walking forward. He was mentally preparing himself to finally scatter her ashes into the waves. The sunset and the stars that quickly followed were her favorite part of the beach. The time was now. Bruce wiped the tears from his face with the sleeve of his jacket and gripped the jar. "We will see each other again, I promise."

Just as the man was about to scatter her ashes his chest tightened up, and the heartbreak that had been squeezing the cavity from the inside slid down into his stomach. He changed his mind at the last second and pulled the jar in to his chest, embracing his love, unable to let her go, but the movement as the tide came in and past his legs caused his world to spin. Bruce nearly collapsed into the water but he saved himself and in doing so accidentally let the jar slip from his grasp. As the water receded back into the ocean it had taken his Katherine as well, he realized as he examined the empty jar.

The old man cried like a baby, collapsing to his knees, his head hanging down in defeat. He lost his wife all over again and the heart wrenching pain that followed was enough for him to follow her into the watery depths, but as that thought solidified into a plan, the tide came back in with a crashing wave. The wave glowed blue, Katherine's favorite color, and Bruce swept the jar into the water out of pure instinct. Nothing but desperation drove the action, but she'd already been lost and it was the best he could do. He brought it up to his face to examine it and his eyes were wide with wonder. There, in the jar that had held his wife's ashes just moments earlier, now held glowing sea water.

When Bruce got home he placed the jar on the dresser and clambered into bed. He struggled with the night's events as he lied there, the soft blue glow illuminating the room. He felt torn. On the one hand, he finally scattered Katherine's ashes like he should've years prior, and on the other, he was not ready to do so. However, the magical glowing water that appeared afterward seemed to be a decent replacement for the man, suppressing the heartbreak he would've surely felt otherwise. His mind raced though as Katherine filled every crevice of his thoughts.

Bruce had never felt so warm or safe from a simple touch, but his late wife had that effect on him. She knew him inside and out, and even when there was nothing to say to each other, her presence filled him with peace and tranquility. More than that though, she filled him with love... an unconditional love he'd never known apart from their children. Strangely, he felt that from the ominous blue glow that emanated from the jar, and soon fell asleep. She held him and whispered sweet words in his ear. Her hand traced along his skin and her lips pressed against his face. They embraced each other on the beach and stargazed for what seemed like hours, bantering back and forth and laughing at one another's quirky mannerisms. As the sun rose, she turned to him and her body stiffened as if a realization had just dawned on her with the new day. She looked at him inquisitively, an accusation on her lips. "Why didn't you answer Bruce? This is your fault!"

Bruce sat up in bed, tears streaming down his cheeks. He wiped them away as he stood up and stumbled into the kitchen. He started brewing some coffee and then sat outside and waited for it to finish. When it was done he went back outside and began sipping it when his phone rang. It was his daughter. "Hi sweetie," he answered.

"Were you able to..." she began to ask and trailed off.

Bruce rubbed his eyes and took a deep breath. "Yeah. Yeah I did it," he answered.

"Thank you, dad, that's really good," she replied. "How are you feeling? Are you okay?"

Bruce suddenly remembered the jar of water. He stood up and carried his coffee into the house and headed to his room. "Yeah..." He choked on the word. "Yes, I'm good, I'm okay. Thank you for asking. Something incredible happened though. You won't believe it," he told his daughter.

"Oh yeah?" she asked. "What happened?"

As Bruce walked into his room though, the first thing he noticed was the absence of the jar. His heart began racing. "Dad?" he heard his daughter ask. Bruce gasped as he noticed the jar on the floor at the foot of the bed, open and empty. "What is it? Is everything okay?"

Bruce felt as though his soul were being ripped in half. "Carol let me..." he stammered. "Can I call you back, please?"

"Okay..." she started to say.

"Thanks sweetie. I love you."

"Love you too, dad..."

He hung up the phone and collapsed to his knees. He started feeling the rug for any signs of spilled water but there were none. The rug was dry. He began desperately searching the floor for spilled water but the more he searched and found nothing but dry floor, the more frantic he became in his search. Tears began dropping to the floor and he sat up against the end of the bed, his breaths coming heavy, and he wiped his face.

"What's wrong?" he heard a familiar voice ask. His heart stopped. The voice was sweet and compassionate, and though familiar, it was oddly foreign. It had a melodic ring to it, but there was no mistaking Katherine's voice. Bruce didn't look at first. What if it was some twisted trick of his brain caused by the overwhelming sadness that she was actually gone now, and she wasn't really there? "Are you okay?" the voice asked again. He looked then, and there in the room with him was something miraculous and out of this world beautiful.

There was a small woman, about the size of a six-year-old girl though it was no child, except it wasn't a woman either. Her skin was blue and reminded him of a jellyfish, and she was glowing much like a jellyfish might... much like the water in the jar had. Her hair wasn't hair but tendrils, like one might see sprouting from a sea anemone, but they were assorted on her head in such a way they resembled Katherine's favorite hairstyle when they were younger.

Other than those obviously inhuman differences, the woman before him was his Katherine. She had Katherine's face... her eyes. Though they were not human eyes they were still Katherine's eyes. She had her smile, and she looked at him with compassion and worry much like Katherine had throughout the decades of their relationship anytime he wasn't okay. She had always known when he wasn't okay, even when he tried to weather the storm on his own. He found no joy in worrying her, and he never sought her pity or attention in that way. Bruce stared in disbelief. "Yes..." he said, unsure of himself. "I think so. Is that really you Kat?"

The small woman tilted her head and studied him. "Kat?" she asked, more to herself than to him. "...I don't know." She came closer to him, never taking her eyes off of him, and continued studying his face. She lifted a hand to his face and touched his cheek gently, much like Katherine would on so many occasions. "What's your name?"

Bruce choked on his words. He couldn't believe what was happening, but it was a miracle! It took every fiber of his being not to burst out in tears before the magnificence of the glowing image of his late wife. Swallowing the emotions clumping in his throat, he placed a hand over her hand upon his cheek, something he would've done before. Other than a smooth texture and cooler temperature, it wasn't too strange. A shudder ran through the woman's body as their hands met, and she looked at him lovingly. "My name is Bruce," he told her.

"Bruce..." she echoed. "Bruce..." She repeated his name several times, and each time she spoke it with more confidence, as if it were a name she'd heard a million times. "I know that name..."

Bruce choked again, a single tear running down his cheek. "Yes, you do Katherine."

The blue woman withdrew her hand from his face and placed it over her heart, or where a human's heart would be. "Katherine..."

Bruce smiled, his lips quivering. "Yes. Do you remember?"

She shook her head. "It's familiar, but I don't remember anything."

An idea came over Bruce and he got up and took her hand. "Come with me," he said. "I have an idea!" He walked her through the house and showed her all the family pictures on the walls, her favorite chair, things of hers that he'd held onto and the view outside the house. Each thing he showed her seemed to send another shudder through her body and she would show signs of recognition, especially when looking at pictures of their children.

They sat outside on the bench they used to share when she was alive. They looked out to the lake and the trees they had fallen in love with when they originally bought the home. The closest neighbors were a quarter of a mile in either direction and Bruce wasn't the least bit concerned about anyone seeing the little blue woman. She gazed out into the lake in awe and stood up, moving slowly toward the water, but with each step her pace hastened.

"Be careful!" Bruce yelled after her before getting up and following her to the shore. She ran straight into the water disappearing beneath the surface. Bruce quickened his pace and attempted to run when she vanished under the water, but he tripped and fell to the ground hard, crying out in pain as he did so. The woman popped out of the water laughing and splashing, reveling in the element that had gifted her life. She flew through the water as if she were a bird flying through the air effortlessly, and grinning from ear to ear all the while.

"Hey!" she yelled for Bruce. "Come join me!" When she got no response, she looked around concerned, and was stepping out from the lake a moment later. She ran up to him when she spotted him. "Are you okay?" she asked alarmingly. She helped him up and he was grimacing in pain. She wrapped him in a hug and her body pulsed with a brighter glow than before. Bruce realized he was being held by a full-sized woman now, one the exact height and frame of Katherine when they had first reunited, and squeezed her back. He began to sob in her arms.

"Oh no!" she cried as her arms loosened around him. "Did I hurt you?" But Bruce didn't let her let go, burying his face into her.

"No, no, no!" he cried in response. "You could never hurt me, Kat." He felt his body lighten. Suddenly, the pain from his fall had seceded, and then the arthritis in his limbs stopped throbbing. His joints no longer fought against him, and his back pain was gone as well. He pulled away just enough to see her body pulsing with light, but with each pulse the brightness of her glow dimmed. "Stop!" he pleaded.

Katherine pulled away and the look on her face told Bruce she was confused and hurt. "No, Kat, I didn't mean it like that," he said. "I feel a lot better, thank you, but you don't need to keep helping me if it's hurting you. Please, just a hug." They embraced one another and her body just continued glowing as it had before. "You're bigger now," he told her. "Was it the water?"

"I think so!" she said gleefully, a wide smile on her beautiful face. "Come! It's amazing!" She pulled him to the water and he stripped down to his underwear. He went in with her and she held him as she moved through the water gracefully, and he found himself grinning just as much as her. The wind against his face as they sped around the lake reminded him of what it felt like to go horseback riding, free and boundless. They laughed together, and by the time they left the water Bruce felt like a young man again.

When they finally went inside, he showed her the family photo album she had put together in her previous life. Looking through it together, it seemed like every page they flipped her eyes got bigger and brighter. "Bruce..." she said suddenly, wearing a knowing smile upon her face. "I remember! Oh

Bruce!" She wrapped him in a hug and kissed him. He held onto her tightly with all his soul, he held her. He buried his face against her neck, his eyes glossing over.

"I'm so sorry I didn't answer your call that day!" he cried. "I had so much going on... I was going to call back but..."

"*Shhhh...*" Katherine shushed him as she rocked him in her arms. "It wasn't your fault honey. Don't do that to yourself." Bruce buckled under the pain of the guilt he'd been carrying around for years, blaming himself for the accident that had taken his wife's life. If he would have answered her call that day maybe things would've turned out differently. Maybe she wouldn't have died, but by the time he was able to call her back it was too late. She was already gone. She'd forgiven him... it wasn't his fault, and she still loved him anyways.

They cried and kissed and held each other for what seemed like hours. They made love, embracing one another, and talked until time itself forgot about them. He told her all about their children and their lives. Then he remembered he was supposed to call their daughter back. Katherine remained quiet as he made the call.

"Hey dad, everything okay?" Carol asked when she picked up.

"Hi sweetie," he said. He looked over and saw Katherine tear up at the sound of her voice. "Yeah, everything is okay. Thanks for checking in. I love you." They spoke for a few minutes before getting off the phone, and Katherine seemed sad that she could not tell her daughter she loved her as well, but so happy to hear her voice.

The next couple weeks were magical for Bruce and Katherine. They spent all their time doing all the things they used to do together, so long as it didn't involve exposing her to other people. She was fine with that because she knew no good would come of it. They held each other like they never wanted to let go, and would lie together talking all night. Bruce's heart was full again. He tried to invite the kids over but Katherine wouldn't let him. They had already made peace with her passing and she didn't want to stir anything up for them.

They spent a lot of their time in the lake. Bruce felt young again every time Katherine pulled him along the water faster than any boat he'd ever been on. She loved being in the water just as much. One of the days when they left the water, Katherine found an injured bird struggling to move. She healed it the same way she had healed Bruce, and it flew away. She felt herself grow weaker, but she didn't mind. She had always had a kind, selfless heart, and she was able to help in a way she hadn't been able to before.

Another day while Bruce napped peacefully, Katherine spotted a familiar dog wandering nearby. It was one of their neighbors' dogs, a lab that the neighbor's children absolutely adored. It collapsed in a thicket of trees and Katherine approached it sensing something was wrong. She felt the animal's heart failing somehow, and her presence didn't disturb the poor thing at all. It just lied there whining quietly. Soon the dog was as good as new and running home.

Another week would pass and Bruce noticed her glow had been slowly fading. She assured him she was fine but he did everything he could to help her. He gave her salt baths in the tub and tried taking her into the lake. He tried everything and anything he could think of, but her glow just kept fading, slowly yet surely. A distraught Bruce begged her to tell him if there was anything he could do to help but she just smiled and told him he already had. Bruce promised her he'd figure something out, but continued giving her salt baths because it was the only thing that seemed to bring some of her glow back.

One night as she laid in the tub there was a knock on the door. She heard Bruce answer it and invite the visitors in. It was their son Jacob and his wife Sharon. She desperately wanted to see him, but she knew it wasn't wise. She remained in the tub and a little while later Bruce came to check on her.

"You're aging," he said sadly. "I don't want to lose you again." He kneeled at the tub, tears welling up in his eyes. "What do we do?" Katherine smiled at him and shook her head.

"None of that... the time we've had has been magical," she replied. "How is Jacob?" One look at the woman and Bruce knew he wasn't going to be able to divert the conversation back to her health.

"He's good," he said. "Carol asked him to check on me, I guess. I assured him everything was fine, but he knows when I'm not okay. He insisted they stay the night." Katherine gave him a look. "I know. I tried telling him it isn't necessary, but he isn't taking no for an answer. They already unloaded the car and..."

Katherine put a finger over Bruce's lips. "Calm honey. Everything will be okay." She pulled him in close and held his head in her hands, kissing his forehead. "Our children love you. Let them love you."

Later that night as Bruce, Jacob and Sharon slept, Katherine sensed something was amiss. She couldn't pinpoint what it was exactly, but it was similar to how she felt when she approached the neighbor's dog, except different somehow. She quietly made her way through the house, following the sensation as it grew stronger and stronger until she got to the spare bedroom where her son and his wife slept. She felt life slipping away, and in a panic, she opened the door thinking one of them was in peril.

Her son and his wife were sleeping peacefully however, and a confused Katherine wandered the room double checking and triple checking that everything was okay. Jacob and Sharon were just fine, but the sensation that life was slipping away was an urgent and alarming one, begging for her intervention. She approached Jacob first, illuminating him in a soft blue glow. Her hands hovering over his body, she checked for any signs of injury but he was perfectly okay.

She moved on to Sharon, repeating the same motions with her hands and stopped as they hovered above her abdomen. She was with child. Katherine's eyes popped open, tears running down her cheeks. They were tears of happiness, and tears of sadness. The fetus was only ten or so weeks old, but something was wrong with it. It wouldn't make it through the night. She had to move quickly.

Placing her hands on the sleeping woman's stomach, Katherine began using her healing ability, and her body pulsed with light as she did so. Nothing else mattered to the mother. As she finished the process she heard a gasp and looked up to see Sharon staring at her with terrified wide eyes... and then she screamed. "What!" Jacob cried as he shot out of bed, waving his arms at an invisible intruder. "What is it?" But he saw the glowing figure in the room as the words left his lips. He just stared at her, tilting his head, not screaming or attempting to rescue his wife. He just looked at Katherine... not with eyes full of fear, terror, or anger, but with eyes full of recognition, and confusion. "Mom?" The words were quiet and uncertain, but Katherine smiled and nodded, tears running down her cheeks once more.

Without asking any questions, he wrapped his mother up

in a tight hug. Bruce watched from the hallway as they embraced each other, Jacob's shoulders bobbing up and down as he sobbed into his mother. Sharon didn't know what to do or what to say, and when her eyes met Bruce's, she finally spoke up. "What were you doing to me?" she asked Katherine.

Jacob finally pulled away from his mother and looked to his wife, and then back to his mom. Katherine wasn't sure how to respond though. Did they know she was with child? She inhaled deeply before explaining herself, but before she could get a single word out, she collapsed.

When Katherine came to, she was greeted by Bruce, Jacob, Sharon, and her daughter Carol. They all exchanged loving embraces, and Bruce, having explained what had happened that night on the beach already, let them have their time with their mother. He knew something had happened as Katherine's glow had greatly diminished, and she had aged quite a bit since earlier that night. He fought the heartache growing within him. "What happened back there?" he asked after everyone got reacquainted with Katherine.

She looked at Sharon, whose eyes were locked onto hers, her hands covering her stomach. "Sharon," Katherine said to her. "You were about to lose your child. I had to do something. I'm sorry if you feel violated at all."

The news came as a shock to everyone, and suddenly there was another reason for everyone to celebrate. The five of them spent the next week together being a family again. Everyone seemed in such high spirits, even Bruce's heart seemed full despite Katherine's condition and its steady decline. He was cherishing every moment he got to spend with Katherine and their children.

Finally, Carol asked what was on everyone's mind. "You

can't stay, can you?"

Katherine held back her tears, shook her head, and hugged her children. "It's a miracle I got to come back at all." She waved Sharon over and placed a hand on her stomach. "And now you get to have a miracle of your own." Then Sharon started crying.

"There has to be something we can do…" Jacob insisted, always the stubborn one just like his father. Bruce wrapped him in a hug, and kissed his forehead.

"There's only one thing left to do." He shocked himself and everyone else in the room. A strange peace settled inside of him then.

The very next evening, after a day of celebration and love, the family parked at the beach. They made their way down to the sand, stepping over driftwood and rocks, until the tide was mere feet away. Katherine was Bruce's age now, and she hugged and kissed each of her children, including Sharon. They said their goodbyes, and she insisted she would always be with them. Bruce and Katherine Swan held each other as they walked into the water, just as they had on countless other occasions. Their relationship, like anyone else's, wasn't perfect, but their love for one another knew no bounds.

They shared one last hug as the moon cast its light upon them. "You're going to be a wonderful grandfather," she told her husband as she gave him one last kiss. "I love you, Bruce."

"I love you, too, Kat," he said as he looked into the depths of his love's eyes for the last time. "I'll see you again." They smiled warmly, and as the next wave hit their feet Katherine's body collapsed into the sea, a glow dispersing with the tide.

Legacy

Alexander Delaney looked upon the view that greeted him one fine afternoon. A lush jungle thrived below the very ridge he stood on, canopies of teals, violets and greens beneath the aqua blue-colored sky. He particularly enjoyed the subtle splash of violet in the heavens. He closed his eyes and inhaled the air deeply through his nose. What a blessing it was to breathe, he thought, one of earth's simplest ingredients for life, yet so often taken for granted.

"Professor!" someone called out. "Professor!" Alex turned to regard the man yelling for him, an eagerness upon his face.

"What is it?" he asked. "Did you find it?"

"We believe so professor!" the young man said hopefully. "Come!"

Professor Delaney wound his way through his excavation site until they reached a new hole that had been started over the past few days. That particular spot had seemed promising to the archeologist as he'd studied the area at length. He leaned down to peer inside. "What do you see?" he called out.

"Professor!" a voice called from the darkness. "It's incredible!"

Alex was already gearing up to drop inside. Once he hit

the bottom he looked around in astonishment. It was the inside of a building from ages past. Directly underneath the hole they'd dug was the dead remains of a tree. Whatever the place had been used for long ago, it had been converted into some sort of sanctuary. The professor and his colleagues searched the place up and down for days, meticulously removing the earth where cave ins had punctured sections of the building over the generations.

At long last, Alex held in his hands the prize for which he'd come. He dusted off the cover of the book revealing one word: Laney. He found a comfortable place to sit and opened the book carefully. It was in surprisingly good condition all things considering. A tear welled up in the corner of his eye as he caressed the page with a finger, and then began reading.

My earliest memory was choking. I was just a toddler. I must've known better, but I guess I just really wanted to see the trees, the sky, the clouds, the flowers... the stars. I remember smiling as I looked up at the trees dominating the outside world, the violet sky overhead, and then collapsing to the ground as my lungs filled with something... else. It was not air. I remember it tasted sweet on my lips but that's all, then everything went black.

My mother used to tell me stories from when she was a little girl. She remembered when the sky was still blue, and animals and people alike were everywhere. Giant metal birds carried people across the skies, and metal fish called boats carried them across the seas. She would go on about the rain, how it smelled, how the rays of sunlight against the skin felt like a soft warm embrace, and about the moon and the stars. She was just a child when it happened, but remembered just enough to appreciate it. I could always tell just how much she cherished what little she could remember. "The smallest things, like the wind against your face. The things most people took for granted, those were the things that turned out to be the biggest things." I often heard her say.

The first signs were birds falling from the sky. By that point it was too late though. People began dropping in the streets, and wild animals began storming through cities in desperate agonizing fits. People would find their pets at home, dead. I guess it only took a few weeks for half the Earth's population to just, stop breathing. It happened so fast that the politicians, the military, the doctors and engineers... all the people deemed important were given sanctuary underground, leaving the rest of us to die.

For a while, people believed it was biochemical fallout, an act of war or terror that proved to be too much for the culprits to control. Then it was believed to be the work of artificial intelligence, our own result at playing god turning against us. The blame seemed to constantly shift, and amidst the chaos, everything that called the Earth home was rapidly dying off. Extinction seemed inevitable. My mom said she had never been more terrified in her life, before or since. She said most people turned into rabid animals, killing, maiming, beating and torturing others, all for the hope of surviving just one more day.

When scientists finally discovered the cause of the Earth's atmospheric changes, more than three quarters of the global population was gone. Just like that. It took less than two months for the planet to nearly snuff us out. It turned out to be the trees, that's it. I'm no scientist but I know life on Earth breathed air, a concoction of natural gasses consisting of mostly nitrogen and oxygen, the former far outnumbering the latter. The plants of the world, through photosynthesis, helped maintain healthy levels of oxygen and carbon dioxide in the atmosphere. The same was once said of trees, the planet's primary source of oxygen.

However, in the span of two or three months, the trees went through some sort of global metamorphosis. They were no longer using the same form of photosynthesis, and began emitting a new gas into the atmosphere. It has come to be called anaégen. It is the very antithesis of oxygen, as if mother nature herself set out to eradicate everything just to rid itself of humanity. Who could blame her? In the four and a half billion years the Earth has orbited the sun, nothing as destructive and careless, that we're aware of, has walked upon her soil. She simply hit the reset button... how many times has the Earth undergone this transformation I wonder?

If anyone is reading this, and god I hope this is the case, then it worked. You need to understand what happened, please. Don't let it have been in vain. My whole life, my family and I lived mostly underground. My family was all I ever knew. When I was five they started bringing me scavenging with them. We used respirators that filtered the toxins from the air, and even then, we had to learn to breathe slowly and with intent. Before then, my father always went alone. He could never be outside for too long, and sometimes his longer trips led us to believe the worst, but we had to remain strong and vigilant in his absence. We would travel, searching for anything from food and uncontaminated water, to packaged seeds and bags of soil from before the collapse of civilization.

It was a wasteland void of life in every direction, but in humanity's absence the trees thrived, multiplying tenfold through the decades. For me, home had always been an underground bunker my father procured years before I was born. It was a comfortable enough living for the most part, but we still needed to venture to the surface for supplies periodically. Those occasions were some of the most frightening, but also exhilarating times *throughout my childhood.*

I was still a teenager when that all changed. We were out scavenging when they found us. Much to our surprise, there were other survivors. We were cautious and weary, and we tried to be diplomatic, but they were savages. It was clear to them that we didn't live on the surface, and to have made it as long as we had there had to be a bunker or something. They demanded information and when my parents refused to answer them, they answered with their lives instead. I begged. I screamed. I cried. I'd never known pain quite like that. There's a devastating emptiness that gnaws at your insides when a loved one is lost. My father had begged me to run, to flee while they covered my escape, but I couldn't leave them. I froze, and to this day I can still see their deaths replay in my mind's eye. I believed myself a goner. Surely, I was next, but as quickly as they had made an appearance they were gone. They left me to mourn my loss. I can't remember how long I cried over their bodies, but as nightfall approached I hurried home.

It wasn't until I was safely tucked away in the bunker that it hit me. I was alone. Truly, utterly, alone. It was a terrifying realization, one that nearly fractured my fragile grieving mind. I snapped into survival mode, something primal took the steering wheel, and everything my parents had taught me was clear, concise, and rushed to the forefront of my thoughts. It was easy to not think, not feel anything at all, just survive. When it came time to leave the bunker for my first solo surface run, I was immediately greeted by my parents' killers.

Survival mode lasted all but a few seconds before they overpowered me. I was on my knees, ready to see my parents again. It was the second time I tasted that strange sweetness on my lips. They removed my respirator, laughing all the while. The end had come, I thought. I started choking on the toxic air, my vision was getting blurry, and I could see the legs of those men approaching the hatch to my bunker. As I scratched at my throat, as if it only needed to be opened, the faint sound of screams erupted all around me. Then I collapsed, the familiar blackness overcoming me.

When I opened my eyes, I thought I was dead, in an afterlife. I couldn't be alive... it was impossible. It wasn't until I got my bearings and looked around that I realized my respirator was back on my face, and I was right where I had been ambushed. Their bodies littered the ground, their limbs bending at impossible angles, blood spatter everywhere. Maybe I should've been scared, but I was more curious than anything. Not far from the scene there was a man covered in blood. I approached him and tried thanking him, but when he turned to regard me I saw that he was not wearing a respirator.

He wanted nothing to do with me, and he told me to leave, but I couldn't wrap my head around how he was breathing. My curiosity outweighed my intelligence, and I followed him. I tried asking him how he was breathing but he ignored me. After following him for some time he finally threatened me. He wanted to be left alone. I continued following him, but from a distance. I needed to know how he could breathe, how he was able to fight off the group that had murdered my parents. I wasn't alone... I didn't have to be alone.

I followed him for so long I had to switch respirators. I picked a couple off the bandits that attacked me, and I started getting nervous when I had to start using the last one. I started panicking and began running after him, but he lost me. He was gone and I was stranded in an endless forest of toxic trees. I cried out for him, but he never came. I didn't know what to do, and in my panic, I started wasting what little use the mask had to offer. Then I felt something on my shoulder, and when I felt around, something started crawling down my hand and I screamed.

I ran until I was out of breath and collapsed. I started crying and screaming for help. I felt my body lift from the ground and all I could see were the backs of his legs as he carried me, and once again blackness took me. When I came to I was in his camp, but there was nobody else, no supplies, nothing. Just the man and junk he had collected in piles under some tarps he'd set up for shelter. I started asking him something and realized I could breathe. I wasn't wearing the respirators, but a new mask over my face. I asked him where the oxygen was coming from, but he declined to answer. He wasn't happy with me, his scowl gave as much away.

I watched him for some time, but I think he hoped I'd leave. Finally, he asked me what my deal was. I explained my curiosity, my gratitude, and my loneliness, but he didn't seem to care. He explained that people were dangerous and I should leave before I cause trouble, that he didn't want to have to hurt me. I tried to convince him that I didn't want trouble, and that I wouldn't do anything to hurt him. He laughed and we didn't talk for some time after that. When we finally did I asked about other people.

He told me there were plenty of survivors out there. There were groups of people, and he avoided them because they always attacked him or attempted to steal from him. People weren't to be trusted. He solidified that belief as he never seemed to take his eyes from me for too long. I tried to convince him that not all people were like that, but he knew better than me. He knew it, and I knew it, but was I not people? I figured if I was ever going to get answers from him that I had to earn his trust, so I stopped asking questions and started helping around camp.

One night as I was sleeping, I felt him unscrew something

from the back of the mask he'd given me, and in a panic, I sat up and questioned him. That's when he showed me the bugs. I had never seen any living creature other than another person before. He called them beetles, and they were big, about the length of my index finger. They were a brown-ish green, had six legs, antennae, and were disgusting looking. They terrified me, but I tried my best not to show him my fear. He told me they fed on tree sap and the byproduct of their meals produced oxygen. He explained that they retained most of the gas in their bodies however, and only produced enough for someone to breathe if contained in numbers and fed. The thing he had unscrewed from the mask contained dozens of the beetles, and I was breathing their... flatulence, to put it mildly.

I began assisting him in collecting the beetles. The trees were covered in them, and we harvested hundreds every day. He escorted me to scavenge for water during the day, and part of me was worried he'd abandon me, but he never did. He still scowled at me and kept a close eye on me at all times, but I could see him slowly coming to trust me despite the stray comments he'd make about returning me to my bunker. It was extra cold that night and I couldn't stay warm. He poured hundreds of the beetles into a pit that he covered with wood. I just watched curiously as I shivered. It was the first time I ever saw fire. The beetles hummed and crackled, but the flames burned, and the wood burned. I had never been so warm in my life. He stayed up and made a point of feeding the fire as I slept.

We spent the next few months together, scavenging and harvesting, but it would prove difficult to get much out of him. He told me his name was Dee, but that was pretty much the extent of it. We ran into another group of people one day while scavenging in the ruins of the old world, and his first instinct was to attack them. They hadn't seen us though, and I talked him into remaining hidden and waiting for them to move on. Surprisingly, he listened. Once they'd moved on we continued our routine. That night, a noise woke me. I heard the sound of people arguing. The group we had seen earlier that day had followed us back to camp. Some of them were arguing with the others. They didn't want trouble, and they wanted them to leave us alone, but the others would hear none of it.

That night, Dee and I both learned a thing or two. At my behest, he offered the people food and water, and tried to send them on their way. They requested shelter for the night though, and against his better judgement, Dee complied. I don't think he wanted me to see him as a monster. We spent the evening talking over a meal, and I found myself feeling sorry for the women. Janet and Alexis, they were kind and they were appreciative, but the men they were with remained silent and scowled at Dee the entire time. I didn't blame any of them for scrutinizing my new friend, after all, I found myself looking at him the same way at times. They tried asking him how he could breathe, but when they received no explanation, they chose to go to bed. The men attacked Janet and Alexis that night, thinking everyone was asleep. The women wanted them to leave us alone, and to leave them alone, but the men got   violent instead.

Dee was too late though. The men had killed Janet in a fit of rage, and fatally injured Alexis as she tried to stop them. One of the men had a device I'd never seen before. It created electrical currents, and they subdued Dee by electrocuting him. He managed to knock out one of the men before collapsing, and I knew if I didn't act then Dee was going to die. My heart pounded against my chest. I don't know that I'd ever felt rage like that before. I wasn't able to help my parents, and I knew I wouldn't be able to live with *myself if I did nothing, so I killed that man before I let anything happen to Dee. My first kill of many. I liked those women, and Dee was my friend... I couldn't let them hurt him or anyone else ever again, so I killed the other man as well. Alexis was gone by then, and it was just him and I once more. Dee learned that there were good people in the world, and I learned that not everyone deserved the benefit of the doubt. Dee helped me bury them that night.*

I learned that Dee could not remember who he was or where he came from. He didn't know why he could breathe, but he knew of the beetles, of science, and had been living alone for years. People were dangerous, and that night made me understand. He tried to save those women, much like he had saved me, but he failed. Not all people were bad, and not all people deserved to die. We became much closer over the next few months. He was finally opening up to me, and he was always there for me. We were always there for each other. He struggled with his feelings, and it often frustrated him. It was as if he didn't know what feelings were, or how to process them. He didn't understand that some felt good while others felt bad, and I comforted him many times over those months. He grew very attached to me, well, we grew very attached to each other. He was my protector, my savior, and my dear friend. I was his teacher in a way, like a counselor, and I loved him. Love was an interesting feeling to see him process, but he expressed it beautifully.

Eventually, he showed me a tattoo he couldn't remember receiving. The letter "D." He wasn't sure if that was his name or not, but it was all he had to go off of. Something happened one day and he was injured. It dawned on me that I had never seen him bleed, but I learned why. His blood was blue. Cleaning his wound caused no pain, and in his manic, Dee pealed some of his skin away to reveal machinery beneath. He wasn't human. So many questions were answered, and he thought I'd fear him, but I could see the pain in his eyes... the struggle he felt was very much human. I had come to love him with every fiber of my being you see, and it didn't matter what he was... to me, he was my Dee.

However, nothing was ever the same after that. He had become depressed, quiet, withdrawn. I gave him the space he needed, but one day I woke up and I was all alone again. I cried out for him. How could he leave me! How? It didn't make sense to me and I started to panic, but then I saw the letter he'd left for me. He said when he learned what he really was, his memories returned to him, and that he believed he could fix everything so that I could live a normal life again. He thanked me for teaching him what it meant to be human, for being his friend, and that he'll never forget me. My heart ached just as it had when I lost my parents, and I decided I wasn't losing Dee too. I wiped away the tears and was about to run into the forest calling his name, but then the forest shuddered and quaked.

Humming, crackling, popping, and moaning erupted all around me as trees were shaken by a thousand miniature explosions on every tree. They snapped and crumbled all around me, fiery bursts bursting from tree to tree, a domino effect that spread for dozens of miles. Suddenly it made sense why he had picked a clearing the night before to set up camp, away from the trees. All I could do was watch in grief, that feeling of loss once again taking hold of me. I read the letter again, clutching it tightly to my chest when I noticed more writing on the back. It read Spitsbergen, Norway. . I didn't know what to make of it at first, and it wasn't until later that I realized something: the explosions, the presence of fire, influenced what trees remained standing. The fire triggered a chemical reaction, inducing changes within the *great pillars of death. They were exhaling oxygen once more.*

I spent the remainder of my life searching for the vault in Dee's letter, spreading word to other survivors and settlements I came across that fire was the key. The trees needed to burn and survive to reverse the change that killed most of life on the planet. It took many, many years to find the vault. I had a family of my own by then, and together we blazed a trail of fire wherever we went. The vault in Dee's letter was just one of many, in fact. The world was littered with vaults containing, not only seeds, but the DNA and tissue samples of hundreds of thousands of creatures that once roamed the Earth beside us. The atmosphere has not yet fully recovered nor is it breathable, but I hope that one day we will get there.

I tell you my story for a reason though. Someday, when the world is once again habitable, I want you to remember Dee, and his sacrifice. He was a machine, but he had enough faith in me, in us, to become the catalyst that would save us all. If you're reading this, please help him. I salvaged what I could—

Professor Alexander Delaney finished reading the journal, his fingers caressing the words on the final page. In her final words, Laney had included the location of Dee's remains, or what was left of them, and his search continued.

Some months later, Alex stood before Dee's new body, the final pieces put in place. He and his team had managed to repair and recover the machine's memory, and its upload was nearly complete. The professor was elated; after all, his entire life had led to this point... to this very moment. Dee opened his eyes.

Dee shot up into a sitting position. "Laney!" he cried out for the only human he'd ever loved... the only thing he'd ever loved.

"Dee," Alex said, "she isn't here, I'm afraid." The professor could only imagine how Dee was feeling. He wasn't quite sure how he was going to navigate the conversation, but he had an advantage nobody else in the world had.

"Where is she?" Dee asked. "Is she okay?"

"She had a good life," Alex answered. "I hate to be the one to tell you this friend, but you've been gone for over two hundred years."

Dee sat back, digesting the information. He remained silent for a minute. "Friend?" he asked. "Who are you to me?"

The professor smiled warmly. "I am Alexander Delaney," he replied, waiting for the gears in Dee's head to calculate. Dee looked at him inquisitively.

"Does that mean...?"

"Laney is a distant ancestor of mine, yes," Alex told Dee. "My bloodline is the legacy of yours and Laney's bond, of your sacrifice. My namesake honors the both of you."

Dee seemed to relax, even seemed relieved by the news. "Did it work? Did we fix the world?"

Alex nodded happily. "You were the catalyst for humanity's survival," he explained. "It is so good to finally meet you."

"I'm very happy to hear that," said Dee, "but why bring me back now?"

Alexander Delaney's face tightened up and took on a far more serious look then, one which wore regret, concern, and desperation. "Will you help humanity once more? Will you help me broker peace with the rest of your kind?"

Vatgeslu

Rain drops echoed, reverberating through her senses. The drops splattering along the roof of the car, the persistent drumbeat of a thousand armies marching to their death. Cracking the window slightly filled the car with petrichor, a welcome alternative to the new car scented tree hanging from the rearview mirror that'd been torn completely open.

She pressed her forehead against the cold pane of the window, the world outside passing by in a blur as her eyes focused on the droplets of rain dancing and swelling upon the glass. The pit in her stomach lived there now, unpacked and comfortable since they'd landed. Before then it all seemed like a bad joke, and she'd just been awaiting the punchline.

Natalie watched the water coalesce into larger puddles on her window, dispersing and spreading into thin streaks before amassing into large globs over and over again as the rain relentlessly clapped against the car. She was watching this process despite not really being present for it, the dread dwelling within her demanding her attention, but as the puddles upon the window formed into what appeared to be a face she watched curiously.

Fully expecting the face to last just a moment before the

droplets continued its dance across the window, erasing the image, Natalie gasped in shock and jumped in her seat as she watched the eyes in the window move to look upon her. "What is it?" Her dad asked. "Nat?" Natalie looked from the window to her dad.

"I…" she started, but when she turned back to the window the face was gone. It was just water running down the side of the car. "Nothing… I thought I saw something, but it was nothing."

"Are we there yet?" Natalie's younger sister asked from the opposite end of the back seat.

"No," he answered.

"How much longer?" she asked impatiently, her voice nearly reaching the tone most would recognize as whining.

"Desi…" their dad said. "We talked about this. There's no airports in Wales, so we have a while to drive," he explained again.

"Why?" Desiree asked. There was no response. "Daddy, why are there no airports here?"

Natalie looked over at her little sister, three years her junior but quickly catching up to her in height, looking hard at her as she opened her mouth to repeat her question when still no answer came. "Let him focus on the drive, Desi!" Natalie answered for him. Desiree tried reaching over to push her older sister but the older sibling easily held her at bay. Natalie and her father's eyes met through the rearview mirror, a silent thank you for silencing Desi's abundance of questions, if only temporarily. Hers was a look of contempt and dread.

"Ow!" Natalie yelled after Desi kicked her when she wasn't looking. "Desi!" she yelled and her sister stuck her tongue out at her.

"Hey!" their dad chimed in. "C'mon guys… Desi, apologize to your sister."

"But daddy! She—" Desi started.

"Now!" their dad insisted. "And look her in the eyes when you say it. Isn't this whole thing already stressful enough?"

Natalie didn't wait for her sister to apologize. "Why did we have to move? Why are we here!"

Their dad stiffened up and sighed, the backseat going quiet. After a moment to gather his thoughts he finally replied. "It wasn't safe anymore," he answered.

"What do you mean?" Natalie asked. "I don't understand, Daddy."

"America…" he replied. "You're too young to understand, but the constitution that protects Americans is being abolished. The shit's about to hit the fan, and we got out before that happened. The whole country is about to collapse…"

Tears welled up in Natalie's wide eyes. "What about Samantha?! What about all my friends?" she cried.

"I don't know, sweetie," he said. "I gave their parents a heads up… that was the best I could do, okay? They're not my responsibility… you guys are." Natalie didn't like the answer, but it was good enough for the moment apparently because a retort never came.

"Daddy, why would shit hit a fan?" Desiree asked, breaking the uncomfortable silence that had grown in the car. He couldn't help but start laughing, and as upset as Natalie was right then, she couldn't help but join in. "What? That's gross!" Desiree started explaining in detail how she'd expect such a situation to unravel.

The remainder of the drive went without incident, and the siblings had fallen asleep. "We're here," their dad said as he woke them. They stumbled from the cramped car and Natalie looked at the old house in awe and trepidation. It was old, nay, it was ancient, and had definitely seen better days. The big house reminded Natalie of a castle, but it was very clearly no such thing.

There were other cars already parked there. Natalie and Desiree were meeting relatives they'd never met before. The reunion was not one any of them were excited about. After meeting aunts, uncles, and cousins, Natalie understood why. None of them really seemed to care about seeing one another, or about meeting their nieces for the first time. It was strictly about business, and when that business became too personal, the children were dismissed, left to wander the house unsupervised.

Desiree was clinging to Natalie's side as the older sister followed a couple of their cousins around the house. Amelia and Thomas were slightly older than Natalie and Desiree, but none had yet reached their teenage years. They wandered the corridors curiously, all except Desiree were intrigued and excited to be out from under their parent's ever watchful gaze. The floors creaked and the wind blowing against the structure seemed to make it groan.

"I'm scared!" Desiree squealed as she tugged tighter against Natalie's arm. "Let's go back!"

"There's nothing to be scared of Desi..." Natalie started, but a chuckle from Thomas stole the remaining words from her mouth.

"What has your dad told you about this house?" he asked.

"Nothing..." Natalie replied. "Only that it belongs to our family."

"My dad said it's been in the family for hundreds of

years!" Amelia chimed in.

"It has," Thomas agreed. "People say mysterious things happened in this house. That it belonged to witches, or vampires, depending on who you ask." Desiree made a whining sound as she clutched onto Natalie.

"It's fine Desi, it's obviously not true. There's no such thing as witches or vampires," she said.

"Bullocks." Amelia snorted.

The children wandered the halls until they came upon a giant portrait of a woman at the end of a hall. She loomed over them like a gargoyle preying upon intruders. She seemed important and strangely familiar to Natalie, but before she could say anything, Desiree beat her to it. "Whoa..." she said admirably as she craned her neck backward to take in the full view of the impressive woman. "Who's that!"

"That's our great-great grandmother Lucille," Thomas answered. "The last matriarch of our family before our great grandparents went their separate ways, and this house became a distant memory..."

"I've heard my dad call it a blemish in our family's history," Amelia chimed in again as she also took in the mighty view of their ancestor.

"What happened?" Natalie asked. "Why did our family go their separate ways?"

"No one really knows," Amelia said. "I've heard people say someone was murdered here, or that our family turned on each other."

"I heard a rumor once that our family was accused of cannibalism, and that the townsfolk were coming to string them all up on the tree out front," Thomas said. Desiree gasped and made a disgusted look on her face. "But every story I've heard has one thing in common: Lucille mysteriously vanished." They all looked at her portrait once more.

"How come my dad never told us about any of this...?" Natalie asked aloud, more to herself than anyone else.

"Probably the same reason our family changed its name since then..." Thomas said. "To keep as much distance from us and our cursed heritage as possible... I've heard my parents say as much, so why are we here? That's the real question."

Natalie squirmed uncomfortably as Thomas and Amelia eyeballed her. "Our entire family knows of this place... of each other... and yet we have never been here or so much as spoken to you before, and now suddenly, we're all meeting here? Seems pretty sus to me. What don't we know?" Amelia asked, directing the question at Natalie.

Natalie didn't know what to say, gulping down the knot in her throat. "The American constipation is about to shit the fan!" Desiree interjected loudly, drawing giggles from her cousins. The cat was out of the bag... oh well.

"I guess my dad's contacts from his military days have been reaching out for a while, and guys..." Natalie's face went serious. "The United States is about to collapse any day I think."

Her cousins' faces went blank and unblinking. "Holy shit," Thomas gasped quietly. "Should we be eavesdropping right now?" The cousins all exchanged stupid looks, as if to ask themselves why that wasn't the most obvious choice after initially being dismissed by the "adults."

"What's leaf droppings?" Desiree asked as the kids scurried back the way they'd come, navigating the maze of hallways and staircases until they reached the front room next to the kitchen and large dining area.

The kids put their ears to the door quietly.

"...world war?" one of the adults finished saying.

"How do you know this isn't an isolated event?" another asked.

"I told you!" Natalie and Desiree's dad answered. "I have contacts all over the world! I trust them... there aren't many places that will be safe. It's not a matter of *if*... *when* this goes down, it—"

"If you have contacts all over the world, why are we here? In this shithole instead of some bunker?"

"Well, firstly!" their dad snapped. "The higher ups don't care much for me..."

"Now there's a shocker!" one of the other adults replied sarcastically.

"Secondly!" their dad snapped again. "I had a very strong feeling this is where we needed to be..."

"Not your feelings again!" the same man snorted in response. "Nothing good ever—"

"Dennis!" a woman's voice interrupted. "We all know there is merit to Michael's intuition..." She paused, and a moment that seemed to stretch on forever seemed to pass. "What was that?"

Natalie's bulging eyes met Thomas's. Desiree looked from her sister to her cousin and got really scared. "What's happening? What does that mean?" Natalie clasped her hand over her sister's mouth. The kids hurried from the door to the hall and around the corner. Still holding Desiree's mouth shut, Natalie poked her head around the corner of the wall to see one of her uncles open the door and look around before closing it once more.

Once the children were a safe distance from the adults, Amelia rubbed some tears from her face. "Did they say war?"

"I think so," Thomas answered.

Natalie could hear her sister and her cousins frantically trying to make sense of the little they had overheard, but the sound of rain against the window at the end of the hall where they stood distracted her. She felt her mind melt away. The sound of voices muffled into background noise as everything went silent except for the rain hitting the glass.

Tap tap tap. She listened. *Tap tap tap.* It sounded like a heartbeat. *Tap tap tap* **tap!** This time louder. The sudden sharpness of that last tap surprised her, and she turned to look at the window just in time to see a watery hand become streams of raindrops running down the glass. She remembered the face from the car ride, previously believing it had been a figment of her exhausted jet-lagged imagination, and started moving closer to the window, slowly, cautiously.

When she stood before the window looking out over the property, she couldn't see anything out there. She squinted her eyes and put her face against the glass to try and get a better look.

TAP!

The tap against the window was so loud she squealed and fell back from the window.

"Natalie!" Desiree yelled. Natalie looked over to see her sister and cousins staring at her. "Hello! We've been saying your name over and over! Don't ignore me!"

"Are you okay?" Thomas asked.

"Yeah... I'm fine," Natalie replied, speaking nothing of either incident to them.

Later that evening, after the parents finished their secret conversation, they showed the kids to the rooms they'd be sleeping in. They weren't told how long they'd be there, but with the looming threat of the political landscape, Natalie figured it'd be a while. Once her and her sister were ready for bed their dad came to tuck them in.

"How are you guys feeling?" he asked them.

"I'm scared, Daddy!" Desiree squealed as she wrapped her arms around him. He returned the hug and kissed her on the forehead.

"I know it's scary being in a new strange place, but everything is okay. You've got your sister and I'm right down the hall," he told her as he held her tight.

"I'm confused," Natalie said. Her dad looked at her, Desiree's head tucked beneath his chin.

"I know you have questions sweetie," he said. "Get some rest, and we'll talk about it tomorrow, okay?"

He kissed them goodnight and left the room. Desiree fell asleep first, and Natalie lied there for what seemed like hours trying to fall asleep, but the house gave her the creeps. She kept feeling as if she were being watched, and she swore she could hear whispering coming from somewhere, but also nowhere like it was so faint, so quiet, that she wondered if her mind was playing tricks on her.

Tap tap tap.

Natalie got out of bed and walked to the window. It was raining out, as it had been since they landed, and she looked down to the front grounds of the property. As the rain fell, she watched it bounce off something, creating an area void of rain drops. The void moved closer to the house, and though she couldn't see whatever it was, she got the sense that it was looking up at her. Then watery hands smacked against the window.

Natalie jumped and gasped, but in the same breath heard

a whisper from behind her. "*Come—*" The whispering continued but grew distant as if it were moving away from her. She followed the disembodied voices through the house. Most of it was indecipherable gibberish, but every now and then she heard a, "*Find me...*" It stopped at a wall in one of the small dens on the bottom floor. The door to the room slowly closed behind her on its own.

Natalie was surprised that she was not afraid, neither of the voices or the door closing of its own accord. Her focus was on the supposed wall the voices had led her to. She placed her hands on the wall, feeling around a framed picture, searching for something out of place... a clue, something... anything. She stopped and took a step back to look at the picture, which was to the right of a bookshelf. There was nothing all that peculiar or special about the picture, in fact, it was so prosaic it seemed strangely out of place among the many oddities and curiosities around the property.

She reached up and touched the frame. There was something strange about the frame. The picture did not sway as one should, as if it were bolted to the wall. When she attempted to move it, the frame went crooked ever so slightly, and Natalie heard a faint click. A portion of the wall had been released from a latch and sat slightly ajar. It wasn't too obvious, but upon closer inspection she was able to see the crease and pushed the wall inward.

A room untouched for decades greeted her on the other side. Cobwebs and dust coated everything within. It looked like an old office. Bookshelves, chairs, and a few strange knick-knacks were inside, but the most prominent thing in the room was a shrine-looking area with a desk and a mirror. The whispers erupted all around her, leading her to the shrine. Natalie walked up to it and brushed the cobwebs and dust from the mirror. The whispers came to an abrupt stop. Natalie peered into the glass, expecting something to happen, but nothing did. She began examining the ancient mirror. A word was carved into the corner of the frame holding the mirror. "Datgelu…" Natalie read it aloud.

Her reflection faded from the mirror and the image of the unused space behind her blurred until it no longer resembled the room she'd found. The air in the room seemed to be sucked away, and Natalie felt a sense of falling overcome her. Her body lurched forward, yet didn't move, the sensation overwhelming her and she began to scream, but no sound came out of her mouth. Suddenly, the momentum came to a halt and Natalie found herself somewhere else.

The girl inhaled deeply as if she'd been suffocating, and finally able to breathe again, she was so focused on filling her lungs with air that she didn't realize she'd been brought somewhere new. When she finally caught her breath and got her bearings, she began to panic. She turned around to see the dusty cobwebbed room on the other side of some sort of window. It was hovering there impossibly, as if by magic, swaying up and down ever so slightly. Or perhaps this was just a dream.

"Okay Natalie," she said to herself, "this isn't real… wake up!" Slapping herself did nothing but sting. She walked toward the portal leading back to the room but every step she took toward the levitating window it seemed to drift further away. She felt her heart begin to race and she stopped. The floating portal also stopped moving away. She took a step back and watched it grow in size just a smidge. "Okay…" she said as she decided to turn her attention to her current whereabouts.

It was dark and foggy, and Natalie wandered around for a

while, always checking on the portal she'd come in through. It was always there, more a beacon of light in the darkness than anything, a comforting pull ever present as she explored the mysterious place. Eventually she came upon an older woman, maybe in her fifties, who seemed very disoriented and confused. "Excuse me?" Natalie asked.

The woman screamed and fell backwards. "What is this?" she asked. "I've never conjured you before! Your face is unfamiliar to me! Speak your name at once!"

Natalie couldn't see the woman's face, but she didn't feel frightened by her either. "My name is Natalie," she told the woman.

"Surname?" she asked.

"Emmerson. Natalie Emmerson."

"Hmmm..." She pondered for a moment, her finger scratching her tilted head.

"What's your name?" Natalie asked.

The woman still looked very confused, as confused as someone could look without fully seeing their face. It didn't seem to matter how close Natalie got to the woman, she either moved or some trick of the darkness or fog kept her face hidden. Still, the confusion was evident. "I..." the woman stammered. "I'm not sure."

"How long have you been here?" Natalie asked, fully convinced she was dreaming now. The woman wandered around as if looking for something, but unsure what she was looking for, scratching her head all the while.

"Emmerson..." she muttered to herself as she seemed to continue wandering aimlessly. The dark misty atmosphere began to clear up as a room began to take shape around them. Bookshelves popped up all around them, a staircase and some furniture, and then a large coffee table and a fireplace. It all seemed to conjure itself out of thin air... or out of the dark fog. Natalie was beginning to worry she was lost, and turned to find the distant beacon still hovering behind her, through the illusion of the library. As relief settled within her, she heard the woman shriek with joy. "Aha!"

Even in the lighting of the library, the woman's face remained aloof from any attempt at identifying her. It was just distorted and blurry, or wrapped in the darkness from before. She held up a book, tapping it excitedly. It looked incredibly old and fancy, and covering the entirety of the face of its cover was some sort of crest... a family crest perhaps? Natalie knew what those were slighly because of her dad's ties to the UK, but mostly due to Harry Potter. At the top was some sort of orb, like a scrying crystal, and from either side of the orb sprouted large dragon wings that stretched down the sides of the cover to the bottom. Taking up the center of the cover, underneath the orb and between the wings, there was a tree. Its roots spread to the bottom of the cover, its branches reaching toward the orb and the wings, and in its branches were three perched ravens.

The woman's hand was extended toward her, and Natalie wasn't sure what she was supposed to do. She slowly reached her hand out toward the woman. She grabbed her hand suddenly, and tightly. "Hey!" Natalie cried. "Stop it! What are you doing?"

The woman prodded a fingertip with a needle-like object, let go of Natalie's hand and let a droplet of the blood she'd produced fall onto a blank page of the book. The blood swirled around the page, filling the book with pictures and writing. The woman handed the book to Natalie. "Take a look, deary."

When Natalie looked upon the book's contents she

realized it was a family tree. She clearly saw her name, except her family's last name did not show up as Emmerson. It read "Emrys." She saw her parents and Desiree, the aunts and uncles she'd just met as well as Thomas and Amelia, and her grandparents she'd never met. She lingered on their likeness for a moment, having never seen pictures of them, before flipping the page. On and on the family tree went through the generations until she came upon Lucille Emrys, and she let out an audible gasp. "Lucille?" she asked the woman. "Is that you?"

The shroud masking the woman's face slowly dissipated to reveal her great-great grandmother Lucille, and along with the shroud, her confusion as well. She smiled at Natalie and took in a deep breath, then basked in her surroundings. "This is real isn't it?" Natalie asked her ancestor. Lucille didn't respond right away, but when she did, she did so with renewed vigor and determination.

"I'm afraid so," she muttered, "and judging by that entry I'd say I've been stuck here for quite some time..."

"A hundred-eighty years..." Natalie said slowly and nervously. "Give or take..."

Lucille turned to regard Natalie closely, studying her. "What do you know of our family dear?"

"Not a lot..." Natalie explained. Lucille flicked her wrist with a finger extended and the book's pages flipped three quarters the way through, landing on a page whose most prominent figure was born more than fifteen hundred years ago.

"Do you know who that is?" she asked Natalie as she pointed to the figure named Myrddin Emrys. Natalie's face contorted in confusion. How was she supposed to know anyone from that long ago? "No matter..." Lucille remarked. "Our family comes from a long line of powerful sorcerers dating back over two thousand years. It matters not how the centuries bend and distort our namesake, our blood speaks the truth through this book: The Grimoire of House Emrys…"

Natalie looked like a deer in headlights. "I'm sorry… what? This is real? You're real? Our family is magic?"

"Try and pay attention dear," Lucille said without skipping a beat. "There are things we must discuss… things you must learn. But first, tell me, do you see the way out?"

Natalie turned to once again see the beacon lingering in the background of the mysterious place, awaiting her return. "Yes," she answered, "but last time I tried to go back it got further away…"

"Very good," Lucille said. "Let's get started."

Natalie emerged from the mirror, once again in the dusty old room of cobwebs, and made her way through the house until she spotted Desiree, Thomas and Amelia. Desiree spotted her first. "Natalie!" She squealed. "It's Natalie!" She ran up to her older sister and wrapped her in a hug, tears running down her cheeks. Seconds later, the adults burst into the room. Her aunts and uncles, and her father all swarmed around her. Her dad lifted her up in his arms and held her tight. He was also tearing up.

"What's wrong?" Natalie asked sheepishly, not sure why everyone was acting so strangely.

"Where have you been?" Her dad asked. "You've been missing for days!"

Natalie's heart sank. Days? It had only felt like hours. "I…" she stammered, unsure what to say. "I don't know that anyone would believe me…" Her dad leaned down to look her in the eyes at her level.

"Nat…" he went on. "I think you might be surprised,

please, we have been so worried." He wrapped her in a tight hug once more.

"I was with Lucille…" she replied. The looks on her entire family's faces said it all. It wasn't disbelief, or doubt even… maybe shock? The shock wasn't disappointment or skepticism either. Natalie didn't know how to read the room, a first for her despite her age.

"Guys…" one of the uncles said. He pulled an earbud from his ear and turned Bluetooth off on his phone. *The collapse of the United States shocked the world just two days ago. The world held its breath and waited for the dust to clear, and then Canada… Russia… Iran… Sweden… the world's governments are collapsing, and I fear it is only a matter of time before the end comes for us all. Keep your loved ones… Oh my God! Just in, I am receiving reports China has launched a volley of nukes!*

An emergency broadcast took over the phone. Everyone ran outside in the rain and watched streaks in the sky tear through clouds as rockets passed overhead. An explosion sounded and a mushroom cloud erupted from the horizon, hundreds of miles away somewhere on the mainland. Desiree, Amelia and Thomas all began crying, and the adults seemed to have resigned to their fates, grabbing the children and holding them close. People all over town were just standing around as well, resigned to their fates, unsure how to react, while others could be heard screaming and wailing.

"I think I know what to do," Natalie told them. "Everyone, form a circle and hold hands."

Nobody questioned her. A moment later her and her family, the House of Emrys, had formed a circle, hands clasped together. Natalie began speaking in tongues, channeling the innate magic dwelling within her family's blood. An invisible dome appeared over them, rain hitting nothing and flowing down its curved sides. "I think we should help." Michael told everyone. "Everyone!" he began repeating Natalie's indecipherable words as she spoke as if on a loop, and the others joined in not long after. It was as if they already knew the language… they just needed to try.

The dome grew until it encompassed the entire property, and grew some more until it covered the entire town. Ordinary townsfolk were looking around terrified and confused, but most were in utter shock. There was no telling how far the dome reached when a nuke hit somewhere assumedly near London, and as the shockwave of fire and debris raced toward them, the sky grew dark. Looking up, they realized the darkness was not coming from the nuclear blast, but that day had become night somehow. The stars were clear and bright, and then the moon appeared in the sky… and then took up the entire sky. In the opposite direction, an Earth on fire was shrinking. The moon passed the town, and moments later they could see Saturn and its rings up close.

Then they were moving through a cloud of debris made of ice and rock, and then the stars began to stretch into noodles, curving around the dome protecting their home. All sorts of colors and lights swirled around them, bending away from the dome, and never once did the Emmersons dare halt their chanting. The lights and colors slowed down, and the lines of stars began shrinking until they were once again dots in the night sky. An enormous nebula was off to one side, and soon the brightness of a star came into view. It grew bigger and bigger until another dot appeared from the light. It too, grew bigger and bigger until it was very clearly another planet. As they entered the atmosphere, the darkness of space turned to day, clouds rushed past the dome and a moment later their town sat upon the surface of an alien world.

"Home…" Natalie gasped, her eyes wide and full of wonder.

Later when everyone slept and Natalie was alone, she got up and left the house. She walked the property with intent. Thomas, Amelia and Desiree followed her from a distance. They watched and listened as Natalie stopped at an old well. "Desmond!" she called into the well. "I know you're here!"

Water rose from the well, splashing over the ground, water dancing around an invisible object… something… someone. No, it was the water. "Hello Lucille," a disembodied voice greeted the girl. "Are you here to make me whole again?" The cousins clasped their hands over Desiree's mouth, tears flowing from her eyes, and quietly planted themselves to the ground, hidden from view.

Back inside the house, behind a wall in one of the bottom floor dens, in a dusty room full of cobwebs sits a shrine with a mirror. Inside that mirror, the silent screams of Natalie pounding her fists against the glass fruitlessly… a tear running down the face of the mirror.

Ascension

Arthur Flannagan, the city's sweetheart and aspiring savior, waved to the people as he stepped from the raised platform where the podium remained. The smile he wore was more for show than anything though. Truthfully, the man didn't enjoy being in the spotlight. The flashing of cameras wasn't just coming from the swarm of people occupying the city's rooftop, but from overhead as well. The Ascendancy's fleet of drones were capable of performing a myriad of functions, but this one in particular was by far Arthur's least favorite.

He raised his arm before his clean-shaven handsome face to shield his eyes from the obnoxious flashes as he was escorted through a sea of the elite, pedestrians, and journalists alike. Without prompting his assistant, the metallic arm extended before the man's face, blocking the flashes so he didn't have to. His other assistant gently pushed the crowd away with extended arms and open palms, keeping the politician's path clear for him.

As they made their way toward the platform's center, Arthur took in the incredible view of the city's rooftop. A majestic tree reached toward the sky from the center, a massive fountain circling the circumference of the tree, its water spouting in arcs and zigzagging around the tree like faithful worshipers performing a ritual to their deity. "Rivers" flowed from the fountain to the four sides of the platform. Smaller buildings were scattered upon the city's rooftop, but it was mostly grass and trees, statues and formations that transcended human creation, harkening to the days of old when mankind believed structures such as the pyramids had been built by gods.

How foolish people had once been, Arthur thought, so quick to pass humanity's extraordinary accomplishments over to false beings simply because the science had been lost to them. Even when they had believed themselves more advanced than any other civilization in history, their misunderstanding of the very science that catapulted them to such heights limited them, keeping the species in a state of primitive ignorance. From this vantage point Arthur could see the clouds and mountains hundreds of miles away rising to match humanity's stubborn ambitions.

Lines of armed men, the soldiers of the Ascendency, posted outside one of the buildings decorating the city's rooftop, making way for the politician's return. The two android assistants, Arthur's body guards, followed behind scanning the faces in the crowd for any potential threats. An elevator closed behind them and they descended into the city below. The transition was always a shock to the politician. Blue skies and clouds, and the luscious views of mountains and forests stretching for miles in every direction, all vanished abruptly as the dark underbelly of the city came into view.

The sky was replaced by a ceiling of skyscrapers hanging like stalactites, the occasional opening for sunlight to seep through, and enormous mega structures spread throughout the city at regular intervals. The megastructures were shaped like pyramids, rising from the bottom and hanging from the ceiling, all connected to one another by a series of immense skyscrapers, creating the shape of hourglasses that provided the city with its foundation and support. The only nature that grew within the city was upon smaller platforms below the openings in the ceiling of the city that rotated with the sun's movement through the sky above.

Bridges and arches stretched between thousands of skyscrapers sprawled across the city, and mountains of residential areas piled on top of the others, haphazardly placed about almost as an afterthought. Along the circumference of the city were strategically built military structures that blocked most of the sunlight from the city's edges, creating the illusion of steel vines, hillsides and canopies that served as the city's defenses.

The lack of overall natural light within the city itself washed the otherworldly place in near perpetual darkness. Still surrounded by the Ascendancy's soldiers, he came upon some street beggars, starving and deprived of all hope. The man showered them with nourish credits, enough to feed a dozen households for more than two weeks. This was his purpose... the amount of good he could do for the needy was astonishing, and there seemed to be an endless supply of them. The armed soldiers escorting him through the city did nothing when they came upon a skirmish between some of the city's lower-class citizens despite its brutal nature. They waited impatiently, even seemed annoyed when Arthur dispatched his mechanical assistants to defend the helpless residents and fight off their attackers.

He'd clawed his way up the social ladder, through blood and grit, but still preferred the anonymity of the lives and goings on of the day to day average citizen. Of course, in Temple City, one found it quite the task to maintain any semblance of anonymity, so much so that it was a highly sought-after set of skills rarely found outside the city's criminal underworld. Luckily for Arthur, he was no stranger to that way of life. Even as he made his way onto the radar of some of the city's largest players, he was a master of his craft and gave them a run for their money. Arthur and his androids easily lost their escorts in the ocean of citizens as they continued through the city's bustling innards, using a protest to slip away.

He made his way to the hyperloop railway station, using a falsified identification chip to get aboard, and found comfort in the customary hiss muffled by the shell of the train as the surrounding atmosphere was sucked out of the tube. Once the tube had become a vacuum, Arthur felt the familiar, yet subtle sway of his boxcar, settle as the magnetic array took hold. He heard a girl sitting with her mother gasp as the train accelerated, their eyes meeting, and as she began to visibly calm down one of the androids stepped between the girl and the politician. There it remained for the duration of the ride, staring the little girl and her mother down with its cold emptiness.

By the time the train reached the city's outer limits, it had broken the sound barrier and still it continued to accelerate. Arthur looked out the translucent tube at Temple City as it slowly faded from view. What an incredible image it was, each and every time. Great waterfalls poured over its sides from its rooftop platform. Trees and vegetation clung to the exterior, failing with every attempt to break through the colossal cube of darkness and its toxic neon lights. The city of promise and intrigue was quickly swept away by lush countryside, the old world reclaimed by nature, vegetation, and wildlife alike.

Arthur let the hum of the magnetic array put him in a trance-like state in an attempt to push away the anticipation rising inside of him. Soon, another city appeared on the horizon, growing quickly. Like Temple City, large megalithic pyramid-shaped structures, serving as foundations, supported a variety of enormous skyscrapers connecting them together, except this city had no walls or ceiling. It appeared as though the Ascendency cared only about fortifying the mega structures holding the city's immense system of buildings together. It looked more like a web stretching across the sky in three-dimensional space resembling that of multiple expanded Hoberman spheres within one another, mostly devoid of any vegetation due to its high altitude.

Upon exiting the station, Arthur was hit by the warm gusts of air that spun through the open spaces of the city in vortices that carried all the city's scents. The food of high-end exclusive restaurants, and the food of street vendors; the smell of putrid steam trying to escape the city, and the oil that kept the city running. Dozens of smells weaved their way through the webbed city... the sweet scent of nostalgia, the politician thought as he inhaled deeply.

He activated a device that he wore on a finger like a ring as he began his journey through the crowded streets. It masked his digital identity, shuffling his appearance to all video feed anytime a person or object passed through a camera's line of sight of him. The androids remained by his side, and when he reached a platform to traverse the distance between that section of the city and another with nothing but empty space separating them, the machines folded in on themselves and clasped together to go with.

The platform holding Arthur and his body guards released its hold from the street and flew through the empty space along thin cords that weaved throughout the entire city, propelled by the very vortices carrying some of the politician's favorite smells. It took them to a deeper section of the city toward its center, and when they came to a stop the three of them stepped off the platform, and Arthur marveled at the sight of his home away from home. The largest building in the city, despite being dwarfed by those connected to the megalithic foundations, was still as imposing as ever as it towered over them. They followed their master inside and ascended thousands of floors until they reached his floor. The androids posted outside, on either side of his door, and Arthur entered his suite.

He breathed a sigh of relief once the door shut behind him. The weight of the world slid from his shoulders as he began disrobing, neatly setting his things where they belonged, and slouching against the island separating the kitchen from the dining room, which was closest to his front door. He poured himself a glass of pristine water, a rare commodity these days, and downed the whole thing. He made his way to the couch and collapsed upon it, before lazily pressing a series of buttons on a remote that activated his suite's security protocols, making his privacy absolute and his home nigh on impenetrable. His arm fell to his side as he melted into the furniture.

Politics is so draining, he thought, and there's no end in sight. Finally feeling safe enough to relax, he lied there decompressing and reflecting on the day's events. The speech that had rallied even more to his cause... to his ambitions. A smirk broke out upon his face as he recalled how many of the elite he had pissed off, and what little they could do about it. How many more he'd made question their own beliefs, and the potential allies he'd make. The ever-expanding bridge between the Ascendency and the people they neglected... the people they overlooked... the people they underestimated. It was all coming to a head, and he was going to be the face behind it all.

After some reflection, and feeling a little lighter, Arthur pulled himself from the couch and continued disrobing as he made his way to the shower. Steam poured from the faucet, fogging up the mirror, and he reveled in the scorching hot water as it rinsed away the filth... the façade he had to don day in and day out. Arthur could feel it burn from his flesh, shriveling into thin wisps of prevaricated unrest, coiling in on itself until it all just fell away as seared flakes leaving him wholly himself once more. He still wore the that same smirk, which then curled ever so slightly into a grin. The Ascendency would help him bring themselves to their knees.

After the much-needed shower, Arthur put on his robe and cleared the fog from the mirror, splashing his face with cold water. He looked into the reflection of his hardened, yet tired eyes and noticed the grin he was wearing. He wiped it from his face as he'd wiped the mirror clean, and stepped into his bedroom. He continued reflecting on the day's events, the lower-class citizens he'd helped, and the lives he had likely saved. Arthur stood before a wall, the furthest from the window that wrapped around most of his room, the godly view of the city of skies and aspiration that washed the inside of his home in natural light. "Privacy," he said, and the window darkened to a soft black that rendered his room into dark ambience.

Reflecting still, his thoughts found their way on the girl he'd made eye contact with on the train. He put his hand on the wall and it lit up from beneath the skin as the wall scanned it. Then a panel near his face slid open and his eyes were scanned next. The girl had recognized him... had looked into his eyes and found comfort. The panel near his face slid shut, and a familiar click sounded within the wall. A seam appeared in the wall as it became a door and slid open. Arthur felt his anticipation bubbling up to the surface as he stepped inside. The room was roughly the size of a walk-in closet. There was a chair, some hanging outfits, a chest, and at the very back there was a safe. Beside the safe, hanging on the wall, a placard with gridlines etched into it immediately grabbed his attention.

The placard was covered in X's, each one crossing out a specific box within the grid. The anticipation sparked into excitement as he brushed a finger across a blank box in the grid. His breaths were coming in heavy, and the politician attempted to ground himself and take control of his mind that had begun running away from him when a subtle flickering of light got his attention. It had come from his bedroom. He returned to the opening in his wall and looked out into the room... nothing. "Huh..." He shrugged as he returned to the secret opening in his wall, but then he felt a sudden shift in the airflow of his private quarters directly behind him. Before he could react in any meaningful way a glowing blade burst through his chest, then receded as he began shifting his body to look upon his attacker, and he collapsed to the floor.

"Who... are you?" Arthur asked, blood pouring from his mouth. He was looking at a figure shrouded in darkness. He tapped the screen on his wristwatch, and the darkness in the window lifted and his room was once again bathed in the sun's fading luminosity, the sunset imminent. A man wearing a combination of old-fashioned clothing and state-of-the-art military style armor, the lower half of his face hidden beneath a mask and a hood draped over his eyes, stared down at him. Arthur struggled to breathe as he coughed up even more blood. "Why?"

The attacker leaned down and looked him in his eyes, and

there was a passion… a rage burning in them. "Because people like you think they can get away with anything," the assassin told him coldly. Arthur's eyes popped wide open as a blade cackling and glowing with energy appeared out of thin air from a device, a bracer that his would-be killer wore, and before the killing strike stole his final breath, Arthur managed to gasp the word "help." Two mechanical slaves ran into the room, and a fight broke out between the murderer and the androids.

One of them attempted to hold the man down, but he tossed a device charged with energy at the other bot, and as it latched itself in place the charges were released, spreading throughout the android. There was nothing it could have done… its body began folding in on itself as it had done earlier, except it continued beyond its capabilities and destroyed itself in the process as it collapsed in the middle of the room. The man didn't wait around and watch it happen however, and he swung his free hand toward the remaining android. It dodged his swing and threw him, but instead of flying into the wall he hit an invisible field, hovering in the air for a moment before dropping to his feet. The android was already on him though, and as it lifted the man up once more, the man kicked at the android. A heatwave washed over the android and it was knocked backward a couple steps. The man took the moment to throw another of the devices. It latched onto the remaining android, it too becoming a crushed hunk of debris on the late politician's floor.

Silence and stillness settled upon the suite, and the assassin basked in it for a moment before heading back into the secret room behind the wall. First, he scanned Arthur's body for any desirables, and pocketed the device he'd worn like a ring. Second, he pulled out a syringe-like object from the belongings he carried on his person, and poked the corpse with it. The blood sample withdrew into the device and lights flashed around its circumference for a few seconds before turning solid. The killer activated the device and tossed it into the middle of the room. The man watched as everything possessing Arthur Flannagan's DNA was vaporized: the blood spatter, fingernail clippings, hair follicles, fingerprints, body oil, the teeth, bones and the entirety of the body... everything, gone, including the device he'd thrown into the room. There was literally nothing left of the politician; not his clothes, not even ash. It was as if he had simply vanished into thin air.

A few objects remained upon the floor where his body had lied moments earlier though, such as a key. The man picked it up and scanned the room before settling upon the chest. He used the key and unclasped the chest, opening it to find a ladder descending into another secret part of the home. As he climbed down he heard something scurrying across the floor. When the room below began to come into sight, he first saw a tripod... then a large area rug... then a mattress... and then some rattling chains. He heard a whimper as he reached the bottom, and looked upon a frightened little girl huddling in the corner of the room upon the mattress. "It's okay Scarlett," he told her as he lowered his mask and pulled back the hood, revealing a tightly trimmed beard that was slightly longer toward his chin, its length matching that of his mustache. Salt and peppered dirty blonde hair was tied back neatly, held in place by ornamental hair clips that doubled as weapons, were he to ever have need of them. His eyes were orange like the sunset, and the features upon his face were soft and warm. He extended a hand to her as he inched his way closer. "My name is Luther. I'm here to rescue you," he assured her. "Can I remove the chains?"

Scarlett nodded and Luther freed her with ease. She

barreled into him in a tight embrace, holding him for a time that seemed to stretch on for far too long. Luther gently pulled her away, and looked her in the eyes at her level. "Let's get you home, yeah?" She smiled and agreed. They made their way up the ladder and back into Arthur's suite. She looked around nervously for the politician, but there were no signs of him whatsoever. "He's gone," he told her. "He will never hurt you again." Scarlett barely noticed the clumps of metal on the floor that were once tormentors of hers as the two of them made their way to the window.

The final rays of sunlight were disappearing behind the horizon, and the city looked like an abstract work of art stretching into the sky. Hundreds of small platforms traversing the gaps between the various sections of the city, and solid ground a few thousand feet below them. Luther pulled his mask back over his face, lifted Scarlett up in one arm, and backed away from the window. With his free hand, he pressed a fingertip into his palm and once recognized as his, a device that had been flush with the rest of his hand lifted from the inside of his glove into his waiting fingers. "Hold on tight." Scarlett did as he said, but confusion erupted across her face, quickly followed by panic as the man tossed the device against the window and began sprinting for it.

As soon as the device contacted the window it split into three parts, repelled by one another upon the glass until the three points made a triangle. They started spinning in an arc upon the window and emitting lasers that connected with its other parts, creating a circular opening large enough for a burly grown man to leap through, and leap they did. As they flew through the opening, Luther reached toward the opening with his free hand and the device reassembled itself and flew back into the palm of his hand before he could blink once, the window appearing as it always had as if nothing had just transpired. Then they fell.

Scarlett screamed as they began their fall, but she held on to her savior for her dear life, just as she'd been told. The clouds beneath them blocked their view of the city's floor, and the wind howling past her ears made it impossible to hear herself, or anything the man may have been telling her. Then their fall slowed abruptly, and when she found the courage to open her eyes she saw that the man's boots were littering the sky with a wave of red energy, and she could feel its heat from her perch on Luther's side. He grabbed onto a platform rushing through the vast openness of the city and they lurched in its direction, disgruntled cries of shock and confusion spewing from its occupants.

As quickly as they had slowed, and had hitched a ride on the moving platform, they were flying through open air again. Except this time, they were not falling. This time, they were soaring horizontally from the platform to the side of another skyscraper. Luther ran across its surface without losing any elevation or momentum, and once he'd reached the other side he leapt once more. His boots made their landing on the rooftop of a much smaller building graceful and soft. "Recognize where we are?" he asked her. She finally let go of him, deciding she was finally safe, and took in her surroundings. She could smell the vendors across the street and noticed the lit-up book sign on another building across the way.

"Home..." she said, and tears began running down her cheeks. She gave Luther a big hug. "Thank you! Thank you for saving me." She looked him in the eyes one last time, his face lit up from the neon book sign. "I'll never forget you."

After returning Scarlett home safely, Luther made his way to a safehouse on the other side of the city. When he strode in he was greeted by a colleague. She was dressed very similarly to him: old fashioned clothing from the renaissance era with some modern flair, and state-of-the-art armor that hugged her feminine frame. "They aren't happy with you," she said as she walked beside him.

"What else is new?" Luther replied dryly.

"This is serious, Luther," she scolded him. "Politicians are off-limits without authorization. You—"

Luther scoffed in her face. "He was a pedophile, Dolores!" he snapped, his face going red. "Damn their authorization! How many more children did that monster have to destroy before he was brought to justice?" Their eyes met, and he could see sympathy, understanding, and agreement in her emerald colored eyes. "How many?" he asked calmly.

"I agree that he deserved to die," she said, "but we both know that the choice isn't ours to make. They have called for an immediate assembly. Everyone is being hailed as we speak. Don't be late, alright." Dolores put her hand on his shoulder, and he sighed. Luther knew he was in trouble, but he didn't care. He couldn't do nothing about people like Arthur Flannigan. He couldn't let the filthy bastard etch another X onto that placard. She gently squeezed his shoulder before they exchanged a nod, but before she went on her way she lingered for a moment. "We've still got some time to kill. I'm going to wash up." And off she went.

Luther knew that was an invitation, and he didn't make any moves to follow her right away. He'd had a rather emotionally draining experience, one that hit harder than others. He seemed to be awaiting a reprimand, and he could still see the terror in Scarlett's eyes when he first looked upon her. He splashed cold water into his face to shake it off... he could use Dolores's comfort; she was always good at that. He caught up with her as the last of her clothes slid from her tight curves, the shower already running and awaiting them. Her back was to him as he removed his armor and undressed. She stepped into the shower, glancing over her shoulder seductively, her green eyes hungry for their reunion. She lowered them to his waste as he removed his undergarments, biting her lip. He pulled her in close from behind as he joined her, his hands exploring her front as he pressed his lips against her tilted neck.

Less than an hour later they were gathered for the assembly. Seven others had joined them, and five others were there as holograms. They stood side by side, all facing the same direction. Three of their organization's leaders faced them, two of which were also holograms. The one present addressed them. "We have assembled because one amongst you have broken the code, and not for the first time." Everyone, including Dolores, turned their eyes upon Luther.

"He was a—" Luther started before being silenced.

"We know what Arthur Flannigan was," they said. "Yet, his aspirations aligned with our own. He would've chipped away at the Ascendency from within, openly I might add. He could have unknowingly accomplished so much for us, but now he is dead... a politician none were authorized to eliminate."

Silence followed the condemning statement. "Luther Lancaster," the leaders spoke after some internal discussion had taken place. "You are henceforth stripped of your rank, and you will not ascend beyond novice until you prove your loyalty to the Code." Rage burned within Luther, but he said nothing. "You understand what this means?"

"Yes," Luther replied.

"You are not to speak to other members unless spoken to. You will carry out tasks befitting your new station. Everyone except Luther and Dolores are excused."

The holograms vanished from sight, and the others retreated from the chamber, not so much as even acknowledging Luther's existence. He'd been warned, not just by superiors, but by his fellow members on multiple occasions. Their organization had been operating from the shadows for thousands of years, delicately and mercilessly plucking corruption at its roots, and steering civilization toward a brighter future, always. What other horrors have they allowed to transpire throughout history in the name of the greater good? Luther couldn't bring himself to stoop to that level, and if this was the price to pay for remaining true to himself, so be it.

Luther spent the next few months running errands for the guild. As unbecoming of his skills as the tasks were, he performed his duties flawlessly. He was a ghost, unheard and unseen, moving through the world and executing his objectives with unbiased precision. He'd often take his frustrations out on petty criminals, trash that killed the elderly during muggings, or that beat their wives and children, people far beneath the guild's radar... people wholly worthy of Luther's blades... people whose absence only made the world a better place. It was on one of these errands that Luther stumbled upon some knowledge concerning a legendary artifact the guild's archive mentions throughout its history, as well as its whereabouts.

The artifact supposedly once belonged to the guild, but was lost hundreds of years ago. There's scripture from the archives dating back thousands of years that mentions the object, and rather than reporting the discovery to the guild, he decided to go rogue and continue down the rabbit hole he'd come across. It led him to the ruins of the old world. Megalithic compounds like Temple City and Nexus City were scattered across the planet, built to house entire states, some of them even countries, an attempt to let the Earth heal from the damn near irreversible damage humanity had wrought. The Ascendency rose from the ashes of world governments attempting peaceful union with the Earth's preservation in mind, and only because there were no feasible alternatives.

The Ascendency controlled the world under one law... one governing body, and they were a beacon of hope for over two hundred years, but corruption slithers its way into all crevices... every crack in the armor was exploited by the serpent, its venom flowing through the veins of society until the Ascendency had become the tyrannical force Luther had always known. They outlawed living in the ruins of the old world, and only they were able to explore the wilds outside the cities, with the exception of agricultural regions of course, though those were heavily monitored and controlled.

Luther made his way to a long-forgotten dam in a desolate barren land, the structure still holding strong after all these years. It was wedged between two rocky cliffs that formed a ravine, the river having long dried up. Despite having been abandoned by humanity centuries earlier, Luther was impressed by its durability as it showed minimal signs of damage. As he approached an entrance he noticed an eagle perched on a skeletal tree near the dam, its head tilted, just staring at him. It must have noticed some prey because it ruffled its feathers, spread its wings and leapt from its branch with its talons outstretched and vanished from sight. The man's stomach began to groan at the thought of dinner, but he quickly overcame the sensation.

After examining the lock on the old dam, Luther went to work on it. Something so rudimentary was child's play, even without the guild's advanced technology. Then, from the corner of his eye as he successfully opened the door, he saw the eagle. It was perched on a skeletal tree near the dam, its head tilted, just staring at him. It must have noticed some prey because it ruffled its feathers, spread its wings and leapt from its branch with its talons outstretched and vanished from sight. The man's stomach began to groan at the thought of dinner, but he quickly overcame the sensation.

Strange, Luther thought, but dismissed any lingering thoughts as he entered the old building. It was silent and still inside, with no traces of activity for a very long time. He launched a device that would scan the place in its entirety, mapping it out for him as he continued exploring. The place was cold and dark, and had a musty smell about it, as if the air was full of moisture, but he knew that was impossible. He followed his newly constructed digitized map to an area deep within the structure. Its ceiling was high, and ornamental statues and carvings were present, indicating to Luther that the chamber held some sort of significance.

Upon the large marble floor was a map of the stars. The marble tiles placed in circular arcs around a center point, and as he studied them something seemed off. The floor shimmered and he nearly lost his balance and collapsed. Then he heard voices speaking a language he did not recognize. "Who's there?" He demanded, but no response came. Everything went bright for a moment and the room disappeared. He dropped to his knees, closed his eyes and covered his head. He could see flashes through his eyelids, but the light was too bright, opening them would be pointless. He felt a rush as if the room had spun with him in it, humming pounded loudly in his ears and he started to scream as he covered his head with his hands until the sound of his cries was deafening to his own ears.

It was as if nothing had just happened. The room was still and silent, dark and musty, and there were no traces of any light lingering in his sight... they were perfectly adjusted to the room's lighting, or lack thereof. His rising heartrate from the experience had settled as immediately as everything else had ceased, and he had to consider the possibility that there was something medically wrong with him. He'd have to be checked out once he returned to the city.

Upon further inspection of the floor, Luther noticed the constellations were out of place. He smirked as he illuminated the room, stepping back and taking in the bigger picture. "Clever," he said to himself as he figured out how the mechanism worked. The circular panels of marble rotated around other circular panels, the center indicating which way to arrange them in regards to north. Just as he finished the puzzle, he heard the same indecipherable voices. "Show yourself!" Luther shouted as he spun across the floor, red glowing blades shimmering with energy popping out of his bracers. His head was on a swivel, looking in every direction, and his breathing was expertly slowed to control his heartbeat and hearing. He stood where he was, arms up and blades extended, waiting....

Once he finished the puzzle, the center piece seemed higher than the rest of the floor. Luther pressed it in and the floor began shifting beneath his feet. It was an elevator that took him to a lower level, which looked nothing like the rest of the dam. There were statues resembling what appeared to be a sentient species he'd never seen before. "What is this place?" he asked aloud. It appeared to have been shoehorned into the damn at a much later date, but in its own way seemed more ancient. Perhaps the dam was built around this place? Perhaps this place was moved here during the construction of the dam? It didn't matter however, because he would never know.

Luther studied the statues. There were four of them, all facing the center between them. One held its hand up, as if it were observing the palm of its hand. Another held some sort of weapon in its hand, holding it up like the first statue held up its hand. The third held its fist up, and the fourth held its hand out horizontally, palm facing the floor. It had to mean something... as he pondered what to do next, he heard the squeaking of a rat and looked in its direction as it had been the only sound to break the chamber's silence. Luther couldn't believe what he was seeing though. He turned away from the statues and put all his attention on the rat. It was frozen. Not in the way water freezes into ice, and not in the way a child freezes when caught in the act of something they weren't supposed to be doing either. The rat was stuck in mid-sprint across the floor as if it had been paused. It squeaked again and Luther nearly tumbled backward.

When he poked it, it glitched like antique CCTV footage, as if it weren't really there but Luther had felt it... had heard it. The same voices sounded off from behind him as the rat bit him and scurried off. "Hey!" he yelled at the rat before spinning around to confront the voices, but there was nobody except him present. He looked back the way the rat had gone and the entire room glitched like the rat had, and for the briefest of moments he saw a different place entirely. "What's going on?" he asked no one again. He returned to the statues to examine them once more. He mimicked their hands and held his over the center. Blood from the tip of his finger where the rat had bitten him dropped to the floor and the floor began to vibrate.

Luther leaned down to inspect the droplet of blood and it was hovering above the vibrating floor ever so slightly. He then examined the statues' hands again. "Of course," and he pulled out a knife. He cut his hand open and held it over the floor, squeezing to pour the blood out more quickly. The floor began lighting up as the blood started dancing across it, forming a pattern. The statues began shifting and moving until they all reached toward the floor, as if beckoning something to appear. The room began glitching again and he looked around in a panic, but then it stopped and when he looked to where the blood had been forming a pattern, there was a golden orb. It was a little larger than an apple, indecipherable markings decorated its exterior, and an impression clearly in the shape of a hand visible upon its surface.

Reluctantly, Luther reached for the object. When his hand rested within the impression an explosion of images flooded his mind. Thousands of terabytes of data were being sent directly to the cerebral cortex for processing, then being redirected to the other parts of his brain as he was overcome by primal emotion, of every variety. He was immobilized by the process, but he could hear multiple voices surrounding him. "Now!" Came a familiar voice. He watched four members of the guild suddenly descend into the chamber, Dolores being one of them. "The artifact is activated," she told the others as she looked into Luther's eyes. "Retrieve it and—" Her voice faded as the others grew louder and louder. Ignoring Dolores, Luther turned his eyes toward the voices he'd been hearing since his arrival.

In the room with him, Dolores, and the other guild members, were beings that were not of their world, but neither did they resemble whatever the statues were. They were pointing at him and talking to one another as if observing. Before Dolores or the other members could pry the artifact from his hand, as data was pouring into his brain, he fought against every command holding him in place, screaming in pain as he defied them. As he turned and twisted his body toward the mysterious beings, the room began contorting and reality began glitching. The beings stopped talking and simply observed, then looked to one another erratically, realizing he could see them. They pulled out a device, but before they could use it, Luther flung his glitching body at them, the artifact shattering in the one hand, and his other grabbing onto the creature's device.

He got one glimpse of Dolores. She seemed utterly confused and terrified, and was in the middle of mouthing the words "I'm sorry," when he brought his other hand to the device, attempting to free it from their grasp. Instead, he watched as time rewound around him. He watched Dolores and the others moving in reverse, and once they were gone things moved too quickly for him to keep up. The environment and surroundings were flashing past faster than he could keep track of what was happening. When it stopped, he was on a battlefield, someone addressed him as sir, and cannon fire exploded all around him. He went flying backwards, landing by a puddle, and when his vision cleared and he got a good look at his reflection in the water, Luther Lancaster wasn't looking back at him. He began to panic, his eyes going wide, then reality glitched again. He looked for the creatures that had brought him there and they were gone.

A woman's face began coming into view, the battlefield slowly fading away, two realities getting mixed up as he tried to focus on one. He could hear the muffled sounds of someone's voice, then felt his body lurch to and fro. "Hey!" he heard as one reality finally settled around him. A woman's face greeted him there, a face he did not recognize. She was pulling him from a cramped space, but he felt weak and helpless. "Wake up already!" Her words were becoming clearer and clearer as the disorientation slipped away, until he was fully present in a new place.

His eyes focused on the woman, then his surroundings. He was in some sort of pod, and all the light he could see was artificial. Beyond that, all he could see was the woman's face. "Who are you?" he asked, and then his face scrunched up in confusion. It wasn't his voice coming from his mouth. "What's going on?" She frowned at him, then helped pull him free of the pod.

He stumbled from the pod and his heart sank. There were thousands of pods surrounding them. Rows and columns stretching for thousands of feet in every direction. He turned around to look at the pod he'd come from, examining it. The name Edmund Smith followed by the date 08/23/1863 was displayed on a screen attached to the pod. As he noticed the name and date they began changing until it stopped on Luther Lancaster, showing a date of 11/29/2376, and a wave of nausea overcame him.

The man collapsed onto the floor that was more like scaffolding than an actual floor. He threw up bile, his body shaking. "Get up," the woman told him. "We aren't safe here... they'll find us." She helped pull him to his feet.

"Where are we?" he asked her. "Who are you?"

"What do you remember?" she asked him.

He tried to recall the last thing that made sense to him. "The artifact..." he gasped. Then his mind was flooded with imagery. An ancient species from the stars, ones resembling the statues, came to Earth tens of thousands of years ago. They helped advance evolution on the planet, helping homo sapiens to reach the level of intellect necessary to produce civilization. They nurtured humanity from its inception, gifted them with powerful artifacts and a map detailing how to find them when the time came. He watched civilization thrive and flourish. They reached a level of advancement they hadn't yet reached in the time he could remember. Then he watched their civilization collapse. Another alien species, ones resembling the creatures he saw with the device that had rewound time, attacked them.

They nearly defeated them, and the aliens limped back to their distant star, but the loss was almost absolute. Humanity, nearly extinct, lingered along for thousands of years, and he watched civilizations rise and fall throughout time, each one's end nearly driving humanity to extinction. "Can you please tell me what's going on?" he asked.

Once he and the woman were safely hidden, she explained. "Look," she told him as she pointed out a window. They were in space. The man's gut tightened up. "I don't have the full picture, but what I have gathered since waking up is this: the aliens abducting us, they destroyed the Earth hundreds of years ago… only problem was, they later discovered Earth held a secret they wanted. So," she gestured around them, pods for miles in every direction, "they recreated the Earth using the memories within our DNA. With enough humans… enough DNA, they were able to digitally reconstruct the Earth and its events as experienced by our ancestors.

"The artifact… it…" he stammered. "They want the map…" His eyes bulged… they knew he held its secrets now. "How do you know all this?" he asked the woman sternly.

"One of them told me," she answered hesitantly. "They

didn't give me a reason, but made it seem urgent that I found you... that I got you out..." Tears welled up in her eyes. "And I did... they knew I would..."

"They knew?" he asked, suspicion sprawling across his face. "How? Why?"

She wiped the tears from her eyes. "I told you I'd never forget you."

Under the Sister Moons

She grit her teeth, digging them deeper into the leather bound dowel, her eyes watering from the pain, as her elders slowly and methodically jabbed her pale flesh with a needle. She was only about eight years old, and she'd been lying there for hours already. They repeatedly dipped the needles, which were the bones of some ancient creature her tribe had held onto for hundreds of years, into a bowl of sea badger oil mixed with soot. She knew the soot had been specially prepared just for such an occasion, the byproduct of burning sacred wood that was said to have come from her people's ancestral home.

Even though she was only eight she knew the importance of the ritual used to prepare the soot. Much of the tribe imbued the ancient wood, or the flames that fed upon it, with the energy they channeled through the synchronized chanting they invoked in their ancestral tongue. Lexa knew not which had been the case... she only knew that these tattoos were vital to her heritage, and upon completion she would be true Snehóvškriátok. Still, even as the elders poked and prodded her skin attentively and meticulously, she could hear the words of her ancestors being sung through the burning in her ears.

She squinted through the glaze in her eyes, quietly grunting through the pain, an icy blue glow surrounding her as she sent her mind elsewhere. She inhaled deeply, steadying her mind, and recalled the recent events that led to her current predicament. She was sparring with another. "Come on then," her spar partner taunted. "Try and hit me." Lexa growled her frustrations and leapt through the air at her opponent. She was quick for a youngling, but not quick enough. They evaded every attempt, laughing all the while, setting the girl's frustrations ablaze.

"You'll regret taunting her one of these days, Aguta," Lexa heard another of her tribe's warriors say from the sidelines.

The youngling dared not let the interruption distract her though, and she attacked Aguta with a renewed vigor. All her life all she ever wanted was to join the ranks of the warriors of the Snehóvškriátok. They were a nomadic people that traversed the vast tundra that stretched in every direction for as far as the eyes could see. The treacherous landscape was all she'd ever known, and she found it difficult to believe there were lands that existed beyond the frigid wilderness, yet she'd heard her people speak of such places. The tundra was a harsh and brutal place riddled with endless dangers ranging from other warring tribes, enormous vicious beasts always on the prowl for their next meal, and the relentless blizzards that came and went as often as day and night. To be afraid was to be weak, and to be weak meant certain death... or worse.

"You misunderstand Anuk," Aguta replied while dodging the girl's attacks with ease. "I will relish the day!"

Lexa heard Anuk laugh from somewhere beside them. "Well hurry it up!" he said, his tone shifting from one of warning to a more assertive one. "Hunting party heads out soon." Lexa didn't miss the wink Anuk gave her.

"Finally!" Aguta cried out happily. "It's about—" A fearsome growl erupted from Lexa, and she dove between his legs, taking advantage of the distraction. Aguta spun to face his fierce little adversary but she wasn't there. "What?" he murmured, confused, as he spun again when he heard Anuk's laughter. Lexa pounced upon him and he stumbled backward in surprise, throwing his arm up to deflect the feisty little beast.

A crowd of people had gathered to watch now, cheering and hollering as Lexa grabbed Aguta's upraised arm, using her forward momentum to swing herself up and around to his back. He spun again, and reached for her, but she reached out and slapped his cheek from behind and kicked off his back, landing softly upon the snow and grinning ear to ear. The cheers were for her, and it was her turn to laugh when she saw the dumbfounded expression he was wearing. She crossed her arms, the smug look on her face inviting the onslaught of praise that was inevitably coming her way. "Does that count?" Aguta asked the others, his face slowly twisting into a grin. "Impressive little Lexaldra. We'll go again later, yeah?" He moved to join his companion Anuk.

"I'm coming with you," Lexa blurted out as the crowd began to disperse, her grin slowly curling into a frown.

"No," Aguta began, "it's—"

"Dangerous?" Lexa snorted. "I earned it! I'm coming with!"

Aguta looked to Anuk for backup, but none came. Anuk shrugged and taunted him with a smile of his own. "You can't deny her, as unorthodox as it is, it's the path she's chosen for herself."

Lexa's moist purple eyes popped open and she cried out in pain as the needle dug into her spine. She forced a grin as she grimaced through the pain, and thought of the hunt. Though it wasn't unheard of for their women to share Lexa's aspirations, they typically leaned toward helping to raise the children, crafting tools and weapons, making leather from animal hide, curing it, and protecting the tribe's camp while the warriors and hunters were gone. The Snehóvškriátok people set no expectations for anyone either way though, and the feisty little girl had always possessed more fight than nurture. It had come as no surprise to anyone when she started down this path, as both of her parents had perished in battle against another tribe when she was still too young to remember their faces. Such paths however, required a degree of hardship, and demanded no less from children as they did from anyone else.

There were a handful of children among her people who, just like her, were parentless and raised by the tribe as a whole. Most of them however, were either much younger or much older than she was. The younger kids tended to fear her while the older ones simply had no interest in her. She felt more comfortable being alone anyway and spent most of her time either listening to the elders weave tales of their ancestors and their endeavors, or the mysterious collapse of their once grand civilization. She would watch the warriors spar with one another when she wasn't actively participating, bask in the harsh elements of the tundra, or gaze longingly and in awe at the night sky. The elders would speak of a time, long, long ago, when the first of their people arrived in this world from somewhere beyond the stars. She'd lie beneath them at times and pretend to know exactly which star they once called their own. Sometimes, if she poured a significant amount of her time and energy into it, she could feel the presence of her ancestors watching over her, or attempting to convey something to her.

She had earned her right to join the hunt, and hunt she did. It was tradition to allow the newest member of the hunt to lead the pack, and to make the kill, and Lexa had done so in spades. It was all too easy for the young girl, and even though some proudly proclaimed that the ancestors were guiding her faithfully and true down her chosen path, there were others who looked down upon her, calling her a fluke... that her luck was mere coincidence and would eventually run out. She'd hear whispers among them claiming she had it far too easy, and if she hoped to survive, the tribe needed to truly challenge her. The words would echo in her thoughts, and they festered there until she believed them.

The tribe gathered at the center of camp for the hunt's return, the icy wind repelled by the large communal fire built there for all to share. Their return had been spotted from miles away, the vastness of the open tundra stretching from horizon to horizon, nothing obstructing their view. The occasional forest or rock face rising from the glacial depths, its ridges casting shadows far across the land, sprouted up here and there, but they were few and far between. The hunters hauled their catch into camp, cheers and praise for Lexa resounding through the place, but she wouldn't relish in them.

"Why are you not feasting with the others, child?" a familiar voice asked, breaking through the wall of doubt that had been building inside of her. They had been back for a few hours and her prey had been skinned, prepared and cooked already, but she was found in the outskirts of camp, alone and brooding. "It was your kill was it not?"

Lexa looked at her chieftain, leader of her people, and frowned. "It was," she replied, though her voice retained the doubt possessing her mind.

"Tell me what it is that plagues your soul young Lexaldra." The chieftain of her people viewed them all as his family. He did what he could to keep the peace between them, while managing their nomadic and, often, barbaric ways. It was a delicate balance, but Chief Atreyu was well versed in the ways of their ancestors, deeply respected among his people, and as fierce as he was wise. "Your absence has not gone unnoticed. Anuk and Aguta have expressed their concern."

Lexa wanted to scream. Tears dropped to the ground as the needle stabbed at her nerves, sending jolts of pain throughout her body. She felt her teeth sinking into the leather-bound dowel as her jaw clenched against it, leaving permanent impressions upon the object. The memory made her want to scream as well, however. She had finally regarded her chieftain, a darkness in her purple eyes.

"Nothing I do is good enough..." she blurted out in frustration. "I hear what they say... what do I have to do? They think I'm weak, but I will prove them wrong!" Tears flowed down her pale cheeks, and flustered growls escaped her lips as she fought the urge to scream at the top of her lungs into the frigid night.

"Sometimes, Lexaladra," Atreyu said calmly, "the only person you have to prove anything to is yourself. Sometimes, that is enough."

Lexa looked her chieftain in the eyes. "Tell me," she said coldly, all emotion having vanished from her young features.

Atreyu sighed and turned his attention to the heavens. "Both of your parents were fierce warriors. They struck fear into the hearts of every enemy they faced, and..." He turned to look upon Lexa once more, a bittersweet smile curling the corners of his lips ever so slightly. "...when you were born, they proclaimed before the gods of this world that you would be the most ferocious of us all... very well."

Lexa's ears perked up, and she gave Atreyu her full attention.

"There's a rite of passage that our people may conduct. It is a dangerous and brutal quest, and many have perished in their attempts over the centuries. There are so few of us left now... it is no longer expected of our people..."

"My parents did it though?"

Atreyu fought the urge to forbid the little girl from following in their footsteps. "They did," he finally confirmed.

Lexa stood up and looked to the stars. "What do I need to do?"

"You'd be the youngest to ever embark on this quest... there is no rush, child."

Lexa closed her eyes, her head tilted toward the sky. She inhaled deeply, the icy air flowing into her body and filling her lungs. She listened to the wind and contemplated her path. She filled her thoughts with those of her parents, the spirit of them, and listened. The freezing air in her lungs grew hot in her chest. The sudden shift in temperature was not uncomfortable, but felt more like an embrace. "I am not afraid," she said with finality. Atreyu looked her over, his face a mixture of sadness, regret, pride and envy.

Lexa squeezed her hands, her nails piercing the flesh of her palms as the needles continued down her mid back. She clenched her eyes shut, bit even harder into the dowel, and groaned as the elders slowly and meticulously turned her body into a canvas.

"You don't need to do this Lexaldra," Anuk told her as she prepared for her quest. "You've already more than proven yourself…"

She shot Anuk with a glare that shut him up. "Tell that to Ohanu and Aiyana…"

"They didn't…" He started.

"…and Evolet! And Nayati, and Hokota, and the others too!" she snapped.

Anuk couldn't believe the girl was only eight years old. She was quite the child, and he'd played a big role in her upbringing he liked to believe, but she was becoming uncontrollable, headstrong, and reckless. He said nothing in return, only nodded, and began assisting in her preparations.

Later that day the tribe wished her luck and saw her off. Anuk escorted her a few miles from the Snehóvškriátok camp before leaving her to her own devices. "Continue in this direction until the landscape gets rocky. Could take a few days, but you'll notice the change in the tundra," he explained to the girl. "Once you reach the chasm, be weary. Chasm shrills don't take kindly to intruders, so try not to startle any. The gleaming frost cap grows in the beast's excrement. One big one should suffice, alright?" Anuk wanted to scold her… to scream at her… to knock her out and carry her home, but she'd chosen her path, and for her to return empty handed now would mean certain embarrassment.

"Thank you Anuk."

Lexa turned to see Anuk where she had left him, shrinking into the distance as he watched her go. She was more certain of her path now than she had ever been. The first day went without incident, and she slept in a snow burrow she dug herself. She built a fire to melt snow in order to hydrate, and on the second day she continued on her way. Eventually she came upon a small forest, and she took in the rare sight with widened eyes. "Whoa..." She'd seen trees before, but she was a lot younger then. The wildlife there was far more active than out on the open plains of the tundra. It wasn't long before she picked up the scent of meat cooking over a fire.

When she reached the makeshift camp, she saw two adults and a child dressed in furs... layers and layers of furs... so much that they looked large and puffy. She nearly giggled at the sight, but then her stomach began growling. She supposed she should do the same as the strangely dressed people were, and procure herself a meal. Then she heard growling and saw that the people were surrounded by wolves. She hesitated... surely, they could take care of themselves... the tundra was an incredibly dangerous place after all. She watched as the two taller figures fought the vicious animals, and chased them away, leaving the child alone. They didn't appear any older than her, and they clumsily held a spear close, looking this way and that.

Before the adults returned to the child, a large lone wolf crept into their camp. Clearly, that kid was no expert with the spear it held, and Lexa looked around frantically for any signs of the people she assumed were the kid's parents. They were nowhere to be seen. Her heart began to race as the wolf inched its way closer to the camp. It became clear to the girl that the child was done for if she did nothing, so she charged the camp. Lexa screamed as she came upon the wolf, who was seconds from lunging at the child, and as the animal turned toward her, the two of them went sprawling aside in a flurry of limbs.

The wolf flung its head this way and that, trying to bite Lexa, its body thrashing around as she fought the wild creature. Its growls and barks deafening to the girl's ears, and she didn't know how long she could hold the wolf's maw away. The growls became yelps as she snapped one of the creature's legs just to get it off of her. "Here!" She heard the child call out to her. She looked just in time to catch the spear and drove it through the wolf's neck.

In the rush of the moment, death having been seconds away, the boy couldn't get a great look at neither the wolf or the girl that had come to his aid, but once the frantic fight between the two had subsided and the world slowed back down, he realized... there were no footprints in the snow where the girl had charged from. How was that possible? When he looked upon her he was greeted by the grinning form of Lexa holding his spear. She was tiny in stature, smaller than him even, and she wasn't wearing any furs... in fact, he would likely freeze to death in a mere few hours if he wore what little she was wearing. Her skin was almost as white as the snow itself, accented by a faint gray-ish blue. His eyes widened as he continued to take in the girl's appearance. Her fingernails were like little claws, and her hair was a wild mess of white. Her purple eyes popped compared to the rest of her, and her grin revealed subtle fangs that reminded him of a cat's, but the dead giveaway was her ears. Unlike his, the girl's ears were long and ended in points.

Lexa saw fear in the boy's eyes as he looked upon her, and the smile fell from her face, replaced by confusion. "Don't worry..." she started to say.

"You're a..." the boy stammered, his voice beginning to quake. "You're a snow elf!"

Lexa rolled her eyes and smiled, her posture relaxing. "Nothing gets past you does it?" She snorted, thoroughly amused. "And what are you supposed to be?" She exaggerated her examination of him and his ridiculous clothes. "You're way too small to pass as a yeti!" She laughed at the absurdity of all the fur he wore. She wondered how he could even move in all of it. It was his turn to look confused, but the fear was clearly still there.

"Hey!" a man's voice screamed from behind her. As she spun to confront the newcomer something heavy hit her across the face. The spear flew from her hand as she tumbled to the ground, and into the snow. She hissed as she recovered and looked upon her assailants. A man and a woman, the boy's parents, had returned. She remained low to the ground, ready to pounce if need be, baring her fangs and studying them; taking a measure of them, their size, their weapons, etc. "Get away from him!" he yelled at her, now pointing the spear at her. "Get outta here you savage little beast!" She saw the boy's mom pulling him into her arms and scurrying to get behind the man. He began thrusting the spear toward Lexa, over and over.

For a moment Lexa had nearly listened to the man and ran off, but with every thrust of the spear a rage burned brighter and hotter within her. She felt every doubt that had ever been cast upon her... every sparring match she'd lost... she felt the way her heart ached when she heard others tell stories of her parents... her face grew stiff, and her eyes sank into slits. She caught the next thrust of the spear and used its momentum to roll away from him, yanking the spear from his trembling grasp. Lexa pounced on him then, driving him to the ground and screamed in his face at the top of her lungs, her fangs glistening in the light bouncing off the snow. She raised the spear up high, her scream becoming a feral growl as she channeled the untapped rage. As she was thrusting the spear tip toward him she heard the woman's sobbing cry, a shriek that reverberated off the trees, and at the last second Lexa stopped. Her chest rose and fell, the adrenaline having taken control, and she looked at the desperate woman and frightened boy in her arms, and then the shocked man beneath her. Lexa cried out in frustration and threw the spear aside before sprinting away and disappearing into the woods.

That night, after continuing her way toward the chasm Chief Atreyu and Anuk told her about, and having left the forest far behind her, the landscape became rockier and rockier. There were ridges jutting up and out of the ground, creating formations she hadn't seen before... formations akin to what she'd heard others call mountains but on a much smaller scale. She sat upon one such ridge, looking to the stars as she did so often, and snow eventually began to fall. The cold meant nothing to her or other snow elves for they thrived in such conditions, but as her stomach growled she thought of the slain wolf, wishing she'd had the opportunity to snag its corpse. She raised her arms and closed her eyes. The wind was the only sound she could hear, but it was within the icy wind, the snowfall, and silence of the tundra itself where one found the company of their long-lost ancestors.

As the snow came down harder, the wind subsided. It was so quiet she could almost hear the snowflakes hitting the ground. Lexa closed her eyes, and through the needle's jabs and the elfish chanting around her, she recalled the moment she found that comfort. It was as if the sky was holding its breath, each snowflake landing with a soft thud, but then came the wind in short gentle bursts as the sky exhaled against her skin. She heard voices on the wind with each of the sky's breaths, but they spoke in a dialect she didn't quite understand. "Yes?" she whispered excitedly. "I can hear you. I'm here!" The indecipherable words in the cold air pulled her in opposite directions. Even though she couldn't understand them, she felt them. She could continue on, or she could....

Lexa felt the warning, the excitement, the yearning, and the sense of belonging pulling her deeper into the rocky terrain... but she also felt the comfort of peace, familiarity, and acceptance pulling her further along. Both sensations felt welcoming to the girl, but something about the warning... the inkling of danger that had always called to her that made her feel alive, had her going deeper into the foreign terrain. The snow elf came upon a cave, and it wasn't difficult for the girl to discern it was a den of some sort. A den meant food. Lexa began salivating as she thought of eating, inciting another deep growl from her stomach as she approached the mouth of the cave.

She drew a hunting knife Anuk had given her, preparing for a kill, and crept further inside. She came upon a large white feline covered in black stripes. The animal could feed a dozen or more children her size, and killing it would be an utter waste, but she hadn't eaten in two days. She would need her strength if she were to face the chasm shrill and live to tell the tale. It was asleep as she crept up on it, but even as it dawned on her that she couldn't kill such a majestic and beautiful creature, Lexa heard the playful noises of cubs. The beast was a new mother, and she watched as four little ones climbed over her and each other to feed.

Lexa smiled as she watched the cubs, sheathing her knife as she did, and when her eyes fell upon the mother again she froze. It had woken up and was staring hard at her, watching her intently. Lexa put her hands up and slowly backed away. She lowered her gaze from the mother as a sign of respect, and continued her slow retreat. Then a vicious roar shook the cave and when she looked up she saw what she could only assume was the creature's mate. He could tear her to pieces easily, and he wasn't happy. She turned and ran faster than she'd ever run in her life. She could feel the rush of air as they both moved quickly through the cave. When she reached the mouth of the cave she leapt from the ridge it sat upon, falling further than a stone toss below... hitting the rocky decline hard and tumbling down and into the snow. Though beaten from the fall, she staggered to her feet, picked a random direction, and ran to the best of her ability right into the butt of a weapon knocking her square out.

When she began to stir, she felt restrained... confined in a small position, her skin burning. The ropes of a net had been rubbing against her exposed skin. Her hands were tied together, and her wrists were tied to her waist... she wasn't cutting through with her nails. She could hear enough to understand the people she had bumped into earlier had caught up to her, and were responsible for her predicament. She didn't know where she was, and she couldn't see as they had also blindfolded her.

Lexa had no idea how long she'd been unconscious, but she waited and listened, and heard enough to know her capture was a product of vengeance. Snow elves had killed many of their people in battle, but she knew her people didn't kill without purpose. Their deaths were likely a result from their people starting a fight they couldn't finish. The snow elf began wriggling around frantically, whining, whimpering and growling.

"*Shhhh...*" she heard from somewhere near her. "They'll hear you and know you're awake." It was the boy she had saved from the wolf. He reached into the net and pulled her blindfold off. He didn't look silly and puffy anymore, she noticed as she studied the boy's face, her purple eyes boring deeply into his being. She thought about asking why he was helping her, but quickly concluded that it didn't matter... she did the same for him after all, so she just offered him silence, and watched as he went to work cutting through her restraints. "I don't care what they say... you were kind to me..." He cut through the restraints tying her wrists to her waist and started on the rope holding her wrists together. "I can't let anything happen to you." Lexa no longer saw fear in his eyes as he looked upon her. She saw kindness, remorse and determination.

Even though the boy was bigger than her, it was obvious to Lexa he was younger than her. To defy his people... his culture... his parents at such a young age, and in such a consequential way... she looked into his almond shaped brown eyes, tears nearly falling from her own, and when she was free from her bonds she hesitated. He looked at her confused, then pointed in a direction. "That's north," he said as if a nomadic snow elf who lived beneath the stars and spent her life wandering the endless tundra couldn't figure it out for herself, but his words seemed to fall upon deaf ears. "You can't stay here!" The boy turned frantically, his voice rising in desperation. "You need to go, now!" Lexa wrapped him in her arms and hugged him like she'd never hugged anyone before. It took a moment, but the boy finally returned the gesture.

"What's your name?" she asked, her arms still around him.

"Luka..."

"Thank you, Luka. I'm—" They were interrupted by heavy footsteps nearby that were growing louder with each step, accompanied by voices filled with pain and cruelty.

"Go!" the boy urged her, and the snow elf was gone.

Lexa thought of Luka as the elders began sinking the bone needles into her face. The cultural milestone was nearly behind her. She clutched a railing in her hands tightly as each prod into her face sent blinding light searing into her vision, but the worst of it was past, and she refused to show anymore weakness.

The next day Lexa found the chasm. Using a system of roots and stone, she climbed down the cliff face of the scar within the tundra, the fall to the bottom so far below her she would surely perish if she were to lose her hold. After some time descending along the frozen cliffside she spotted an opening, a large crevice in the side of the chasm. It didn't take her long to reach, and she landed on its ledge with a grace only an elf could. As she crept further inside, as silently as a cat stalking its prey, she realized it wasn't so much a cave system as it was a deep shelf embedded within the tundra, and no beasts in sight. There were a couple tunnels leading to smaller areas further inside, one of which contained an empty nest, but otherwise seemingly abandoned.

Lexa approached the ledge and looked around the chasm. She could see no other openings, and she followed Chief Atreyu's directions perfectly. She didn't understand... her heart sank as she wondered if the creatures had migrated elsewhere despite the chieftain's certainty. She crouched upon the ledge, watching, waiting, and remained so until nightfall. It wasn't until darkness had spread across the land that a shimmering glow from within the crevice grabbed her attention. It came from one of the deeper chambers down one of the tunnels. Confusion washed over her as she came upon a massive beast, the blue glow fading as she approached it. How was it possible? Lexa couldn't make sense of it, but she didn't have time to wonder either, as the beast turned its gaze upon her lithe form.

It had the head of a massive bird, its beak alone bigger than she was, a primal intelligence reflected in its icy blue eyes as it cocked its head and studied her. Its white and gray feathers spread from its face to its front legs, which ended in enormous taloned feet, and down the front half of its body. The feathers seamlessly transitioned into long wavy white and gray fur, dark ring looking spots speckled along its lower half. Its hind legs reminded Lexa of the great striped feline she'd found with its cubs. Its long spiny tail resembled the creature's forelegs, and sprouted long dark hairs at its tip. The chasm shrill flexed its talons, its body shuddering as it appeared to become more and more agitated as Lexa just stood there watching it, too afraid to move. It shrieked so loudly that Lexa's world went dark and quiet, replaced by a sharp ringing in her ears after a moment of sheer pain.

Lexa turned and ran from the chamber and down the tunnel toward the main shelf in the cliffside. She heard the large creature's body scraping along the tunnel's walls behind her, until she didn't. A bright blue light erupted before her as she reached the shelf, and the chasm shrill appeared out of thin air and blue energy that resembled lightning. She slid to a halt and gasped, wide eyed and unsure what to do. The chasm shrill's body was transparent, dark like a silhouette, and glowed with blue light, and as the glow faded its body became less transparent. "What are you?" Lexa cried as it swung a talon at her. She managed to dive under its huge leg and then it whipped its tail around, hitting the snow elf in the chest. She flew toward the ledge, hitting the ground hard. As the chasm shrill approached her it unfurled its impressive wings, covered in its white and gray feathers, and beat them against the cold air. Lexa's small frame slid backwards toward the ledge as the beast's wings flapped, and the creature slowly advanced on her. It struck at her with its beak, and ended up catapulting her from its home.

Lexa squealed as she was shoved from the ledge and fell a ways before snagging some roots on the cliffside, still a long way from the bottom of the chasm. The shrill pierced the quiet with another of its high pitched and deafening screeches as it dove from the ledge toward Lexa. It flew down to her and tried swatting her loose with its talons, its beak, and its tail but each time Lexa rolled across the cliff's surface, the tangle of roots kept her easily perched in place. The shrill began trying much harder, using its talons to tear through the roots until Lexa was barely holding on. The creature flew out to await her demise, and she watched it defecate as it hovered in place, the droppings plummeting to the ground far below. If she didn't act fast she would splatter against the bottom as surely as its excrement was about to.

She was not going home empty handed. Lexa growled as she kicked off the cliffside, launching herself at the beast faster than it had thought possible. As she wrapped her limbs around the chasm shrill, grabbing tufts of feathers and fur tightly in her hands, it cried out and convulsed in flight. It flew upside down, slammed its body into the side of the chasm a few times, and fell into a steep dive. Lexa held on for her dear life, but she was losing her grip. As soon as the creature felt free of the snow elf's stubborn grasp, it became transparent, glowing blue, and vanished.

Lexa, dangling from the shrill's tail, dug her nails in just as a blue light encompassed them both. Darkness overcame them for the briefest of moments before something Lexa could not wrap her mind around exploded all around them. She saw worlds upon worlds in a sea of infinite stars, layered one after the other, all connected by glowing strands that weaved in every direction. The shrill jerked suddenly, realizing the snow elf was still attached to it, sending Lexa's body flinging around, and she got another incomprehensible view. One of the ethereal strands with no end in sight dangled from her chest as the beast flew haphazardly, but she could do nothing except hold on as she got whipped around relentlessly. As quickly as the strange tapestry of worlds had greeted her, she was back within the chasm, the shrill in a dive once more.

Its momentum slightly slowed by its progression through realities saved her. It finally flung Lexa from itself as they neared the bottom of the chasm, and she slowed herself further by falling through strange plants jutting out of the cliff before hitting the ground, the wind blasting from her chest. She lied there choking on the absence of air in her compressed lungs, unable to breathe or move, until she managed to roll herself onto her back. She watched the shrill fly around looking for her through thick branches above before giving up and disappearing from sight.

Lexa waited for a time before daring to move, taking the opportunity to learn how to breathe again. Once she finally did, a smile found its way to her battered face. Strange icy blue mushrooms were growing from old shrill droppings scattered upon the chasm's floor, and they were glowing with a similar light she'd seen surrounding the shrill, as well as the strange place it had taken them.

Upon returning to her tribe with half a dozen of the gleaming frost caps, Lexa was celebrated for her success. The elders wasted no time preparing her for the most sacred of ceremonies: receiving the ancestral runes of her people, a tradition the snow elves had passed down since before the collapse of their once great civilization. Lexa gritted her teeth against the dowel as they finished inscribing her flesh with the elven runes. As the dowel was removed from her mouth, Chief Atreyu greeted her with a tea made from the mushrooms she had gathered on her quest. As the contents flowed through her body the runes began glowing an icy blue, like the others surrounding her.

"The cold connects us all to the powers our ancestors once wielded," Atreyu told her. "No Snehóvškriátok would dare question Lexaldra again. Your parents would be proud, child."

A tear ran down her cheek and she smiled her thanks. "Just in time for the festival too!" Atreyu added gleefully. The timing was perfect! "You know this eclipse only honors us with its presence every twenty-five years!"

With the eclipse imminent, Lexa found herself seeking some solitude despite the festivities and celebration all around her. Some were dancing by the fire, others were demonstrating the feats of their kin now passed, and children were entertained by stories. Some of the tribe's warriors were engaged in trials of strength, a pass time activity where they tested their unarmed skills against one another. The sounds of fighting, laughter, storytelling, children gasping in awe and wonder, the fire crackling, conversation, love making and howls in the distance all danced in her ears like the elven songs of old.

Lexa listened to it all, smiling and gazing at the blanket of stars above. In this moment, everything seemed so perfect, yet her mind would not find peace. She thought of the human boy and the majestic creatures she encountered on her quest, but the things that haunted her was the warning on the wind that second night, and even more so than that, the place the shrill had taken her... the infinite worlds, or realities, swimming among the stars. Lexa watched a meteor shower, and the northern lights dancing overhead, laying there with her head resting on her hands and feet dangling back and forth over the edge of the pile of snow she built and occupied. This was her home; this was where she belonged, and as ferocious and brutal as her people were, they were equally as compassionate.

"You seem different somehow," Anuk said as he joined her. "You know, I never doubted you for a second."

Lexa smiled up at him but she never diverted her attention from the sky. He followed her gaze, and looked upon the two moons that would soon align. "Thank you Anuk... for believing in me even when others didn't." He looked back to the girl he helped raise, pride swelling within him as her runes illuminated him in an icy blue glow. Before he could respond, the camp's festive celebration quieted around them until silence spread like a plague. They looked at each other inquisitively, then sat up looking around, curious as to what was happening.

Lexa's pointy ears perked suddenly when she heard snow padded footsteps approaching just outside the camp, and stood up to see what was going on much like everyone around her. A large man dressed in furs head to toe entered their camp, and many snow elves glared at him, hands upon their weapons, ready to attack at the first sign of aggression. "A human..." Anuk said distastefully. "How dare—"

"Not all humans are bad." Lexa's unexpected retort silenced him.

They watched the tall man greet Atreyu as if they were old friends. She could only see above the man's waist from her vantage point, but she noticed some of the other kids pointing toward the man's legs. She began moving around to try and get a look without disrupting whatever transaction was taking place, but Anuk grabbed her arm and when she looked his way he was shaking his head. Her chief and the man shared a friendly exchange of respect, a sign that the stranger was well accustomed to her people and their ways, and that he was welcome, yet the snow elves remained silent and on edge. She didn't know what to do so she just waited beside Anuk and watched as the man walked to the center of camp. It wasn't until he did so that she could see what the other children had pointed at. Walking beside the newcomer was a large familiar animal, a great white feline with black stripes covering its body. He crouched down to eye level with the animal and when he stood up, it began wandering the camp on its own.

She was so confused... what was happening? Never before had Lexa seen her people so quiet and attentive, so she didn't act upon her nagging impulses as she watched the beast slowly make its way toward her, sniffing and ignoring others of her tribe. Her purple eyes went wide as it came right up to her. Anuk watched curiously as the animal and the girl looked into one another's eyes. It was the most beautiful creature she had ever seen. It sniffed her then sat down before her and looked around to the man waiting at the center of camp. When he approached, his companion stepped aside, and he knelt down to greet her. "Hello," he said smiling, "what's your name?" Lexa looked to some of the others and they nodded their approval, then looked to Anuk and he shrugged. She returned her attention to the stranger. "Lexaldra," she answered. "Who are you?"

"I am Jarik," he replied, "and this is Nyx. Didn't take her long to find you..."

Lexa began to panic.

"Come," he said softly. "We have much to do." What? She was confused, and her whole world began crumbling around her.

"I didn't do anything!" Lexa cried. "I didn't hurt them!"

Jarik looked at her, his face full of regret and compassion. "Do not fret child—"

"She isn't going anywhere with you!" Anuk told him, a threat looming within his voice.

Jarik stood up to face Anuk, towering over the snow elf as he reached his full height. Despite being covered in furs, it was obvious to the elf that the man was huge, his body corded with muscle.

"Enough Anuk!" Chief Atreyu scolded him for involving himself in the transaction. He nodded sternly to Anuk, a gesture Anuk knew to mean he needed to remove himself from the situation immediately. Once Anuk was gone, Atreyu pulled Lexa to her feet. "The Snehóvškriátok have been indebted to this man for a very long time..." He was sad, Lexa could tell. "They have chosen you, child. You must go with them now. Remember where you came from, yes? May our ancestors guide you."

A few hours later, miles from home, Lexa and Jarik sat upon the tundra watching the two moons come into alignment. "It is time," Jarik said to her.

"I hate you!" Lexa screamed at him, her voice fuming, spewing venom with each syllable.

He grabbed her and knelt down to her level like he'd done back home, steadying her despite her struggles. "It is nothing personal Lexaldra," he explained to her, "but greatness calls upon you... the Lady has chosen you. One day, you will be the fiercest woman in all the land, mark my words."

Lexa heard Chief Atreyu's voice in those words, how her parents once made that exact claim, and she ceased all struggles as she calmed down. She watched Jarik lift his arms above his head as he gazed toward the eclipsed moons. "Bare witness," he called out to the moons, "the manifestation of my love; the culmination of my devotion!" He sliced his hand open with a knife and returned to the chosen girl, taking her hand in his. "You will do incredible things, little cub."

She gasped as he cut her hand open as well and placed their open wounds together. Lexa felt something flowing into her hand, rushing throughout her body. He released her after what seemed like minutes to the girl, and she staggered backwards, the world spinning around her, and collapsed into the snow. The eclipse gazed into her soul from above, an anchor in a world that was spinning out of control. Her body bent and lurched from side to side, and she began screaming in pain. Lexa dug her fingers into the snow to steady herself and she struggled to breathe as whatever had rushed through her body began attacking her from within.

A moment later she lay still and gasped for air, and as she reacquainted herself with the act of breathing, she opened her purple eyes to return the eclipse's gaze. The celestial phenomena watched the purple of Lexa's irises flee from her face, an emerald fire burning in its place.

Cargo

Long before the collapse of natural order and the peak of the technological revolution, in a mysterious land teeming with creatures and spirits untouched by civilization, an airship transporting perilous cargo flew through the heavens. This was no ordinary airship, nay, this was a pirate ship. They were freebooters, buccaneers, and raiders alike... the scallywags of the skies. The Tainted Thunder would normally prey upon cargo ships and other transports, the occasional diplomatic vessel, and from time to time they'd encounter privateers who had received bureaucratic backing via royal decree to put an end to them. Obviously, no such luck had befallen any privateer as of yet, and despite the Tainted Thunder crew's customary raiding, sacking and pilfering; their merciless and lawless savagery, a staple of their attacks always ensured someone lived to relay their words. This boastful and prideful signature of theirs, showcasing their tendency to escape any lawful justice unscathed, even going as far as to taunt entire governments that would stop at nothing to see them fall from the sky, ultimately led them to their most profitable venture yet. It required no plundering or murder; no deception or acts of terror, no... it was a much simpler task. The Tainted Thunder was commissioned by one of the governments that had hitherto hunted them across the globe to transport the cargo they carried, and in doing so would not only be pardoned for every crime ever committed, but granted land, the means to maintain it, and enough coin to spend the remainder of their lives comfortably. *Some cargo.*

A young deckhand aboard the Tainted Thunder leaned on the railing at the stern of the ship, his mop and bucket also leaning lazily beside him, as he gazed out astonishingly from the aft of the ship. The Tainted Thunder left arcane vortices in its wake that slowly dissipated and rained down upon the land far below. Clouds seemed to bend around the craft as it flew, parting right before the bow made impact and then disintegrating within the trailing vortices. The boy could feel the splash of mist as the clouds came crashing together at the rear before vanishing. He laughed gleefully, wearing his smile wide upon his face as he threw his hands into the air and cheered, his celebratory cries muted by the ship carving its path through jet streams. He looked up and squinted, shading his eyes against the sunlight, and spotted winged creatures in the distance far above them, and had never felt happier in the disadvantaged life he'd lived up until then... dragons! Real life dragons! They paid them no heed however, for dragons were incredibly intelligent and social beings, and they understood that this particular ship, the one known as Tainted Thunder, had never once taken up arms against their kind. To do so would be a special kind of suicide, but besides that, the boy had heard rumors that Captain Astraeal had gone to a dragon's aid in his youth, forever forging an understanding and respect with the serpentine species. He waved at them, but whether the majestic creatures noticed or not, there was no response.

The boy looked starboard and port side, and nothing but an infinite stretch of open sky greeted him. When he looked down he saw nothing but the canopies of trees, the uncharted spirit wilds where no man brave enough to enter had ever returned. Civilization existed in pockets all around the world, thriving peacefully beside the mystical wilds that claimed the majority of the planet. Stories from a bygone era, told primarily by word of mouth for hundreds of years before modern storytellers began documenting them, each differing in their own unique ways, warned humanity about a time in the distant past where they had aspired to conquer all of the land. Even with industrialized tools, weapons, and even armies at their disposal, the stories all mention the very near extinction of men. Their hubris led them to war against the planet itself, for the spirits and creatures of the wilds are said to be the planet's own children, or that they and the planet are one and the same, depending on which story one listened to. Modern civilization understood the balance that must exist between humanity and the wilds, and the stories teach them to respect and fear them. Some are predisposed to challenge this normal of course, organizing and leading rebellious groups hellbent on proving such stories as fables, into the wilds never to return or be heard from again. Those stories are also well known and documented, serving as further warnings against such foolish aspirations. Still, there are some who venture into the wilds with peaceful intentions, a search for enlightenment... to join the spirits and become one with the planet themselves. Their successes and/or failures, due to the very nature of their motivations, would forever loom over humanity as a mystery.

"Aye!" a large burly man yelled at the boy. "Quit yer daydreaming and get back ter work!"

The boy stiffened up when he heard the man snap at him, and then fumbled to retrieve his mop. "Y-yes, sir!" he replied.

The man eyed him with annoyance and a look upon his face that told the boy he had erred. The boy felt his heart pounding in his chest, barely managing to keep his hands from visibly trembling. The man leaned in. "I ain't no *sir*... get back ter work!" He walked away laughing, clearly amused at the terror he'd induced within the deckhand.

After what seemed like hours, the boy headed into the bowels of the ship to return the mop and bucket to a janitorial closet. As he was headed back the way he'd come to return to the cabin where the berthing compartments as well as the crew's communal area and lounge resided, he heard a strange noise. He looked around to ask if anyone else had heard it, but the rest of the crew was above deck, so he mustered the courage to investigate the sound himself. Letting his ears be his guide, the young deckhand wound his way deeper into the bowels of the ship until he came upon the cargo hold, the noise growing slightly louder as he navigated his way through the Tainted Thunder. His heart stopped in his chest and he held his breath as he came upon a door with a fog rolling out from beneath. A humming sound, accompanied by the occasional guttural cry of some creature, could be heard coming from behind the door.

Too young to understand this was the moment to report the strange finding to an adult, anyone really, he found his resolve and bolstered the nerve to push the portal open. The fog caked the floor inside the room, which appeared to be the brig, and inside the brig was a strange looking cage. The cell, much like the ship's propulsion, seemed to be a fusion of technology and the arcane, magical restraints showering down from its ceiling upon the most terrifying thing the boy had ever laid his eyes on.

It was some sort of quadruped demon! It was slightly larger than one of the apex felines he'd seen in books back home. Its black oily flesh seemed to leak wisps of shadows. Long tendrils protruded from its front shoulder blades, waving around impatiently, a long, barbed tail that ended with something resembling the toothed pod of a carnivorous plant whose name was escaping him just then. The pod pulsated, a crease appearing ever so slightly around its circumference as the creature inhaled and exhaled, revealing sharp teeth-like extremities hiding behind the opening he knew was there. Rows of bone-like ridges ran up its face, growing in size as they continued down its back, seemingly becoming the barbs along its tail. Horns jutted from the sides of its head, which was half covered by some sort of exoskeleton, rows of glowing eyes, varying in size, beside the bone-like ridges. Its legs were muscular and its feet were shaped strangely, as if they were also hands. It wasn't until the boy noticed the rows upon rows of razor-sharp fangs within its massive maw, that he realized the fog was coming from its mouth. The creature's rows of eyes were locked onto him... he had its full attention, and there seemed to be intelligence behind those malicious eyes. He felt his curiosity swell inside him.

In front of the magical cage sat a man wrapped in as much darkness as the monstrous beast. He noticed the man's glowing green stare, the inhuman eyes looking right at him, and gasped.

"Is it the Erybai that scares you child?" the man asked with a cold emotionless voice. "Or is it me?"

The young deckhand didn't know how to respond. They both frightened him, for they both radiated a sense of dread... there was nothing natural about either of them... but it was caged, and the man seemed to be guarding it. He wasn't sure if he was scared per se. "W-what's an Erybai?" he asked.

"Come closer," the man replied. "It can't hurt you, see?" He held up his hand and clenched his fingers into a fist. The magical restraints tightened around the Erybai, squeezing until it stopped swaying... until it stopped moving entirely... just stared down the boy, patiently. The boy approached against his better judgment, the creature's eyes following him as he did so, until he was only a couple feet away from the man and surrounded by the unnatural fog. "See its tail?" he asked, and the boy nodded. "That bulb can open up like a second mouth, and its clamp is like a vice grip. Inside the bulb are retractable quills that produce an acidic toxin that can dissolve flesh." The boy's eyes filled with awe and trepidation. "The spines along its back are as tough as steel. Those tendrils act as additional eyes and limbs, and emit sound waves at frequencies humans can't hear. They can cause confusion, nausea, disorientation, and sometimes induce hallucinations, depending on the subject." The boy gulped. "Each of its eyes can see in a different spectrum, its sense of smell rivals that of the most competent dire wolves, and it can open its jaws nearly ninety degrees."

"Whoa..." The boy gasped, his eyes full of wonder and apprehension. The Erybai just lied still, its unblinking eyes latched to the boy. "Why is it looking at me like that?"

"Erybai are creatures of chaos and darkness," the man explained. "They are not of this world. There are layers to reality, and your primitive brain is only capable of perceiving this one. The Erybai is of the Void. It is a place of darkness so absolute, so wholly malevolent, that the very fabric of the realm spews corruption and decay. Aberrations like this Erybai are spawned from the Void itself to spread its corruption however it may. It is looking at you like that because you are undoubtedly the most innocent thing aboard this vessel." The man's words lacked any empathy, his voice so full of indifference that the boy wasn't sure if the darkness was coming from him or the Erybai.

"What are you? How do you know all this?" the deckhand asked.

"I am a Nullifier," he answered. "Myself, and others like me exist to resist the Void... it will never cease in its attempts to spread its decay. Its hunger for worlds like yours is endless... it knows no bounds, and will stop at nothing until it consumes everything... until all there is, is the Void..." The boy's eyes filled with utter terror. "It has consumed many worlds, but its appetite is insatiable." The boy looked at the Erybai, the creature's eyes still locked onto him in a malicious gaze, watching intently, patiently. Then he looked to the Nullifier, not sure what he was either, suddenly conscious of the fact he had never been in a more helpless predicament in his life.

A whistle broke the tension from somewhere behind the boy. "Godsdamn!" one of the pirates squealed obnoxiously. "You really need to learn to lighten up!" he said in an uplifting tone, laughter at the edges of his words. He patted the Nullifier on his shoulder and the man of darkness craned his head to look up at him with his expressionless face, glowing green eyes regarding the newcomer. The crease of his lips tightened, and his eyes narrowed slightly after a moment.

"You shouldn't touch me..." the Nullifier warned.

The man raised his hands disarmingly into the air between them. "Alright, alright... don't get all dark and broody again..." He exaggerated a shiver as his body convulsed for a second. "We'll leave you to it then! Always a pleasure friend! Nice to have you onboard... you really bring a special kind of charm to the place! We'll have to exchange some stories over some sunfire-peach moonshine later!" He pulled the boy from the brig and back into the cargo bay area, his hands clasped gently upon the deckhand's shoulders as he led them from the deepest depths of the ship's belly. "You know you shouldn't have been down there Smitty..."

"I know... I'm sorry Jedidiah," Smitty replied. "I was putting the mop away and heard that... Erybai thing."

Jedidiah squeezed the boy's shoulders affectionately, but assertively, and gently shoved him along. "You're lucky I was the one that found you down there," he answered, flashing Smitty a disarming smile. "Get outta here kid." He watched Smitty scurry away, relieved he found him when he did. Those two were trouble, he knew, as he stopped and looked back toward the brig in contemplation. Eventually, he made his way back above deck where he made eye contact with the first mate, a lean, mean brute that wore his older age in his complexion as opposed to his hair, as he had none. The first mate's muscles were tightly toned rubber bands, and the man's weapon of choice was his own body. He'd trained with monks deep in the Jaded Torre Mountains for years, the only thing any of the crew really knew about him other than the fact he was terrifyingly ruthless.

"Jed!" he called to him. "I need you—"

His orders were cut off however, as the ship quickly lurched starboard, throwing a few pirates to the deck. The normal comforting sound of the Tainted Thunder was replaced by an even louder one, a sound that came from somewhere else entirely. Jedidiah ran to the edge of the airship to spot whatever was causing the disturbance, as did many others including first mate Gaeleath Novak. Jedidiah couldn't hear his orders over the sound that was now drowning out the Tainted Thunder's own. Captain Astraeal joined his crew above deck the moment an enormous militarized airship dawning the crest of Corenthia rose above the clouds. It nearly tripled the size of the Tainted Thunder, igniting a frantic shock among the pirates. They had never seen an airship so massive, and until then, didn't know such ships existed.

It all happened so fast. Jedidiah ran below deck to find Smitty, got thrown around into bulkheads as the ship got attacked. All he knew was that the boy didn't deserve this fate, but then the ship fell into a dive, and as he braced himself the bulkhead flew away from the airship leaving a gaping hole in its place. Jedidiah tried to hold on to a railing in the corridor but was ultimately sucked out the hole and into a freefall above the spirit wilds. He must've been a couple thousand or more feet above the canopies of the trees when he hit open air, the wind rushing past his face. The adrenaline caused his mind to think a thousand times faster than normal, but really, there was only one thing he could do. He pulled on a tab near his shoulders and a bunch of rounded tent-like air brakes lifted from his suit, followed by a parachute, but the parachute was damaged and sent him twirling through the air at even greater speeds. His only chance now was to cut himself loose from the failed chute, and the forest was racing toward him from below.

When he awoke he found himself entangled in a swarm of vines hanging from the tallest trees he'd ever laid his eyes upon. He pulled a knife from a sheath on his ankle and cut himself loose, dropping a dozen feet or so to the bed of the forest. It was considerably darker beneath the canopies and he couldn't see very well, but his eyes were slowly adjusting. The smell of smoke was unmistakable however, and so he followed his nose, stumbling his way through the spirit wilds until he came upon a body. He rolled them over only to see the Nullifier staring back at him with his glowing green eyes.

"The Erybai," the Nullifier stammered. He craned his neck to look toward his abdomen. A large jagged piece of debris had impaled him through the gut, black fluid was dripping from his lips. "You have to…"

Jedidiah scoffed. "Oh no," Jedidiah waved his hands and laughed nervously. "Me? Really? That's your plan?" He looked around frantically. "You got the wrong guy! If you're putting your faith in me then we're all doomed!" He laughed and continued looking around. "It's probably dead… besides, there are worse things out—"

"No!" the Nullifier cried out. "There is nothing worse, and it must be stopped by any means necessary." The Nullifier pulled Jedidiah by his collar until their faces were only inches apart. Jedidiah couldn't swat the man's hands away or break free… the dark warrior's strength was uncanny… impossible even. "Left unchecked… the… Erybai will spread corruption… the forest so… pure… will decay and the Void will… spread until it claims this world. You must stop it… this… vessel has expired… I cannot—" The strength fled from the Nullifier's grasp and Jedidiah nearly flew backwards but caught himself. He watched as the corpse seemed to deflate and the green glow in its eyes evaporated into the air, dissipating as it slowly rose until nothing was left.

Jedidiah's jaw hung agape. He reached down with his right hand and unclasped the holster that held his trusty revolver, slowly pulling it out as he lowered his eyes back down to the flattened corpse of the had-been Nullifier. "Oooooooookay…" he said to himself nervously as he held the gun close to his chest and stared, purely dumbfounded by the scene before him. "That just happened." He reached out with his right foot and tapped the toe of his boot against the body, the squishy feel of it sending a shiver through his entire body as he recoiled the foot and gagged, standing on a single foot like a flamingo. He remained as still as a statue as he listened to the sounds of the forest: birds and other creatures chirping and chattering in the distance, psithurism in all directions as the brush and other plants rustled and swayed, and the bugs making all their creepy sounds. Despite the absence of city buzz, the rumblings of factories, or street music playing, the forest was incredibly noisy, he realized. Then the body shuddered as it expelled some gas, Jedidiah squealed, and ran from the scene more grossed out than afraid.

Continuing toward the wreckage, Jedidiah found it easier to see as flames danced upon foliage and metal alike... he heard wood crackling and people faintly crying out in the distance. He felt a sudden sense of urgency overcome him, not because he felt the need to provide anyone with aid, but he realized if he did nothing he'd surely be stranded there alone. Regardless of whether or not he liked his colleagues, each and every one possessed a set of skills the others did not; they all had their uses.

As he made his way closer to the primary crash site, he kept his head on a swivel, looking everywhere and scanning his surroundings for any signs of immediate danger. Mushrooms larger than he was tall, some two or three times his size, were scattered all around, a forest in their own right apart from the massive trees. Enormous tree roots rose from the ground, weaving this way and that, creating a web of wood in every direction offering any number of predators an advantage over him. Some of the leaves dangling from some of the plants were as large as dragon wings. At one point he saw a bug as big as a cat dart around a tree trunk. He cocked the hammer of his revolver back, *click*.

A scream erupted from somewhere behind him, *"heeeeeeel—"* and it wasn't until he focused his attention in that direction that he realized someone, or something, was charging him. *"Meeeeee—"* He spun around and fired his gun with deadly accuracy. The body, covered in flames, dropped to the forest floor with finality.

"Dammit!" Jedidiah cursed. "Why'd you do that?" It was one of the Tainted Thunder's crew. He left them there for the fire to feed upon, and continued toward the crash site. As he approached the hulking wreckage, a hand grabbed his ankle. He looked down with pity as the mutilated pirate stared up at him, desperation in their eyes, a silent plea for help. He ripped his foot from their grasp and continued searching for anyone that might be of any use to him.

Jedidiah climbed into the burning remains of the Tainted Thunder, ducking under debris, and weaved his way through twisted metal and dancing embers. Bodies lay scattered amidst the wreckage, some burning, some in pieces, and his hopes of finding anyone began to dwindle. Then he spotted Smitty, his hand reaching out for him, lying halfway buried under some debris. The kid wouldn't be of much use to him, but he was a kid and he didn't deserve any of this. He rushed over and grabbed his hand. "I got you kid," he said through gritted teeth. "C'mon!" He tugged on Smitty's arm, pulling his torso free of the debris, and fell over and onto his ass. Smitty's lifeless gaze looked right through him, the expression of terror permanently imprinted upon his young face, and Jedidiah gasped, looking away and breathing heavily.

The faint cries he'd heard before were no more. He wasn't sure where to look, or if there was any point, but he continued on. "Jedi... diah... is that... you?" He heard after some more searching. He rushed over to the voice to find a woman named Agatha sitting against a twisted bulkhead. Half her body had been burnt pretty bad, but it seemed as though she could make it.

"Agatha!" he cried as he knelt before her. As she looked up at him, pressing a hand against her chest, he offered her a kind smile. "Are you going to be alright?"

She coughed in an attempt to laugh. "Didn't realize you cared," she teased before groaning through the pain.

"You were always pleasant to the eye... though..." He pulled back a bit and looked her over, examining her current state. "Not sure your looks are gonna do you anymore favors." He grinned as she stared him down.

"You're..." She laughed and choked. "...such an ass."

Jedidiah slapped his hand over his chest. "You wound me," he retorted.

A noise off to the side stole their attention from one another. Then Jedidiah's world began to spin and he collapsed to the ground beside the injured woman. Agatha groaned and slammed her head against the bulkhead. Straining against the disorientation, Jedidiah managed to open his eyes and see the Erybai stalking toward them, its tendrils erect before it. Its eyes were slits as it slowly approached them, and Jedidiah fumbled for his gun. The Erybai's bulbous tail swayed back and forth, the crease in the bulb expanding to reveal fang-like quills within.

"What in the actual—" Agatha cried out before the Erybai whipped its tail, sending a quill flying through the air at them, hitting her square in the shoulder. She started screaming in agony as her flesh began to burn, and both her skin as well as the clothing surrounding the impact began sizzling and melting away.

Jedidiah cocked the hammer of his revolver and fired at the monster. The shot hit the beast, but whether it phased the thing in any way, it didn't show... it just kept advancing toward them, a fierce rumbling growl emanating from its maw. Its rows of eyes were locked on the injured woman, completely ignoring its attacker, and as its muscles flexed, Agatha pulled her own gun out. "Get outta here!" she screamed, and Jedidiah didn't need to be told twice.

He saw the blur of the monster's leap from the corner of his eye as he fled the scene. Agatha's screams lasted all but a couple seconds before they became gurgles, and then utter silence. Jedidiah climbed from the wreckage back into the forest and ran, his heart pounding in his chest. He kept looking behind him expecting to see the Erybai not far behind, but it was never there. After running for about ten minutes, he stopped to catch his breath.

"Jed!" He heard another voice call out to him. It was Gaeleath Novak, the first mate. He seemed to be all in one piece, and any injuries he had sustained in the crash were minor. Perhaps his luck hadn't yet run out. Now there was a man he'd like by his side in the trials to come.

"Novak!" Jedidiah answered, a resounding relief riding his voice the way dragons rode the skies above. "Thank the gods..."

"Shut it and help me," Gaeleath snapped at him. His foot was lodged in a strange plant that had clamped itself around his ankle. "I can't get it free!" he exclaimed to his fellow pirate.

"Hold up," Jedidiah replied. "Let me see what I can do."

He attempted to pry the plant open to no avail. The stubborn thing was as sturdy as welded metal.

"Gods damned spirit wilds..." muttered Gaeleath.

Jedidiah pointed his revolver at the plant and fired. An unnatural cry erupted from the plant, and the ground around them rumbled. They looked at each other frantically, but as quickly as Jedidiah pulled his trigger, the plant opened impossibly wide, and a feminine looking humanoid face appeared from the opening. It hissed at Jedidiah, and vines slithered up Gaeleath's legs before vanishing back into the strange plant. As it did so, it pulled the bald man with it, his body sinking into the open plant. He reached out for Jedidiah, who grasped his hand and began pulling with all his strength, but it was no use. A moment later the first mate had disappeared into the ground, and the plant shut behind them.

"Bleeding harpy tits!" Jedidiah cried as he staggered away from the plant, a look of horror stamped across his face. He had no time to contemplate what had just transpired however, for immediately afterward he heard the Erybai's growls in the distance closing in. All he could do was run, and he did just that.

As the man fled through the cursed forest, leaping over gigantic roots, dodging suspicious looking plants, and slapping low hanging vines out of his way, he wondered if he'd lost the monster as he could no longer hear it. At one point he punched some random creature that he hadn't noticed until its body popped open around its face, making it seem several times larger than it actually was. It took him by such a surprise that he instinctively swung at it before it knew what had happened. Jedidiah had thought it was just another vine, but it was more akin to a snake. Layers of its skin, or scales, or whatever unfurled from its face, and opened faster than he could blink. He imagined it would've looked like some giant spiky low hanging fruit, as claw-like appendages curled outward from its expanded body, but he didn't stop to take a closer look at the thing.

So quick was the encounter, that he didn't realize the creature was about to feast on a blissfully ignorant entity frolicking among the flowers along the vines. It was about the size of a hummingbird, had the alluring frame of a siren, and all aspects of the small tantalizing creature were objectively appealing. Even its eyes, twice as large as other sentient beings, relatively speaking, seemed to only add to its beauty. It wore only tiny flower petals over its chest and around its waste, and flapped its wings as quickly as an insect. Jedidiah's sudden and frantic reaction to the predator's shocking transformation allowed the feminine creature to flee unscathed, but as she did so she realized the large fumbling idiot had become the beast's prey. She contemplated letting the foolish outsider suffer his inevitable fate, but only for a moment before her conscience berated her for musing such a thing.

It didn't take long before it became blatantly apparent to Jedidiah that the thing he'd hit was coming after him. His chest burned, his breaths came sharp, and his legs were getting wobbly as the adrenaline began to fade. He cocked the hammer of his beloved weapon and flung around to face his new enemy, beads of sweat running down his face. He looked around nervously before spotting the beast. Unlike a snake, the thing had branching tentacle-like parts of its body at its lower half that resembled plant roots, and its open face resembled some sort of budding plant or fruit. It seemed obvious to the pirate that the thing likely spent most of its time camouflaging itself, awaiting its meals to come to it. Compared to a lot of other things

Jedidiah had seen in the spirit wilds up to this point, the creature wasn't all that massive in size, though it could surely take its time feasting upon him if it were to successfully incapacitate the man.

"Not today," Jedidiah said determinedly, and aimed his pistol. The little flying woman appeared suddenly and started squeaking in his ear insistently. He couldn't understand anything she was saying and tried shooing her away. "Go away, *shoo!*" He wasn't about to break his line of sight. He applied pressure to the trigger when she began tugging on his ear. "*Ow!*" He snapped at her, waving her away with his hand. The snake creature made a hissing sound, the tiny woman tugged on his ear again, and Jedidiah's heart pounded in his chest as his finger slipped from the trigger, a blur of motion striking at his peripherals. "*Stop!*" he yelled desperately, as if words alone would freeze time and save him.

It was not time that stopped the snake-like creature from striking him however, it was the Erybai. When he heard that all too familiar, other worldly guttural growl as it snatched the thing mid-strike, both Jedidiah and the little flying woman looked in horror at the monstrosity from the Void, and then at each other. Jed's knees buckled as the Erybai's tentacles unleashed a flurry of silent, but incapacitating sound waves. The world spun around him, his stomach tightened, and his temples began to throb. He collapsed to his knees as he grabbed his face in his hands attempting to apply pressure and hold the world still. The last thing he saw before it all went black was the Erybai's powerful jaws mutilate and twist the snake thing's body with a single crushing bite as it turned its many eyes upon him.

"He's awake!" Jedidiah heard a woman's voice grow with excitement. When he opened his eyes, he was greeted by several winged women, the very same as the one that had been tugging on his ear, except they were no longer tiny. They were all wearing little to nothing, only their breasts and groins covered by leaf-like garments. His eyes popped open widely as he struggled to process their immense beauty, their flawless skin, their perfect curves... the luscious hair, and their dazzling large eyes that seemed to really work for them. Standing over him, he was able to see their wings for the first time, and they reminded him of butterfly wings, except they didn't seem as fragile; they seemed strong and sturdy, the colors changing depending on the lighting and the angle.

"Does it speak?" another asked as she cocked her head and studied him.

"Of course I speak..." he replied.

There were five of the winged women, and they all cooed excitedly at the revelation. One reached down and touched his foot... his bare foot with her hand, massaging his arch and sending a wave of relaxation and comfort through his body. "Where's my—" He stopped abruptly as another grabbed an ankle and firmly stroked up his calf. They giggled as Jedidiah's tension melted away. Another took his hand in her own and began massaging it, while yet another placed her hands upon his abdomen, applying generous pressure and working out all remnants of stress. His eyes rolled into the back of his head as he basked in the ecstasy of the moment. The one that touched his abdomen reached up and began pulling the sheet, or blanket, he then realized was woven from the same leaves their garments were made of, down his chest. It was confirmed, he wasn't wearing any clothes, but it wasn't an alarming revelation, just one that could wait a little longer as he let the scene unfold.

The one that had begun massaging his hand brought his fingers to her lips. The one that had yet to touch him approached him and began playing with his hair, her smile kind, genuine, and thirsty. "Gods..." Jedidiah breathed with pleasure as three separate sets of lips began to press against his thighs, breasts falling loose from leafy captivity in his face. Had he died and ascended to some higher plane of being, he wondered. His body had become their playground; the object of their curiosity, and they were taking full advantage of the opportunity, when...

"Hey!" he heard a voice cry out, and suddenly, his sense of ecstasy became one of guilt, like he was a child again and had just been caught stealing from the bakery. The five winged seductresses scattered from the now naked pirate, and he snapped the leaf blanket at his side, covering himself as he looked upon the newcomer. It was the one that had been tugging on his ear when... the clouds in his mind began to secede... the Erybai! His eyes widened as they met his savior's, and he looked to the others, then back at her.

"I was just..." he stammered. "Asking about my clothes, and... the concept seems a bit foreign to..." He trailed off, not sure why he was spouting off a lie. She crossed her arms as she hovered in place, and then he noticed she was holding some clothes, but they were not his... they were also made of leaves. She threw them at him. "Hey!" He retorted as he caught them. "What are these? Where are my clothes? Where is my pistol?"

"Now he wants to talk." She rolled her big eyes and left

the... room? It occurred to him then that the space they occupied was no mere building... but the inside of a giant hollowed out tree? The others covered their mouths as they grinned, whispering amongst themselves, and looked upon him from the corners of their eyes, but they made no more attempts to seduce him.

Jedidiah put the clothes on and followed after the one that had thrown them at him. He found her outside. "Hey..." He greeted her. "Can you tell me..." Again, the words left him as he registered his surroundings. They had not grown to his size... he had shrunken to theirs! A moment of silence passed before he found his wits once more. "What—"

"What was that thing?" she asked, cutting him off.

"...thing..." he echoed, his eyes falling toward his groin, his cheeks turning flush. "*Uh...*"

"Not that, you..." She let out a frustrated growl. "That thing that took you down with its gaze! It was unnatural! A perversion..."

Jedidiah smiled sheepishly and nodded back the way they'd come. "Your friends know a thing or two about perv—"

The woman closed the distance between them in a split second, hovering just above him so she looked down upon him, her eyes slits. "Tell me what you know." Her words were cold and dangerous, and he was unarmed.

He lied to her. He claimed complete ignorance, only mentioning that it was aboard the Tainted Thunder when it was attacked above the forest. After calming the woman down considerably, and leading her to believe the Erybai posed no more a threat than any other apex predator, she showed him to his things... an odd situation as he could fit into one of his pockets. His pistol was left behind and he considered going after it when she offered to return him to his normal size, but he agreed to remain with them for the time being. There was a degree of security among the women, as well as its many perks. He figured he'd bide some time with them, enjoy the time to its fullest, and eventually move on when he felt confident that enough time had passed, and the Erybai was long gone. He learned her name as well: Zhaasmin, and though he seemed to grow on her, she would still remain skeptical of him. The others however, couldn't get enough of him, but his interest in them would eventually wane as several weeks passed by and a connection grew between he and Zhaasmin, and he felt her judgment anytime they got their way with him.

He'd listen in on their conversations when he could, learning as much as possible from the little big-eyed women. Beings called Fey were apparently the most ancient and powerful among all the inhabitants of the spirit wilds. They talked about them as if they were deities, but he knew better than to believe such things. Apparently, they were ageless, the first settlers of the spirit wilds thousands upon thousands of years ago. He learned there were several prominent races in the forest, all rich in culture, societies of their own, cities (not like the ones he was accustomed to, certainly), and despite their many differences they lived side by side harmoniously. There were the elves, several different kinds actually, the centaurs, the gnomes (whom, from his understanding, the dwarves living beside humans outside the spirit wilds had originated from), the Anura (a frog-like people known for their savagery and mystique), and the Malia (the least civilized and most animal-like of all of them) to name a few he'd overheard.

After gathering berries, nectar, and the other things the women either consumed or used regularly, one day, he overheard the mention of a dryad. From the context of the conversation, he deduced that dryads were plant-like creatures that lived within, and controlled, well, plants. His mind went to Gaeleath Novak... the poor bastard. Except, this particular dryad was in distress, for her budaklé, whatever that was, had escaped. He entertained thoughts of the cold brute defying whatever fate had befallen him in the plant that day, and wreaking havoc throughout the forest. The thought made him smile.

One night, Zhaasmin invited Jedidiah out to one of her favorite spots in the forest. It had been a couple months since they'd met, and in that time, he'd remained safely within the trunk's protective walls while his new "friends" left for food, materials, etc. There had been no sightings of either the Erybai or any other survivors of his crew, and he thought it was a good opportunity to gage the situation, so he agreed to tag along. Jedidiah's mind was fracturing though. On the one hand, this was his chance to feel safe enough to move on and find some way out of the damned spirit wilds, and on the other hand, Zhaasmin's sincerity, kindness and intelligence made him question that motivation. Whenever he caught himself pondering that sentiment however, he embraced any available distraction as to not confront such a ludicrous philosophical rabbit hole.

Upon their arrival however, they discovered parts of the forest was decaying... a darkness was spreading and feeding upon the innate properties of the magically imbued land, and its enchanted inhabitants. What was once vibrant and full of life had become a brooding dull and eerily silent place devoid of any life. Something powerfully horrific had desecrated the section of the forest, and as Zhaasmin shrieked and cried out in anguish, Jedidiah swallowed the guilt that attempted to nestle in his throat. After all, this wasn't his doing, right? At the center of the infestation was a pulsating and unnatural sack, slick and black in appearance, with tendrils stretching from it in several directions. The sickly umbilical-like appendages penetrated the ground, and the sides of trees and other plants causing lesions that absorbed and defiled everything.

"We have to destroy it," Jedidiah said as they watched the sack throbbing with its stolen energy. There was clearly something moving around inside the unnatural womb, which became even more apparent when it reacted to the sound of Jedidiah's voice. They gasped, looks of disgust and horror upon their faces. They were powerless to do anything... they were too small.

"Why do I get the feeling you know what this is?" Zhaasmin asked, eyeing the man carefully as she spoke each syllable. Jedidiah hesitated... a first for him. He couldn't even bring himself to make light of the situation... perhaps he knew the attempt would only make his situation worse. "Why does it look like the thing that attacked you that day?"

Jedidiah didn't know how to respond. The silence didn't last long though. "If it isn't destroyed, everything you've ever known will be." With that, he turned away from the flying woman and began his trek back to the trunk. It was time for him to go.

When he returned to the trunk the other winged women approached him with their insatiable thirst, but he had to put his hand up and shake his head. "I can't." They all pouted and went about their usual routines until Zhaasmin showed up shortly afterward. She'd followed closely behind Jedidiah, contemplating their next course of action.

"So, you're leaving?" she asked Jedidiah, clear distaste exuding from the words.

"If you return me to my normal size," he replied. "I would like to go home."

"I'll return you to your normal size..." she agreed. "I know that you know what's happening, and I think it's far worse than you're letting on... but go on. Run away, coward."

Jedidiah tensed up, but offered her no response.

"Before you go," she said, breaking the silence that grew between them as she escorted him to his things, "I'm taking this news to the Fey." Jedidiah tensed up again. The Fey? His curiosity was piqued, and he didn't know if he should be concerned or not. "Please, come with me and tell them what you know." He thought about her request for a moment.

"Will it be safe for me?" he asked.

"You'd be helping. You will be safe."

He sighed and mulled it over for a minute. "Okay." Zhaasmin breathed a sigh of relief. "But return me to my normal size first."

When Jedidiah arrived in Fey territory, the fairy riding upon his shoulder, he was greeted with friendly words lacking any sense of surprise at the presence of a human. They looked similar to humans, but their skin was a myriad of different colors and textures. Some seemed more wood-like, while others seemed more stone-like, or more gem-like; some seemed as if they were made up of soil or snow, but he knew none of this was true. Their ears were shaped like daggers, and their hair (well it wasn't hair) resembled glowing crystals. Their eyes glowed the same color as their "hair." They were the most bizarre looking creatures he'd ever seen, and he knew some female dwarves personally.

Upon explaining what he knew of the Erybai, and between the alarming looks upon their faces, and the judgmental and disappointed ones from Zhaasmin, the pirate was ready to go. There was nothing else he could do to help, and he wanted no part of it. Facing the Erybai again was the last thing he wanted to do. So, when the Fey requested his participation in the effort to clear the infestation from their lands, he turned them down.

"I am an inconsequential man," he explained to them. "What could I possibly do that you can't do better?" They acknowledged the truth of his claims, and offered him sanctuary among their people as they sent word to the many races of the spirit wilds: a call to arms. At their behest, he remained to impart any additional information to the assembled forces.

As the next couple days passed he relied heavily upon Zhaasmin for security, reassurance, and companionship as more and more of the other races arrived. Almost all the ones he'd learned about from the fairies showed up, some even bringing stories of the sickness he knew to be the void, spreading through the wilds. Species he hadn't heard the fairies mention showed up as well. Jedidiah was impressed... perhaps they could do something about the Erybai and infestation in its wake, but he still wished to leave. The abundance of support from the varying races of the wilds only made him more confident in his decision. He no longer needed to feel guilty, even if Zhaasmin struggled to look at him the way she had just days before.

A couple days later as himself, Zhaasmin, and several of the other races' leaders gathered before the Fey, a looming shadow stretched over them, growing and darkening a massive area around them. Jedidiah looked up in terror as a dragon came in to land beside them, powerful gusts of wind blowing at them in bursts as its wings flapped to slow its descent. He trembled at the sight, but none of the Fey seemed bothered by its presence at all. When the beast landed, the wind subsided, and he finally got a good look at the majestic creature, a familiar face appeared from atop the thing.

"Captain?" Jedidiah gawked in disbelief. "Captain Astraeal?"

"Jed!" his captain greeted him joyously. "You survived!"

"The rumors..." Jedidiah breathed. "They're true..."

"Yeah, well," the captain went on, "from a certain perspective anyway." He placed a palm against the dragon's face. "Grizephwyvar and I go way back!"

After much deliberation and catching up, Jedidiah still chose to go his own way. He did everything he could, and all present were far more equipped for the situation than he, even his captain. Zhaasmin stayed with him though, to help navigate him through the wilds, while Captain Astraeal and the others sought to cleanse the forest of the Void. Perhaps that made him a coward, but he was okay with that.

As the two traversed the wilds together, they eventually came to a lake where they stopped to freshen up and rest. As Jedidiah rinsed his face off, he noticed something peculiar. It was his beloved revolver! Before he pondered how it may have gotten there though, he wrapped his fingers around its masterfully crafted frame. The familiarity of the device had him grinning from ear to ear, and he nearly shed a tear. "Zhaas!" he called out to her gleefully. "You'll never guess—"

"Jedidiah!" she cried. "Look out!"

He was suddenly jerked from his feet and flung wildly, hitting the ground, a tree, the ground again and then flung from his weapon, which dangled from one of the Erybai's tendrils. His world spun around him and his head pounded. Blinding light seared through his eyes, and he knew he was done for if he didn't recover. He watched Zhaasmin fly at the beast to distract it.

"Go!" she called out to him.

It was as if time itself froze around him. To flee, or not to flee. It was simple, a primal instinct that had catapulted every living species forward throughout all of time... and he contradicted it.

"What am I doing!" he growled as he ran toward Zhaasmin. As if in slow motion, Jedidiah watched the Erybai turn its attention on his small friend, who was foolishly sacrificing herself for him. He didn't deserve such a selfless act of nobility from her, and he wouldn't allow it. All he could do when the time came was smack her out of the way. He screamed in agony as the Erybai's maw clenched around his arm, its many rows of teeth piercing slowly through his flesh and into muscle, tearing tendons and crushing bones. All five of his senses went dark as it whipped its tail at his face, its bulb open, a quill penetrating the side of his face and exiting through an eye socket. He couldn't hear the sound of his skin sizzling and melting from his face.

It was dark. The air felt musty and cold. He couldn't really feel though. How could he? He didn't have a body. Already, the events that led him here were fading far from his mind... his mind, it was collapsing in on itself, and he felt how close he'd come to completely ceasing to exist when a voice brought it all back together.

"*Not yet,*" the voice said. The words didn't seem to make sense at first, but as the voice continued, the fragments of his mind began coalescing and reassembling itself. Green vapor surrounded him... observed him. "*You're not done yet. Let's try this again.*" As his mind repaired itself and the words started making sense, excruciating agony blazed through every crevice of his being, even his thoughts felt as if they were on fire. Darkness became green wisps of smoke judging him from the slits they formed into. "*We'll be in touch.*"

First came the sound of his sizzling flesh, and then the sounds of Zhaasmin's cries beside him. The smoky green eyes became a lens from which he now viewed the world, partially at least. He could still feel the quill protruding from his socket, the pain strangely subsiding. He yanked it out before realizing his eyeball had been melting around its tip. He ignored

Zhaasmin's horrified confusion and brought a hand to his face where the Erybai had stabbed him. His hand was made of ghostly green smoke he noticed as he did so, and his heart stopped. Panicking, he turned around and looked into the lake. The reflection he saw was a monstrosity.

A third of his face matched his new arm, decorated by patches of remaining flesh and bone, and one of his eyes was glowing a recognizable green, wisps dancing around the phantom orb. He sensed the Erybai stop dead in its tracks nearby, half of his arm still dangling from its mouth.

"Well, shit."

Reckless Abandoned

He followed the deer tracks, as he and his friend had been doing for the past hour or so. "Vion, *pffftttt...*" Gareth mumbled to himself as he pulled an arrow from his quiver. His beloved friend and hunting companion Asta insisted on offering their god of the hunt not only a prayer, but a small sacrifice in the hopes of invoking the deity's blessing. Vion didn't deserve any credit for any of his successful hunts, and Gareth had been adamant about this on countless occasions. As much as he'd grown to question the gods' existence, he envied Asta's unwavering faith and devotion to them. She participated in both solstice ceremonies every year, the harvest rituals every few months, and the daily sermons. Sometimes, her blind faith in their gods annoyed him, but even he couldn't deny the appeal of such character. They'd known each other their entire lives, all twenty or so years, and they were often inseparable. Asta's devout nature wasn't uncommon though, for the small village they called home, like many of the neighboring communities, had worshipped and praised the same gods for a millennium.

It is said that the gods once blessed their people in appearance; that the answers to their prayers, devotion and sacrifices were palpable. Vion, dressed in the furs of long extinct beasts, blessed their hunts, and the prey would fill the bellies of each and every villager, the elderly as well as the youngest children, and everyone in between. Eudora herself would endow the fields with her essence, enriching the land with fertility, but not just the land. It's said that Eudora would, on occasion, bless a devout woman with the same fertility that brought rich harvests, and the goddess's sister Zihses would watch over her and bless the life she brought into the world. Zihses blessed every childbirth, supposedly, but gifted these special children with names of her own choosing. Gareth had never met someone named by the goddess however, because the last one died of old age before he was born, ushered onto the next life by Erebus... supposedly.

The stories were real, or at least they had been once upon a time. All Gareth's life all he'd ever known was the struggle of keeping a healthy harvest; the struggle of returning home with enough meat to feed those most in need. They got by of course, but his life looked nothing like the lives of their ancestors in the stories passed down generation after generation, and he found himself wondering if there was any truth to the stories at all the older he got. Not Asta though... in addition to altruistically blessing the hunt in his stead, she'd then perform rituals to invoke Zihses's blessing for a fruitful day of foraging, and gathering of medicinal herbs, spices, and other prized flora that he couldn't deny benefitted their people greatly. That was the balance to their friendship: He would hunt, and stalk his prey silently as the girl that filled him with warmth, joy, frustration and madness, filled her bag with all the goodies their people actually cared about.

"Vion..." Gareth mumbled again as he rolled his brown eyes. "If you're really out there like everyone says, then let's see a white mammoth elk... that ought to feed the entire village. Come on then." The boy nocked the arrow, his fingers lightly pulling on the bowstring, as he looked around and waited. "Surprise, surprise..." he quietly said some moments later when one failed to show up. He doubled back for a few minutes until he spotted Asta, a habit they both grew accustomed to when they were young to ensure they never lost one another. He recalled the time he'd wandered too far and couldn't find her. He'd been terrified, more so for himself at that time, than for her. He'd always felt courageous and strong when she was with him, but the moment he was alone he'd felt lost. He shook away the shame as he watched his friend with a smile.

She had mastered the art of silent foraging, as to not interfere with his hunt, but whether it was his imagination or some trick of the wind, watching his friend gather the necessary plants for herself and the other healers brought to life a melody he couldn't quite wrap his head around. She wasn't singing or humming... she'd learned long ago that his hunt didn't go very well when she did that, but he heard it nonetheless, a rather strange phenomena that made him feel all fuzzy in his chest. Was it all in his head? He shrugged it off and took one last look at the girl he adored so much, before returning to the tracks that had split in multiple directions.

The ones he chose to follow led to a creek, a rather large one at that, and he stopped for a drink. He scouted the vicinity for more tracks on the other side, but the deer must've gone downstream for some time. Sunlight shone through the forest's canopy in beams all around, the sun wasn't going down anytime soon, and having just checked on his friend, Gareth decided to continue downstream in search of the tracks. He spotted plenty of wildlife, none of which that would've passed as decent spoils however, and so they paid him no heed as he walked the banks of the flowing water.

It didn't take him long to find the deer, and it was a pretty large buck. *Perfect.* He pulled the bowstring and raised his bow, steadied and... a faint scream that lasted all but a fraction of a second resounded through the woods. He barely heard the flapping of wings somewhere as flocks of birds fled from their perches, "Asta...?" Gareth said aloud as his brain began calculating the meaning of what had just transpired, and then he glanced up suddenly when he heard the buck fleeing the scene. In the chaos of the moment he'd released the arrow, spun around wide eyed, and was in a full-on sprint without hesitation. "Asta!" Gareth cried as he ran back the way he'd come. "Asta!" Her scream had come from further away then he'd realized he'd gone, it was quick, and then all was silent apart from his frantic running and yelling. "No, no, no, no!" Gareth cried as he traversed the forest, and when he finally approached her last whereabouts, she was gone. "No!" Gareth yelled defiantly. He nocked another arrow to his bow and pointed it straight ahead, turning this way and that, desperately hoping to spot someone, anyone!

Nothing... Gareth ran in a direction for a minute, then repeated his frantic search. "Asta!" Then ran in another direction, all the while aiming his bow at nothing. The helplessness that overcame him was on the verge of breaking the boy. "Asta!" Tears welled in his eyes and he collapsed to his knees. "No!" he screamed. "No..." The defiant denial grew weaker and weaker. "No..." She was his rock... his best friend... and she was gone. Gareth began balling at the overwhelming sense of loss that overcame him, and this would continue for a few minutes before he started thinking rationally again. Then he ran back to the last place he had seen her and began investigating the area. Following Asta's tracks, he found some blood speckled upon some bloodroot at the base of a tree nearby where she'd been harvesting horsetail. "Asta!" He screamed again, his heart sinking at the thought of failing to protect her. He searched the area more thoroughly and discovered a blood-soaked cloth beneath a stone.

Gareth studied the cloth, even hours later when the moon had risen into the sky, sitting upon his bed. He'd returned to the village, not only empty-handed, but alone. The villagers had heard the rumors... that people were being taken from their homes from other communities, but their village had remained untouched... until now. Nobody knew what happened to the taken, because none were ever seen again. It had been weeks since the last reports from their sister village, and that report had consisted of zero disappearances... complacency had taken hold. There was nothing anyone could do. Gareth was both devastated and outraged. He was heartbroken and filled with grief, for the thought of never seeing his friend again shattered his soul. The regret began to settle in the pit of his stomach. He never told her how he truly felt about her, and now he'd never get the chance.

As the days went on, Gareth struggled to keep up. Time didn't adhere to the woes of man. Time just carried on, caring nothing for those it left behind... forever forward. There were days Gareth couldn't bring himself to get out of bed, and the days he managed to do so he avoided Asta's family. They weren't any better off than he was. They were far louder in their grief, and they looked at him as if he were to blame. He felt guilty for not grieving as loudly... for having failed to protect her... for everything. One night he joined a community grieving ritual around the communal fire where he listened to the people he'd known his entire life go on and on about Erebus, their god of death. Rage simmered beneath the surface, slowly cooking him from the inside until his blood was boiling in his veins. How could they assume she was dead! How could they just give up! And what do the gods have to do with anything! The gods had abandoned them long ago, and yet they continued honoring them with their worship, and their faith!

"Enough!" Gareth yelled angrily, and dozens of his neighbors went silent, their prayers and chants halting abruptly like a rapid inhale followed by the nervous holding of the breath. "You all speak as if Asta is dead!" The words spilled from his lips the way lava spilled from the crest of a volcano, and his words condemned them all with accusation, venom dripping from every word. "You all pray to the gods as if they're not dead! I can't...!" The boy's voice began to tremble as he yelled at the families gathered to mourn the girl they all loved.

"Gareth..." A voice broke through the silence. All the boy saw was red, and all he could hear was his heart pounding in his ears. A hand rested upon his shoulder and he opened his eyes to see one of the village elders looking upon him, compassion overflowing in their tired gaze. "Even if she were alive, she is lost to us. We are not warriors, fighters, or god-kissed, son. We are just farmers, grazers, and shepherds. We are the gods' humble servants... what you're feeling is perfectly normal, son. Come, grieve with us..." He waved the boy over.

Gareth returned the compassionate gaze with one of contempt. "You and your gods are weak!" He snapped in the old man's face. He scanned around the communal fire, at the shocked looks on everyone's faces, stopping on Asta's father. "She might still be alive, and you sit around doing nothing but wasting your breath on gods that abandoned you a long time ago. It's maddening!" The elderly voice full of compassion and grief reached out for him once more, but the boy was past listening to fools. Asta's father had nothing to say, looking away in shame. Gareth stormed off into the night.

He gathered his things: his bow and arrows, a waterskin, and some rations. His parents died when he was young, but his guardians had held onto his father's leather armor, if it could be called that. Even for leather, the material seemed flimsy and weak, but it was the closest thing to pass for armor in all the village, and it would have to suffice. He slipped it on, donned the quiver, stole a couple butcher knives, and headed to the well to fill the waterskin. "You're leaving then?" Asta's father asked him as he sealed the waterskin. The man took the boy by surprise, and Gareth looked to him suspiciously. "My duty is here, protecting my wife and Asta's siblings. With the failing harvest, and the disappearances, I can't leave them... but here." Asta's father presented Gareth with a bag. "There's medicinal herbs, tinctures, oils and the like in there, some of which were prepared by... by Asta herself."

The man choked as he said his daughter's name, but recovered quickly. "There's even a vial of poison... don't get that mixed up with the others, okay? Please Gareth... find my Asta and bring her home."

Gareth nodded his thanks, and affirmed the man with the determination radiating from his very being. As he turned to leave, the man spoke up one final time. "Head north," he said. "Most of the disappearances are reported from our neighbors to the north. Good luck." With that, Gareth headed north, alone for the first time. The adrenaline had driven his action, but as he ventured into the darkness of the wilderness by himself, he felt his courage and fierce determination begin to slip away. It was strange... if Asta were beside him he could do anything, anything at all! He drew his strength, courage, and confidence from the girl... she knew how to inspire him; how to invoke that primal masculinity from within him, but now he had only himself to rely on. It was a daunting thought.

Gareth headed in a northerly direction for a few hours using the stars to guide his steps. He clutched his bow tightly anytime he heard a wolf howling to the moon overhead, or when he heard rustling in bushes. The silence of the night out in the wilds sent chills up his spine, the hairs of his body standing on edge, and anytime something disturbed the eerie silence, crickets ceased their song and the creatures of the night responded in kind. Wings flapped around him, nocturnal predators squealed and screeched from afar, and deep guttural growls reverberated off the trees. There was no way to tell where any of the sounds came from, but anytime he found himself shaking in his boots and on the verge of prayer, his fear was replaced by anger and resentment, driving him forward.

The tree line grew thicker and thicker the further north he went until the light of the moon, and the stars, were no longer visible. Gareth felt as if he'd been wandering the woods aimlessly for hours before he saw the flicker of firelight. As he crept toward the light, he began to hear voices... the dialect was spoken in an accent he was unaccustomed to. He snuck closer for a better look and saw the emblem of a griffon upon their armor. They were soldiers alright, foreign ones too.

"How much longer you s'pose we'll be scouring these pathetic villages?" one of the men asked the others.

"Expansion doesn't simply end," another said. "It isn't about time or numbers."

"Aye," another man chimed in. "It's about domination. It ends with the extermination of the bygone eras clinging to their old dead ways. They'll see... they'll all see when—"

Gareth held his breath, unsure what had happened or if they'd heard him. A bead of sweat ran down his face as he kneeled in some brush not far away, but definitely out of sight. He began to tremble, his eyes watering, and he quietly reached for an arrow. "You idiot!" the man finally said, snapping at another after what seemed like minutes. He went on talking to the other men and Gareth breathed out a sigh of relief... they hadn't heard him... he was okay.

The men began mumbling quietly as they lit a torch before putting out their fire, and moved on. Gareth continued tailing them for a while, listening when he could. "...what good's a slave if they're broken? Just dead weight at that point. So, I just put them out of their misery!" The man laughed, and Gareth's blood began boiling. They spoke of people as if they were nothing but tools! He thought of Asta, and what may have happened to her if she were injured... just discarded like she was nothing! But wait... did that mean... she was alive? Hope, the first hope he'd felt since she was taken, swelled within him. "What?" the man asked one of the others. "The bodies will fertilize the land...maybe then these people could actually grow something worthwhile!" A belly laugh erupted from the man, the others joined in, and Gareth nocked an arrow to his bow.

He waited for an opportunity, driven by his anger, and finally one presented itself when the loud man left the others to take a piss. He leaned against a tree with one hand as he relieved himself, and an arrow plummeted into the bark next to his hand. "What the..." the man gasped. When he turned in the direction it had flown from Gareth was there, just a few feet away, pointing yet another arrow at him.

"Tell me what I want to know and I'll spare your life," he said through gritted teeth.

"Okay, okay..." the man replied, his hands up like one does when they don't want an arrow in the gut. "Lower the arrow and we can talk." The man said as he took a step toward the boy.

Gareth drew on the bowstring, readying another shot. "No," he replied. "Stay put! I mean it. Another step and I let it fly."

"Okay kid," he answered. "What do you want to know?"

"The people you take..." Gareth started, "where do you take them? What do you do with them?"

Gareth could tell the man was smiling, even in the

darkness of the woods at night. "Depends…" he replied. "Who wants to know?"

"I'm asking the questions!" Just to reiterate his point, he released his arrow at the man, and it passed through the space between his legs. The man did not flinch, and he was smiling no longer. "Where—" Gareth began asking as he reached for another arrow, but as he did so the large man charged him. Gareth shot the arrow at the man's chest and it bounced off the man's armor, and he continued toward the foolish boy. Gareth tried to run, but the man was quicker then he was. He was knocked down, and the wind was knocked out of him as he hit the ground hard under the weight of the large man's heavy foot. Gareth felt excruciating pain explode in his chest as he watched the man ball his hands together and bring them down upon him. He gasped for air, coughing and hacking, but it was no use. He began slipping in and out of consciousness as he felt his body sliding along the ground.

When he came to, he was bound in chains. He could hear voices, but they were muffled as his senses were still recovering. As his eyes adjusted to the lighting, it became clear to him that he was in a cave, and he had no idea how long he'd been unconscious. His hands were bound and raised above his head, and his feet were bound at the ankles. He was helpless… how could he have been so stupid?

"He's awake," a voice said.

"This is going to be fun," another said.

When he finally saw the men around him he was surprised to find that they did not look as he'd expected. He imagined them as twisted, evil men, barbaric and wild, but they were none of those things. On the contrary, they were well groomed and looked at him as if they felt some sort of empathy for him or his predicament... all except the large man of course. "If we're going to kill him, I want to be the one to do it. He had no qualms about putting me down," the man said as he spit to the side of Gareth's face.

"Let's not be so hasty," one of the others said. "He may be of use to us."

"I'll never help you!" Gareth yelled at them defiantly.

One of the most reserved men, the leader of the group Gareth assumed by the additional décor on his gear, approached him then. "You would've made a fine addition to our ranks, what, with that fighting spirit and all... but you've attempted to kill one of my men already, and your defiance makes you more trouble than you're worth." He leaned down to look Gareth in the eyes. "Oh, we'll get what we need out of you, and then we will relieve you of your pathetic existence." The man turned away. "Gregor, he's all yours."

The large man that he'd tried to shoot stepped forward, unrolling a sheet of leather, various tools assorted upon it. Gareth strained his eyes trying to see what Gregor was doing with them, but his position didn't grant a very good view. When Gregor returned he held what looked like pliers, and a jagged knife. His smile betrayed his lack of civility... he wasn't like the others, and it was blatantly evident. "You can pray to your dead gods now," Gregor taunted him, "like all the others." The man laughed and brought the knife down to his chest. He tore his shirt open and began carving into his chest. Gareth screamed, and Gregor grinned. "This one doesn't seem to waste his breath!" Gregor said to the others. "Your gods...“

Gregor's words faded from Gareth's ears as the pain

dominated his mind. Gregor's face came in and out of focus as Gareth's vision was intermittently blinded by the sharp pain rushing up his chest, but he heard the word "gods" between his cries and as his rage and his fear bubbled to the surface of his being, and the cave suddenly vanished. He saw an infinite void, dark and inviting. He felt compelled to reach out with his mind, and felt he was not alone. Then the pain in his chest brought the cave back into view as he cried out. Even though he was looking into Gregor's eyes he saw the vast pit of darkness in his mind, the presence extending itself.

"...are weak!" Gregor laughed.

"Damn the gods!" Gareth roared back, tears falling from his face onto the table he lied upon.

Stars showered down upon the void and black ribbons unraveled before him, twisting and winding downward in a vortex, a road that offered him an escape. The presence seemed to awaken and grow with his cry damning the gods, and then he heard it while simultaneously feeling the knife slicing him open. *Good... now invite me... ask me to help you.* Gareth cried as Gregor carved his flesh.

"Tell me which village you hail from boy," Gregor said at long last, "and I'll stop... maybe." He laughed.

"Help!" Gareth cried. Gregor laughed at the absurdity of the request.

"Nobody can hear you... nobody is coming to save you!"

Gareth sent his mind down the black ribbon road. "Help me dammit!" He screamed in desperation, his cries and groans fading as Gregor mocked him and pressed the knife further into his chest. The moon shined brightly above him suddenly, and the raining stars glistened in the moonlight washed over the black twisty path spiraling into the darkness, and the road glowed silver... then it was gone and all the pain stopped abruptly. Was he dead? He no longer felt cold, or the cold steel of the knife against his skin. He didn't hear Gregor breathing, laughing, or speaking. The world had gone mute, just as his senses had. Then a silver swirl spiraled into view before melting away. In its place stood a creature unlike anything Gareth had ever seen. Its eyes were red, and its skin was as black as the infinite void he'd seen with his mind's eye. Horns rose from its scalp in various directions, jagged and twisted. It appeared humanoid, but animal-like in many ways. In some ways it reminded him of a werewolf, what he'd heard of them anyway as he'd luckily never encountered one before, except it had less hair and its face wasn't so wolf-like. Its clawed hands looked deadlier than any weapon he'd ever seen, and when he finally met its eyes he saw its lips curl into a smile.

"What are you?"

The otherworldly entity cackled, an awfully raspy and guttural sound that assaulted Gareth's senses. "I am many things, but your little mind would hardly make sense of it. Let's just say I share your contempt for the so-called gods your people love so much."

"Are you a demon?" he asked, remembering the stories of fallen deities, divine relatives of Zion, Eudora and the others... corrupted gods whose names have been long since forgotten.

"If that explanation pleases your insufferable curiosity, sure."

"Why help me?" Gareth asked.

"Ahh, now there's a question that makes sense. Why indeed?" it said coyly.

"You want something…"

"You aren't as dumb as you make yourself out to be," it replied, its smile growing into a grin. "Here's the thing…" it said as it put an arm around Gregor, who until then seemed far away from him, but now stood there frozen in time, holding the knife to his chest. "I'll save you from this unfortunate predicament you find yourself in… Hells, I'll even accompany you on your noble quest to rescue the damsel in distress. I'll protect you from any harm all throughout the endeavor, and see to it that you reach her safely, but then you belong to me."

Gareth dropped his head to the table. "What worth am I to you?" he asked after a moment of silent contemplation, lifting his head once more.

"Not you per se," it said, "I'm more interested in the essence you carry around in that vessel of yours… I believe your kind refers to it as a soul. What do you say?" It said as it leaned toward the boy, a sparkle in its red eyes.

"What do you want with my soul?" Gareth asked.

The demon grew irritated, its red eyes narrowing dangerously as it withdrew its arm from around Gregor and leaned over the foolish helpless boy. "Enough with your intolerable questions boy!" Black flames erupted from its flesh and its eyes widened in frustration. "They are tiresome, and…" The demon waved its arms around, gesturing to his captors and predicament. "You don't have many choices here."

"…but my soul…" Gareth breathed. "Let me—"

"Never mind then," it interrupted, snapping its fingers and vanishing.

Time continued as if nothing had just transpired, and all the pain... the excruciating pain hit him like a ton of bricks all at once, the knife carving his flesh. Gregor paid no heed to his deafening screams and wailing as it came rushing back. "Okay!" he screamed, but nothing happened. Gregor looked at him curiously for a moment, easing on the knife, but only for a moment before he went back to his torturous deed. "Okay! I said okay!"

The demon appeared beside him as Gregor continued. He put the knife aside and brought forth the pliers, opening and closing them in Gareth's face, then brought them to his fingertips. "Say we have a deal," the demon said. Gregor began pulling his fingernail out ever so slowly. Gareth didn't think anything could hurt more than the knife carving into his chest, but he was so wrong. He began howling in agony.

"It's... a... *deal!*" he cried with every syllable.

Everything stopped. The pain in his finger and his chest, the overwhelming agony coursing through his body, the sound of the world, and the cool air brushing up against his skin. Time itself stopped once more, and the demon slashed the chains, freeing Gareth from his bindings. Red eyes watched him as he sat up and brought his arms down, holding them as if they'd stretch away from his body at any moment. He felt for the wounds upon his chest but they were no more, only scars remained in their place.

Gareth watched as the demon walked around Gregor, still standing at his side, pliers in hand, and traced his claws across the man's body. The man's skin peeled open all over, blood visible but remaining beneath Gregor's skin. It sliced the man's hand clean off and it remained attached as it continued gripping the pliers. The demon then slid two of its claws into Gregor's eyeballs about an inch, before moving onto its next victim.

The next man wasn't so lucky, if what happened to Gregor could be labeled as such. The demon smashed its hands on either side of the man's skull, crushing it to half its normal size. It carried on with its sickening slaughter of Gareth's captors, tearing off limbs, opening chest cavities, and pulling spinal cords from out their backs. Gareth couldn't watch, but neither could he look away. A moment later, time resumed and blood erupted all over the cave walls. Bodies and body parts collapsed to the floor with gruesome splatters, sickening wet sounds echoing throughout the cave. Gregor's gurgling screams lasted a few seconds before he lay still at Gareth's feet, his innards sliding onto the floor through the many openings across his torso. Gareth's legs gave out and he collapsed, landing in them, and he vomited aggressively as he slid around trying to get back up.

"Worth it," the demon chuckled.

"I suppose you know the way then?" Gareth asked later on, once he'd had the opportunity to clean himself up and retrieve his belongings. The sun had since risen, and Gareth found it difficult to be in the presence of such an entity in broad daylight, where he could see every diabolical detail.

"Leading you astray would only elongate my torment," it said. "I don't want to deal with you or your stupid questions anymore than you want to deal with me. The faster we find this..." The demon twisted its face as if it were going to be sick, and shudders physically manifested upon its limbs, flowing down its body in a wave of cringe. "...*love* of yours, the better."

"She is not my love," Gareth retorted.

"Ahh, but you wish it were so nonetheless. Shame you'll never see it."

Gareth ignored the demon's words despite the anger they just sparked within him. The anger nestled in his throat, swelling into an ache he had no choice but to swallow and move on. "So, what am I supposed to call you?"

The demon looked at Gareth suspiciously, mulling the question over for a moment before responding. "I have been called many things over countless millennia, but you may refer to me as Kalídagonía."

"Kalida what?" Gareth answered. The demon rolled its eyes and shook its head. "I'm not calling you that. Kali it is." Kali offered no response, and Gareth took what little victory he could gather from the moment. "Say, Kali, is there anything you can do about that?" He made a gesture toward the demon.

"About what?" Kali answered apathetically, another small victory for the young village boy.

"*That!*" He pointed again at the demon. "If you're going to be here, can't you at least be less..." Kali eyed him dangerously. "...I don't know, distracting?"

"I suppose I can tone down my superior qualities..." Kali said in his apathetic tone. "As entertaining as it'd be, pissing yourself every time you look at me would ultimately delay us." He snapped his fingers and most of the horns jutting out from his scalp disappeared, his face contorted until it resembled a measly human's, clawed hands became more human-like, and his stature shrank dramatically. He didn't stand much taller than Gareth now, and with the exception of a couple small horns sticking out of his forehead, the red eyes, dusty black skin, his tail, small canine-like fangs and a forked tongue, Kali looked pretty much human... he even donned some tasteful hair atop his devilish head. Whereas he hadn't been wearing anything before, now the demon wore a stylish tunic of grays and burgundies that contrasted his skin tone quite nicely. "Happy?" Kali asked sarcastically. "Or would you like to continue with your

Gareth looked at Kali somewhat amused, but mostly annoyed. "The tail's a bit much don't you think?"

"You're lucky we're bound by contract," Kali groaned.

The two unlikely companions traversed the countryside without incident the first day. Gareth had dried fruit and nuts to munch on from the supplies Asta's father had given him, and he hadn't needed his bow since his encounter with the imperial soldiers. Things were going smoothly despite the ever-looming thought that this was it for Gareth. His life was forfeit, but he reminded himself he'd be dead now, or worse, and at least now he gets to rescue Asta from the clutches of the imperial bastards... and he'd do it in style, he thought as he glanced over at Kali. The demon was many things, but boring was not counted among them. They stopped to make camp as the sun dropped toward the horizon, and Gareth sat close to the fire, drinking from his waterskin he'd recently refilled in a stream.

"So..." He broke the silence finally. Kali groaned and gave the boy his attention. "...if the gods are real, then why did they abandon us?"

Kali's groans grew louder to the point of exaggeration. "It's always the gods with you people!" His limbs shook, little black embers dancing upon his skin. "Ever think that maybe, just maybe, they have other things to do than cater to your pathetic species? What makes your people so special?"

Gareth swallowed his snappy retort and exhaled slowly, slumping down a tree trunk in an internal retreat. "I was just asking... we can't be that pathetic if you want my soul so bad..."

Kali snickered.

"What?" Gareth asked. "What's funny?"

"There's nothing special about your soul, especially the vessel in which it resides. Just another soul, and there's no shortage of those. I just saw an opportunity to stretch my legs." Kali laughed as he started stretching his limbs. "You humans have an exaggerated sense of importance when it comes to your species, for as low as you are on the totem pole. Never ceases to amuse though, always makes for a good laugh."

"Shut up!" Gareth snapped suddenly before collecting himself.

"Ahhh!" Kali squealed, covering the left side of his chest with a hand. "You wound me..."

"Stop."

"The words..." Kali fell to his knees. "They hurt so bad! Why human? Whyyyyyy..." He collapsed to the ground, his voice shrinking as he reached up toward the stars, extending the final word for an absurd amount of time. "... yyyyyyyyyyyyy—"

"You can stop now," Gareth mumbled, "I get it... you got me, alright?"

"Well... okay then," a voice from behind their camp

said. "I'm not sure how you heard us, but uh, if you hand over everything you got, we won't hurt you." It was a man's voice, leaning toward the elderly side if Gareth were to guess.

"Who's we?" Gareth replied, surprised at his utter lack of fear, but seeing the intrigued look upon Kali's face, he figured it was just a symptom of knowing he couldn't be harmed.

"There's a handful of us!" another voice called out from the shadows. Then three people walked into the light of the fire. One reached out, curling their fingers repeatedly in a "give me" gesture. "Come on kid. Give us the bag, the bow, and whatever else you've got."

"And the boots!" the third person added. "We want your boots too."

"You don't want to do this. Just turn around and walk away, please." He urged them to listen. "Nobody needs to get hurt."

The three thieves laughed as they moved closer to Gareth's camp. "Don't be a fool," the older voice he'd initially heard replied. He nodded to the others and they drew weapons as they continued their approach.

"Please don't do this!" Gareth tried again, for he knew the lengths people would go to feed their families in these hard times. The many neighboring villages to his own had been ignored by their gods for years, and their crops have dwindled, harvests have given them little to nothing, and even the fishing towns along the coast weren't catching anywhere near what they had just a few years before. Imperial soldiers have been snatching their loved ones for months, possibly longer. The quality of life for Gareth and all the people living in the surrounding area had been on a steady decline for a long time, and he didn't blame them for turning on their own and grasping at straws. There weren't many options, but people like them deserved the repercussions for the choices they made, even if he understood why. "Stop!" he shouted, hoping he could save them.

They only stopped for a moment, but his shout seemed to fuel their desperation and the younger of the men charged Gareth. He raised his weapon, but he couldn't bring it down upon the boy's skull. "Huh?" he blurted out in confusion, fighting against an invisible force holding his arm upright. Then his arm snapped in half and he screamed in pain and terror as he watched his broken forearm twist until only tendons held the two pieces together. His screams became high pitched wails as the tendons tore apart and the weapon in his detached hand was thrust into his skull through the temple, silencing the man's screams. The body fell to the ground in a bloody heap just inches from Gareth.

The boy sighed. The others cried out as they attempted to flee the nightmarish scene, and Gareth looked away and tried to block out the blood curdling screams and gurgles that followed. As the silence settled, he looked up and Kali was nowhere to be seen. "Kali?" Gareth yelled out. "What are you doing? Come back!" Then he heard a quick high-pitched scream somewhere not far from camp. It lasted but a moment and then Kali appeared beside him. "They weren't a threat!" Gareth scolded the demon. "You don't have to kill everyone!"

"One of them got away because of you," Kali scolded him in return.

"That's fine, let them go."

"And if they return with a mob of your countrymen carrying pitchforks and torches? What then?"

Gareth sighed. "I don't know." He was defeated. "But not everyone deserves to die, even if they initially come across as threatening."

"How are you still alive?" Kali asked incredulously.

Gareth ignored him, and moved toward one of the bodies. "Can you help me with these?" he asked.

"Why?"

"Because I don't want to sleep next to corpses..."

"How is that my problem?" Kali retorted. "I actually think they liven' up the place quite nicely... the way your mother might stick some disgusting flowers in, you know, one of those stupid flower things."

"My mother died when I was little..." Gareth replied before instantly regretting it.

"Ooooooh! Juicy!" Kali squealed enthusiastically. "Probably for the best though! *Ooooh!* Tell me how it happened, I love me a good death!"

Gareth ignored the demon once more, continuing to drag the bodies away from camp. He tried ignoring the demon's comments and complaints when he didn't get his way, but eventually he just zoned the demon's voice out. He thought about his mother for the first time in a very long time. He could hardly recall what she looked like anymore, but he remembered her laugh... he remembered the way she'd sing to him and twirl him around... the kisses that would linger upon his cheeks long after she'd planted them there. It wasn't fair how she was taken from him so young, and the thoughts brought tears to his eyes. He tried pushing her from his thoughts, but that only made him think of Asta, and how she'd taken it upon herself to comfort him after she'd died... how she replaced the cheek kisses when they were little.

It took him a while to move all the bodies far enough from camp on his own, but once the task was finally complete he rejoined Kali by the fire. He thought about all the death he'd seen since summoning Kali and the deal for his soul, then looked at the blood upon the ground, and the trails leading to the discarded bodies. "Why not take their souls?" he asked the demon.

Kali groaned. "Must you always prod? Why should I tell you when you don't answer my curiosities, hmm?"

"Is it because you can only have the souls that you barter for?" The look on Kali's face was one of annoyance and surprise. Kali didn't give Gareth enough credit it seemed.

"Go to sleep," Kali replied, and sleep he would, a smile upon his face for yet another small victory.

Gareth drifted off to thoughts of Asta, and how wonderful it was going to be to see her again... to free her. He thought about how scared he's been without her around, and how her presence had always filled him with joy and comfort, even despite their disagreements. Their differences in opinion had never caused rifts between them, but had complimented their friendship. They challenged each other's views of the world, kept one another on their toes, and lifted the other up when one felt pressed down by the weight of their gloomy reality. Their friendship just worked... how he missed her so.

Thoughts of his beautiful friend slipped into his dreams. They were together again; laughing and teasing one another on one of their routine outings into the woods surrounding their home. They ended up on a river bank. The sun shone brightly overhead, and he watched her remove her garments and run into the refreshing water. "Don't just stand there like an idiot!" she called out to him. "The water feels amazing! Come on!"

Gareth removed his own garments and ran in after her. She splashed him as he shivered, taking his sweet time to get to her, and she laughed when Gareth attempted to block the water. "Don't be a baby!" She giggled as she splashed him again. He would not tolerate being called a baby! He jumped into the water beside her, and the next thing he knew they were floating there together, gazing into each other's eyes. She draped her arms around his neck, and he felt tingles course through his body. "What are you thinking about Gareth?" she asked when the silence between them had gone on a little too long.

"I..." he stammered. What was wrong with him? *Tell her!* "Asta, I..."

Asta laughed and put her forehead against his, the tips of their noses touching. "I feel the same way Gareth," she said softly. Her lips pressed against his as she squeezed him close, then pulled away in surprise. "Oh?" She gasped. "What's this?" She brought a hand from around his neck down into the water, and began stroking his manhood. He looked her in the eyes, utterly shocked at the development. Her sweet innocent features seemed gone then, and her smile was no longer a loving one, but one of hunger or thirst.

"What—" He started, but she blinked and her eyes were red when they opened. He opened his eyes and Asta's face was replaced by a woman's resembling her somewhat.

Her skin was black, and her eyes were red. Two small horns jutted from her forehead, and canine-like fangs revealed themselves when she smiled at him. She was almost entirely naked, gray and burgundy undergarments hardly hiding her feminine bits.

"Good morning handsome! Having a nice dream are we?" She giggled, a finger nail tracing down his chest toward his nether regions. "Pitched a tent I see."

Gareth yelled out in a horrified shock. "Kali!" he cried out angrily. "Why!" He jumped up and stormed away feeling utterly violated. He kept going until he could no longer hear Kali's amused laughter. Finally, he stopped and roared his frustrations, shaking and convulsing from the repugnant start to the day.

Most of the next few days went by smoothly, other than Kali's despicable behavior, and inappropriately timed comments. The two continued their journey, only stopping a couple hours before sunset so Gareth could refill his waterskin. "Someone's approaching." Kali told him, and then the demon shapeshifted into the likes of a small black cat with little horns and a very contradictory tail. He hid behind Gareth's leg as the boy turned to regard whoever was approaching them. They were on horseback, and after a minute had arrived beside them. They donned the griffon emblem he'd seen on the imperial soldiers that had captured him.

"Traveler!" the leading man called out to him. "Haven't you heard? The road is quite dangerous around these parts. Where are you headed?"

"Nowhere in particular... wherever the road takes us. Looking for—"

"Us?" the man asked suspiciously.

Gareth's heart stopped for a second before Kali meowed and curled around his leg. "Yes. My cat and I."

The man eyed the cat suspiciously. "That's not like any cat I've ever seen..."

"It's a... kith mutt... the runt, abandoned by its mother..." Gareth trailed off as he began eyeing the soldier suspiciously. "You said the road's been dangerous?" he asked. "How do you mean?"

The soldier continued to look the boy and his cat over suspiciously, waving his fellow imperials over. Three other men slid off horseback and approached them. They all turned around and spoke quietly before addressing him. "So, you haven't seen any suspicious characters lurking about? At all?"

"Can you please define suspicious?" Gareth answered, crossing his arms.

"Tell you what friend," the man said. "How about we escort you to our fort, it's maybe a few hours ride from here." He pointed in a north easterly direction. "We can provide protection and some good company."

Agree. Gareth heard Kali's voice inside his head.

"That's awfully kind of you, sir! We're headed in that direction anyway, thank you."

"Don't mention it kid."

They got further the few hours they rode on horseback than they'd gotten in a few days on foot. Gareth took the opportunity to converse with the imperials, and try to subtly probe information from them that might help him find Asta. They hadn't revealed much, other than the fort they were headed to was just a checkpoint along their route to the imperial capital, a place to rest and eat, gather supplies and the like. At some point along the way, a group of freedom fighters using guerilla tactics, ambushed them. One of the horses stepped into a trap, halting abruptly and collapsing onto its forelegs, sending the soldier atop it from their saddle. He fell into a pit and cried out. Some stakes had been planted there, but the man had managed to miss them. Roars erupted from the sidelines, from beyond a hill not far from the pit. They swooped down shooting arrows and throwing spears.

"Watch out kid!" one of the men yelled as he shoved Gareth down just as an arrow flew by. "Stay down!" Gareth crawled away and toward the pit where the fallen soldier was yelling for assistance. He managed to reach the ledge and see the man reaching up for a hand. Gareth contemplated leaving him down there, but quickly dismissed the idea as doing so would likely turn the soldiers against him, rendering this little venture of theirs obsolete. He reached down and grabbed the man's hand, but he was too heavy to lift, wearing all the armor. They could hear a battle ensuing around them, but Gareth couldn't pull him up, groaning heavily and sweat dripping from his brow. Kali swirled around his arm, and then around the soldier's arm and Gareth fell backward, the trapped soldier rising from the pit and sliding onto his chest.

"Thanks, kid," he said, and then swung his sword beside the boy, striking down a freedom fighter. When they collapsed beside Gareth, very much dead, the air was sucked from his lungs. He recognized the face! It was someone from his sister village, one of the fisherman's boys. He looked at the other aggressors, and recognized another as well. His heart sank... what was he supposed to do? Then an arrow thudded into his chest, and he looked down at it confused. Kali, still wrapped around his arm, had taken control of the limb and caught the arrow in the nick of time. One of the attackers stopped when they saw Gareth for the first time, confused, as he'd clearly recognized the boy. A moment later he was struck down, his near lifeless body falling limp at their feet. Gareth looked into the dying boy's eyes, whom clearly recognized him, and was consumed by shame. The boy tried to speak to him, accusation and contempt in his eyes, and he grabbed Gareth's leg before a sword was buried into his neck.

Gareth leaned over and vomited. He remembered a time he and the boy had played together when they were young children. *Kill them!* He imparted his thoughts to Kali. The demon refused, and Gareth wanted to scream. He could've helped them; he and Kali could've saved them!

They were foolish to attack these men. Their deaths were inevitable. Kali told him. *Their deaths contribute to your cause.*

Gareth felt himself slipping away. Was this the price of selling his soul? Was it worth it? He had to ask himself as he looked into the boy's dead eyes. Yes… if it means Asta will be free and safe, it had to be worth it. He couldn't consider any alternative. "I told you to stay down!" the soldier snapped at him as he was yanked to his feet. "You're lucky you were not killed, boy." None of the soldiers had perished in the fight, though one of their horses had suffered fatal injuries and had to be put down. They continued the rest of their way in silence.

When they arrived at the fort, the soldiers guarding the entry saluted his escorts and opened the gate, and they eyed him suspiciously as they rode in. It wasn't a large compound, but the place was packed full of soldiers, horses, and prisoners.

Cages full of people were scattered all throughout the fort. The soldier he'd pulled from the pit noticed him looking at them and nudged him. "We were gonna throw you in with that lot," he laughed, "but I think you proved yourself trustworthy today. We're transporting them to the capital in the morning. How about joining us? The empire could use another soldier with that kind of strength." He winked at Gareth who said nothing in return. Gareth could still see the dead boy staring at him as if he were a traitor, the life leaving his eyes as the sword sank into his neck. "Think it over at least," the soldier said as he walked away.

Later that evening, as they all sat around the communal fire eating better than the entirety of Gareth's village had in months, the soldiers addressed him again, as he'd remained silent since their arrival. "Did you think about it?" the soldier asked him as he bit into his dinner.

"Yeah right!" another soldier he'd arrived with chimed in. "He hasn't spoken a word since we showed up. He ain't got the stomach for this life." Some of the other soldiers laughed as they continued eating.

"Actually, yeah I have," Gareth answered, and the soldiers went silent as they turned their suspicious eyes back upon the strange boy. "I accept your invitation," he said as he stared at his food. He hadn't eaten very much. He didn't have much of an appetite, but he couldn't waste it either, so he reluctantly took a bite.

"Alright then!" the soldier cheered, lifting his ale to the boy. "This kid has quite the arm ya know," he said to the soldier beside him. "Where did you say you're from?" he asked Gareth.

"I didn't," he replied. "I've never really—"

"That voice…" a quiet voice called out from a cage nearby. "That's him! The sorcerer! The one that killed my entire family without even laying a finger on them! I told you!"

Well shit, Kali groaned. *This is worse than pitchforks and torches!*

The soldiers stood up, all having gone silent, and looked at Gareth questioningly. Gareth lowered his food and looked up at them, not sure what to say or do.

"Sorcerer!" another prisoner cried.

"Stay right there," the man ordered Gareth, and walked over to the cage. "I'm sure this is a misunderstanding." He went to retrieve the prisoner who identified Gareth and brought her over by the fire. "Is this the man that slaughtered your family with his mind?" The girl strained to recognize him, and the soldier tugged on her roughly. "A false accusation of such magnitude could cost you your life, peasant!"

"She doesn't know what she's talking about…" Gareth said.

"I'm certain of it!" she said with the utmost confidence. "I'll never forget that voice."

The soldier threw her to the side and stalked toward Gareth. "I thought there was something fishy about you!"

"Kill him!" Cries came from the cages.

A soldier lifted Gareth by the scruff of his neck and dragged him across the ground. Kali, once more in his cat form, hissed at them and one of the soldiers kicked him away.

"String him up!" a voice yelled out.

"Burn him at the stake!"

"Gut him!"

Gareth got punched in the jaw a few times, and they started tying him up to a pole. A soldier paced back and forth, brandishing his weapon and spitting at Gareth. "You die tonight! The empire will not suffer the likes of you!"

Gareth looked past the angry mob of soldiers, at the cat approaching them, and began to laugh.

"Kill him now!"

The soldier was already raising his sword to gut the boy, but a moment later his sword was driven through his skull, and he collapsed to the ground at Gareth's feet. Soldiers began to rush him, and heads began popping, bodies tore apart, and in the chaos the girl released the other prisoners. Most fled, but some armed themselves and joined in the frenzy. Gareth lowered his head as Kali flew around the camp, a mass of black flames ricocheting from one body to the next like a comet flashing through the night sky. Dozens upon dozens of men and women splattered to the ground in pieces, their screams and their cries becoming wet gurgles, and as the seconds passed, the horrific sounds quieted in a wave throughout the encampment, until silence was all that remained.

Gareth's limbs were freed and he rubbed his wrists, not bothering to take in the awful sight, or to regard Kali in any manner. "Let's go," he said, but Kali stopped him in his tracks.

"Let me make something very clear to you boy," he said as he poked him in the chest. "All these people are dead because of *you*." He reiterated the point with another poke. His scowl became a grin then, and he skipped around the piles of corpses, splashing blood around as he did so. "Your pain is scrumptious!"

"I'm glad you're enjoying yourself," Gareth said,

drained of all emotion.

"Now, take this armor," Kali told him as a body dropped beside him. "Put it on. It's time for this soldier boy to return to the capital!" He took on his feminine features and batted his eyelashes at Gareth. "Let's save your girly friend and be done with this."

After Gareth put the armor on, Kali disintegrated the body with its black fire until nothing was left. Gareth didn't even bother asking why, nor did he attempt to wonder. Kali was pleased.

A few days later they arrived at their destination. The capital was huge, and was protected by a very impressive wall. A palace was visible from miles away, nestled snuggly and safely within the perimeter. It wasn't difficult to gain access, as a stream of soldiers transporting prisoners were heading inside. Gareth simply blended into the company, just another imperial soldier returning home. Gareth wasn't prepared for what he'd find inside however, for he'd never laid his eyes upon such a large community. He saw more people in mere seconds, than he'd seen in the entirety of his life. The noise, the rush... it was all so overwhelming, and it took him a minute to collect himself.

Gareth had made it at long last. The armor he'd taken from one of the imperial corpses wasn't quite his size, but it did its job. He'd made it into the heavily fortified imperial compound. Shackled slaves were hard at work everywhere. They were building walls, weapons, and all manner of things for the empire. He looked around, his heart heavy, at what'd become of his people.

"Don't get any ideas," Kali told him. "We have a deal.

We aren't here to liberate anyone other than your girl."

Gareth looked at Kali hard, but the demon was right. "I know," he agreed. "We just have to find her..." He tried to keep his voice down as there were hundreds, if not thousands of people surrounding them, imperial and slaves alike. He couldn't draw too much attention to himself. "...there's so many though... where do we even start?"

"Hey!" someone nearby shouted. Gareth ignored them though. They could've been talking to any number of people. He continued walking through the crowd of imperial soldiers, people who looked more like priests and priestesses, as well as imperial civilians. A hand grasped his shoulder and spun him around. "Hey soldier, I'm talking to you. Show a superior officer some respect!"

Gareth looked at the man and came to attention, saluting the way he'd seen before. "Yes, sir!" he answered. "Apologies sir, I didn't realize you were addressing me... sir!"

"Fine... fine. At ease," the officer said, and Gareth relaxed, lowering his hand. "What are you doing? What's your assignment?" He asked as he looked Gareth up and down suspiciously.

"I... uh..." Gareth stuttered, not sure how he was supposed to answer the question.

The officer stuck a finger into Gareth's chest, smeared it an inch or two along his armor, and brought his finger up to his face. The blood! Why didn't he think of cleaning it? "Just come in from the field with the latest company?"

"Yes, sir," Gareth answered, relief settling in. "We were attacked by some of the local trash, but we made quick work of them," he said.

"Very good," the officer said, suspicion still thick in his voice. "Were you injured?"

"Well…"

"Best to swing by the infirmary and get checked up. Come by the guardhouse afterward for debriefing and reassignment. Dismissed."

"Yes, sir, thank you, sir," Gareth said, then he turned around and began walking away. That had been a close call, and he wanted to put as much distance as possible between him and the officer as quickly as possible.

"Are you daft soldier?" the officer called out to him. Gareth froze….

"Sir?"

"The infirmary is that way," the officer pointed. "You get hit in the head or something?"

"Oh right!" Gareth answered. "I might have. Thank you again, sir." He walked off in the direction the officer had pointed.

"And soldier!" he heard. Gareth stopped and sighed. Kali groaned his frustrations as well. Gareth turned to face the officer once more. "Get your armor refitted. It's a bit big on you." The officer didn't wait for Gareth's response before walking away.

They wound their way through the crowded streets until the infirmary came into view, all the while scanning the faces of every woman they passed. A large greenhouse sat beside the building, surrounded by a lush garden. A few slaves tended to the garden, among others, and Gareth beelined for it, knowing Asta would likely be drawn to such a place.

When he saw her, his heart leapt from his chest. He was

overcome by both happiness and sorrow. Seeing her face brought tears of joy to his eyes, but also sadness for he knew what was to come. Fear began swelling within him at the thought, but he was determined to free her from this place. He rushed up to her.

"Asta!" he called out to her, his voice shaking. She looked up at him in shock. "Asta, it's really you!"

"Gareth?" she asked skeptically.

"Yes! It's me!"

"Gareth!" she cried happily and hugged him in a loving embrace. "But how?"

"Not now," Gareth replied and grabbed her hand. "We need to get you out of here!" He began to pull her away from the garden but felt resistance. When he turned to face her again, she looked upon him with pity, sadness, and shame. "What?" He asked.

"I can't..." she answered.

Then Gareth saw what she was wearing as if for the first time, he'd been so fixated on her face. She was dressed in a blue and gold tunic. He looked at the slaves helping to tend the garden and they wore filthy brown rags. "No..." Gareth breathed, horrified by what it all might mean.

Kali began laughing hysterically, and all of a sudden, the world went mute again. The hustle and bustle of the crowd, the clanking of the armor upon all the soldiers, the wind... it all ceased. "Oh, the irony!" Kali wheezed.

"What..." Asta cried. "What's happening Gareth?" She looked around at all the people frozen in time, and then her eyes fell upon Kali. "What is this?"

Gareth fell to his knees. Kali reclaimed his natural form,

growing in stature, twisted horns growing from his contorting head, laughing all the while. "I'll tell you what's happening! Your pathetic little friend here offered me his soul in exchange for saving his life so he could rescue you... only to learn that you do not need rescuing!" Kali howled with glee.

"No!" Asta cried. She looked to Gareth, love and regret flowing from her eyes as tears. "No, no, no!" She wrapped her arms around Gareth, crying into him. "Please don't!" She wept. "Gareth why did you—"

"As heartbreaking as this is, I really should get going," Kali said. "Time to go, boy."

Asta lifted her face from Gareth and eyed the demon desperately. "Take mine instead, please!"

"Asta, no!" Gareth snapped.

"Please!" Asta pleaded with the demon.

"It's too late." Kali laughed. "It is done."

Gareth pulled Asta's chin toward him so their eyes met one last time. "I'm glad you're okay," he said softly, attempting to smile. "I lo—" His face lifted as his head tilted backward, his mouth agape and his eyes wide open.

Kali's clawed hand hovered above Gareth, pulling on the boy's essence like a puppet master pulling the strings. Wisps of white ethereal light poured from Gareth's mouth until it danced around in Kali's palm, his long fingers moving back and forth as the essence weaved through them.

He looked at Asta and smiled. "Who knew this ending would be so delightfully tragic! I can't thank you enough my dear!" Kali's roars of laughter faded as time resumed, and Gareth's body fell over, landing beside the imperial healer.

Consumed

A monstrous howl pierced through the calm night, sending the residents of a village from a tranquil sleep into a collective frenzy. Damian Grey sprung from beside his wife and immediately began putting his trousers on. "They're back?" she asked him, but he didn't waste his breath answering the question, for it needed no confirmation. The noise had rattled their bones, and the flickering of torches could already be seen through the window shutters; voices filling the outside as much as the firelight. "I'll get the kids!" she said as if her mind had taken an extra moment to grasp the situation, and threw her nightgown over her naked body.

When Damian was fully dressed he beelined for the family room. "Daddy!" one of his daughters cried out as she ran to him and buried herself into his leg. He leaned down and wrapped the girl in his arms, and she nuzzled her face against his large beard where she knew she would be safe. "I'm scared, Daddy."

Three more of his children were in the room now, as well as his wife, Malinda, and they awaited his orders. He pulled his youngest from him and smiled at her. "Your dad's not gonna let anything happen to you, you understand?" he told her, her eyes meeting his as he leaned down to her level. She nodded and looked upon her hero with awe and admiration, feeling safer for having embraced the man and hearing his words of affirmation. Damian stood and looked to the rest of his family, nodded, and turned his attention to Malinda. "Get them to the bunker. Lock it. Keep quiet, and wait for me. Do not come out until I give the okay." Malinda nodded, her eyes lingering upon her lover. "Be safe, and come back to me Damian. I love you," she told him as she began ushering their children away.

"Dad!" one of his sons called out to him. Damian turned to the boy. "Give them hell."

Damian nodded and rushed to retrieve the axe he'd only ever used to cut down trees, until recently anyway. Blood still stained its edge from the previous encounter, a reminder to the man that he'd become far more than a simple logger... all the surviving men of their village had... they'd become killers, hunters. Those who'd resisted that reality left their children fatherless... their wives, widows. There was no choice.

The men of the village gathered outside, brandishing what weapons they'd accumulated over the years, most of which were simple logging, fishing, and harvesting tools such as axes, spears and scythes. They carried torches, pitchforks, and other non-combatant tools as well, the only true weapons being bows and arrows they used for hunting bucks, and occasionally, the rare mammoth elk. "Damian!" one of the men called out when they spotted him. The man trotted up to Damian and spoke as they hastily made their way toward the edge of town with the other men of their community. "I've been itching to sink my axe into one of these beasts again!"

The man chuckled, slapping Damian on the back.

The full moon shined brightly in the midnight sky, the cosmos speckled across the heavens, its light reflected off the surface of the nearby lake. The cries of cattle sounded off into the night as all the excitement had them stirring and agitated. The endless trees surrounding their village in nearly every direction swayed with the cool autumn breeze, blowing Damian's long brown hair about as he regarded his friend. "This isn't a sport Cale," Damian replied sternly. "Our lives, the lives of our loved ones, and our livelihoods are on the line. Get your head on straight."

He and Cale exchanged an incredulous look, a knowing one that stretched on for a moment before Cale flashed his old friend a disarming smile, one that nearly lifted the corners of Damian's lips in turn. The mob of men traversed the dense woods surrounding their homes in the direction the howl had come from, skirting along the eastern edges of the lake. Eventually, the ground dipped below the lake, a steep incline to their west, cliff faces scattered here and there, rocky ledges and outcroppings in abundance until the ground returned to its initial elevation. Moonlight began shining through the thick canopies above, the trees thinning out as they approached one of the forest's edges, a clearing nearby.

"You're not fooling anyone ya know," Cale told him. "You've slain more than any of us, like it's been your calling all along. The others look up to you... your mere presence bolsters everyone's resolve... some even fear you now," Cale snickered.

"Shall I count you among them?" Damian asked Cale. He hid his smile behind his stoic nature. "Gods man, you gonna get on your knees next?"

Cale visibly relaxed, the last question surely being a jest, and he chuckled. "You—"

Another terrorizing howl pierced the silence of the night, followed by another, and then another, each sounding closer than the last. The last one sounded a couple miles away, if that, and the husbands and fathers tightened their fingers around their mediocre weapons, tightened their formation, and looked about nervously. "There!" one of the men called out quietly, and the others followed his extended finger to a hilltop about a mile away, just north of the lake's shores, and nothing but open fields between them.

There, atop the hill bathed in moonlight, stood a lone creature, its limbs long and its stature large. "Put out your fires!" Damian called out quietly, yet sternly, and led by example. He only hoped the trees and the brush had shielded the dance of their torches from the beast's prying eyes. Nobody needed to be told twice, and a moment later they stood in the darkness, watching the creature look about in the general direction of their homes. Damian watched intently, studying the creature's odd behavior.

"What is it doing?" Cale asked.

"It's just standing there," another chimed in.

"What are we waiting for?" another man asked. "Let's go!" The man's words stirred some courage from some of the others, all of whom had likely lost loved ones to the monsters, their vengeance clouding their judgement.

"No!" Damian snapped. "They'll come to us."

"How can you be sure?"

"Why would they go around the lake?" Cale spoke up for his friend. "He's right."

"Aye," Damian confirmed. "We'll make our stand here."

More howls erupted from the hilltop. They watched in horror as more than a dozen of the beasts appeared beside the first. There had never been more than a few at a time, and some of the men began visibly shaking from sheer fear alone. One last monstrous howl came forth, and then a wave of monstrous beasts descended the large hill, and to Damian's credit, they were headed directly for them. "Prepare yourselves!" Damian told them. "We are the last line of defense."

Cale swung his axe in a circular motion, his eyes fixed on the creatures that would soon be upon them, the humor and the thirst for battle having abandoned him. Without diverting his attention from the coming horde, he addressed his friends and neighbors surrounding him. "It was nice knowin' ya lads!" His voice broke as he finished the sentence. "Truly," his voice now a tremor, "it's been an honor." His concentration was only broken when he looked at the hand upon his shoulder, its strong firm grip giving as much affection as inspiration. Damian nodded to him, and Cale knew the depth of it, even if no words had been exchanged.

They'd retreated a bit the way they'd come, until they were in the bowl, cliffsides to their left, to minimize angles of attack, and a moment later the beasts were upon them. Rabid, wild things... the werewolves swarmed them, and the men didn't wait, striking first and with all their fury. Damian heard the cries and the gurgles of his friends and neighbors as canines tore through flesh, and ripped out throats. They were tall, reaching heights of seven or eight feet, covered in fur, and their limbs long and corded with muscle. They attacked ferociously, swiping with their long claws, biting with their sharp fangs, and they were quick too. Damian tried focusing on one at a time, and quickly buried his axe within two of the beasts right off the bat, but there were so many, even more so as men dropped around him… still, they far outnumbered the things and he could only hope they'd be enough, even if nothing was left standing by the end of the confrontation, at least their families would be safe.

Damian sunk his axe through a werewolf's neck, kicked his boot into its side, pinning it against the cliffside, and yanked it from the corpse. It dropped in a bloody heap at his feet. He turned to find his next victim and saw Cale swinging away at the beasts, and one flanking him. Their eyes met just as Damian flung his axe in his direction, but his friend didn't flinch, nor did he take a moment to thank him. His axe intercepted the sneaky werewolf's face just as it was opening its maw to clamp it shut around Cale. The surprised beast roared out in pain, and attempted to remove the weapon from its face, but crumpled to the ground before it could do so.

The hulking lumberjack spotted another axe a few feet away, laying beside the corpse of one of his neighbors. Damian swooped it up just in time to swing it at an advancing werewolf. Their eyes radiated a rage… a hatred that shimmered in their unnatural irises, and this one barely flinched as the axe bit into its side. It had caught his arm just as he'd made contact, and it lifted the man off his feet. Dangling from the beast's clawed grasp, it laughed in his face. What was this? Damian's deep gray eyes widened in shock. How could this be! Werewolves weren't meant to be sentient… they were feral, mindless things, yet this one was studying him… mocking him. "Ah," it cooed. Damian's heart stopped beating in his chest. "*Lupus Interfectorem!*" The words glided coolly from its maw, neither anger nor hatred spilling from them, but more so a curiosity, an observation. It spoke! Damian struggled to grasp the revelation, his brain still processing its words, spoken in a low rumbling as if straddling an imminent roar, raspy and cold. "Watch, wolf slayer!" It snapped in his face.

The werewolf easily lifted Damian high off the ground, its clawed hands wrapped tightly around his forearm, and it turned him so he could see the battle nearing its end. Dozens of his friends and neighbors decorated the cold ground, their lifeless bodies torn to shreds. Their guts spilled around them, the heat still permeating the cold night air, visible streams of heat rising from the fresh corpses. Those were the lucky ones. Some still screamed in pain as the remaining monsters butchered them slowly. "What do you want?" Damian cried as he dangled helplessly from the werewolf's hand.

"Not I," it replied. It turned to face the cliffs then, and Damian watched alongside all the others, as each and every wolf seemed to fall in line and silence overcame the gruesome scene.

A noise from above caught Damian's attention, and just as he looked that way the blurry image of another wolf intercepted his sight, and a moment later the largest of them all stood before them. It had been watching from up above the entire time, Damian realized. The pack released a volley of howls that shook the man to his core, and left his ears ringing for some time afterwards. "*Lupus Interfectorem...*" He couldn't quite hear the words, but he knew that's what the alpha had said as he stood before him. "Bring him," the alpha said to the wolf Damian dangled from, before turning its attention back upon the helpless man. "You'll wish you'd died with your brethren here when I'm through with you." Its golden eyes flared with a malevolent lust as it stared daggers into Damian's soul. Then he was thrown over the beast's shoulder, and he watched in horror as some of the slain werewolves scrambled back to their feet, their wounds slowly healing, and wind rushed past his face as the pack made haste for his home.

Damian was beaten and battered, and the bones in his arm felt as though they'd been shattered beneath the wolf's brute otherworldly strength. He slipped in and out of consciousness until he was thrown to the ground, and he could hear screams all around him. The werewolves were laying waste to his village, women and children were screaming, and then they were silenced. His thoughts went to his family. Malinda, and his beloved children, and he desperately hoped they were all okay. He'd been the best father and husband he knew how to be, often times believing his best didn't suffice, but he never stopped trying. Before Malinda, Damian had been lost, drowning himself in his sorrows, wallowing in the transgressions and pain of the past, and more often than not, finding comfort at the bottom of a bottle. She'd saved him, and she'd given him a family; a second chance at life, and he loved her all the more for it. He was truly blessed.

"*Aspectus divinus*... where are they?" the alpha roared in Damian's face. He had no idea what the creature was asking for, and his face must've given it away. It growled its frustrations, and kicked a dead woman's corpse in its tantrum. The body went flying across the village, and Damian's heart sank. He'd known the lady. Hilda... her husband Brand had died bravely in their fight against the beasts. They'd just announced her pregnancy with their first child within the past month. He looked around hoping against hope he wouldn't spot his family. "The god-kissed!" the alpha roared at him finally. "You must know! Tell me!"

Damian choked on the swelling bulge in his throat, and tried moving, but screamed when he moved his arm, grabbing it with his good hand. "Problem?" the alpha wolf asked as he cocked his head to the side, examining Damian's injured arm. The wolf grabbed the arm and pulled, drawing screams of agony from the bearded man, then squeezed.

"Please!" Damian cried. "Haven't you done enough? Just—"

His screams grew tenfold as the alpha dug its claws into his arm, squeezing all the harder. "The god-kissed! You will tell!"

Damian wanted to spit in the beast's face and be done with it... the pain was too much, but he had to know his family was okay. With as much determination as he could muster, revulsion spilling from every syllable, he eyed the despicable monster. "You just kicked her, you disgusting bastard!" Debilitating agony coursed through his body as the wolf tightened his claws, and he would've sworn he could hear them scraping against his bones, but then the alpha let him go and turned to retrieve the woman.

"We should turn him!" another wolf exclaimed, stopping the alpha in its tracks. A few muttered their concurrences of the suggestion, while others remained silent, even readying themselves to withdraw.

"*No!*" the alpha boomed. "If anyone turns the wolf

slayer," the alpha paused, looking at each and every wolf in his pack. "It'll be the *last*! The end for you!" Once the pack unanimously lowered their gazes from their leader, he retrieved the crumpled remains of Hilda, holding her body to his nose and inhaling deeply. "*Lies!*" The word erupted with savagery and reverberated off the buildings, so full of madness it was. He threw the body down the street and roared furiously in Damian's face once more. The alpha's rage was reaching its boiling point.

"I swear!" Damian tried to say, but the alpha was having none of it. His rage consumed him.

"You lie!" The alpha grabbed Damian's arm once more, drawing more screams from the man, squeezed tighter and tighter, basking in the man's cries, and then tore Damian's arm clean off. Strangely, the act had relieved the worst of the pain, and Damian found himself staring dumbfoundedly at his own limb in the hands of the monster. The alpha then waved it before Damian's face. "You will tell me, stupid man."

"I thought it was her!" Damian yelled. "We all did!"

The alpha let loose a blood curdling sound, a cross between a roar and a howl, a sound of pure frustration. Damian watched his disembodied hand rise behind the beast, and then into his face, hard. "Where!" the alpha roared, smacking him across his face with the limb once more, even harder than before. "Is!" Again. "The!" Again. "God." And again, each time hitting the man's face harder than the last. "Kissed!" The wolf was heaving heavily, foam and saliva spewing from its maw.

Damian toppled to the ground, unmoving, and waited for the end to come. The alpha wolf raised his foot above

Damian's head, screaming obscenities. This was it, Damian thought. The bitter end was coming for him, and any second his brains would litter the ground around his body. If his family survived, and this was how he saved them, so be it.

His life flashed before his eyes. He watched his father beat his mother mercilessly until she was gone. He never even cried over her... doing so would only direct the man's anger toward him. He and his sister buried her in the field behind their cottage, their father watching from the patio. He watched himself beating his sister for his father's praise. He watched as he punished himself beneath the barn. He watched he and his sister murder their father and leave his corpse for the crows. He watched as she sold her body for man's pleasure every night just to feed them, and he watched himself allow it as he wasted away at the bottom of a bottle... for years. He watched his sister whither away, as her soul was stripped apart little by little until there was nothing left of her. He was too drunk to stop what came next... couldn't even lift his head, and watched her take her own life. He watched as he spiraled into insanity and flirted with death's kiss over and over again. He watched as other drunks picked a fight with him in an alley, and he smashed a glass against their skulls, and stabbed each and every one of them without hesitation or remorse, leaving their bodies where they fell.

Damian left the city, and aimlessly wandered the countryside. He eventually ran out of food, water, and alcohol. He'd watch as animals came and went, but hadn't the will nor the drive to obtain sustenance for himself. He watched as he stood on a bridge, peering down into a deep ravine, and he watched himself climb over the ropes and nearly plummet into its depths... but then he heard her voice. It was Malinda, and she was calling out to him. He watched as she nurtured him back to health. She fed him, bathed him, gave him a safe place to overcome the alcoholism that had taken over his life. He watched her cradling him through the cold sweats, the shivers, the convulsions, and he watched himself slip in and out of consciousness for days until he was okay again. He watched as she introduced him to her community; his acceptance there, and how he found a purpose serving the people there. She slowly, patiently, and lovingly peeled away the walls he'd built around himself over the course of years as he stubbornly turned away her advances. He wasn't worthy of her love, or her affections, and she deserved someone better than him.

He watched as his rejections hurt her over and over again. She prayed for him every day and every night, but he was too stubborn to let go of his past and accept her love, in all its forms. He watched as she eventually gave up on him, and how she began to distance herself from him. He watched his friend Cale talk sense into him over the course of weeks as they worked in the fields and chopped down trees. He felt the divine gift of forgiveness as Cale's words followed him around incessantly, and he watched Malinda's tears of joy fall from her eyes when he finally let go of his past. He watched the birth of each and every child of theirs, and how his family grew more and more rich in love. Each saved him over and over again, and as the love grew between them all, his past and its toxic hold over him faded into a long-forgotten dream, the ghosts of his mother and sister following him around no longer haunting him. He watched the miracle of his youngest's birth, and how she had been accompanied by the presence of a goddess, whom bestowed the newborn with a name. She'd been blessed… kissed by a god.

"Daddy!" His daughter's voice snapped him back to reality, the alpha's foot hovering above his head. The wolf lowered his foot and turned his attention to the little girl.

"Melodie!" Malinda cried. "No!" She chased after their youngest and threw herself over the girl, finally realizing they were now surrounded by more than a dozen werewolves. Damian's head was not smashed beneath the alpha's foot, but the realization of his family's presence, and what it meant, crushed him more than the werewolf ever could.

"Leave them alone!" Damian cried desperately.

The alpha wolf cackled as he looked from Malinda and Melodie, to their broken husband and father. "What's this?" his deep raspy voice asked. He waved his finger at the other wolves, a gesture that meant 'round them up.' The wolves grabbed Malinda and Melodie, ripped them out of one another's arms, and pulled them away.

"Mama!" Melodie screamed.

"Melodie!" Malinda cried. "Let us go!" She screamed at the wolves.

Damian felt more helpless than he'd ever felt in his life. "Sweetie!" he yelled as he attempted to get up. His limbs barely responded, pain shooting through his body. Blood poured from the stump his forearm once attached to, and he stumbled back to the ground. "No!" he cried as he tried to move once more, but this time he was hit with his arm again, and collapsed into the dirt.

"Daddy!" Melodie cried, and then her cry turned into one of pain, and she screamed in agony as the wolf holding her still dug its claws into her shoulders.

"Leave her alone!" Malinda roared, but another wolf smacked her so hard, she too, collapsed to the ground.

"No!" Damian screamed in horror, and he was hit yet again.

"Leave her alone!" Damian heard his oldest son scream suddenly. He looked up just in time to see him rush the wolf that knocked his mother to the ground, only to be impaled through the neck by a wolf's claws. His eyes bulged from their sockets as he watched the wolf rip the boy's throat out as a child might pull the petals from a flower; with such ease that all hope remaining within the man was immediately vanquished. His eldest toppled to the ground. Tears poured from his eyes.

"No!" Malinda screamed a blood curdling cry, the pain over the loss of her son reverberating through the remains of the small village, and across the lake.

"How many of them are there?" the alpha asked amusedly over Malinda's and Melodie's cries. He looked to some of the other wolves then. "Go check." Looking down at the beaten and broken man, the alpha lifted his chin with the detached arm. "Why lie?" he asked Damian. He watched the wolves drag three other children out from where the dead boy had been hiding, kicking and screaming, and crying to their mommy and daddy. "Now you suffer, *lupus Interfectorem*. Who is it? Tell, or another dies."

"No!" Malinda begged and begged for her remaining children.

"None of them," Damian answered. The alpha gave the others a signal and they moved to another of his sons. "Why don't you believe me!" Damian sobbed angrily as he watched his son be placed on his knees before them. "Why! Please! Stop!"

The alpha leaned down to eye Damian in his swollen, broken face. "I'm told they're here..." he told the man. The wolf watched Damian closely, analyzing his reactions. "...I'm told they're female." The alpha gave another signal, and Damian watched his second eldest son die, moans, groans, saliva and snot spewing from his face. "Understand, stupid man, nobody else has to die. Tell me."

"You're a liar!" Damian sobbed.

"Probably." Another gesture, and he watched his youngest son get put on his knees.

"Daddy!" his son begged. "Mama!"

"Please! Stop..." Malinda pleaded with them, her screams were piercing, agonizing sounds. "Please..." Her voice grew weak and shaky as her and her son's eyes met. Her and Damian watched him meet his end as well. Damian felt his soul shattering, rage and hatred filling the void, but gasped in shock when he heard Melodie's voice.

"It's me!" she cried. Her mom and her sister looked upon her in horror. Damian felt his breath fail him... he couldn't breathe, and he couldn't think. "It's me! Please let my family go!"

"No, no, no, no, no, no!" Malinda cried, and then her words became gurgles as a claw slit open her throat, and she joined her deceased children upon the cold ground.

"You will all die!" Damian growled, spit flinging from his quivering lips.

"Daddy!" His eldest daughter cried out to him. "I love

you, Daddy." Then he watched his eldest daughter's death as well. He and Melodie were all that remained, but before he could witness her fate, the alpha knocked him out.

When he awoke, the sun had risen, and looking upon what remained of his village was pure nightmare fuel. He spent quite some time crying over his family's bodies, unable to locate Melodie's, and eventually, a primal force overtook him. He no longer had any thoughts, and he was no longer in control of his body. Damian made his way to the healing house and began gathering supplies. He brought them over to the fireplace, and after some time struggling due to a missing arm, he finally got a fire going. Then he began cleaning his stump, and the severity of the pain threatened to send him reeling back into unconsciousness many times as he nicked exposed nerve endings and whatnot. The reality of what needed to be done hit him hard once he realized he could not efficiently or sufficiently clean the wound. It had been an uneven and messy severance.

Once the fire turned the hatchet's blade bright red, Damian bit into a leather-bound dowel, took a couple deep breaths, and gave his severed arm a clean cut. The bright red hatchet cauterized his arm as he left it pressed against the fresh wound. His skinned sizzled, and he groaned in agony throughout the duration. After the room finally came back into focus, he cleaned it and wrapped it up before gathering a number of weapons. He sheathed them on his person, hung them from his belt, and staggered to the building that had dried meat hanging outside. He ate some jerky as he made his way to the well, drank some water, and then made his way to the place him and the other men had battled the werewolves.

All the men remained in heaps across the ground, as well as the few werewolves they had managed to kill. Damian immediately spotted his axe, and after retrieving it, noticed a blood trail leading from the corpses toward the cliffs. It ended at some bushes, but nothing was there. Damian picked up a scythe and cleared the brush, revealing the entrance to a cave that went underneath the lake. With daylight overhead, Damian could see something not far inside, and it was clearly too big to be human. It was hunched over, and as his eyes adjusted to the darkness, Damian could see subtle movement. He brandished his axe and crept toward the figure, but when he neared it, readying his swing in case the beast was to attack, the movement became screeches and the flapping of wings. Bats had been feeding on the dead werewolf, and Damian's presence had disturbed them. They flew toward the mouth of the cave, a flurry of claws and fangs nipping at him and ricocheting off him, and he swung the axe around wildly until none were left.

The werewolf, wearing what was left of some very familiar garments, was quite dead, and the revelation drew growls of frustration and sorrow from the man. Upon searching the cave further, he discovered an abandoned den, and a bear's carcass rotting within. He roared and began swinging the axe at the corpse. Where did they go? A sound from outside the cave got his attention, and when he returned to the scene of the battle, he readied his axe once more and looked around cautiously.

"Damian?" He heard a man's voice. "Damian! You're alive!" It was Cale! His friend didn't sound good at all, and he rushed over to the man. Unlike him, Cale seemed to be in one piece. His friend didn't miss that fact either as he examined the man's stump. "What happened—"

"Do you know where they went?" Damian asked Cale.

"I don't…"

When Damian and Cale returned to the village, Cale was struck by the overwhelming devastation, and utter loss of his home; his loved ones and neighbors, their families, everyone… dead. Damian no longer flinched at the horrendous scene, and his face remained the same emotionless and blank expression. He took Cale to the healing house to tend to the man's wounds, and assess the damage. Cale's shoulder was missing chunks, surrounded by deep fissures where a werewolf's fangs had bitten him. The revelation didn't surprise the men at all, even if Cale seemed deflated by the discovery.

"If I turn—" Cale started.

"I'll end it." Damian said with cold certainty.

Over the course of the next few days, the two men buried their loved ones and burned the rest. They would feed one another's thirst for vengeance, and planned their next excursion in search of the monstrous pack that had taken everything from them, and Damian dared to hope Melodie might still be alive out there. The excursion became a collective and singular purpose between the two men that lasted weeks, as they had no reason to return to the forsaken village. It wasn't until nearly a month had passed that they received a tip from someone in another village roughly thirty miles north of theirs that they found the pack. Apparently, a group of hunters had stumbled across them the previous evening, and luckily they went unnoticed. After warning their village, many up and left, and many others had begun preparations for an attack that never came. They had kept eyes on the werewolves though, and were very much still in the area. Damian had inquired whether a young girl was seen among them, but the hunters couldn't say.

"You ready?" Damian asked Cale after they'd received all the information they needed to locate the pack's exact whereabouts. After a month of relentless searching, and a shared hunger for vengeance, Cale's silence perturbed Damian. He gave his friend an inquisitive look, watching the wrath and commitment evaporate from Cale's face.

"It'll be damn near nightfall by the time we reach them..." He finally answered. After a short pause, he continued. "The full moon rises this night."

Damian finally understood... he'd be facing the pack alone then, unless... "Guess we better move fast then, yeah?"

"I'll try," Cale told him. "But if we don't make it, remember what you agreed to."

"I know Cale." Damian answered apathetically. "I won't let you turn. You have my word."

They weren't far from the pack's last known location as the sun began to set, and it was evident they wouldn't make it in time for Cale to taste sweet vengeance. Damian offered to wait until the last possible moment, but Cale didn't want his predicament to possibly compromise the rescue of his daughter, or hinder their objective in any way. Damian still had a chance if he wasn't a cause for concern, and he requested Damian end it before the sun finished setting. They looked one another in the eyes, and Cale smiled weakly at his friend. "I am glad you found a home among us all those years ago, and I'm grateful to call you my friend." Cale told him.

"You're a good man, Cale." Damian replied, nodding to his friend, denying the tears that threatened to come forth. The two friends said their goodbyes and Damian made it quick.

Before the last rays of daylight vanished behind the horizon, Damian ventured into a makeshift camp full of men. It was in a clearing hidden by trees and rocky hills. The men regarded Damian as he approached them, one of which pointed at the man's stump, and the men began laughing. A tall burly man approached Damian, the rest watching impatiently as the two spoke.

"I didn't expect to see you again so soon." The tall man called out to Damian.

This was all the confirmation the one-armed man needed. "Where is my daughter?" he asked.

"The god-kissed is no longer with us." The man said matter-of-factly.

Damian roared, and with lightning-fast reflexes, he hurled the axe into the alpha's chest. It may have killed him or done far more damage if the alpha hadn't caught it before burying itself too deeply in his flesh. The others growled and advanced, but the alpha kept them at bay with an upraised hand, and pulled the axe from his chest without hesitation. He transformed as he did so, becoming taller and mightier in his wolf form.

Damian put up a good fight one on one against the alpha, but he was never a match for the werewolf. Perhaps he just had a death wish; to rid himself of the pain and loss they'd left in him to rot, but instead of taking his life, they left him outnumbered and defeated. "Tell me why!" Damian demanded. "What use is a god-kissed to you?"

The alpha watched the final rays of sunlight vanish from the world. "Wasn't for me..." The alpha answered. "For an... employer... someone far more dangerous..."

Damian couldn't believe what he was hearing. Even if he had successfully defeated the bastard, his vengeance would've been unfulfilled. Someone... something else was behind everything! "Who?" he asked sternly.

The alpha laughed at the absurd question, but thought about it for a moment and figured answering the doomed man would be of no consequence. "Have you heard of the Erdastraz?"

Damian racked his memories for the reference, his face scrunching up in confusion. "From old children's stories?" Damian asked incredulously.

"Oh, I assure you, they're very real." The alpha said. "... and they aren't as extinct as the stories would lead you to believe."

"Even if this is true," Damian retorted, "the Erdastraz were peaceful... they were protectors... what you're saying is nonsensical, but if you're telling the truth, tell me what the Erdastraz have to do with my daughter!"

The alpha felt a surge of power course through his body as he watched the full moon rising into the sky behind the foolish man with the death wish. "Until the divine's ambitions no longer aligned with their nature. Now they're driven by vengeance..." The alpha said. "How ironic..."

His entire family died over an ancient feud between the celestial divine and an immortal species born of the planet... he wanted to scream... he wanted to burn the world down. He felt the blood in his veins boiling, and his vision went red. A feral cry erupted from his lips.

"What is this?" The alpha asked, taking a cautious step backward.

An enormous limb ending with a clawed hand grew from Damian's stump. Ripples broke out beneath his skin as his bones shifted and snapped, and the man let out a guttural roar, one of both pain and rage. His face began contorting, elongating from his skull, and hair began sprouting from every pore on his body. His deep gray eyes became a bright mustardy-yellow, bloodshot, his pupils stretching into slits. Damian felt himself slipping away as the enraged beast residing within him took control. He tried to fight it, but he was no match against the furious beast's rampage within his mind and body. Gigantic leathery wings grew from his long arms, and a moment later a quadrupedal creature unlike any seen before stood amidst the pack of werewolves, a monstrous bat sporting long razor-sharp fangs, and incredibly long, curved talons from a digit on either hand. Crouched on all fours much like a wyvern, its wings folded along, and around, its lanky arms... claws protruding from various points along the massive wings as well.

Damian Grey ceased to exist that night, but so too did the ones who'd stripped him of his humanity.

The Erdastraz were next.

Synchronous

I was on my way home. It was overcast, and maybe an hour before sunset. It wasn't too chilly out yet, but I was wearing shorts and a t-shirt, so I wanted to get home before it got too cold. I'd opted out of wearing a sweatshirt for some reason, so I decided to cut through alleys and side streets. I had nobody at home waiting for me, except I guess my cat Leeroy. I've had relationships here and there, and some of them were pretty good, but I've just never been much of a people person. I never really know what to say, and then I feel bad when it feels like the people around me are expecting me to say something. Leeroy doesn't care if we don't talk so long as I feed him... and give him water... and clean his litter... well, he likes his coat being brushed too. Come to think of it, Leeroy talks more than I do. He'd probably greet me with a bunch of meows and leg rubs when I got home.

I've just never understood people. Growing up, my parents never really talked with me. It was always about necessary things like homework, or chores... or whatever, you know? Listening to other kids talk to each other felt strange to me. In a way I was jealous, but at the same time I was relieved it wasn't me they were talking to. I don't really have friends, but I get along with coworkers, and sometimes I will go out with them after we clock out, but I'm usually one of the first to call it a night and head home. It's simple that way. Me, Leeroy, my books, comics, video games, and massive DVD collection. Maybe there was an extra oomph to my steps because I had just started a new campaign with some online folks. I'd call them friends, but I'm a realist, and we don't really know anything about each other than the fact we love slaying digital beasts together.

I avoided any crowds as I made my way home along the new route I'd chosen, and believe me, if you're bored and think my life is mundane as all hell right about now, I'd say you aren't wrong but hang in there. I was crossing a street, and there were some little kids kicking a ball around, nothing out of the ordinary, but as I made it to the other side of the street, I heard a commotion from where the kids had been playing. I turned just in time to see the ball fly toward me from a passing car, and land in a ditch right by me. I'm not sure I fully comprehended what I'd just seen, but then again, I hadn't really been paying attention. The kids waved at me as I made it clear I was going to retrieve the ball.

I looked down into the ditch and wasn't sure I was seeing clearly, so I rubbed my eyes. Half of the ball was missing, not like it had been torn in half or something, but like the other half was hidden behind something, but there was nothing there. I tried getting a better angle as I moved toward it, but I couldn't find an angle that revealed the missing half of the ball. It was as if I was looking at a hologram that kept its face toward me no matter which vantage point I found... that's the only way to explain it. I was more intrigued than anything and strode right up to the ball. Scratching my head for a second, I examined the strange phenomena before reaching down to pick it up, but as I did so I felt the ground rush toward me, and then the sensation of falling in several directions overcame me. Vertigo was nothing compared to this feeling, and as I recovered from the disorientation, it dawned on me that I was no longer in the ditch. I was no longer outside at all!

I raised my head from a crawling position and took in my surroundings. I'm not sure I'd ever experienced true terror until this moment. I was in a strange building with very unpleasant colored walls. They were yellow, but not a sunshine and rainbows kind of yellow, or even a sunflower kind, but that sickly disturbing color people were so fond of in the 70's or 80's. I half expected to see flavorless wallpaper lining the place, but there wasn't any. I found my footing and wondered how it was I came to be there, but even the memory of the kids' ball was quickly fading from memory. "Hello?" I called out, my voice wavering slightly as I fought against a heaviness growing in the pit of my stomach. There was nobody else there. I was in a long hallway, and there were no windows. I started down the corridor for a while before I found a door leading into a large empty room. It reminded me of the sort of rooms that were used in call centers, and there were even desks and cubicles, but no sign that anyone had ever been there.

At this point I hadn't seen anything scary, but the heaviness in my gut grew heavier and heavier, and I got an awful feeling like I wasn't supposed to be there... like nobody was ever supposed to be there, and I couldn't even recall how it was I got there. It was so quiet, and the dull, gross colors everywhere only added to the uneasiness. I found myself hoping to come across a different color more than I was hoping to come across another person. I wandered the empty building for what felt like hours, but in all honesty, there was no way to keep track of time there. Every room I found was like the first. All were slightly different, but always empty and unused. Some had stacked boxes full of blank paper the same color as the walls, and other rooms had random cords lying around, but they led to nowhere and connected to nothing.

"Hello!" I screamed into the void often. "Anyone! Please!" There were never any replies. My voice never even echoed off the walls. What happened to me? I roamed the labyrinth of hallways, explored nonsensical rooms, and even went up and down flights of stairs that only ever seemed to lead to more endless mazes of hallways. I wanted to cry, but somehow, I managed to hold myself together... until I began hearing what sounded like someone else's footsteps coming from somewhere anytime I was moving. I knew they weren't mine because there weren't echoes in this place. My heart began thudding against my chest. I'd stop and listen, and there was never anything to be heard when I did that, but I'd start moving again and I swear I heard them... every... time! I was going mad, I thought. I started running, and the footsteps started running after me.

"Leave me alone!" I screamed. "Who's there?! Show yourself!" I collapsed into a corner of a hallway and tucked my knees up against my chest. I had a view of both directions, but I didn't want to look. I could imagine any number of things coming toward me, and I started crying at this point. This wasn't making any sense, and I just wanted to leave. I never wanted to walk down another hallway ever again. Then I heard a crash come from one of the rooms down one of the hallways. I gasped and sat upright, stiff as a board, every hair on my body standing on edge… even my breaths were nearly silent.

"You aren't supposed to be here." A voice whispered behind my ear, and I screamed bloody murder, but there wasn't anyone there. I knew there was no one there… I was sitting against the corner in the fetal position. Then I heard the crash again, and this time it was closer. Lights started flickering, and then there was another crash, even closer now. I held my breath and waited for whatever was going to happen to happen. "Go!" The same voice I'd heard urged me to move, but where was I supposed to go?

I heard the beep of an elevator that hadn't been there before, across from me in the opposite direction of the crashing sounds, and the doors opened. I stared in confusion for a second, maybe, but didn't need to be told twice. I got up and ran into the elevator. I was hitting the close door button repeatedly as I heard the crashing noise nearing where I had just been sitting, and the doors closed. "How did you get here?" The disembodied voice asked me.

"I…" I tried to remember, but for the life of me I couldn't explain. "I don't know. I can't remember. Who are you?" As I asked the question, I felt the elevator's descent speed up until it felt like I was falling. A shadowy figure seemed to walk through the side of the elevator and walk up to me. It was holding a strange object in one of its hands. It was about the size of a golf ball, spherical like one, but looked like black marble. It glistened with what I could only describe as the universe as light bounced off it at different angles. There were metallic looking rings that wrapped completely around it in several asymmetrical places, thin and flat like the rings of Saturn, and neither the sphere nor the rings ever touched the other. The dark figure held it up for me, and then the lights in the elevator went out and we were falling through what seemed like space. Everything had gone black, except the figure was no longer a shadow... it was me! The sphere glowed a strange darkness, and the other me placed it over my chest, and then it sank into my chest and vanished.

I sprung up in bed grabbing at my chest, but immediately breathed a sigh of relief. It was just a dream! I've had some bonkers dreams before, but that one put them all to shame. Leeroy greeted me with his usual purrs as he pounced onto my bed and rubbed his face all over me. I welcomed the distraction. Before leaving for work, I refilled Leeroy's food and water bowls. "Leeeeeeroy Jenkins!" I called out to him since he hadn't sprinted for his dishes upon hearing the food. He moseyed on over finally, stretching and yawning, and I felt bad for interrupting what must've been one hell of a nap. I scratched him under his chin. "I'll be back later. Don't get too crazy."

The dream quickly faded from my mind as I went about my day. I was sitting at my desk chatting with my coworker Elise, whom I'd been training the last few weeks. We got along pretty well, and for not being much of a people person, it was nice to have someone to banter with. My job was boring for the most part, except for when we were "in season" and things got hectic in the office, but I work well under pressure. I never really looked forward to my job though... not that the thought of going to work was a miserable one or anything, it was just meh. I found that I looked forward to hanging out with Elise though, which made the thought of getting to work an enjoyable one.

"Don't you have work to do Justin?" My incredibly annoying supervisor asked. She was a control freak and micro-managed as much as humanly possible. I was, in particular, a favorite of hers to get after. I think it was because I was so efficient at my job that I afforded myself down time, and I think she was jealous... or just disliked that I did things my own way instead of hers.

"I am working Anna." I replied as I commenced the tedious task of checking on my studies and running my numbers. We were data analysts at a big company, and our job was to manage the various studies everyone in the call center outside our office were calling households regarding. It's all rather boring really. "Everything is looking good." Elise said nothing as Anna and I went back and forth, just sat there quietly, and I don't blame her. She's new, and she didn't yet understand the work dynamics between the people there.

"Why don't you run Elise through the status reports." Anna said.

"She knows how to do those, Anna. She's watched me do them for two weeks... but, okay." I replied, thoroughly annoyed, and just wanted her to leave us alone already.

"What are the sticky notes on the desktop for?" Elise asked me. Anna knew, and we heard her disgruntled groan as she lingered for another moment. "Nobody else uses them."

"Well, my padawan," I replied and smiled as Anna rolled her eyes and left the office. "Watch closely."

"Of course, Master Yoda." Elise replied and giggled.

I'm sure Anna regretted assigning me to Elise's training, but with her hours I was her only option really, and I know deep down Anna knows I'm excellent at my job and she hates it for some reason. I've always found it quite strange. The end of the shift marked the beginning of the weekend, and though I was excited to join my online friends slaying in our campaign, Elise was on my mind as I made my way home after work, which I knew was probably not ideal. For one, she had a boyfriend, and for two, I never dipped my pen in company ink. I've seen that scenario play out and blow up in loads of people's faces and that wasn't something I was about to entertain.

I swung into a small local family-owned pet store near my place before going home. It was a routine of mine to grab Leeroy a tasty treat on Fridays after work, and the employees knew me by name there. It always felt good to see them, as brief as our encounters always were. "Hey Justin!" the owner's son greeted me. "How's it going?"

"Hey Mike!" I answered. "It's going pretty good, thanks. How are you?"

"Oh, you know," Mike said, "living the dream!" He laughed sarcastically. "Any exciting plans this weekend?" he asked as he scanned Leeroy's treat. I didn't even need to grab it anymore; they always had it waiting for me.

"Some friends and I are gonna play Legends of Arcanum all weekend." I blurted out before I could stop myself. I held my breath and laughed nervously. Tell them you don't have a life without telling them you don't have a life Justin, I thought.

"Oh sick! That's the one that just dropped that new

campaign, right? Uhh, what is it…"

I perked up. "The Trials of Lithinostoranj Garden!"

"That's it!" Mike laughed. "No way I was going to remember how to pronounce that. Looks epic! Let me know how it is."

"Alright, you got it, thanks Mike." He handed me the bag. "Have a good night, man," I said as I left.

Leeroy was happy to see me when I got home, or maybe he just knew it was Friday and he was getting his special treat, but he was all over me when I walked through my front door. I changed into something more comfortable, made myself a drink, and logged into the game. My party was already waiting for me. I turned my headset on and put it on, taking a sip of my drink.

"Mags!" a voice said cheerfully in my ear. It was The Gay Tellytubby.

"Hey Tubby!" I replied. "Hey Eternity! Hey Fisted! What's up?"

"Just waiting on the Gorgonite Scum to log in," Fisted (By Edward Scissor Hands) answered. "Ready to slay for like ten hours straight?" She laughed.

"Wooooo!" Tubby cheered.

"I've been looking forward to this all week!" Eternity chimed in.

"Oh yeah!" I replied. "This is gonna be dope, guys."

Once Scum joined us, we began our long and tumultuous marathon. At one point we were fighting a major boss, and it had taken a lot of effort and coordination to reach that point, and then Leeroy hopped across the room and knocked my drink over. "Leeroy!" I blurted out alarmingly.

"Jenkins!" Tubby and Scum yelled out in unison.

"Mags! What are ya doin'! We need you!" Fisted cried out.

I was flustered, trying to wipe my drink off me and play at the same time, and got us killed. I blame Leeroy, but the loss led to us taking a little break as we'd have to repeat a lot of the game to get back to the boss. I ended up taking a walk to the gas station down the road for some food and some beer, as that drink had contained the last of my liquor, and I needed food. Something in the road caught my attention as I made my way there though. It shimmered in the streetlights, and I gasped as I got closer. It was a small spherical object, and reminded me of... my dream, as a fragment of it came back to me. There was no way....

All thoughts of food, alcohol, gaming... everything, fled my mind. I couldn't believe what I was seeing. I walked up to the object and picked it up, my mouth hanging agape. It was the exact same object from my dream... but how? Before I could make any sense of it, I was blinded by headlights, and before I could react, my life flashed before my eyes. It happened so quickly that I couldn't register a single thought. I heard the car slam on its breaks as I hit the front bumper, the windshield, and then flipped through the air. I couldn't scream, but I felt the cool wind against my wet skin as I flew through the air, lights circling me as I flipped around and around. Then I hit the ground with a hard thud, my body unresponsive to my commands.

I tried to take a breath, but it sent searing pain through my body. I heard the muffled screams from onlookers and passersby as my vision became distorted. I tried to speak, but I started choking on the blood that had begun seeping into my lungs. I was literally about to die in a matter of seconds, and this realization brought a tear to one of my eyes... it was all I could muster. I thought of Leeroy then... not my parents, nor my siblings or any other relatives... not any of my ex's, nor friends or colleagues... just my cat. How sad is that? My body felt like ice, but I couldn't shiver. I watched someone's feet approaching me with urgency as I felt myself drifting from the realm of the living. This was it... I closed my eyes and reached for the steadfast embrace of death's unbiased appointment with me.

The cool night air filled my lungs as a peaceful acceptance was robbed by the blaring of a car's horns as the vehicle swerved around me, barely missing me. I stood there like an idiot, in utter shock and confusion, in the middle of the street. "Get out of the fucking road moron!" Someone yelled at me, but my body struggled to do much of anything in those first few seconds. Finally, enough awareness returned to me, and I shuffled back over to the sidewalk. What the fuck just happened? There was nothing in my hands and experiencing my death just mere seconds earlier haunted me. I had felt the impact of the car, and my body hitting the windshield and the ground. I'd heard the car slam its breaks, the breaking of glass, the crushing and snapping of my bones, and the cries of the same people I could see walking around at this very moment. I could still taste the blood in my mouth, and the sensation of it all draining into my lungs, and pooling around me... the pavement beneath my broken body.

Fuck the gas station. Fuck the beer. Fuck eating. I was terrified and confused, and as the minutes passed on my way back home, I started feeling more and more normal. I opened my front door and locked it behind me, relieved to be back in my safe space. I thought it was strange that Leeroy wasn't greeting me, but I dismissed that and rushed to my headset. "Guys... something fucking crazy just happened to me." There was no response. "Hello?" Maybe they were all still eating? I checked the party, but there wasn't one. "What the hell?" I pulled up my friend's list and only Fisted showed up. "Okay..." She was online so I opened a party and sent her an invite, and a moment later she popped in.

"Hello?" she asked.

"Hey Fisted, what happened to everyone? What's going on?" I asked, trying not to sound upset.

"What do you mean?" she asked.

"What do you mean, what do I mean?" I asked frantically. "Eternity? Scum? Tubby? Our campaign?"

"Holy shit, bro," she said, thoroughly concerned. "Is everything okay?"

"No, I don't think so," I replied, on the verge of panic. "Something really fucked up just happened, and now you guys are fucking with me or something... it's not cool, ya know?"

I heard her take a breath, and her background noise go quiet. "What happened? Let's try and figure this out... you have my attention."

"Fuck!" I yelled, holding back the tears. "You, me, Scum, Tubby and Eternity... we had the whole weekend planned out. We were playing for hours, and then... c'mon Fisted, please stop fucking with me, it isn't funny."

"...and then what happened?"

"...we took a break, and I..." I lost my breath. She

waited. I could hear her breathing. "I was walking to the gas station down the street, and I was hit by a car."

"Oh my god!" she cried. "Are you okay?"

"I... died..." I felt stupid saying it out loud. That's the kind of shit I need to keep to myself or I'm gonna end up in a looney bin but Fisted and I were arguably the closest out of our little gamer group, and based on past conversations we've had, I felt safe telling her. "...but then it was like it didn't happen, and I was back, and the car missed me..."

"That is a goddamn mind fuck bro."

"I sound crazy, don't I?"

"Here's the thing," she said. "I don't know who Eternity or Scum are. You and Tubby are the only names I recognize, we haven't been playing a campaign together and... you and I have only ever played together a few times."

"Okay, now I know you guys are fucking with me!" I yelled. I could feel my blood boiling, and my tears welling up. I wasn't going to be able to hold them back much longer. "It's not fucking funny!" My voice began to crack. "Please stop... please..."

I heard a meow and looked over to see Leeroy finally come out from wherever he'd been hiding. I couldn't handle whatever fucked up game they were playing with me anymore, so I left the party and scooped Leeroy up and hugged him. "Leeroy," I cried, "hey, boy." He began to purr and let me cuddle him for a while as I calmed down. I spent the weekend avoiding video games, hanging out with Leeroy, and thinking about the car incident. I was still mad at my friends as Monday rolled around, and I wasn't sure I wanted to play with them anymore.

Things got really weird when I showed up to work though. First thing I noticed was a bunch of new faces throughout the call center. Then I got to my desk and logged in, or tried to, but my password wasn't working. I growled in frustration. "Can I help you?" I looked over to see Anna standing at the threshold.

"It's my password," I replied, not at all excited to see her. "It isn't working."

"You... don't work here. I'm getting security." She pulled out her phone.

"Anna!" I snapped, and she looked at me alarmingly, a disturbed look upon her face. "It's me! Justin!"

I ended up getting dragged out of the building by security, but I held my tongue. I felt as if I were going crazy, and maybe I was... but I needed to be smart. I wasn't about to be locked up. I straightened out my shirt as they ushered me out the main entrance and made my way back toward the parking lot that wrapped around to the main part of the campus.

"Justin!" I heard a familiar voice call to me excitedly. Oh my god! Thank you! It was Elise, and she recognized me! Maybe I wasn't so crazy after all. I turned to see her approaching me from the parking lot, a big smile on my face.

"Oh my god, you have no idea how happy I am to see you," I said, thoroughly relieved.

She wrapped her arms around me, putting her lips close to my ear, and whispered, "What's gotten into you?" She sounded pleased, and I felt her breath against my skin as her lips touched me. She pulled away and kissed me. My knees nearly buckled as I started to melt, but I was so confused that I barely returned the kiss before pulling away.

"Don't you have a boyfriend?" I asked suddenly.

Elise rolled her eyes clearly annoyed by the question. "Since when does that matter to you?"

"What!?" I asked incredulously. "It matters! I've gotta go, I can't do this right now."

She looked at me as confused as I felt, her face a mixture of anger and sadness. "Wait, Justin... didn't you come here to see me?" she called after me. "What just happened? I'll leave him! Where are you going?"

I ignored her, but I had no idea where I was supposed to go, so I headed home. As I came upon the pet store near my place, one of the employees was vaping outside and waved at me. "Hey Justin!"

"Hey Victoria," I replied.

"How's Chewie?"

"Who?"

"Your cat, dingdong," she laughed.

My heart sank. I said nothing to her and rushed home. I shut my door behind me and started to cry, hoping this was a nightmare. "Wake up! Wake up!" I said over and over as I clenched my eyes shut and slapped myself across the face. I looked at the tv and realized what an asshole I must've been to Fisted the other night. I powered up my gaming console and found a message in my inbox from her:

I did some digging and found the other players you were talking about. I'm sorry in advance, but I told them about our conversation the other night. We'd all like to talk to you if that's okay. Hope everything is okay.

I sighed and started a party, sending them all invites,

and waited. It wasn't long before everyone had joined. "Hey guys," I said, defeated. "Sorry about the other night Fisted."

"Were you really hit by a car?" Tubby asked.

"And died?" Scum asked next.

"Guys!" Fisted scolded them. "Really?"

"It's fine, Fisted," I told her.

"Just call me Sammy," she said, I had never known her real name before then.

"I'm Justin," I replied.

"Alina," Eternity chimed in.

"Toby," added Tubby. That made everyone laugh. Leave it to The Gay Tellytubby to lighten the mood.

"Christian," Scum said.

"Wow..." I said. "It took my whole life turning upside down to learn your guys' names."

"We've been talking about that all weekend actually," Sammy replied. "We have a theory."

"Are you familiar with quantum physics?" Christian asked.

"Vaguely," I answered.

"So, there was this experiment done in the 70's or something where they shot electrons through these slits right?" Christian continued. "And they reacted differently based on whether they were being observed or not. Basically, all particles exist in every possible position until they are observed..."

"I'm not sure I'm following," I replied. "What does electrons have to do with everything that's happening?"

"Some theoretical physicists believe that every position still exists even after they're observed to have chosen one."

Toby added.

"Think of a position as an outcome," Christian said.

"Okay…" My brain was beginning to hurt. "How is that possible?"

"What if different outcomes, the different positions all exist simultaneously, but in different universes?" Alina asked. "Have you ever heard of the Mandella Affect?"

My jaw dropped. "I have…"

"We think, when that car hit you," Sammy said, "that somehow you jumped universes, and this one is different because…"

"Because different outcomes created it…" I gasped.

"Exactly!" Sammy exclaimed.

"But how?" I asked.

"Yeah, that part is anyone's guess." Alina said.

"Whoa…" I sunk back into my couch and tried processing the theory. It made sense but it sounded insane. They let me sit in silence for a minute before speaking up.

"So, we were all friends before?" Toby asked. "In your universe I mean?"

"Yeah… we all play together all the time, for the most part. Sometimes Christian… wait, you're still married with kids, Christian?" I asked.

"Yeah, that hasn't changed. I'm curious what else might be different though!"

"That's all we really knew about you."

"Wait, what?"

"Guys," I went on, "none of us really shared too many details about our personal lives with each other. I can't remember why, that's just how it was, and it kept gaming together fun and simple."

"Makes sense..." Sammy agreed.

"What is different about our universe than it was in yours?" Toby asked.

I told them about my cat, my job, Elise, and how I was too scared to leave my place over the weekend. We spent a while going back and forth covering details about mundane and minute things like childhood cartoons, books, video games, movies and the like, and we found quite a few conflicting details between our universes. Apparently, they had no clue what Leeroy Jenkins was a reference to, so that explained my cat's name. We all chatted for hours, and then, just as I was beginning to feel relieved and okay with my predicament, a shadowy figure that seemed to distort the very fabric of reality around its form, dropped through my ceiling into my living room. I screamed and fell off the couch.

"What is it, Justin?" Sammy asked. "What happened!"

"A... *uhh*... a shadow thing just fell into my living room..." I whispered. It had no face, and I couldn't tell if it was looking at me or not.

"A *what?!*" Toby yelled.

"It isn't doing anything... it's just standing there," I said.

The shadow spoke then. "Target acquired."

"Get out of there!" Sammy and Alina cried in unison.

It lifted its hand toward me, and I screamed, rolling out of the way as a blast of energy tore through my couch where I'd just been sitting. As it continued its attacks, I got the impression it was intentionally trying to miss me, but just barely, like it wanted me alive for some reason. I ran in front of the window and let it blast an opening for me to escape from.

As I tried hopping from the hole in my home, I suddenly froze. It captured me in some sort of gravitational field, spun me around to face it, and extended a hand toward me once more. "Acknowledged," I heard it say with its head tilted down slightly, then it lifted it until its eyes, where I imagined they might be, were aligned with mine. "Release the Synchronous Orb at once!" It opened its palm and waited for me to comply.

"The *what?*" I asked.

It blasted a hole in my ceiling. "I will not tolerate feigned ignorance, thief. This is your final chance." It held its palm out once more.

"Thief?" I gasped. "I didn't steal anything!"

The dark figure squeezed its fingers into a fist, and I felt an energy pulling every little part of me in separate directions. It was agonizing... a pain unlike anything I thought possible, and I would've been okay with death in that moment. It was as if every fiber of my being was being pulled apart, or like the atoms I was composed of were being dismantled. Then I watched as the spherical object I'd seen in both my dream and upon the street right before the car hit me, began drifting from my chest. It was the key to everything, I realized! I couldn't lose it... "No!" I screamed despite the pain. "I need that!"

"The Synchronous Orb does not belong to you, and once it is extracted you will pay for your transgressions against both The Watchers and The Weavers." It said almost tauntingly, as if I were supposed to know who they were, and that it wasn't a good thing by any stretch of my imagination.

"Please stop!" I pleaded as half the orb had already left my body. I'm not sure how exactly I managed to do it, but I brought my hands toward my chest. It was like trying to sprint at the bottom of the ocean, if the ocean was made of sentient mud pulling on all my limbs at once; it wasn't easy, but I managed to bring my fingers upon the object.

"Impossible!" I heard it gasp. "What are you?"

As my fingers wrapped around the object, I felt the effects of its gravitational field weakening, and I didn't know what else to do but try and push the object back into my chest. As I did so however, the field grew stronger as if it were an extension of the thing's will, and then Chewie came to my rescue. I heard him hiss and growl as fiercely as a house cat was capable of, and my attacker's grunt as I fell to the floor. I wasted no time, hopping through the hole in my living room and across the yard outside.

"Justin?" Hearing Elise's voice made my heart sink. "What—?"

"No time!" I yelled, interrupting her. "Let's go!" I grabbed her by the wrist and started running, and I heard her scream beside me.

"What is that!?" she yelped in terror.

I looked back and saw the shadowy figure step outside, blasting the ground at Elise's feet. I watched as it raised its hand for another blast, knowing it wouldn't miss her this time, and I shoved her out of the way and took the full brunt of the attack. I knew it would annihilate me at once... so be it.

The world came rushing back to me and I was outside inhaling the fresh air of an undisturbed neighborhood. It was quiet and peaceful, and I understood I was now in yet another universe... in another me. I also understood that I'd only bought myself so much time.

"You okay, Justin?" Elise asked beside me. Of course

she was. "Babe?"

Babe? I sighed. "Yeah, everything's okay. Just thinking."

She leaned in and put her face against mine, embracing me lovingly and passionately. "I was thinking about how happy you make me. What are you thinking?"

Not gonna lie, it felt amazing. Somehow, I didn't need to ask... I just knew that we were together in this universe. It was a thing, and there was no sneaking around, or compromising our integrity. She hovered her lips near mine, and I kissed her, and then I pulled away, grabbed her hand, and started rushing us away from the neighborhood. "Something bad's gonna happen if we stay here," I said to her.

"Something bad?" she asked. "What do you mean?" She used her body as an anchor and slowed us down. "Justin! What's going on?"

"I don't know," I lied. "I just got this feeling..."

Then, a few hundred yards behind Elise, I watched as the shadowy figure appeared. She must've seen it on my face, because she followed my eyes and saw it as well. She cried out and I steadied her and looked her in the eyes. "Go! Get out of here!"

"I'm not leaving without you!" she retorted.

"Go!" I snapped and started running away from her.

I didn't put up much of a chase before it caught up with me, but at least Elise was safe. It didn't shoot any blasts or use a gravitational field this time however, it opted instead to restrain me with these electrical cuff things made of energy. They weren't physical in any way, that much was evident, but I could do nothing to fight against them. Then the world went black.

When I came to, I was in some sort of interrogation room. I don't know how long I sat there before someone else joined me. I was surprised to see someone who resembled a human, though I wasn't convinced. I remained silent until they decided to address me.

"Justin Miller. Born August 10th, 1994. No spouse, or children. Data analyst. Self-proclaimed gamer and film buff. Feline enthusiast. Fantasy and science-fiction aficionado. Bit of a lone wolf... estranged from nearly all relatives. Shows signs of multiple personality disorders including schizoid personality disorder, antisocial personality disorder, avoidant personality disorder, obsessive-compulsive personality disorder, and suffers from chronic social anxiety. Has lived alone for most of adult life." The man paused, and then looked up from his paperwork and acknowledged my presence for the first time. "How is it, someone such as yourself, came into possession of the Synchronous Orb? Please be as detailed as possible."

I didn't know where to start, or what to say for that matter. I was still in shock that it seemed as though they were addressing me, from my original universe, and neither of the Justin Millers I had become... and schizoid personality disorder? The *fuck?* I pondered on a reply for a moment. "I don't even know what a Synchronous Orb is..."

The man gave me a doubtful look, mocking me, and sighed. "Justin, Justin, Justin," he said, shaking his head. "You expect me to believe you don't know anything about this object you believe resides within you?"

"That I believe..." I echoed to myself, scrunching up my face confused.

"The cosmic device that synchronizes every version of

yourself across the multiverse?" The man read off the paper in front of him, a humorous look upon his face. He reached up and massaged the bridge of his nose between his thumb and index finger.

"Whoa..." I said as I studied the man before me. "This is the first I've heard the description... that's... pretty cool though," I said. He looked up at me with pity written all over his face. "Right?"

"Justin..." he said. "This façade of yours isn't good for anyone. Your delusions are what landed you here in the first place..."

"You're fucking psychotic," I said angrily.

His face straightened up real quick. Oops... He stood up and walked over to me. I couldn't turn to see what he was doing behind me, but I could tell he stopped. "Look," I said, "I don't know anything about no multiverse, and I definitely know nothing about no goddamn orb—" Suddenly, my face slammed into the table in front of me, sending blinding light through my eyes and then searing pain across my face. I put my hands on the table to try and lift my head up, but I felt the man's grip tighten around the back of my head, holding my face in place against the table's cold surface. Warm fluid began running down my face.

"You're delusional," he told me as he lifted my face and slammed it back into the table hard. "You're sick," he said as he did it again. "You need help Justin." Then he did it a fourth time, and I felt bones in my face crack, and I started whimpering, and bloody teeth fell onto the table.

"I don't know—" I felt my face lift from the table a fifth time, but my eyes were swollen shut, and I couldn't see as he slammed my face back down again, but the world went black and I was suddenly sitting in the chair across from him again. I could still feel the pain in my face as it receded into the fog of memory. "You psychotic fuck!" I screamed at him.

I don't know how long the interrogation went on for, or how many times and how many ways he killed me, but I always ended right back in that seat across from him. With each death, and with each Justin, came brutal physical and psychological torcher, manipulation, nonsensical questions and accusations, and each time I was treated as if I were the sick one in the room. As this went on and my mind became more and more numb, I retreated into the recesses of my fragmented mind. I felt fingers open my mouth, and I was forced to swallow pills. I was strapped into a wheelchair and rolled out of the room. I felt a needle prick me in the neck, and next thing I knew I was in a white padded room. I couldn't focus on anything as I slipped in and out of consciousness, and when I attempted to make sense of what was happening and build myself a mental map of my situation, I didn't know what was real and what was fake.

After a while, hours... maybe days, a slit in the door opened and a woman's face appeared. She had much softer features than the man that had tortured me, and she had a kind voice. "Justin, please, you can end all of this."

"How?" I didn't recognize my voice. It was slurred and strained, but if she was offering a way out of this, I was all ears.

"I believe you can bring your fantasy to a conclusion by removing the orb yourself," she said. "Symbolically speaking, of course, and hopefully bring yourself back to reality. The doctor is willing to reassess your condition if you just show some effort and try."

"Okay..." I agreed. I saw her eyes light up briefly.

"Good boy, Justin," she said hopefully. "That's it," she said as I put a hand upon my chest. I didn't know what I was supposed to do, or how I might do as she was asking of me. Was the orb real? I wasn't sure anymore... the only thing I was sure of was that I was in pain. I was confused, and I didn't know who she was or who the man had been... or who anyone was anymore. I was weak, hungry, dehydrated, and disoriented as all hell. I could barely get my tongue out of my mouth enough to lick my lips, but when I did, I felt how dry and chapped they were, but my tongue felt just as dry and I wanted to cry. My hand dropped from my chest to the floor. "Justin!" she said sternly from her little slit. "Come on, Justin!"

I lifted my hand back up. "There you go, Justin!" she encouraged me. Then I gave her the birdie and tried to laugh, but no sound came out. "You fool! The Watchers won't be so reasonable!" she snapped and slammed the slit closed.

The Watchers...

The words repeated in my head over and over again. The words became a point of reference... a foothold for me to stand on as I tried desperately to ground myself somehow. As pieces of my mind came together in some sort of cohesive way, I was able to focus on my surroundings for the first time in I don't know how long. Once the room was no longer spinning or blurry I sat against the far wall and continued my mental battle, trying my best to make sense of everything. As I did this however, one part of the room remained blurry and out of focus. It didn't track with my eyes as I scanned the padded room, but remained stationary. That didn't make any sense...

I crawled over to the disorienting spot that seemed to defy what little logic I had managed to piece back together, until it was only a couple feet away. I stared at it for a minute before deciding, fuck it. What was the worst that could happen? I reached out for it, the wall rushed toward me, I lurched in several directions as a falling sensation overcame me and landed in a yellow hallway. Suddenly, and all at once, my mind was whole again. "Fuck!" I screamed... *Not this place again.*

I started running down the endless halls. "Hey!" I yelled desperately. "Come on!" I cried as I ran, checking empty rooms, and banging on walls. "Where are you?!" I hoped against all hope that I'd spot an elevator somewhere... anywhere! I spent what felt like a few hours roaming the place when I heard the chime of an elevator somewhere, but I couldn't see it. "Hey! I'm here!" I started running with a renewed vigor, and then the other footsteps started following me. As I ran down a hallway, a door opened, I screamed, and someone pulled me into the room.

I was staring at myself. It was the strangest thing ever... well, never mind, I take that back. It was the version of myself that had originally given me the sphere. "Who are you? What is this place?" I asked frantically. "What did you do to me?"

"Listen closely," he said, "there isn't much time." I just nodded. "We're in the backrooms." My blank stare said it all. "You know when you're playing a game, and you accidentally clip into areas players aren't meant to go?" I nodded, of course I did. "This place is that, but for reality... all realities. Nobody can track us here, but we aren't supposed to be here. That's why we need to make this quick. The Synchronous Orb is the key to our salvation. Yes, I stole it, but for a good cause, and from an incredibly vile organization. A monopoly spreading throughout the multiverse. You've met them already."

"What?!" An anger rose inside me. "Those psychotic fucks that tortured me and locked me up?"

He nodded. "That's the key to stopping them; to putting an end to all of it," he said as he pointed at my chest. "I need to take it..."

"Whoa," I started apprehensively. "Everyone is trying to rip this thing out of my chest!"

"But they can't, can they?" he replied.

"No... why?"

He laughed nervously. "It's not just me, okay, there are others banding together to fight back. That orb isn't the only cosmic wonder we've come across, and there are more out there still. In our attempt to procure another, it evaded us. We underestimated its... capabilities."

"What is it!"

"It's you!" he replied. I was dumbfounded. "Well, you were already you, but it chose you, for some reason. It was supposed to be me, but it's you." His voice grew weaker as he finished the sentence.

"What is it?" I asked, more sympathetic now.

"That is too complicated to explain right now, but it's the reason nobody can take the orb from you, but I need you to give it to me. You need to trust me."

"How am I supposed to trust you?"

He removed a device from his wrist and held it up to me. "We make a trade." He fidgeted with the device and the elevator appeared beside us, at the other side of the room. "This will send you back to my team, in my universe, and the orb will enable me to reach the one I need to complete my mission. I needed you to safeguard it for me... thank you."

"Doesn't that mean... you won't get to go back?" Something began pounding on the door and I nearly jumped out of my skin.

"We're out of time. Please..." He pleaded for me and reached out to me. "Help us save the multiverse."

I pulled the orb from my chest, and he began fidgeting with the device in his hand. We made the trade. He slapped the device around my wrist even as he pressed the orb into his own chest. The elevator chimed and its doors opened. "Go!" he insisted desperately, shoving me toward the elevator just as the door to the room burst open. I watched in horror as a ghostly monstrosity wearing a thousand random objects as armor, its many limbs mimicking the sound of ordinary footsteps, stalk toward the other me. Its grotesque face, nearly human looking but elongated and horrifyingly twisted, stretched its mouth open impossibly wide and snatched him from his feet. As it devoured him, I snapped out of my stupor and started pounding on the close door button, nearly pissing myself as it whipped around and began sprinting across the room for me. The doors closed just in time.

Everything went black, and billions of stars passed by as I seemingly traversed the cosmos, and then I heard a familiar voice.

"Mags!"

And others as well...

"Can you hear us?"

"Are you there?"

The elevator chime dinged, and I heard the doors open behind me. When I turned around, I was greeted by a group of people I didn't recognize. My eyes were fixed on one face in particular though. It was a woman around my age. She was smiling at me, and her eyes were watering. She threw her arms around me, and I returned the embrace. Who knew a hug could feel so damn good?

"It's so good to finally meet you, Justin." I definitely recognized her voice. "Everything's going to be okay now," Sammy told me.

And I believed her.

Tales Around the Hearth

THE GLOOMSTALKER

Three riders on horseback raced the sun as it soared across the sky. They hoped for daylight to accompany them once they reached their destination. Castor Donovan, a renowned warrior of the fabled gloomstalkers, begrudgingly kept a close eye on his protégé Theoden Elidyr, a half-elf. The young man was a promising addition to their ranks, and was a skilled enough warrior and survivalist, but Castor was not an oblivious fool. Ever since they had volunteered to escort the elven priestess Amara Llewel, the boy had been enamored by her, and even though she didn't return the sentiment, she was still a distraction to young Theo… and in their line of work, distractions got you killed.

The two had been bantering back and forth for some time, and a smile found its way upon Castor's face when his protégé tried using their shared heritage as a way to woo the elf. He wondered whether the young half-elf realized Amara was roughly two hundred years his senior. "What do you know of our kind young Theoden?" she asked him, thoroughly amused by his tact.

"We were—"

"Is it we now?" she teased, her golden-brown eyes squinting in his direction as she muffled a laugh.

Theoden laughed off her remark. "Elves introduced civilization to the world nearly five thousand years ago. They brought an end to tribalism among humans and dwarves, shared their knowledge of agriculture, and helped the races develop their social and economic structures. Elves were the first to grant the anurans amnesty, and their alliance lasted for two thousand years until the Great Agonias Upheaval..."

Castor and Amara exchanged an exasperated glance, but Theoden didn't seem to notice as he continued to recite as much elven history as he could. Castor sighed as the minutes seemed to stretch on for hours, practically praying for a run-in with some beast or another. "They were the first to harness the power of the fell stones, and introduced the first school of magic..."

"That's great," she told Theoden, a smile appearing across his young face. "...had I asked for a history lesson." His proud smile fell away. "We experience the passage of time far differently than humans... and even dwarves. Even with your elven blood, you will not live to see half of my lifespan. You will never look upon the world the way we do..." Theoden looked wounded then, and Amara offered him an apologetic smile. "How could you? It is no fault of yours, Theoden. It is the way of things."

The rest of the ride was relatively quiet, and Castor was grateful for that. Sol would shine upon the wasteland for another couple hours as the overgrown remains of Kratorsyr's spires rose in the distance. It had been one of the first safe havens from the gloom, a rising tide of monsters and beasts that had swarmed over the land when a star fell from the heavens and crashed into Cedara hundreds of years prior, and it was the first of them to fall. All that remained were the city's bones, most of which lied in rubble, and Cedara reclaimed the place as her own. Trees, plants and fields swept across its foundation, and giant lianas or vines seemingly held the skeletal towers up in their stubborn grasp... a warning for those who turned a blind eye to history's woes.

The gloomstalkers and priestess left their mounts outside the old desolate city, and as they ventured into its depths, Castor drew one of his longswords. A simple incantation made the runes upon the blade glow as he slid his left hand along its length. Theoden would receive his own fell fragments to set into his gauntlets when he became a full-fledged gloomstalker, but he did draw his own blade and repeat Castor's incantation and hand movements. Amara spoke some elfish words and the grains of fell stone encapsulated at the point of her scepter began swirling in place, and the amethyst and peridot stones surrounding it, each inscribed with their own distinct runes, began orbiting the fell dust in various directions. "This place gives me the creeps," Theoden said as a shiver crawled up his spine, gripping his weapon all the tighter. "It's hard to believe it was once a Paragon..."

"It was one of the strongest," Amara replied, in an almost absent manner. "Its magnificence could not to be overstated. A true marvel... and now stands erect amidst the wasteland, a shadow of its former self, and a smear upon elven history."

"You speak as if you've seen it..." Theo gawked at her.

"She's an elf. Don't be such a fool," Castor retorted for the priestess. Theoden's shoulders sagged, and he didn't speak another word.

"This is why I'm here," she replied, nodding.

The gloomstalkers kept a careful eye on their surroundings as they followed Amara through the ruins. They were there for one reason, and one reason only: to protect the priestess at all costs. They were permitted to slay any beasts if there was no other choice readily available, but the priestess could not perish. Her death was simply unacceptable.

Castor spotted a few beasts scurrying about here and there, but they didn't seem organized, and steered clear of their party, giving them a wide berth to go about their business. Still, the man watched for any signs of an archprimus, a more powerful monster with the ability to rally the beasts around it, the greater their influence, the more powerful they became. Some archprimuses were known to build themselves massive armies, but the last of the grand archprimuses were slain by the gloomstalkers decades earlier. Castor, and the other veteran gloomstalkers, kept those tales at the forefront of their guild's minds however, for complacency would be the death of them all.

Amara led them into a decrepit structure that seemed to have served as a temple once upon a time. Castor and Theoden's jobs were simplified greatly as there was only the one long entrance, and some holes in the ceiling. The elf rummaged through debris, collecting little trinkets here and there, but had one prize in mind. "You might want to hurry, Priestess," Castor called out to her. "I believe..." Then a dozen or so beasts stormed through the entrance. "We'll keep them at bay, but get what you came for! Quickly!" Castor yelled as he and the half-elf prepared to engage their sworn enemy.

Amara summoned the power of her fell-imbued scepter, chanting a few elfish commands, and a magical barrier hummed with arcane energy as it flickered into existence, separating her from the danger as she continued her search with a renewed vigor. They came fast, and though Theoden had seemingly put all his weaknesses on display thus far, he was much more impressive in combat, his instincts possessing more wit than his conscious mind. Castor knew the young man would eventually learn however, and had the utmost faith in his protégé as they fought side by side, protecting one another's backs. That is all that mattered to the veteran in the moment.

A beast came flying at Castor with relentless savagery, and with one powerful swipe of his glowing sword, the experienced man silenced it forever. And so it was, two gloomstalkers felling beast after beast, unyielding and stubborn in their stand, not allowing a single one to break through and reach Amara. "I found it!" she cried out gleefully. "Let's go!"

"Those weren't the last of them," Castor replied. "There's an archprimus here." Amara gasped, becoming visibly and audibly shaken, but a determination planted itself across her elegant face as she raised her weapon and prepared to fight alongside the two men. "You are wise to be afraid," he told her before looking to his protégé. "Get her out of here! See to it that she returns to her people safely!" Amara's stance relaxed as she digested the gloomstalker's sensible words, and looked toward the ceiling instead.

"I'm not leaving—"

"Go!" Castor ordered him. "I'll catch up!"

As Theoden and Amara headed for the ceiling, her magic aiding in their ascent, another dozen or more peons flooded the entryway of the old temple, but none got past the veteran gloomstalker. The man watched knowingly as a monstrous form crouched into the crumbling building, barely fitting, and began running the length of the temple's passage on all fours. Castor let out a battle cry as it approached…he could not allow it into the temple just yet. Its roar was deafening as it barreled into the man, crying out all the louder as the man's blade sunk deep into its flesh. However, it was far too powerful for Castor, and they both stumbled into the temple, the priestess's barrier disintegrating.

He couldn't spare a glance toward the ceiling to see whether or not the others had already fled, and the two faced off in a fierce battle. The gloomstalker slashed at the giant once, twice, thrice, and rolled out of the way as it swung its mighty fist toward him. He circled the beast, chanting another incantation, and blasted it with a magical force that sent it reeling on its heels, nearly toppling over. Then he attacked its ankles, and as it fell over Castor was attacked by another barrage of minions.

They successfully inflicted several wounds as he killed them one by one, but then the runes upon his sword were distinguished. "Dammit!" Castor cried out, grunting away the pain, and blasted the few left standing into the far wall opposite that from where the archprimus was stirring. He immediately pounced upon their leader, driving his longsword deep into its flesh to the hilt over and over, desperately trying to end its reign. He felt large fingers wrap around him, squeezing, and could hear the straining of his breastplate. His blade clanked against the temple floor, and the beast lifted him toward its mouth, now wide open. He wriggled a hand free just as sharp teeth began closing around him, its foul breath stinging his eyes and nostrils as it assaulted his senses. His adrenaline was enough to push through though. He repeated his earlier incantation and blasted a hole in the back of the monster's throat with his one free hand just as its teeth began scraping against his armor.

With another heavy fall, the archprimus's knees hit the floor and shook the temple's foundation. As its torso began its descent, Castor forced himself the rest of the way into the creature's mouth, its fleshy walls protecting him from the impact as the heavy mass collapsed against the floor. He braced himself as the shockwave from the fall reverberated through the building. A moment later, as it lied still, the gloomstalker climbed out of the wet, gory hole in the back of its throat and retrieved his fallen weapon, sheathing it beside the other upon his back. It came as no surprise to the man that the smaller beasts had dispersed upon the archprimus's death.

"Dhumos's balls!" Castor laughed. "You're a big one, aren't you?" He drew one of his daggers and carved into the monster's back, his arms disappearing into its flesh until he reached its heart, groaning as he pulled with all his remaining strength until it came free. He had never seen such a prize... it was the largest fell stone he'd ever claimed from the gloom, slightly larger than a human head.

The structure groaned, and cracks spider-webbed

across its walls, the floor and the ceiling. Dust and debris showered down around Castor as the floor gave out, and he collapsed with it as the building crumbled around him. When he came to, he found himself in some sort of subterranean system illuminated by a strange green glow, a stark contrast against the fell's typical blue radiance. He spotted the fell stone easily for this reason, and traversed the corridors in pursuit of the glow's source until it opened up to a wide chamber with hieroglyphs he'd never seen before, etched into the walls. The glow came from some candles that sat upon a dais, except it wasn't fire dancing upon the candle wicks. They were arranged in a very intentional manner, and a strange artifact sat in the center. "What is this?" he asked aloud as he set the fell stone down to further examine the place that must've gone untouched for thousands of years.

The green glow atop the candles stretched into the empty space of the chamber much like roots reached into the earth, branching and twisting, but on a much smaller scale. Bathed in its mysterious light, he brought his index finger to one slowly, and as he touched it the artifact in the center began crackling and resonating with some sort of energy. It created a bridge with the fell stone on the ground, and Castor could tell it was feeding off of the stone. "No, no, no!" he shouted. "Shit!" The green energy turned blue as it sapped the power of the stone, and the room seemed to fragment as the process took place. Castor looked at his hands and as he moved them there were multiple images of them overlapping, shimmering in and out of view. Everything seemed to be resonating with the foreign energy, and then the bridge between the artifact and the stone began groaning with pleasure, as if it were coming to life.

"I'm done with this!" Castor shouted to himself and smashed the artifact upon the dais. The bridge of energy collapsed abruptly, retreating from the fell stone, and found Castor's eyes instead. He screamed in agony, falling to the floor, his hands clawing at his face. The resonating energy ceased all at once, and the whole room went dark, only the blue glow of the fell stone remained.

"Castor!" Theoden yelled as he and Amara rushed into the chamber. "What happened?"

"By the wisps of Eldora... what is this place?" Amara gasped as all concern for the gloomstalker was replaced by her fascination, and she looked around in awe at the ancient discovery.

Theoden ran over to help Castor to his feet. "Are you okay, Castor?" he asked, but when his teacher looked up at him, something was wrong. Castor's eyes were glowing with the absence of light somehow, and seemed to burn, wisps of darkness dancing upon the orbs. Green tendrils writhed beneath the man's skin, reaching out from his eye sockets as they had from the candles. He lifted Theoden off his feet by his neck, Castor's fingers wrapped around it tightly, squeezing. "Ca-s-tor!" Theoden gasped as he struggled to breathe, his feet dangling limply.

"Not Castor!" the man barked, answering in a voice neither Theo or Amara recognized. "No more Castor!" he yelled angrily as he threw Theo across the chamber. The half-elf slammed against the wall hard, unmoving upon hitting the floor. "Asajrej!" he announced maniacally, gleefully. His eyes came upon Amara then, and he smiled deviously, lifting a finger into the space between them, his elbow bent at a right angle. "But you! You can call me Asaj." He looked her up and down, inhaling deeply as he circled her. "Be a darlin' won't you?" He reached out and grabbed Amara's face, his thumb pressed against her bottom lip, slowly pulling it down and separating her lips from one another. "It's been ages..." A moan hummed from between his lips.

Theoden groaned as he stirred, wheezing as he tried to get up, and Asaj snapped his attention toward the half-elf. "After I take care of that." He looked at Amara again. "This will only take a moment." As he strode over to Theo, Amara swooped the fell stone up and channeled its power fiercely.

Several Years Later

Castor sat in a corner of the seediest tavern of one Paragon, drinking alone. Except he was never alone, a hard truth he'd been struggling to accept for years. He was once a respected protector of the people, practically worshipped and praised wherever he went, but now he was only tolerated at best. Most feared what he'd become, and he'd been expelled from several Paragons already. He was running out of places where he could escape the gloom and rest.

The shell of a man could feel what had taken up residence within him stirring, likely due to his mood in particular, but he'd grown accustomed to keeping the entity at bay when he wasn't in a heightened state of emotion. Still, its thoughts would intrude his own at times; its will played games with him, influencing him whenever he let his guard down. The bottle helped keep him numb, and that's what he focused on, so he didn't notice when a certain gloomstalker made his way over to him.

"You look like shit," Theoden told him.

Castor didn't bother looking at the half-elf. "Why don't you come a little closer and say that to my face?" he replied apathetically. "Or better yet, take a seat." He kicked the chair across from him, scooting it out from beneath the table.

Theoden shifted uncomfortably where he stood. "I'm not here to catch up," he told his old teacher.

"You've come to bring me in then? Is that it?" Castor asked him, and finally turned his attention from his bottle to his old student, a dare in his dull green eyes. "Well come on then! You're a full-fledged gloomstalker now aren't you? It is your duty is it not?" Castor brought his hands out in front of him, as if waiting to be restrained. A gleeful anger bubbled up within him, and he found himself hoping for a violent confrontation with his former protégé. "What are you waiting for? Do it." Castor felt his fingers wrapping around Theoden's neck, squeezing the air from the man's lungs, and lifting him from his feet. It felt so real, so palpable, despite existing entirely in his head, and a laughter crept up his throat at the thought. Castor's hand trembled as he fought the urge to indulge.

Theoden took a half step back. "I'm not here for that. I'm here on behalf of a party interested in your services."

Lies. "Why?" Castor asked. "They already have a gloomstalker doing their bidding, *clearly*. Why don't you pull the job?" The need to feel the half-elf's throat between his fingers was overwhelming.

"It's your... unique... set of skills they... seek," Theoden stammered, clearly uncomfortable with his situation. Castor knew why, clenching his hand into a fist, the very one that had nearly killed the man. No... he willed the intrusive thoughts from his mind.

He looked Theoden over for a moment, sighed, emptied his bottle and stood up. Jobs were becoming more and more sparse as of late, and his coin purse would soon dry up. He couldn't afford to keep himself numb for much longer, and he couldn't afford to be sober either. The drink was his power over the cursed entity inside of him. "I suppose I can hear them out."

The half-elf led Castor to the rendezvous location. "Wait here," he told Castor, and approached a hooded figure, several others beside them, also hiding their faces. "I've done what you asked. We're even now. Farewell." Castor watched the gloomstalker take his leave, sparing a final glance to his former master before departing.

"What is this?" Castor asked the hooded figure. "Who are you? I don't work for cowards. Show yourself." They approached the man slowly, and the others remained where they were.

Amara lowered her hood and looked up at the man with pity. "Oh, no. No, no, no!" Castor snapped. "I'm not interested." He turned to leave.

"Castor Donovan!" Amara barked. "I think—"

"Haven't you done enough?" Castor retorted. "I'm not your lab rat anymore, elf!" *Annihilate her. Make her pay for what she's done.*

"I think I may know a way to help you."

Lies! Asaj's words nearly reached Castor's lips. The

former gloomstalker's breath caught in his throat. *She only brings you pain... put an end to this!* What if? His eyes betrayed his state of being as he fought it.

"Listen to me Castor!" Amara cried firmly. "Not to that... *thing* inside you."

"Why do you want to help me? After everything you've done?" Castor spat, desperately trying to find something, *anything*, to grasp hold of. He couldn't overpower Asajrej forever.

"This would never have happened to you if we'd never met. If I'd never recruited your services. Let me help." He breathed easier then, and a calmness washed over him.

After hearing what the elven priestess had to say, Castor headed back into the wilderness of the wasteland, feeling something he hadn't felt in a very, very long time.

Hope.

THE LORE KEEPER

Nestled between the shimmering sands of the great Kamali Desert and the endless azure expanse of the Sunfire Sea, Azhara stands as a gleaming jewel of prosperity and culture.

The sentinel led the secretive woman far from the shores of Azhara. For four days and three nights they traversed the treacherous and seemingly endless dunes, like ocean waves frozen in time, hardly speaking a word to one another. It wasn't his job to ask questions, only to fulfill the duty of his clan, the Sentinels of the Dunes. Payment came in many forms: gold, silver, and copper mostly, but there were times when a customer paid with rare jewels. The desert sentinels were known for their love of rarities, but even then, sometimes they were paid in the form of investment opportunities...if there was something the clan valued more than the grandeur of ancient gems, most of which promised to contain the purest form of arcanic dust within, it was the opportunity to obtain even more leverage over the gears and wheels that made the clockwork of Azhara tick. The city rose upon the sands they called home, for their clan had wandered the Kamali Desert for thousands of years, or so they were told. They'd spent a millennia building a reputation among the Azharan elites, proletarians and poverty stricken alike for their trustworthiness, and unparalleled knowledge of the desert, its secrets, and how to navigate it. Some might say Azhara would've never survived long enough to flourish into the majestic and thriving enigma it had become if it wasn't for the Sentinels of the Dunes, and their unmistakable value to the bustling civilization and all its occupants. The clan's cradle wasn't even in the city. Nobody outside of the sentinels knew where it was they called home, and every person who'd ever attempted to tail a sentinel to find out had either disappeared never to be seen or heard of again, or damn near perished wandering the dunes aimlessly until they were lucky enough to be found by a passing caravan headed to Azhara. It had become a common superstition among Azharans, not to even attempt something so utterly foolish. The sentinels treasured their privacy and seclusion above all else.

To add to the woman's mystique and intrigue, she hadn't offered the clan any of these things. Very few clienteles had sought out the sentinels with what she was offering in hundreds of years. It was unlikely that many people knew of the old sentinel custom known as yahkdaqi...even more so the ancient term for it: ruhdayn, roughly meaning, 'to swear an oath upon one's soul and bound to fulfill the debt whenever called upon.' Outsiders might hear the translation and think it a metaphor, or figure of speech, but then again, any outsiders familiar with the old ways were thought to have died with the knowledge generations ago. Learning of the word and knowing how to use it were two very different things, and knowing how to use it meant she knew it was no play on words. Ruhdayn was a magical binding of the debtor's soul to the creditor, and could not be altered or cheated, and could not be lifted until the debt was repaid. Ruhdayn was not to be taken lightly, and as an extremely secretive people themselves, they expected she knew this was the case and did not intrude upon her own privacy when she'd incited the old custom. Having bound herself as payment for the sentinels' services, they fulfilled their end of the bargain and escorted her to her desired destination. A great mountainous dune stood before them.

"Of course it's buried," she muttered. "How are we supposed to get to it now?" She asked herself more so than her companion, even though she turned to regard the man.

"Start digging," he responded nonchalantly. After taking in the incredulous look upon the woman's face, but before it was replaced by defeat, the man laughed. "Typically, we do not allow outsiders the privilege of bearing witness, but as you are bound by ruhdayn the matter is moot. Stand back."

She did as she was told, thoroughly intrigued, not sure what to expect, but anticipating something remarkable.

"Further, if you will, unless you want to be buried, that is," he told her, shrugging as if it mattered not to him. She heeded the warning and backed away until he nodded his approval. Then he placed a hand upon the dune and lowered his head as if he was connecting with an untamed beast. He began walking the perimeter of the dune, his fingers combing its side until he came to a stop elsewhere before the mighty mound. Then he placed both hands against the wall of sand and began speaking in tongues. The ground began to rumble beneath her feet and she nearly cried aloud, but found her footing instead as sand began pouring down the dune, but after a minute the sand began pouring out from the bottom instead.

The sentinel was performing some sort of maneuver with his arms, his hands flicking this way and that, bending at the wrists in fluid motions as if he was somehow reaching into the dune and beckoning the sand to obey his movements. As the sand did just that, an opening in stone appeared from behind the sand, and the woman wobbled on her feet as the very sand she stood upon rose beneath her. It continued to rise as the sand continued flowing from the opening, and all she could do was maintain her balance as she watched the miraculous feat in awe. Though the dune he'd led them to still stood as tall as a mountain, with every passing minute she rose to meet its peak, the sun cooking her all the more the higher she got. Then the man looked up at her and flicked his hands in her direction. She nearly panicked as she began sliding down toward him, but then realized the sand was carrying her to the slipface at its base. Keeping her feet steady, she was soon standing beside him, and between two formidable mountains of sand.

"I shouldn't ask…" she started.

"You're right."

"…but as a scribe of the—" she went on before he abruptly continued.

"You shouldn't ask," he added sternly.

As a scholar of the Scribes of the Sapphire Quill, and an honorary Keeper of Lore, she felt an unquenchable thirst for understanding what had just transpired, but she knew better than to prod any further and buried her curiosity. Whatever she'd just witnessed was a Sentinel secret, and she understood the weight of having witnessed such a feat. With her soul on the line, and firmly in the clan's hands, she would take their secret to the grave. Even so, their infamous ability to avoid detection and lose those shadowing behind them on their turf became abundantly less mysterious… no less impressive, however. She peered past the man into the opening, which now resembled the mouth of a cave. "Whoa…" She breathed as she looked from the opening to her escort.

"I believe what you're looking for is through here," he said flatly, wanting to be done with his mundane task. "Let's get this over with, follow me."

"Did you know this was here?" she asked her guide.

"No, but my people have discovered many like this hidden beneath the sand. The desert is littered by places such as this. Come," he answered impatiently.

They lit a couple torches and made their way inside. The two wound their way through a subterranean tunnel until it opened into a larger cavern. A wall of sand covered most of the area to their right as they entered, and stone surrounded the remainder of the cavern except for a large gap in the stone at the far end. The gap was blocked by yet another wall of sand. Large, elongated rocks protruded from various points of the cavern, and all pointed at various angles, many of which collided with one another above them, creating a sort of makeshift ceiling. Streams of sand slid from between the gaps in the rocks above here and there, but they were sturdy enough to keep the dune from collapsing onto them. The most significant thing sat at the center of the cavern however... the very thing the scribe was after: an ancient ship, or shipwreck rather, was nestled there, its bow crushed by the wall of sand to their right.

"A ship? It must be thousands of years old..." The guide gawked. He couldn't believe his eyes. "Is this what you were after?"

"Four-thousand, two-hundred years..." she replied, and he shot her an incredulous look. "Give or take a few decades," she added with a wink. "It's not the ship I'm interested in per se, but what wonders might we find within?" she asked rhetorically. She was stunned by the view... by the revelation! The smile that spread across her face was beginning to hurt her cheeks, but she had never been more excited about anything in her life. "So, it's true after all," she thought aloud, "the desert was once at the bottom of the sea!" She squealed with joy.

"My people have suspected this for many generations, but never have we found such concrete evidence," the man said as he shared in the woman's wonder. "How did you—"

"Ah, *ah, ah*," she teased, wagging her finger. "You have your secrets, and I've got mine." *Years of research,* she thought to herself, smiling all the while. They exchanged a look of mutual respect before turning to face the decrepit ship once more. As they approached the vessel the man stopped, motioning for the woman to do so as well. "What is it?" she asked.

"Do you feel that?" he asked her.

She cleared her mind and reached out with a hand before her. The air seemed charged with something; a slight tingle hung in the air surrounding the ship. "A little…"

"My name is Kalid," he said suddenly, unexpectedly. "Who are you?"

"I thought I was owed my privacy?" she asked, confused about the sudden change in the dynamic between them. "I thought secrecy was your clan's whole thing…"

"There may be danger ahead, and I need to know we can trust each other," he explained. "I'm going no further without—"

"It's Radiya," she answered.

"Can you fight, Radiya?" Kalid asked.

The woman scoffed at him. "Don't worry about me," she answered, "I've been training for a Lore Seeker position for a long time." She whipped out some daggers and began twirling them between her fingers, wearing a grin upon her delicate face.

"Have you ever had to use those," he asked skeptically as he looked her up and down with a raised eyebrow.

"Well, I—"

Kalid sighed. "Never mind, on second thought, I'd rather not know what you were about to say. Let's do this."

They entered the ship through an opening in the hull, and it was like stepping into another world… another time.

Skeletons that should've been ground to dust were sprawled about across the wooden deck. The wooden beams creaked and groaned under their weight as they made their way through the ship's innards. Finally, Radiya and Kalid found the captain's cabin and living quarters. Radiya's heart began racing as she imagined the treasures that might lay within, and began picking the lock of the great cabin's portal. With a thunderous roar, the door burst into pieces as Kalid kicked the thing off its rusted hinges, and a surprised Radiya glared at him once she'd regained her composure. "That was barbaric!" she scolded him. "This ship is a relic from ages long forgotten!" Kalid put his hands up apologetically, surrendering to her admonishing temperament.

As they explored the large room beyond, Radiya began pocketing all the valuables she spotted: artifacts such as a ship in a bottle, a spyglass made of emerald and gold, some old books off a shelf, little knick-knacks she'd never seen before, and a large map she rolled up and slid into a container lying beside it. She put them all in a sack she'd carried with her, disappointed with her find until she spotted the captain's spectacular remains. "Ooooooh!" She cooed excitedly as she danced over to the decorated skeleton. The first thing she noticed was the fancy old tome gripped in both of the captain's bony hands, but when she attempted to pry it from its grasp, the bones began to rattle, and she hopped backwards gasping.

"What is it?" Kalid called from across the room, but when he looked her way, he didn't need an answer.

A fire had been lit in the captain's empty eye sockets, and it rose to its feet. Its jaws repeatedly opened and closed, its teeth making an awful sound as they collided against one another. The skeleton groaned and began waving the book in both hands. "This is mine!" it yelled in a low scratchy voice. "If you wants it, lass, you'll have ter pry it from me cold dead fingers!"

"Uhhh..." Radiya searched for the words, looking to Kalid for backup, but nothing but a shrug came. "I don't know how to say this, but... you've been dead for over four thousand years..."

"Nonsense!" the skeleton yelped, its voice was higher pitched this time, as if an entirely different person had spoken. "Tha'. . . canno' be!" Yet again, a different voice.

"It is true... I'm sorry, but—"

"Screw this!" Kalid snapped and drew his swords, charging at the skeleton.

The captain threw the large, ancient tome to the floor and growled, drawing his own weapons forth. "To yer cap'ain lads!" It roared in its deepest voice yet. "Off yer lazy arses!"

A moment later a cluster of skeletal soldiers were ready to defend their captain in death. Kalid went for them. "I'll take them! You handle that one!" he called to her and engaged with the crew.

Radiya and the captain brawled for a minute, clashing their weapons together, and Radiya thought she might reason with the captain. "Surely there's a way we can all be happy!" she said.

"You tried ter rob me blind, you did!" the captain barked at her and swung its blades at her neck. She dodged just in time, bringing her blades up to parry the next attack. "There isn' no way to settle this lassy! No' in no way tha'll make you happy an'way!" The skeleton laughed maniacally and attacked again. As the dead captain spoke, and its voice cycled between the same four different voices, Radiya examined its remains at every opportunity. From the wide-brimmed hat, flattened on one side, a missing piece on the other as if a beast had taken a bite off it, and a feather sticking out the top to the strange clothing it wore: from the cloth covering its scalp beneath the hat to the sparkling silver tooth on its lower jaw, and the many rings on all the bony fingers. The captain took her by surprise and pinned her against the wall, about to open another dialogue no doubt, but Radiya slammed her fist into the captain's jaw, knocking the lower jaw from the skull and it flew across the room. The captain watched it go, and then stared at her with its flaming eyeholes. She imagined it was yelling ferociously at her. She heard piles of bones falling to the floor across the room as Kalid took the crew down one by one, and then she noticed something...each time Kalid destroyed a crew member, one of the captain's rings flashed ever so subtly. It was her turn to take the offensive, and she had the bony man reeling backwards, and with a feint attack from her left, she quickly sliced its right hand free of its wrist with her other hand. It lifted its wrist in front of its face as the blade from that hand fell to the floor, as if shocked she had done such a thing. Then the captain raised its one remaining hand to attack the distracted woman, or so it thought, but she smashed its severed hand with her foot, crushing the ring she'd noticed flashing whenever a crewmate collapsed to the floor.

The few remaining crewmates, as well as the captain, all collapsed into a pile of bones simultaneously, and Radiya fell backwards in relief breathing heavily as the adrenaline wore off. "Nice one," Kalid praised her, "whatever you did!"

"Thanks," she gasped.

"You alright?" he asked her.

"Yeah," she replied. "You?" He answered with an approving grunt and nod and looked around the room. "The tingling is gone. I think it's safe now if you want to get out of here... I'm just going to grab a few more things first."

"I'll be right outside." He nodded and left the room.

Radiya slid the rest of the rings off the captain's fingers, removed a few necklaces from around its neck, checked the trouser pockets which had some other little trinkets, and pocketed them all. She found some jewel studded earrings lying on the floor where she'd originally found the captain and grabbed those as well. Then she took the hat, smiling, and put it on before fetching the tome, the one prize she was really after. On her way out the room she noticed something gleaming from the corner of her eye and went to investigate. It was the lower jaw she'd punched off the captain, and the silver tooth attached to it. She threw the jawbone in her sack and met Kalid outside the ship.

"That's ridiculous!" He laughed when she joined him, wearing the captain's wide-brimmed hat.

"I make ridiculous look good though." They shared a laugh, and Kalid escorted her back to Azhara where they'd part ways. "Until next time," she told him as they went their separate ways, words meant to carry little weight. Neither of them missed the irony though, knowing that he and his people would indeed see her again.

Radiya made her way back home, to her guild house,

where the Scribes of the Sapphire Quill coalesced with their collection of worldly artifacts and near-endless knowledge. It was her job as a Keeper of Lore to look after the rarest and most valuable of the guild's collection, perform any necessary reparations, and make duplicates the guild could safekeep elsewhere if any misfortune were to befall their beloved temple. It was an honorary position...one she was ever so grateful for. She'd proven herself immensely priceless to the guild, for she was incredibly gifted in all that she did for them. As far as repairing ancient texts went, she was unmatched among the scribes, and she'd often wondered if that had become her greatest detriment. When she found herself in her private chambers she hung the hat on a hook, set the sack of loot between her bed and the wall, and traced her fingers along the edges of the large, precious tome. This would be the prize that would put her on the fast track to becoming a Seeker of Lore, the thing she yearned for more than anything else in all the world. The Seekers of Lore was the sect that traveled the world in search of knowledge from all corners of the globe and brought them back to Azhara to further enrich the lives of everyone in the city with hidden knowledge. By procuring the tome from the ship beneath the dune she'd killed numerous birds with a single stone.

"Where did you procure such a magnificent tome?" the guild master asked her when she presented it to him.

"Guild master," she said as she lowered her head in respect. "I found it clutched in the hands of a dead sailor, aboard a decrepit ship, beneath the sands of the Kamali Desert."

He stared hard at her. "Radiya," the guild master

started, "please tell me this isn't an attempt to persuade me once again to allow you to join the ranks of the seekers..."

"Guild master, please..." Radiya pleaded. "I spent years researching leads that led me to that ship. Not only to prove the controversial theories claiming the desert was once a seabed, but to find knowledge so ancient, no other seeker alive can claim such a prize as this tome! I'm ready!"

"Radiya!" The guild master snapped. "It has nothing to do with how prepared you might or might not be! It has nothing to do with how capable you are or are not! You are a *woman!*" He roared as if the word explained everything. "Women are not seekers! Women stay right here!"

"But guild—"

"Enough!" He roared once more, his patience wearing thin. "This is the last I want to hear of this! Do you hear?!"

Radiya's spirit flickered out in that moment. Her shoulders sagged, and it was everything she had left inside her not to cry right then and there, but she wouldn't shed a tear until she was alone. She certainly wouldn't empower the old righteous fart by doing so before him. "Yes, guild master."

"Now, now..." he said, his voice softening up. "You will be recognized for finding such a valuable relic, and be rewarded, don't you worry Radiya." The old man reassured her. "Perform reparations on this tome right away! The other guild leaders and I must learn all we can from it as soon as possible! And then we shall speak of a deserving reward. Go on, child. You make us all very proud!"

"Yes, guild master," Radiya said as she bowed, and then rushed to her private chamber where she burst into tears, her face buried in one of her lush pillows.

She'd spend the next couple weeks working on the reparations as ordered by the guild master, isolated from everyone as the head of the keepers were given all the privacy they required for their work. Then she stumbled across a page that the captain of the ship had desecrated. They'd circled an image and some text, then scribbled a note in a long dead language others of the guild would most certainly decipher in due time. Upon closer inspection though, she realized the object in the image the captain had circled was a tooth. A shape...no, a rune of some sort was carved into the tooth. She hurried through the guild house to her private chambers, closing her door softly behind her, and dived across her bed. She rummaged through the sack she'd been too depressed to look through and pulled forth the lower jaw of the dead captain. She held it in the candlelight of her chamber and saw something etched into the silver tooth. She stuffed it in her shirt and rushed back to her reparation chamber to further inspect it and compare it to the drawing in the old tome. Side by side the runes were identical. She gasped, not sure what it meant since she was unable to read the text and stood there examining both the tooth as well as the book for some time, at a loss as to what to do. She pried the silver tooth free of the jaw and then traced the rune with a fingernail and felt a slight, very subtle, vibration emanating from the tooth. She frustratingly slammed it against the book and gasped again when the captain's writing began reacting to the tooth's vibrations. The characters slithered around, lines breaking apart and repairing themselves in letters she was familiar with!

With this tooth, I can be anyone I need to be. The voice is the key. They will perceive what they hear.

Radiya had an idea suddenly then. She didn't even think about it. There was nothing to think about. With one of tools readily available to her, she groaned as she gripped one of her own teeth between the jaws of the pliers. Sweat beaded down her forehead, and she took a few very deep breaths...then she began ripping the tooth free from its roots in her gums, blood flowing from her mouth. She cried and groaned, shuddering and wriggling from the self-induced agony. She whined and began bellowing between pursed lips as the tooth slowly came free. Her whole body shook from the pain, and then she keeled over and vomited violently, blood, stomach acid and phlegm pooling onto the floor. Once she recovered and the bleeding stopped, she was ready to install the silver tooth. She sought the help of a friend of hers in the guild of alchemists, who gave her something for the pain, and something that would expedite the healing process instantaneously. Then they secured the silver tooth for her. The friend had owed her, and so no questions were asked, and as quickly as she had arrived, she was back in her private quarters trying to figure out how to make the damn thing work. Her fingernail tracing the rune had done something...so she used her tongue to trace the rune instead, felt it flicker to life, in a way, and focused on making her voice more masculine.

"I will be a seeker," she said smiling as she heard a man's voice speak the words.

THE SHADE

Witching hour, the time of early morning when most were in a deep sleep; the time for creatures of darkness to lurk, and for predators to stalk their prey. The sliver of a moon shined dimly in the early morning sky; a curtain of blackness hung overhead. Clouds blocked out the stars, and the city was mostly silent, except for the sound of a crisp cool breeze rolling in from the bay. The streets were lined with lanterns, flames dancing with the salty wind, and other than the occasional drunk stumbling for a warm hole to collapse into, they were empty. A caravan crept its way out of town, slowly, quietly, and even the horse was silent. The driver shivered as a gust of wind hit him, chilling him to the bone. He pulled his overcoat tighter around his frame and looked over his shoulder this way and that, assuring himself that he was not being followed. A couple miles out of town, he turned off the beaten path and continued for another half mile or so until he found the meeting spot, surrounded by a thicket of woods. The lights from the city were barely visible. He lit a couple of his own lanterns hanging from the caravan and walked around to the back of the cart. He opened the back and held the lantern up, revealing a few people gagged and tied up. A few were children, and the rest were women, all wide eyed with tears running down their faces. "It is nothing personal," he told them. One of the women began screaming as much as she could, squirming and trying to break out of her bindings. "Enough!" the man snapped as loudly as he dared, and when she did not yield, he smacked her across the face drawing whimpers from the little ones. The look in his eyes promised they'd be next if they tried anything.

Eventually, other caravans joined his own. Few lanterns hung around the area offering enough light for the men to carry out their transactions. As they stood in the center of all the wagons discussing their "wares" and negotiating with one another, the air became eerily still. At first, the sudden absence of the breeze went unnoticed, but when one of them laughed, they all realized. The trees had stopped swaying, the howling of the wind was no more, and when the laughter came to a stop the silence raised the hair on the backs of all their necks. They just stood there silently, alarmingly exchanging looks of confusion, remaining still as if anticipating something to happen. Then a darkness consumed the immediate vicinity. The flames of the lanterns still fluttered about but they were barely visible through the unnatural dark. The darkness grew like a cancer, spreading across the area and engulfing the wagons. Suddenly one of the men gasped and collapsed to the ground at the others' feet. Looking back up to where their colleague had just been standing the remaining men saw two yellow slits in the darkness, full of venom and animosity, squinting at them.

The men began screaming, and one by one they fell silent, collapsing to the ground with a loud thud until only one man remained. "Please!" the man begged. "You can have them! Just please don't kill me!" The darkness that had consumed the area receded, and as the light from the lanterns filled the area once more, the man hissed aloud and shielded his eyes. He looked around confused, albeit relieved, and couldn't believe his luck. Whatever had just transpired, he'd been spared and was left the entirety of the cargo for him alone. A smile crept upon his face as he began imagining the wealth he could amass. He leaned over and began removing valuables from his fallen colleagues, and when he was satisfied with the loot, he turned to check each of the wagons. As he turned to check on the first one his blood ran cold. Between the two wagons he was facing was a blackness so deep that no light penetrated through. It was a void, plain and simple... it was nothingness, blackness. Out from this void, as if stepping down from some invisible stairs, a figure came forth. It was black. The skin, the hair, the features, the clothes; they were all just an extension of the darkness now trying to cling to the thing's body as it stepped into the light. Streams of darkness flowed from the figure like flames clinging to dry wood. Gulping, the man stumbled backwards, his eyes scanning up the dark figure until they locked onto those yellow slits in the place where a face should be... where the eyes should be. "What do you want?!" the man screamed to the darkness incarnate.

A split second later the figure was inches from him. He was able to see the silhouette's features then: dark, almost ebony, ashen toned skin, the clean-shaven face of a slender yet stout middle-aged man, wearing what appeared to be black leather armor. Black hair peeked out from within the hood of a tunic that had been torn away at the chest, leaving only the hood. The figure held a large dagger in each hand. "Wait! Please!" the man cried. "I can pay you!" The man barely registered the movement of the dark man's arms slash at his throat, but he felt the blood flow freely from his neck as he gurgled on his words and slumped over. The shade stepped through the shadows to the back of one of the wagons and drew the canopy open. Yellow glowing eyes glanced around its contents. The people bound and gagged stared wide eyed at him, and then he vanished. He opened the next one… still not what he was looking for, and just as he had with the first, vanished before the terrified captives. He appeared behind the third wagon and as he pulled open the canopy, a child attacked, screaming as they did. The shade caught her arm in mid swing and studied the girl for a moment. "Vivienne?" he asked, and though she did not respond, she told him all he needed to know. He pulled her from the wagon, threw her over his shoulder and began walking away, drawing the darkness around them.

"Wait!" she protested. "You can't just leave them!"

The shade paused for a moment. "I'm not here for them." he said coldly.

"We should free them…" the girl said, defeated.

"You freed yourself," he told her apathetically. "They'll be fine." Then they were gone.

Later that morning…

"Vivienne says you left the others?" an older man asked.

The shade shrugged. "You didn't pay me to free them." He opened the pouch of gold the man had just tossed him. "This isn't what we agreed on…" Darkness swirled around the shade threateningly.

The man put his hands up and shrugged in return. "That's because I stumbled upon a lead. Think it's promising. You're going to want to check this one out," the man explained.

The shade didn't move. He contemplated the man's claim for a moment and then tied the pouch to his belt. "How?" He stalked over to the man who was now leaning against a massive table. The table held many artifacts, scrolls and maps sprawled out across its surface, and a model of an airship sat atop one of them. The room was very large, a fireplace adorned with immaculate carvings of sea beasts on either side sat perpendicular to the table, and bookshelves lined the walls. Piles of books that didn't fit on the shelves were scattered across the room, and a door to a large patio overlooking a forest at the foot of a mountain, a city on the other side and the ocean beyond that, was right behind the shade before he moved to the man's side.

"Do you recognize these symbols?" the man asked as he turned to a page in a tome and showed the shade.

He couldn't deny that they were somehow familiar in a strange sense, but not even in a tip of the tongue kind of way. "No. What are they?" the shade asked. The man sighed. "Arthur," the shade said sternly. "...what are they?"

"I thought you might recognize them," Arthur answered, disappointed with the shade's answer. "...but from what I've been able to decipher, it speaks of a fortress in the heavens..."

"Okay... and?"

"Kadaj..." Arthur sighed. "How long have we been helping each other? This is the closest I've ever come to finding your answers, see? The symbols speak of a door of shadows to another realm..."

"You're sure?" Kadaj asked, trying to keep the surprise from his voice.

"That... or some sort of gateway to the infernos of a hellish abyss," Arthur admitted, shrugging. Kadaj tensed up, agitated with the man's inconclusive translation. "But!" Arthur continued excitedly, turning the pages frantically, and stopping to show Kadaj an artifact on a page. "This device has a vital scientific importance, maybe even keeps the fortress afloat," he explained. "If you could retrieve it, I would be forever in your debt."

Kadaj sighed. "...and how am I supposed to reach this fortress if it flies?"

Arthur chuckled, excited that he had talked his friend... colleague rather, into this new endeavor. He would have gladly gone himself like in the good old days, but decades of adventures and exploration, tomb raiding and the like, had taken a toll on his body. He was getting old and fragile. He hated being confined to his mansion, but Kadaj had been a blessing in disguise. Arthur was able to live vicariously through the shade, or at least that's what he chose to call him. Kadaj couldn't remember where he'd come from, and had been wandering aimlessly for years, living job to job before he met Arthur. Together they had slowly chipped away at the mystery of the shade's past. Truth be told, they hadn't learned much. Most leads ended up disappointing them, and Arthur was beginning to suspect that Kadaj had given up hope. He knew the shade would never agree with the old man's sentiment, but he considered the shade a friend and found some solace in Kadaj's reignited hope, even if it was only a minor spark. "There's an airship scheduled to transport goods in a couple days. It will be going in the direction of these coordinates," Arthur explained, slamming the book down beside Kadaj. "...if you commandeer the airship here..." Arthur pointed to some charts next to the book. "...you should be able to reach the fortress by altering the ship's course here..." The old man squealed excitedly, looked up to see Kadaj's expressionless and unamused face, then glanced back to the chart, clearing his throat. "What do you say, old friend?"

Kadaj walked to the balcony and stepped out into the darkness. The wind blew his black hair aside, and the shade closed his glowing yellow eyes, inhaled deeply and hung his head backward thinking, deep in contemplation. He opened his eyes and gazed into the cosmos, the blanket of stars glistening in the heavens. This was indeed the best lead Arthur had ever given him. This could be the best chance he'd ever had of learning who he was or where he came from. Door of shadows? Another realm? Well... if it were a hellish abyss, he supposed he could always persuade a demon or a devil to point him in the right direction. He'd heard of such things as hellish fiends offering their assistance to mortals as they had access to a great deal of knowledge and power. Simply reading his soul could lead to answers, but they always demanded a hefty price. If anything, the artifact would be worth it, he surmised... hopefully. He exhaled and leaned against the balcony railing. "Okay," Kadaj answered. "Let's go over all the details..."

From behind a painting on a wall, a little girl's eyes watched in awe and wonder.

The Merkon

A spiritual prequel to 'The Transall Saga'
by the late Gary Paulsen.

It wasn't the skittering sounds of insects across his floor, or the suffocating restriction of his cell that tore him from his slumber, but the sound of grating metal as the slot in the door opened. He sighed as reality settled over him, but he didn't move a muscle. "Warden says he's putting you back in general population today," the guard told him through the opening. The prisoner's eyebrows rose. "Says you've been good in there."

"Thanks, Thomas," he answered. "Any word from Hanna?"

"She's safe," the guard answered. A relief flooded over the prisoner upon hearing the words and immediately, he breathed easier. "It's getting ugly out there, Marek. She said we wouldn't be hearing from her for a while."

Marek tensed up at the words. "Her location?"

"She was in Sedona, but she's heading to a bunker near the border."

Marek nodded, finally leaning forward from his wall. "Nogales..." he said absent-mindedly.

"Yes, I believe so."

"And they're still not going to relocate us? Or quarantine us?" Marek asked the guard.

"I haven't heard anything. So far, most cases are in densely populated cities. It hasn't reached Arizona yet, but the media is downplaying the whole thing."

"Of course they are. Thank you," Marek answered, and Thomas grunted a reluctant acknowledgement, but the slot in his cell door remained open.

"One more thing, Marek," Thomas said. "You've got a new cellmate."

Later that day, Marek O'Neill was escorted back to general population. He held his head up high, and only the most dangerous, wicked, and legitimately insane men looked him in the eyes as he made his way back to his cell. They were surprised to see him out of solitude so early, he could tell, which would've surely thrown a wrench into some of their plans for him. He just smiled smugly, thoughts of seeing the life drain from their eyes filling his mind.

A loud buzz erupted through the wing and his cell door opened. Marek stepped into his cell and the door shut behind him. His new cellmate looked at him and smiled, then glanced to the guard outside the cell and waved. "Thanks, handsome!" he called out to him. The guard said nothing and walked off. The man looked Marek over and took a seat on his bed. "Marek O'Neill, in the flesh."

"Who are you?" Marek asked.

"Oh, nobody important... just a fan of your work. Name's Jim."

"Wonderful," Marek groaned. "You better cut that

faggot shit out around me, you hear?" He pointed his finger toward Jim, and the man raised his hands in surrender.

"Alright, that's not a problem," he answered. "But I promise you'd like it—"

Jim began choking as Marek's fingers wrapped around his throat, and he began tapping against Marek's forearms as if he were tapping out of a wrestling match. Marek looked him in the eyes and squeezed his hands tighter, a frenzy overcoming him. As Jim looked into Marek's mad eyes he began smiling. The man would die happily at the hands of Marek O'Neill.

The revelation pulled Marek from his stupor, and his grip on the inmate's neck loosened as the craze within him subsided. Jim's smile turned upside down as Marek backed away a couple steps and stared at the man dumbfoundedly.

"You alright?" Jim asked.

Marek opened his mouth to respond, more than once, but he just gawked at the mad man as he could form no words.

"The look in your eyes was beautiful..." Jim said. "Like something primal took possession of you. Where'd you go?"

It dawned on Marek then that he hadn't actually put his hands around the man's throat. It had all happened in his head. Of course, it did... he couldn't afford to head straight back into solitude, not with Hanna out there amidst the ensuing chaos of the pandemic. He had to get out. He had to find her. Marek ignored his cellmate and laid down on his rack, brainstorming in silence as the hours passed by.

It wasn't until later that evening that they spoke again. Marek could feel the man's eyes on him the entire time, as if waiting for him to do something... say something. "What can you tell me about the pandemic?" Marek asked Jim.

He sprung up excitedly. "They're comparing it to the Ebola virus." Jim lowered his voice as he continued, smiling from eye to eye. "I saw it on the news once, someone dying from it. It causes people to bleed from every orifice." Jim squealed and clapped his hands together. "It's a fucking blood bath out there!" He laughed maniacally. "I heard they're bombing cities in some places, to try and stop the spread!" He tried to muffle his laughter, a snort squeezing through his chapped lips. "Hundreds of thousands of people, if not millions, caught in the blasts... and the virus continued to spread anyways! The irony!"

Marek listened intently. He had no idea the severity of the pandemic... an extinction level event if nothing were to change. His heart nearly stopped beating as he listened to Jim, not because he feared death, but because he feared for Hanna. He likely deserved such a fate, but she did not. What was he to do? "Who's they? Who's dropping bombs?"

Jim grinned wickedly. "Everyone."

The days would pass as Marek planned his escape, and tried as he might catch a glimpse of any television, it appeared as if the warden had strictly forbidden them from playing the news. Thomas had no updates for him, and his good graces with the guard were on its last legs as it was. He'd be alone in his endeavor, and he'd be executing the plan with no further information on Hanna's whereabouts, but at least he knew where she'd been headed. That night as his cellmate, and every other inmate there slept, he looked down upon the sleeping Jim, disgust smeared across his face. The time had come if his plan was going to work. The guards were making their rounds, leaving the minimum in his wing present, so he had to act fast.

Balling a sock up in his hand, Marek pried Jim's mouth open and shoved it all the way in. Jim's confused wide eyes focused on Marek and he tried to fight back, but Marek pressed his thumbs into the frightened man's eyes, pushing them further and further until he felt his eyes rupture, and pools of blood drained from the sockets. Jim's wails of agony went unheard through his muffled mouth. He flailed his arms and legs around wildly, albeit weakly, as Marek heard his muted whimpers. He pulled out a toothbrush he'd sharpened in preparation for this moment and systematically stabbed into each of Jim's ears and nostrils so that blood flowed freely from every orifice. Jim was barely moving or making any sounds at this point, and made no objections when Marek removed the sock from his mouth. "Kill... me... Please," Jim begged, his words barely audible.

Marek started carving the inside of Jim's mouth with the shiv. He cut his tongue over and over, the insides of his cheeks, the roof of his mouth... even sliced the fleshy flap underneath his tongue. Jim tried to wail, but only coughed up blood in his attempts. Marek pocketed the shiv and began calling out for help. "Guards!" Marek cried as loudly as he could. "Guards! Something's happening in here! Help!"

When a guard reached his cell, he blanched upon seeing the terrifying scene. Marek huddled against the wall opposite of Jim, and the mutilated man groaned as he reached out with a hand, blood pouring from his face. "What the fuck!" the guard cried as he looked back and forth between Jim and

Marek. "Holy fucking Christ!"

"What is this?!" Marek cried out. "He started coughing and then blood started pouring out of his face! What the fuck is this! Get me out of here!" The guard covered his mouth, his eyes wide, and he hesitated as he looked Marek over. "Now goddammit!" Marek snapped. The guard nodded and opened the cell, his keys dangling from a hoop on his belt. At this point every inmate in his wing was awake and buzzing with alarm, a commotion of inquiries and antagonistic howling.

As they left the cell, the guard just stared at Jim dumbfoundedly. If the virus had made it into the prison, and that man had just suffered from its most severe and final symptoms, then they were all exposed. He froze... he had no idea what he was supposed to do. As he turned around to usher Marek elsewhere, the inmate drove a sharpened toothbrush deep into the guard's neck. He reached up to apply pressure, but he wasn't going to make it. He staggered a couple steps and then collapsed to his knees, gurgling sounds escaping from his mouth as he tried to breathe, drowning in his own blood instead.

Marek took the keys and fled through the wing, threats and pleas from the other inmates as he did. It wasn't long before the alarms sounded, and just as he was making his way to an exit, he found none other than Thomas standing between him and freedom. "I can't let you go, Marek!" he said as he pointed a gun. "Stand down, O'Neill!"

"Come on, Thomas," Marek said as he put his hands up, taking a cautious step toward the guard. "I like you. Don't do this." He took another step.

"Not another step Marek!" Thomas yelled, his hands

shaking as he continued pointing his handgun at the prisoner.

Marek stopped, and stood there analyzing the scenario. "You don't have to die tonight Thomas," Marek told him.

"I'm the one with the gun Marek. Back up!" Thomas ordered him. "Turn around and put your hands behind your back!"

Marek did as he was told. When he heard the handcuffs, he spun around and slammed Thomas against the wall. The guard tried pulling his gun on the man again, but Marek kicked it from his hands and brought the shiv down and into the man's throat as he had done to the other guard. He dragged Thomas into a holding room and began stripping off his clothes. A minute later he was strolling out the exit as a guard.

He fled into the midnight desert heading south, according to his limited knowledge of the stars. There weren't towns for miles upon miles of the prison, and the nearest city was about fifteen miles east. This was as far as he'd planned, but he was confident he could find shelter before sunrise. He made it two or three miles into the dry darkness before he heard vehicles on his tail. "Shit!" he muttered to himself as he picked up his pace, but he didn't get very far. A couple jeeps with armed guards pulled up to him, screaming orders and pointing their guns. Marek spat at them and flipped them off and shots were fired.

Marek didn't know how many times he'd been shot, but he fell to his hands and knees, coughing blood onto the sand, now illuminated by headlights. Just as his vision began to blur, he heard a sharp popping sound from somewhere far above them. Then a strange tube struck the earth beside him, jolting him to attention, his awareness rejuvenated by the adrenaline. It left cracks spider-webbing around the point of impact, and Marek reached out and touched it. It wasn't hot... it wasn't even warm, but cool to the touch. Just as he looked at the swirling lights of energy encapsulated within the object, a blue light engulfed the area....

The sky shone brightly above, and Marek had to raise his hands to block the sudden shift in brightness. What happened? As his eyes adjusted, he looked around to get his bearings. No longer was he in a desert... no longer did he seem to be on Earth. The sky was a yellow-ish color, and the grass and foliage had a red tint to them.

"Where the fuck are we?" Marek heard behind him. He spun around to see three of the guards, half of a jeep and some limbs lying about.

"How the fuck are you not dead?" another asked, and cocked the hammer of his gun.

Marek checked himself for gunshot wounds, but other than the holes in his clothes, there was no evidence he'd ever taken the bullets. He patted himself down and laughed. "I don't know," he answered them both. How was it possible? How was any of this possible? How was he supposed to find Hanna now?

After subduing and restraining him, the guards began wandering the strange place, Marek in tow. They eventually came across an alien field of what could only be flowers. They were large, colorful, and had strange tendrils sprouting from them. From the center, petal-like needles spiraled upward in abundance, like giant strands of pollen, and at the tips were bulbous appendages. They were beautiful, but terrifying at the same time.

"This is crazy," a guard said. "This can't be Earth... what even are those?"

"Yeah..." another replied. "Some weird ass flowers." He approached one and started tapping a flower with his foot.

"I don't think you should be doing that," the other guard said. "We know nothing—"

The guard tapping the flower began screaming. The tendrils hanging from the strange plant slithered around his foot and up his leg, gripping it tightly, other tendrils slithering onto him as well. "Get this thing off me!" he screamed at the others and pointed his gun at the flower. When he pulled the trigger, the gun backfired or something, as if the gun powder in the bullet ignited in the barrel and exploded in his hand. He screamed bloody murder as the remains of the gun dangled from his mangled hand, and his screams persisted as the other guards attempted to pull him free, but to no avail. They backed away as the bulbs at the ends of the long-spiraled petals began to slowly spin down the lengths of their stems. They released objects into the now tube-like "petals," like the chutes banks used to use, and the two remaining guards as well as Marek, watched as they shot into the base of the flower and through the tendrils until they pierced the trapped guard.

His screams for help became howls of agony. His veins bulged beneath his skin, turning purple as they spread across his skin, and a sickly yellow film spread across his bulging eyes as he choked on his final breath. When he died, the tendrils let him go and resumed dangling from the flower as if nothing had disturbed them, leaving sharp quill-like objects sticking out of the dead guard.

The remaining guards threw their guns and huddled closely, trying to avoid touching any of the enormous flowers. "Take these off," Marek told them, and they shot him an incredulous look. "We don't know what we'll be up against out here, and you may need my help. Why render me useless?"

"Who do—" one guard started.

"He's right, Jorge!" the other guard snapped. "He needs us as much as we need him."

The guards removed the cuffs and began wandering through the field cautiously. Marek watched them go for a moment before returning his amazed look upon the dead guard, stupefied by what they had all just witnessed... looking upon the grotesque form sent shivers down his spine, and sent the hairs on his arms and the back of his neck standing upright, but he couldn't look away.

"Hey!" a guard called back a minute or so later when they realized Marek was so far behind. "We need to stick together!"

Marek caught up to them and they wandered the strange new world for hours. They'd hear the occasional animal, or this world's equivalent, in the distance from time to time. Marek didn't want to know what was at the top of the food chain there, and hoped whatever they were, that they kept their distance. Though he knew that they'd need to find something to eat eventually, and kept a lookout for anything that might provide the nourishment.

It wasn't long before they came upon thickets of trees where seemingly harmless critters were eating fruit-like objects growing from the branches. The three men managed to secure a bundle of the objects and decided it was worth the risk. The fruit would sustain them for a few days as they continued traversing the alien landscape aimlessly. They found "wood" and other materials to burn during the night, and took turns standing guard, though Marek knew one of the guards were always awake when it was his turn, and he didn't blame them... he would do the same in their shoes.

On the fourth day the trio entered a valley of sorts. There were trees on either side of them, and they continued their descent between the forested ridges. They came upon a large stream in the valley and stopped to hydrate. The liquid looked like water, though it had a slight violet hue to it, but that didn't stop them. They followed it to a decent sized lake, and as they took a break and lounged around near the "water," Marek watched as Jorge began skipping rocks. A noise nearby stole his attention however, and when he investigated he noticed a creature watching them. It resembled a warthog to an extent, but also had features that reminded him of a cougar... maybe it was the way it stalked them.

He thought about announcing its presence to the others, but chose to remain silent as they stared each other down from a few dozen yards. It crouched between some bushes, and seemed more curious than agitated. Then Marek heard a *thump* from the water as one of Jorge's rocks hit something in the water. Immediately, the pig-lion thing began snorting and heaving agitatedly, and rushed them. It stopped short of attacking them though, and squealed, or roared at them, digging its feet into the ground.

"What's gotten into it?" Jorge asked.

As if to answer his question, the pod-like thing he hit with a rock in the lake burst, making a wet popping sound as it did, and thousands of buzzing insects swarmed from the object and headed right for them. The sound was almost deafening, the buzzing of thousands of the bugs. The pig thing squealed a sharp piercing squeal, and another, and another frantically. "We need to move!" Marek snapped. They began running from the lake, but the pig-lion continued its mindless frenzy as if it were stuck somehow. The swarm collectively dived for the creature as if a single organism, and a cloud of clicking wings encompassed the beast as the men ran to find whatever cover they could. Nothing but slimy bones remained of the creature as the swarm rose from the picked-clean corpse and headed for them once again.

"There!" the guard up front yelled. Jorge and Marek couldn't see what he was talking about as they kept glancing toward the swarm that was quickly closing in on them. "Looks like holes or burrows or something!"

Marek looked ahead to see the guard pointing. Somehow, he'd gotten way ahead of them, and he watched as the man dove into the ground. When he looked back again it became clear that he and Jorge weren't going to make it before the swarm reached them, so he did what any sane man would do in his situation. He slammed Jorge in the face with an elbow just as he was turning to face him. Marek heard the crunch of the man's nose beneath the impact, and Jorge cried out and collapsed to the ground. "You bast-ar-d!" Jorge tried to scream at him, but the cloud of insects was already upon him. Marek dove into the burrow after the other guard.

The man's screams were drowned out by the swarm's

buzzing. It wasn't nearly as loud in the burrow, but they could still very clearly hear the insects. "Where's Jorge?" the one remaining guard asked Marek. "Jorge!" he screamed, but Marek cupped his hand over the man's mouth.

"Shhh!" Marek urged him. "He was right behind me, but by the sounds of it, he didn't make it. The swarm hasn't moved from that spot. Let's not be their next meal." He felt the guard nod and withdrew his hand. The guard kept quiet, and Marek kept a close eye on him, and his ears on the swarm. It didn't take them long to finish with Jorge, but neither did they disperse and flee the scene. The men huddled in the small burrow for what seemed like hours, listening to the swarm fly around the area above them.

Eventually, the men fell asleep while waiting for their chance to flee. Marek awoke to a cold knife against his neck. The guard, whom still remained unnamed to the former prisoner, held him at knifepoint, the blade resting against his jugular. "He was right beside you!" he snapped. "He's dead because of you!"

"If you truly believed that," Marek retorted, "you'd have killed me as I slept, or you're just stupid." He let the words weigh upon the man, both logical as well as threatening. "This fucking place killed him, not me. We'll probably be dead soon too, so if you're going to kill me, do it already." Marek's eyes narrowed as he moved toward the guard daringly. The movement caused a thin red line where the knife was digging into him. It fell to the floor of the burrow suddenly as the guard gasped and got yanked backwards into the far wall opposite Marek. He watched as large earthworm-like tendrils slithered from the "earth" and wrapped around the man...

squeezing him as they attempted to pull him through the wall of dirt.

"Marek..." he gasped. "Please..."

Marek eyed the knife at his feet, contemplated his next move for a brief moment, then drove the knife repeatedly into the wormy tendrils, white blood or guts oozing from each wound, until they released the guard and retreated. He fell to his knees gasping for air as he quickly scurried away from the wall toward Marek. "Thanks..." He offered his savior.

"Don't thank me," Marek told him. "It was the smart move. If we are to survive here, we need to stick together." He handed the knife back to the guard. "You'd be wise to remember that."

The guard took the knife and nodded. "You're right, I'm... I'm sorry," Marek said nothing, nor did he turn to acknowledge the man's apology. "I'm Max by the way," he said as he moved past Marek to the opening in the ground from which they'd come. Marek still said nothing, just watched Max begin to pull himself back to the surface. Marek watched Max's body shudder and go limp, before falling back down.

"Max?" Marek asked. He rolled his body over and made eye contact with the man. His eyes were flickering back and forth, his body twitching here and there, and there was enough light from above to see a nasty gash in his skull. "Fuck." He muttered to himself. Then he heard someone yelling outside the burrow. It wasn't in any language he'd ever heard, but it was a sign of intelligent life. He wasn't alone. Marek quickly retrieved Max's knife and sheathed it in his pants. The voice grew agitated as if they knew he was down there. Marek inched his way toward the opening, not wanting to suffer the same fate as Max, but the moment he tried to peak outside he was lifted by rough, firm hands.

Daylight blinded him as he left the burrow and he looked down to shield his eyes, and as his sight adjusted to the light the first thing he saw clearly were the slimy remains of Jorge a couple yards away. Nothing but the man's bones remained, and he reminded himself he'd be among them had he not acted to ensure his survival. As he looked upon Max's killers, he was stunned by the sight... not entirely surprised, but stunned nonetheless. They were certainly humanoid, as he'd suspected they might be, but they definitely weren't human... close though. Some had different shades of skin tone, some pale blue and others burnt orange and all kinds of shades between, if skin was the right word for it. The texture was different. He couldn't quite think of a satisfactory word for it, scale-y? That word didn't fit either, but it would have to do.

Their noses were flatter than human noses. Their eyes seemed slightly larger than a human's eye in proportion to their faces... they wore accessories in their faces like tribes across the Earth had. Some were bones; some seemed to be handcrafted ornaments, and they donned markings on their flesh as well. Based on their attire and rudimentary weapons, Marek compared them to hunter gatherers from before Mesopotamia times, but it was too early to tell. The one before him began screaming in his face and lifting its hand threateningly. "I'm sorry," Marek replied. "I have no idea what you're saying." This only seemed to make the 'man' angrier, and Marek was at a loss. He didn't know how to respond, or what they wanted. They pointed at his face and yelled even louder, drawing curious banter among the others. There were dozens of them. "I'd love to help, really..." Marek began, but then everything went black.

Marek spent the next few days in restraints, a prisoner once more, except he wasn't alone. These people had accumulated dozens upon dozens of prisoners from other communities, and some of them looked a lot different as if they were a different species entirely. Most shared the same qualities such as two eyes, one nose, two ears, a mouth, two arms and two legs, etc. They fed them just enough to keep them moving, and water breaks were few and far between. If anyone lagged behind or fainted, they were put down like a rabid dog. Marek kept to himself and pulled his weight, determined to make it through whatever this ordeal was.

That was, until one night when he took Max's knife and began sawing away at his restraints. Then he froze as he spotted a female watching him curiously, but continued when she made no move to stop him. Then he was hit hard across the face by another of his captors. They confiscated his knife and reinforced his restraints, and beat him some more for good measure. Marek tried looking for the female captor that had been watching him, but she was gone.

Later that night she visited him while the others slept. It seemed as if she were asking him a question. "We've tried this before, remember?" he replied.

She pointed at herself. "A-SH-EL-YN." She pronounced slowly, emphasizing each syllable.

A smile spread across Marek's face. This had been the first time any of the natives had attempted to communicate with him without their fists. "Ashelyn?" he repeated after her. "That's your name, right? Ashelyn?"

She made some sort of gesture excitedly and then pointed to herself again. "Ashelyn," she said happily, and then pointed to him.

"Marek," he said as he pointed to himself. "Marek O'Neill."

"MUH-ERK-ON-L." She tried to repeat.

Marek almost corrected her, but decided against it. "Merkon will do! Yes, good job," he told her as he smiled. She studied his face and copied him in her best attempt to smile. He nearly laughed in her face, but decided against it, perhaps wisely so. She gave him extra rations and attempted another smile before saying more words he couldn't understand, except one: Merkon. Then she was gone.

As they continued dragging him and the other prisoners along, they traversed vast distances over the course of weeks. Every few days they stopped in what appeared to be villages, but not the ones they'd burn down and capture even more prisoners, but villages that seemed to belong to their own people. The further they went the smaller the gap between the villages. Wherever they were going, they were getting close. The entire trip would've been hell if not for Ashelyn. She visited him every night and gave him extra rations and more water. At first, her visits had been short, but after a week or so, they were spending hours together every night. She had even begun teaching him their language, and he was beginning to get the hang of it, though it was rough. He spoke like he was a toddler, and would often induce her species' equivalency of laughter from her.

"Do you have anyone special in your life, Merkon?" she asked one night.

"I did," he replied. "Hanna, my daughter."

"Did?" Ashelyn asked. "What happened?"

"I don't know… I'm afraid I will never know, but the last news I heard of her was promising," he answered.

"Well I do not give up on hope that you will reunite in the future," she told him, a softness in her words.

"That is kind of you to say," Marek replied. "Listen, Ashelyn… what can you tell me of my fate? Where does this road end for me?"

Marek didn't miss the sagging of her shoulders. She remained silent for a moment before answering. "You are chosen for tribute," she said.

"Tribute for what? What does that mean?" Marek asked.

"Some become servants: builders, cookers, maids, carriers, herders, and the like… and sometimes… Killers," she went on to explain, and Marek perked up at that last one. "But… they see your face." She shifted uncomfortably. "They see you are different. They do not understand. They don't care to understand like I do." Marek's patience was wearing thin, but he took it all in and let her build whatever context she cared to give. He had all the time in the world after all. "Some are used for practice." Her expression became dour as she said so. "This is worst, but this is not tribute. Tribute fight other tribute to please the four faced god. You will have to kill…" Ashelyn looked visibly upset as she told him, her eyes glossed over slightly when she looked him in the eyes. "You must kill, Merkon. If you please the four faced god, they spare you."

Marek laughed, drawing a confused look from Ashelyn. "What is funny?"

"Ashelyn," Marek said ominously. "Where I come from, I am a well-known killer... so this won't be a problem for—"

"You kill?" Ashelyn gasped. "For fun, you kill?"

"Well..." Marek started, but Ashelyn had heard enough and stormed off into the night.

Days passed and she did not visit him. On a few occasions he'd seen her, and on fewer occasions their eyes would meet, and she looked upon him with contempt when they did. There were times he'd try to get her attention, but other captors of his would beat him for acting out of turn. Sometimes he got beaten just for looking different. One night, as they seemed to near the end of their journey and before the others slept, he spotted Ashelyn nearby.

"Psst!" Marek tried his best to be as quiet as possible. "Psst! Ashelyn!" he hissed in a raspy voice. She looked at him and turned away. "Oh c'mon! You tear people from their families and homes and enslave them, and you're judging me!" This got her attention.

Ashelyn snuck over to a smug Marek angrily, glaring at him. "You have no right! You do not know—"

"Listen!" Marek interrupted. "When my daughter was very little, her mother passed. I became a full-time father and her and I were very close. As she got older she attracted every boy she met. I didn't know how to navigate this part of her life without her mother's help. I could've been better, and sometimes I'd piss her off..."

"You," Ashelyn chimed in. "...*piss* on your Hanna?" Her face scrunched up in confusion.

"No, no, no..." Marek continued. "It's a... it means I angered her. The way I reacted to some of these interactions.

Then one day after she'd had enough of it, she told me I could trust her to respect herself and make good choices... that she had learned how she deserved to be treated, because she had an amazing and loving father..." He choked, but he cleared his throat and turned away to hide it from Ashelyn.

"Why tell me this?" she barked at him.

"Please!" he urged. "I'm getting to the point." He waited to see if she had heard enough or if she would stay. She stayed. "After that, I backed off. I put my trust in her, and she put her trust in me. One day, she came to me and told me about a boy that hurt her."

Ashelyn's eyes widened in concern a bit.

"This boy defiled her... he'd broken my girl." As he spoke the words the anger reverberated through them more and more as he went on. "He did unforgivable things to her! After convincing her to give me his name, I found him, and I made him pay!" His face was trembling then, and Ashelyn wrapped her arms around him, catching him completely off guard, but she took the edge off his mounting rage. "The thing is though, I *loved* it. I was good at it. I enjoyed killing that boy for what he did to my Hanna..."

Marek shook in Ashelyn's arms, but she held him tight. "You kill other tribute. You please the four faced god, and you live. Then maybe, you see Hanna again."

He returned her embrace. "I don't know if that is possible Ashelyn. I don't know where we are, or where home is. I come from a place where buildings reach into the sky, a blue sky, and our cities are lit up at night. In my world, if you get hungry you can get food almost anywhere." He paused, thinking how he took so much for granted. "My world is called Earth…"

"Your Earth sounds… odd… but nice. My people call our world Transall," she explained in kind.

They arrived at their final destination just a couple days later, and prisoners were dispersed, splitting into several groups and escorted away. He was taken to a thriving city, albeit rudimentary and ancient by Marek's standards, but a city nonetheless. He could see mountains, and he could hear a river somewhere nearby beyond the hustle and bustle of the people. Trees had been cleared in many places for the city's growth, but a forest still loomed just beyond the city, near the mountains. He didn't get much more of a look than that however, for he and others were taken somewhere underground, and out of sight.

It was down there that Marek truly understood what was happening, for it was eerily similar to ancient Rome. He'd become a gladiator. First, he was taken to a subterranean pool where maids, other servants he suspected, washed the captives… every inch of his body was scrubbed clean. They took sharpened stones to his hair, shortening the length considerably. Then his wounds were tended to thoroughly, strange ointments and oils rubbed in certain places, and all the while not a single person looked him in the eyes, or at his face for that matter, but stared through him as if they were mindless drones.

After the pampering, they led the prisoners to individual makeshift cells. Other prisoners attempted to speak with Marek throughout the night, but he ignored them, as if he didn't understand them. At some point, while the others slept, he heard a *'psst'* outside his cell. It was Ashelyn.

Marek rubbed his eyes and approached her quietly.

"I made this for you," she whispered as she handed him a mask. "Don't let them see," she said as she pointed to his face. A point became a brush with a finger, and then she held his face in her hand. "You wear, and you kill. You live. Please live, Merkon." Then she was gone.

Marek looked the mask over, admiring her craftsmanship. It was made of cloth and would completely cover his head like a ski mask. Flame-dried clay ornaments decorated its face. There was a large mouth sewn into the cloth where a mouth should be, painted black and red and grinning an eerie smile, each tooth shaped individually. The smile reminded him of the one she had attempted when they first started talking. Clay discs, painted black, slanted inward like a scowl circled the eye holes, and other strange ornaments decorated it as well. He didn't understand their meaning or significance, but from a certain perspective she'd made it intimidating, and he appreciated that.

The next day the prisoners were escorted into a large fighting pit that indeed reminded him of the Roman colosseum, just on a much smaller scale. Hundreds, if not thousands, of natives were in attendance, and as he looked around the arena he took note of certain details. Those strange flowers that had killed one of the guards when they'd first arrived were scattered throughout the arena, as were a number of stone-tipped spears. The prisoners looked back and forth at one another, unsure what it was they were supposed to do, but Marek knew.

A horn sounded and more than a dozen of them took off running for a weapon. As Marek reached a spear, a man who'd nearly beaten him to it attempted to snatch it from him, and Marek drove it through the man's chin. As the body fell to the ground, Marek tried pulling it free, but it would not budge. Others were fighting all around him, and he shoved his foot into the corpse's throat to yank the spear free. Just in time too, for another man came upon him from behind. He screamed and thrusted the spear at Marek repeatedly, but Marek dodged and blocked with his own.

Just behind him was one of those flowers, and Marek realized he was being backed into it. The man was relentless, and Marek knew he couldn't beat him, so he kept backing toward the flower while feigning a thrust here and there. Then he stopped backing up and watched the confidence grow on the other man's face. He charged Marek, but Marek used his spear to vault past the flower. The man realized his mistake too late and tumbled into the flower's tendrils. They wrapped around him and sent their toxic quills into his body. It was just as grotesque the second time.

He watched though, unable to divert his gaze as the man's veins bulged and discolored, spread across his body and he was dead within seconds. The tendrils released the body and retreated to the base of the flower, swaying patiently for their next victim. He pulled several of the quills from the corpse just as another tribute stalked toward him. They had him on his toes quick however, and Marek retreated across the arena. Soon there were only three of them left, and both the others had their sights on Marek, because of course they did.

They cornered him, and came from opposite directions. If he didn't think of something quick he was done for. They closed in on him, and once they were both within thrusting range with their spears, Marek whistled loudly and threw his spear nearly straight up. One of them followed the spear with their eyes and Marek clutched the quills he'd been gripping between his fingers even tighter and dived at them, punching their calf as he did so. Immediately, they screamed in agony and pulled at their leg in horror, but it was too late, the toxins were already spreading.

Marek snatched their spear and his final opponent impaled themselves on it as they rushed him from behind. "You... cheat..." the one he'd poisoned struggled to say, but he shrugged and walked away the victor. The crowd went wild for him. He raised his fists in the air and screamed, "Merkon!" His name was roared over and over again.

Marek was forced to fight in several more gladiator style fights in the arena over the course of the next week or so, nearly dying in a few of them, and every time he managed to win by outsmarting his opponents, but only barely. Upon surviving the final fight, he was greeted in the arena by what he suspected to be a leader among the barbarians. The highly decorated man stopped before him and grunted his approval. "Merkon."

Marek nodded and puffed out his chest in pride. He thought it ironic how he was praised here for killing, and imprisoned on Earth. The people of Transall loved him, though he knew their love could be easily swayed elsewhere.

He held out his hand and waited. Marek instinctively handed over his spear, and the man nodded his approval. "You have proven worthy tribute. Are you ready to stand victorious before the four faced god?"

Marek didn't respond.

"Speak, Merkon!"

"Merkon!" he roared with his fists in the air, nearly tumbling over from exhaustion, and the crowd roared his name.

"Hmm," the man conceded. He led Marek through a gate, and as they walked further and further up, the mountains, the forest, and the city came back into view. They followed a path that wound around a cliffside that overlooked the arena. "You have pleased the four faced god, and you will live to kill in their name."

Marek took in the words, but remained silent as he followed behind. Somewhere along the path, another man awaited their arrival. He was even more decorated, and Marek surmised he was the equivalent of a shaman, or a religious figure equally as important to these people. "The Amnokai," the first man announced to Marek. The Amnokai dismissed the other man and he left them, heading back the way they'd come.

"Remove the mask," the shaman said calmly. Marek just stood there maintaining his façade of ignorance, but decided to shrug. The shaman approached Marek and pulled the mask off of him. "Hmm," he contemplated aloud. "Your face is troubling to me," he told Marek calmly. "Come," he said and continued down the path until they reached its end. He spread his arm out toward the mountain and Marek froze. "The four faced god sees your face as I do." On the side of the mountain were four faces staring down upon him. He could hardly breathe, and his vision came and went as the reality of what it meant sank in.

"It is true, you'd be useful," the shaman continued.

"But... your face." The Amnokai turned around and peered at his four faced god. "The people of my world will not accept you. You will be a burden to me... to my reign. I will sacrifice you before my god, Merkon, then—" The Amnokai gurgled on his words as Marek drove a toxic quill into his throat.

"You shouldn't have turned on me," he said into The Amnokai's ear. The shaman's eyes bulged open wide, and even as he fell to his hands and knees, he could see his veins bulging beneath his skin. Then he was no more. Marek returned his gaze upon the mountainside, deep in contemplation. Everyone and everything he'd ever known was long gone. Whether Hanna had survived the virus was no longer relevant. He turned and looked at the fallen shaman then, just as deep in contemplation.

"The Amnokai, huh..." Marek thought aloud. The shaman had done well with his limited knowledge, but he could usher the people into a new age... like leaping from the stone age directly into the bronze age. No more huts or shacks... no more stone-tipped weapons... no more four faced god. He made up his mind then and there that they would be the first to go, and then the world was his for the taking, and nobody would ever know who or what he truly was. He leaned down and pulled the mask from the Amnokai's dead fingers and put it back on. No... not the Amnokai, not anymore. "The Merkon," Marek said and smiled.

He grabbed a large rock from beside the trail and began smashing the shaman's neck with it until he could remove the head. Some of the spinal cord came with when he ripped it away from the body, and then he pushed the body off a cliff. He returned down the path and to the arena, except he climbed to the top, until he was overlooking the crowd that was waiting in suspense for their return. He raised the shaman's head into the air and screamed for all to hear.

"Your god deemed me worthier than your Amnokai!" His voice boomed across the arena for all to hear. They remained silent. "...and they required a sacrifice to realize my place as his successor... as your Merkon!" The crowd began to buzz excitedly. "The Merkon!" The buzzing among the people began to grow louder, on the edge of eruption. "The four faced god gave The Merkon visions of our future! Together we will conquer the land, far and wide! A new age is on the horizon, and The Merkon will lead you to glory!" The people roared and cheered then, and his claim would not be challenged. He tossed the shaman's head down into the arena among the dead tribute and toxic flowers.

Later, as Marek washed up in Amnokai's living spaces, easily the most luxurious place within the city, a knock sounded on his door. "Enter!" he called out, for he was expecting company. Ashelyn entered his quarters and rushed over to him, embracing him in a hug.

"I was worried," she told him. "...but... how... your face..." She brushed his face with her hand. "I do not understand why the four faced god would favor you in this way." She buried her face in his chest. "The people will not either. If they knew what I know... it does not matter. I am happy you live."

"They didn't," Marek said plainly as he coddled her face in his hands, petting her cheeks affectionately.

"What do you mean?" Ashelyn asked calmly, cooing in his clutches.

"I'm sorry it has to be this way, truly." A tear nearly formed in his eyes, but he knew what must be done... he'd prepared himself for it. There would be no loose ends. Before Ashelyn could pull away and turn her inquisitive eyes upon him, Marek mustered all of his strength and snapped her neck in one quick motion. So began The Merkon's reign.

Snowfall's Embrace

The sister moons hovered high above the young girl as she fled her captors. She could hear them barking orders to their bloodhounds, whose growls bounced off the forest's many trees. Her breaths came heavy, and her heart felt even heavier in her chest. She came to an abrupt stop next to a great oak, a pale hand planted against its cold bark as she gasped for air, trying desperately to push her rising anger away. This was the time for clear thoughts and focus, not for seeing red. Her hand slid from the bark and joined her other upon her knees. She closed her purple eyes and focused on her training. She steadied her breaths, inhaling deeply through her nose, hold, and release... repeat.

Her pointed ears flickered at the sound of the bloodhounds as they once more picked up her trail, a fresh vigor in their howls and their growls. Even the men found their spirits rejuvenated as the hunting dogs took off excitedly. Her rest was short lived however, and she forced herself to continue running through the moonlit woods. Her heart pounded in her ears and drowned out the men's gleeful cheers behind her. As her vision blurred, the alarming sensation felt all too familiar to her. "No, no, no!" Lexa gasped between breaths. Blotches of darkness invaded her sight, which only reinforced the memory bubbling to the surface of her mind. Try as she might ignore it, the blotch was all she could see, and then it took on another form altogether.

The eclipse bore into her soul as she grappled at the snow, desperately trying to anchor herself, but the compulsion to let go was overwhelming. Something akin to a woman's voice spoke within her mind, except there were no words... just a mother's affectionate embrace. Tears streaked down her pale cheeks as she began convulsing uncontrollably. "Mo–th–er?" Lexa groaned as her blazing emerald eyes slammed shut, and her piercing scream rang into the night. She felt the impending punishment of a mother's disciplinary scold.

Lexa felt her face grow hot, despite the frigid midnight snow encompassing her writhing body, as a tremendous pressure took hold of it. She thought her face might explode, and she tried to cry out for someone... anyone, but the effort sent the stabbing pain of a dozen knives into her throat. She didn't know who she'd tried calling out for, but she heard the words come out as a virulent series of snarls instead. The faint bluish-red behind her eyelids grew darker as the glowing runes covering her body were snuffed out, a dark furious red taking its place and quickly followed by the sound of snapping bones.

Lexa nearly screamed aloud, reenacting the memory playing in her mind's eye as she raced between trees looking for some place, any place, to take cover and hide. They'd be on her soon enough she knew, and frustrated tears of rage and sorrow escaped her emerald eyes, a low rumble spewing from between the elven fangs behind her knurled lips. She spun around just in time to slash a pouncing hound with her dagger-like nails, inciting a yelp from the animal. She charged the canine as it recovered from the unexpected parry, and both elf and hound tumbled away in a tangled mess of claws and fangs, the vicious animal relentlessly gnashing at her, its growls echoing through the night.

She felt the bones in her face cracking and twisting, an explosion of agony paralyzing her where she lied beneath the eclipsed moons. She tried grabbing at her face as it contorted, both collapsing in on itself and bulging outward, but she could not as the bones in her arms followed suit. They too, bent this way and that, breaking and reforming as she roared at the apathetic moons gazing down upon her. Every pore on her body flared with a strange sensation as white and black fur sprouted everywhere, covering the entirety of her small frame. "It's okay, little cub," she heard Jarik say from somewhere far, far away. "I am here. I'm right here. Don't fight it... just let it happen."

"No!" Lexa screamed in the hound's face. It snapped its maw open and closed repeatedly, trying to tear her to shreds. "No!" She screamed again, even more insistently. She caught the dog's jaws in either hand and began pulling them apart, her scream a blood-curdling one, digging her nails into its flesh as she did so. The hound began wriggling its body frantically in an attempt to escape, but could not break free of Lexa's grasp, its whines barely audible to the girl. Then another hound attacked her viciously, its maw clamped around her leg. She gritted her teeth through the pain and pulled with all her remaining strength, and heard the popping of the hound's jaw dislocate but before she could finish the job, yet another hound was upon her.

Their sharp teeth tore into her legs as they shook their heads back and forth, and Lexa cried out as her strength gave out. She couldn't keep her eyes open as the hounds gnawed on her and dragged her body toward their masters, whom were not far. She tried to ignore the excruciating pain searing through her body and find something else deep within her... something worth fighting for. She opened her eyes, unsure what had happened.

"Ah," Jarik said, breaking the silence as well as the confusion. *The eclipse!* Lexa looked up into the night sky, but the alignment had ended and the moons had gone their separate ways for some time. The girl's face scrunched up as she tried recalling the lost time. "You're awake! How are you feeling?" He towered over her, a man built of corded muscle. His hair was tied back and fell past his shoulders. His beard was braided in several places and tied together and still reached below his neck. He knelt beside her and when he attempted to examine her, Lexa recoiled from him.

"Get away from me!" Lexa snapped at him, and indeed he took a step back. "What did you do to me? Why can't I remember what happened?" There was pain and mistrust in her purple eyes as she scowled at him, but there was also resentment, a look the man knew all too well. He'd taken her from everything she'd ever known.

"Only what the fates had in store for you, Lexaldra." Jarik replied. "It wasn't I whom chose you." Jarik looked into the distance toward his feline companion, who was scouting the perimeter. "Nor was it Nyx. You're special, Lexaldra..."

"I don't want to be special!" Lexa spat at him, furious

with his rhetoric, and for avoiding any blame. She wanted answers... she wanted to go home. She glared upon the large, muscular, human man with a hatred that burned in her viridescent eyes. "What happened?" she asked again, coldly, venom dripping from the words as her chest rose and fell dramatically. "Why can't I remember?"

"You received a gift, a... blessing." Jarik chose his words carefully. "The blood of the borealis tiger flows through your veins now, child..."

Lexa's emerald eyes flared as her chest rose and fell more rapidly. "What does that mean!" She screamed in the man's face. "Tell me what happened to me!" Lexa felt a familiar sensation in her face, followed by an incredible pain. Every pore of her body tingled and she cried out in horror. Her body seemed to have a mind of its own, and she began hyperventilating as fear and confusion became her masters.

Jarik reacted swiftly and knelt beside her, grabbing her chin firmly in one hand. He turned her face so their eyes were locked onto one another's. Lexa tried to pull away... flee from the man, but she was no longer in control of her body. "What's happening... to... me?" Lexa asked as her body began twisting and snapping apart. Jarik ignored her question as he stared into her eyes and began chanting in a language she didn't understand. She watched as his brown eyes took on a bright blue hue, and she felt her body return to normal... no more pressure behind her face, no more tingling all over, and no more blazing red behind her eyes.

"You are a changeling, Lexaldra," Jarik told her plainly. "It may not feel like a blessing now, but you'll learn to see things differently in time. It will be hard work, and take a lot of discipline, but with my training you will learn to maintain control and—"

"A... changeling?" Lexa scoffed alarmingly. "What are you talking about!"

Jarik exhaled deeply and rubbed his eyes. "It's better if I show you." He distanced himself from Lexa and removed his many layers of furs, folding them up and placing them neatly at his feet, remaining only in a loincloth. His brown eyes became a bright piercing blue once more, and he began growing, his limbs and face changing drastically as he assumed the form of a giant bipedal borealis tiger. Lexa was in awe at the sight of the mighty beast, her anger having dissipated in the wake of her intrigue.

"It doesn't hurt?" Lexa asked once she'd recovered from her stunned wonderstruck.

"No," Jarik replied, his voice deeper than it had been in his human form. "It will only hurt until you and your tiger reach an understanding... until you both learn to accept one another. The symbiotic connection takes years to accomplish for some, but I'll be here to help you along the way." Jarik returned to his human form and put his clothes back on. Lexa was torn between fascination and calamity. She had been changed forever, and she had no say in it whatsoever... it wasn't fair.

Weeks would pass as Jarik and Lexa traveled further and further away from home, periodically hunting and resting during the day, and training hard in the evenings. They'd spar, practice stealth, and hone her heightened senses. Jarik would induce Lexa's transformations so she might learn to grow comfortable with it, get to know her inner tiger, and hold on to whatever consciousness she could while the tiger was in control. Sometimes they'd stay in a particular camp for a few days at a time and double down on Lexa's training, but no amount of praising the girl or letting the occasional attack slip through his defenses would win her over. She maintained an aura of contempt towards the man, but he never gave up trying to do right by her. He treated her as if she were his own child, and the tough love was one of necessity... neither could afford to be soft. He kept her safe and her stomach full, and did everything he could to ease her pain whenever she changed forms.

"How do you bring me back?" Lexa asked one night as they sat around their campfire. "When I lose control, I mean. What language is that?"

"It is my native tongue, but it is not the words that bring you back," he explained to her as they ate their catch of the day. "It's a gift not many possess, but in time you'll learn as well."

"Right..." Lexa retorted bitterly. "...because I'm *special.*"

"It is a gift passed down from..." He paused in contemplation. "Alright, fine." Lexa perked up, leaning forward, hungry for his secrets. "When the time comes remember this, child: center yourself. Find a balance... return to your roots... who you are, and where you come from. We are not just the present. We are the sum of all our experiences... I hear you speaking to your ancestors sometimes—" He looked up and Lexa scowled at him dangerously. "Don't worry! I never listen, but bringing someone back from that place, where they lose themselves in what has become of them... requires you to channel yourself from a fundamental place. Reach deep within yourself and find a marriage between your past and your present. Then find it within them. Chanting just helps me focus."

Lexa regarded him with a blank stare. "I don't get it."

Jarik chuckled. "You will when you're ready, and when the time comes, try speaking to them as you'd speak to your ancestors." Though she continued to show Jarik disdain wrought of resentment, he understood the interaction had taken their relationship the slightest shift in a more positive direction, and he'd take what he could get.

Lexa was a fast learner, and over the months she caught on quickly when it came to finding the balance within herself necessary to make the symbiotic connection with her tiger. She wasn't quite there yet, but her level of control was unlike anything Jarik had ever seen, in regards to how quickly she was progressing. Her fits of lost time after shapeshifting diminished considerably for someone so young, and so freshly turned. She'd even shown signs of awareness and control in her tiger form, but was never able to maintain it for long. As talented as the young girl was she was just as stubborn, rebellious, and defiant. Jarik knew she'd do and say things just to hurt him out of spite. He knew she resented him for taking her from her people, but he had no choice... he only hoped she'd see that someday, and come to see him as he'd come to see her: like family.

He gave her breaks where he would tell her stories, myths, legends, all hiding valuable lessons she'd need to learn sooner rather than later. Over the course of many more months, Lexa's disdain toward him dwindled bit by tiny bit, though her stubbornness proved as steadfast as she was fierce, and their bond remained one of master and reluctant student. Lexa insisted on keeping him at arm's length, even when he could clearly see her desire for a connection beyond that, determined to internalize everything and do it all on her own. His lessons, stories, advice, sympathies, and affections all went unacknowledged.

One night as they slept, Lexa was awoken by a strange feeling. She shot up and focused on her heightened senses, listening intently for whatever may have caused her to stir. It was a silent night, still, and warmer than most. Lexa got up and looked to the heavens, inhaling deeply through her flared nostrils. "Ancestors... why can't I hear you?" She feared her connection to her people had been severed and without their guidance, she needed to rely on her instincts. Lexa held her breath and listened. A subtle sound came from somewhere deeper in the woods surrounding their camp, and she sprinted across the snow as only a snow elf could, leaving no trace of her passing through it, nor any sound. It was quiet, and there was nothing out there. She thought perhaps she was being paranoid, but when she turned to return to camp, she found a large footprint in the snow. It wasn't human... nor was it hers or Jarik's tiger's. She looked back into the dark woods, her eyes lingering upon them for a long moment before she shook the feeling of being watched and returned to camp and slept.

"I think we're being followed," Lexa told Jarik the next day. "I felt something watching us last night, and I found a large footprint of some kind of animal."

Jarik erupted with a booming laugh and offered the girl a smile. "What kind of animal do you suppose could take on either one of us? The mighty Jarik and the fierce Lexaldra." He knelt down to her eye level and ruffled her hair. "You are the apex predator out here, Lexaldra."

The apex predator.

The bloodhounds tore at Lexa's flesh with teeth and claws as she began to resist. She was alone, but she didn't have to be afraid. Her purple eyes flared with an emerald fire, and as her body began changing its shape, her less severe wounds knitted themselves closed. The bloodhounds tried latching themselves onto her with clenched maws, but Lexa's transformation pushed their teeth from her flesh and they skittered aside, unsure what to do next. No longer was Lexa a lithe little elven girl, but a bipedal tiger, black and white like Jarik's, nearly a foot taller in the beastly form. She opened her own maw, full of razor-sharp teeth, and growled angrily at the hounds. They neither attacked nor fled, but stood their ground and waited, and when Lexa pounced upon them the forest echoed with their cries.

"There she is!" a voice called out from the night.

"Get her!" ordered someone else.

Lexa swiped at the bloodhounds one last time, looked at the fast approaching men and their weapons, and fled. She covered a lot more ground in her tiger form, but she wasn't in complete control either. Arrows zipped past her, thumping into trees and missing, but they weren't missing by very much. One grazed her side as she leaped through the woods and she growled angrily, bringing her padded fingers up to examine her blood-soaked hand. She saw red and lost control.

"On your feet, Lexaldra," a deep voice ordered the girl. They'd been at it for hours, and Lexa had already gone through all the basic forms he'd taught her again and again, all while struggling to keep her cool. She missed the days when his feline companion would come to her aid, growling at the man and reflecting her frustrations. Nyx was long gone though, having been ordered to return to her home, and thanked for her services. "Attack me." He wore heavy furs, but still managed to move with the grace of a seasoned warrior. He pointed his lance at the girl he'd grown so fond of. Lexa puffed out her chest, bared her fangs with a hiss and ran across the snow in a way that almost made the man jealous. She leaped upon him with a ferocity that made him proud. "Disarm me!" He yelled at her as he batted her off of him repeatedly. The girl got swung several feet away landing with a hard thump.

"This is impossible!" she screamed frustratingly. Flashbacks of all the times she'd struggled to hit her opponents growing up, the warriors of the Snehóvškriátok tribe, flooded her mind and filled her with the childish frustration that she'd felt so many times before. "You are so much bigger than me!" The man stabbed his lance into the snowy ground and stared hard at her.

"Size is irrelevant, Lexaldra." The girl winced as he spoke. "Once you realize this, you will be the fiercest woman in the realm!" With an alarming speed the man swept the lance from the ground and lunged at her once more.

"Jarik!" she screamed as she barely managed to evade his attacks, but he did not relent. She growled her frustrations as Nyx once did. She continued evading his attacks until he left her an opening, and without hesitation she closed the distance between them, swooping into his reach and latched onto his enormous arm. She flung herself up and over his arm and onto his shoulders, locking her legs around his neck and squeezed her thighs. He reached up and tried grabbing her but she hissed and dug her fangs into the flesh of his hand. The lance dropped to the ground as he recoiled his hand in pain. Lexa began beating his scalp with her fists and he dropped to his knees before rolling over and squishing her under his weight. "Jarik!" she wheezed angrily.

He stood up laughing and was about to reach down for the lance when the snow elf pounced upon him with frightening agility. She stabbed him in the chest over and over with her fingernails as if they were knives, breaking the skin and drawing blood. She had lost her temper, and she was losing control.

"Lexaldra, stop!" he snapped, but she could not hear him. Her purple eyes morphed into a raging green inferno and her face began to contort. Jarik threw her a dozen or more feet away and pulled the furs off before gracefully shapeshifting into an enormous white tiger, letting out a powerful roar that sent birds fleeing from their perches. Lexa screamed as her bones snapped and her skin tore apart. The tiger's coarse fur burst through her pores as her body surrendered to the beast that lurked within her. Only seconds passed before the enraged cub attacked the behemoth Jarik. With her enhanced speed, she was difficult to pin down. She climbed all over him, biting and scratching, but it wasn't long before he pulled her away and held her by the neck in his pawed hands. "Enough!" he screamed in her face as she thrashed around wildly, squeezing her throat until her body went limp.

She was still breathing when he set her down. He began chanting in his native tongue as he'd done so many times before, and she painfully reverted back to her elven form, crying. "I'm sorry Jarik!" she groaned as tears streamed down her face. Though she'd never admit it to either of them, she hated disappointing him. He knelt beside her and coddled her in his large arms, comforting her as a father might comfort his daughter.

"There's nothing to be sorry for, my child," he said soothingly. "These things happen, but you'll get past it. You're a strong, fierce girl. It has been an honor getting to know you these past couple years, and you've shown levels of control I've never seen. It may not seem so, but it is the truth." He embraced her in an enormous hug. "Let's call it a day. Go fetch some firewood, and I will prepare your favorite stew. How does that sound?"

Lexa grinned and kissed him on the cheek. "Please call me Lexa," she told him before scampering off into the woods. Jarik, still in his tiger form, watched her go and beamed silently until a scent abruptly hit him in the face. He was immediately on high alert and looked around for the source. An arrow plunged into his chest and he roared in pain. He yanked it out as another flew past him. The arrowhead was masterfully crafted, and made of pure silver, burning his chest even after removing it. Jarik looked back in the direction Lexa had gone and saw her running back his way.

"Go!" he screamed at her. "Go Lexa! Run, now!" Then nearly a dozen hunters surrounded him, stalking toward him with cautious, calculated steps. Bows were cocked by even more men further away, blades drawn by those nearest him. The howls of hunting dogs rang in the distance, and Jarik chastised himself for his foolish complacency... he should've sensed them much, much sooner. He let out another mighty roar as they attacked. Mere seconds passed and three lied dead at his feet, but he was quickly overcome by their silver inlaid weapons, and their foreign tactics. More arrows plunged into his flesh as he fought ferociously, and Lexa watched as his head fell from his enormous body that had already begun changing back to his human form as it collapsed into the snow. She was shook to her core, her glossy eyes bulging open widely in horror. She wanted to scream... tears streamed down her cheeks, but his voice reverberated through her mind. She knew she couldn't linger... already, the sounds of the hunting dogs grew louder in her sensitive ears.

When the snow elf came to, she was lying somewhere deep within the woods, covered in blood. She quickly checked herself for any injuries, but they had all closed as the transformations expedited a changeling's healing abilities. A thorough sniff told her it was not hers, but the blood of multiple individuals she did not recognize. She tried to recall what happened, but her tiger had taken full control of the situation, wholly suppressing her awareness. She curled up into the fetal position against a tree and cried into her lap. "I'm sorry, Jarik... I'm so sorry."

She sobbed for a long while, and it began to snow. The icy-blue glow of her runes were visible through her eyelids, and only became more pronounced as the temperature dropped. "I shouldn't have been so mean to you!" Her sorrow evolved into fury and she screamed curses into the early morning sky. She slumped against the trunk and her shoulders bobbed up and down as she cried some more.

"Why can't I hear you?" she asked the sky more calmly

than before. As she spoke in her ancestral tongue, her runes glowed brighter for a moment and the snowfall reacted, avoiding contact with her skin. There was one direction where the snow embraced her with its soft, soothing kisses, she realized as she moved her hand in an arch before her... but if she moved her hand back another way, the snow danced around her once more. "What is this?" She breathed quietly. "Ancestral arcanum..." She paused in thought and turned back toward the snowfall's embrace... As Lexa got to her feet and oriented herself, listening and following, the snow guided her through the woods until she saw something familiar... giant footprints in the snow. With no destination or Jarik to guide her wherever they'd been headed, she followed them, her curiosity far outweighing her sense of dread.

Eventually, the tracks ended and Lexa tried and tried again to repeat whatever incantation she'd spoken before, but nothing. Just as a heaviness was settling in her chest, she heard the sound of children laughing. She followed it to a clearing, and sitting in the clearing was a village. Her heart nearly leaped from her chest in gleeful relief, and she began to run from the tree line toward the buildings, then stopped. Backpedaling slowly back behind the trees, Lexa remembered the dangers of people. She looked at the dried blood upon her hands and her arms and started scrubbing herself clean with fistfuls of snow. From her vantage point she could see a bunch of buildings, the largest of which was furthest away and centered between the others, human people pulling carts, another person pulling a bucket of water from a hole, and some small children reaching for it excitedly. There was a communal fire much like back home, and people tending to a field nearby. There were other smaller fires where the remains of an animal were being cooked, and the smell made her stomach rumble, pleading with her to feed it.

She watched the man tending to the cooking meat as he went back and forth, seasoning them and turning them, and caught herself drooling. She waited until he disappeared from sight, scanning the immediate area until nobody else was in a direct line of sight of her, and sprinted for the food. She had to hide behind various supplies, stacks of hay, and beneath tables when the man returned to his duties. It wasn't long before a crowd gathered nearby and the food was dispersed among the people, and she could do nothing but watch from her hiding place, listening to her stomach's quibbles.

"Here," a voice right beside her said. It was a girl's voice, and Lexa's heart stopped.

She turned to see a hand lowering a piece of roasted meat for her, glanced back to the gathering and decided the people were too preoccupied with their feast to notice her retreat. She grabbed the meat from the girl's hand and skittered from her hiding place, catching a brief glance of the girl as she did so before quickly returning to the tree line. She was roughly her size, had long straight hair the color of leaves in the autumn before they fell to the ground, and kind green eyes. The girl had smiled nervously at her, but Lexa hadn't stuck around to exchange a greeting or even a thank you. She tore into the meat when she was safely hidden by the trees, and when she finished, she found a spot where she could see the sky and lied there on her back, her stomach full, and her thoughts drifting away from her.

She must've fallen asleep, because she hadn't heard

anyone sneaking up on her, and she was very startled when the same voice spoke to her once more. "Are you out here by yourself?" she asked in a sweet, but concerned voice. Lexa almost jumped out of her skin, sprang up and froze in place, unsure what to do or say. She decided it was best if she fled, and the girl must've reached a similar conclusion. "Please don't run away." She took a seat right where she had been standing, just feet away from Lexa, making no moves to advance on the snow elf. "I'm Maeve. What's your name?" Lexa looked past Maeve and back toward the village. "Don't worry. It's just me, I promise."

Lexa visibly relaxed and took a good solid look at the girl for the first time. She was a little bigger than her but not by much, and her hair was straighter and cleaner than any hair she'd ever seen. There was a look about her, something so... innocent, and recognizing it warmed her heart. "My name is..." She contemplated giving the girl her formal name for a moment. "...Lexa."

Maeve studied her for a moment and smiled. "Well it's nice to meet you Lexa. I've never met a kid that wasn't from here. Are you lost?"

"You... you aren't afraid of me?" Lexa asked her, and the girl giggled.

"You don't seem very scary to me. Hungry, and maybe a little dirty," Maeve laughed again, "but not scary. You're just a kid, like me."

Lexa smiled. She couldn't help it, but it only lasted a moment. "I wasn't always alone, but the... my... my father's gone now."

"It's just you?" Maeve asked, a sadness in her voice.

Lexa nodded and fought away the tears threatening to fill her eyes. "Can I come closer?" she asked, and again, Lexa nodded. Maeve scooted to Lexa and gave her a hug. "I'm sorry Lexa." When she pulled away she finally saw how filthy Lexa truly was. Her white hair was a mangled and dirty mess undoubtedly filled with knots. Her pale features were hidden behind layers of dirt... even her ears and eyelids were filthy. When Maeve looked into Lexa's eyes though, she stopped analyzing the elven girl, her eyes lingering on Lexa's. "You have such pretty eyes!"

Lexa didn't know what to feel, but she looked away, her cheeks growing hot. "I like your hair," Lexa replied awkwardly. "It looks so... smooth."

Maeve giggled. "Wait here, okay? I will come back when everyone is asleep. I don't want my parents to get suspicious. Will you wait for me?"

"Yes," Lexa replied.

Maeve nodded and smiled, and was about to get up before turning to face Lexa again. "How old are you? I'm eleven and a half."

"I think I'm ten?" Lexa answered. Jarik had said it'd been a couple years, and she was eight when he took her, so it was her best guess.

"I think you could be eleven," Maeve told her. "Stay here. I'll come back for you."

Lexa lied back down smiling. Maeve was the first human she'd ever met that wasn't afraid of her or that tried to kill her... or that stole her away from everything she'd ever known. There hadn't been a speck of hatred, anger, fear, disgust, or ill will directed toward her... only kindness. In a strange way, Maeve reminded her of home, the last place she had known only kindness. Not that Jarik wasn't kind to her, but he came with a lot of mixed feelings, especially since he never told her his true purpose in taking her in the first place. She supposed she'd never know now.

A little bit after dark, once the village had gone quiet for an hour or so, Maeve returned. "Lexa?" she whispered into the darkness. "Lexa, are you there?"

"Yes, I'm here," Lexa answered as she stepped into the moonlight cast by the closest of the two moons overhead.

Maeve grabbed her by the hand. "Come on!" she said excitedly as she tugged Lexa toward the village.

Lexa wanted to ask her if it was safe, or if she was sure whatever they were doing was a good idea, but decided she could trust the girl. Maeve led her to a small shack that stood on stilts, a fire burning beneath it. Lexa had never seen anything like it before, it was bizarre in every sense of the word. Inside, a hanging lantern bathed the room in a soft pleasant glow, and a large tub of water big enough to fit two adults took up almost the entirety of the shack. A pile of clean clothes was folded up on a bench beside the entrance along with a basket full of herbs and plants she didn't recognize, and some other objects she wasn't familiar with either. "What is this?" Lexa asked, her interest piqued.

"It's called a bath house. My father and some of the other adults here built it when I was seven. It is the most amazing thing ever, trust me! You are going to love this." Maeve smiled and picked up the basket. "Get in the water."

Lexa started to climb into the tub and Maeve laughed. "How can you get clean if you keep those dirty rags on? I promise I won't look." She turned around and covered her eyes. "Tell me when you're in the water."

Lexa removed what had once served as clothing, but between the bloodhounds and her transformations, they did look more like rags than anything else. She looked over her shoulder to see Maeve turned away and covering her face with her hands, then stepped into the water. Never in her life had she experienced hot water before, and the feeling was sensational... She moaned aloud, for it was a spectacular feeling indeed. She sunk down to her chin. "Okay," she said.

Maeve turned and smiled. "Feels good huh?" Lexa nodded, hiding her smile from the girl. "My ma loves the bath house. She will spend hours in here sometimes, if she can." She laughed as she gathered some of the things from the basket. She sprinkled some herbs in the water. "This is lavender. Ma says in addition to its wonderful fragence... frag... erm, scent, it can help with burns and rashes, but isn't useful like this. This is for the smell. Smells good huh?" she asked Lexa.

Lexa's senses were heightened after Jarik turned her into a changeling, and there was no mistaking it, the lavender's scent was strong, but it was pleasant all the same. She nodded as she watched Maeve go through the basket.

"First, I'm going to treat your scalp, and then I'll wash your hair." She pulled a jar from the basket filled with some sort of thick creamy paste. "This is used to scrub the scalp. It's good for it for some reason. It might sting a little. Ma makes it with stinging nettles, but it's good, don't worry." Maeve lifted a bucket. "Look up."

Lexa did as the girl instructed, and Maeve poured water over her head, soaking her hair without getting any in her face.

She repeated it a couple of times and then scooped some of the paste out of the jar with her fingers and grimaced a bit as she rubbed her hands together. "Are you okay?" Lexa asked.

"Yeah, they'll break up and wash right off in the water." She began scrubbing Lexa's scalp with her fingernails, and massaging the cream in with her fingertips, and Lexa audibly groaned. "I love when ma does mine too!" She giggled. After a thorough scrub she rinsed her hands off in the tub. "Okay, as that sits, I'm going to clean your face if that's okay." Maeve took some cloth from the basket and soaked it in the tub, then carefully rubbed down Lexa's face when she did not object, making sure to get the hard-to-reach places her dad never thought about getting when he's the one washing her. She was careful around her eyes and nose, and then got her ears as well. Setting that cloth aside, Maeve grabbed a clean one from the basket and pulled out another jar with a different substance within.

She explained to Lexa what it was made with, just as she had with the first cream. It was a combination of various plants and roots that was good for the skin. She laid it across Lexa's face. "Let it sit there while I rinse this out of your hair."

Maeve would go on to treat Lexa's hair with multiple other products her mother had made from the native foliage, and then let Lexa wash herself with more of the same, concocted specifically for different parts of the body. Lexa genuinely felt cleaner than she'd ever felt in all her life and took mental notes of the names of all the plants and roots Maeve had mentioned, and what they looked like. "Your mother sounds like a very smart and caring woman," Lexa said to Maeve as the girl pampered her.

"Yeah, she's great!" Maeve beamed. "What's yours like?"

Lexa got quiet. She didn't know how to respond to that. "I don't remember," she answered finally.

"Oh... I'm sorry Lexa, I didn't mean to—"

"No, it's okay. Don't be sorry. I grew up hearing stories about her and my father. They were great warriors, and beloved by our people," Lexa elaborated.

"Warriors?" Maeve cooed. "Sounds like they were impressive!"

"I believe they were."

"...but, I thought you said you were with your father until recently?" Maeve asked.

Guilt came over the snow elf, remembering the lie she'd told her just a few hours before. "...not my real father, but he was kind of like one to me." Lexa grew quiet, her guilt multiplying exponentially for having never reciprocated the feelings.

"So... where are you from?" Maeve asked as she rung out and dried Lexa's hair. She grabbed a brush made from animal bones and began working the knots out of the elf's hair.

"The tundra plains." Lexa told her, trying not to melt into the water as the girl brushed her hair, another sensation she was unfamiliar with, and one that eased her mind from her guilt-ridden thoughts and self-reflection. "My tribe is always moving around and following the herds. We slept under the stars every night."

"Wouldn't that be cold?" Maeve asked.

"Not for snow elves." Lexa said more enthusiastically. "The cold doesn't bother us at all. The elders used to tell us stories of our ancestors from long ago who lived in magical palaces made of ice that reached high into the heavens. There were tens of thousands of us back then."

"Whoa!" Maeve gasped, beaming at the majesty of Lexa's description. Once she got the knots out she began methodically combing the brush through Lexa's hair. "Are there not a lot now?"

"No," Lexa answered.

"Do you have any brothers or sisters? I have two brothers. They're crazy! But also really sweet."

"No, just me. I'm alone now."

"No you're not," Maeve told Lexa. "You have me now, and I'm sure ma would love you."

Lexa wasn't sure how to respond to such open kindness, so she didn't, but she couldn't hide her smile. Once Maeve was done pampering Lexa in the bath house, and Lexa got dressed in the clean clothes she'd set aside for her, Maeve snuck her into her room in her family's home. Lexa had never worn proper clothes like that before. It was almost like they were hugging her, and they smelled good too. She was sure this was all some fantastical dream, and none of it was real; nothing felt this... normal. They eventually fell asleep after talking through the later hours of the night, laying side by side. Come morning, Maeve was awakened by her family stirring about. She sprang up nervously and wondered what she would do, but as she looked at Lexa she just smiled.

The snow elf slept peacefully, quietly, bundled beneath the many cotton blankets and furs upon Maeve's bed. The sunlight peaking in through her window shutters reflected off the elf's now clean, dry snow-colored hair... white wavy locks that were now to her shoulder blades when her hair had only been to her shoulders prior to her bath. As if seeing them for the first time since she'd met the snow elf, Maeve saw the faint markings covering Lexa's face, her neck, and the rest of her body that she could see. "Whoa..." She mouthed silently to herself as she examined them.

"Maeve!" her mother called out to her. "You up?"

Maeve scurried out of bed and left the room. Sometime later, when Lexa woke up, she was happy to see Maeve beside her. Was this real after all? Lexa combed her fingers through her now smooth clean hair and felt flutters in her stomach, a pleasant feeling. "Good morning sleepy head!" Maeve greeted her. "How'd you sleep?"

Lexa yawned and stretched. "That might be the best sleep I've ever had." She laughed at the absurdity. Was this how regular people lived? It was nice, she thought.

"So... don't be mad, okay?" Maeve blurted out suddenly. Lexa shot her a confused look. "I told ma about you. She's waiting to meet you, come on!"

Maeve led Lexa out the bedroom and was greeted by a delicious smell, and more smiling humans. An adult woman, and two children maybe half her and Maeve's age. "Good morning, Lexa! I'm Maeve's mother, Aeryn," the woman greeted warmly. "My heavens, aren't you a precious thing! Are you hungry?"

Lexa nodded, her mouth salivating. "Thank you," she said, a bit overwhelmed.

As they all sat at a table with food in front of them, Maeve's mom passed utensils out. "Maeve tells me you're an orphan?"

"Ma!" Maeve barked, giving her mother an embarrassed look, silently pleading for her to stop. "I'm sorry Lexa…"

"No, it's okay," Lexa told Maeve before addressing her mother. "Yes, and I don't mean to be trouble. I can leave—"

"Oh, don't be silly!" the woman interrupted. "We don't get many visitors here, and we definitely don't get to meet many elves! You're no trouble at all. Please, eat up!"

She didn't have to tell Lexa twice. As Maeve and her siblings grabbed their utensils, Lexa dug into her food with her bare hands, shoveling it all into her mouth. It wasn't until she'd eaten half the food in front of her before she realized nobody else had eaten. They were watching her, looks of bemusement on their smiling faces. Lexa looked to Maeve beside her, the girl's face scrunching up in a grin, and then everyone started laughing. "What?"

"I've never seen such enthusiasm!" Aeryn chuckled. "How long have you been on your own?"

Lexa looked to Maeve, who was holding her utensil up, emphasizing it as she scooped up her food and put it in her mouth. Lexa looked down and found hers sitting not far from her food. "Oh!" She laughed embarrassingly. "I… it was just my… Jarik, a man that had taken me in, it was just us for a while, but he's gone now. It's only been a few days."

"Oh…" Aeryn looked as if she was going to cry. "You poor thing. Well, it isn't anything special, but you're welcome to stay here with us for as long as you like."

"Really?" Lexa and Maeve both asked excitedly.

"You'll have to help out like everyone else, but I don't see why not." Aeryn watched Lexa scoop some food onto her utensil and shove it in her mouth.

"Thank you! I can hunt! I can cook! I can—"

"No need, child," Aeryn told her. "Those are jobs for the men, but I'm sure we'll find you something that compliments your skills. Now eat up, there's lots to do."

"Hi, Lexa!" Maeve's little brother yelled from across the table as if he'd been ready to burst.

"Lexa!" Maeve's other little brother chimed in. "Want to play tag with us later? Please! Oh please?"

"That's Declan and Finn," Maeve introduced them.

"You have really pretty eyes!" Declan said.

"I like your hair!" Finn added.

Aeryn and Maeve started laughing as Lexa seemed to shrink from the attention. "How about we let Lexa get settled in first, shall we boys?" their mom said as she scooped them into her arms and started roughhousing with them.

Over the course of the next few days, Lexa was introduced to their neighbors, their father, Liam, sat in on lessons that were required of all the children every morning, and got acquainted with the task she'd be doing as part of her contribution to the village. She wasn't unfamiliar with sewing as many of the women of the Snehóvškriátok back home were the ones crafting the every day necessities, and she'd learned how, but it wasn't until she'd met Maeve that she actually enjoyed it. Before, she just wanted to be a warrior, but she'd come to enjoy the simplicity of Maeve's people and the lives they'd built for themselves in their comfortable little village, a sanctum safely tucked away from the many dangers she was accustomed to elsewhere. She felt liberated of the burdens she didn't know she'd been carrying her whole life, free to just be another kid.

The village seemed a bit weary at first, but no less inviting or accepting as Maeve's mother was. They used similar tools to sew as her tribe had: tiny sharpened bones, and though she hadn't sewn in a long time, the skill quickly came back to her. She used techniques the Snehóvškriátok women had taught her, techniques the village people were unfamiliar with but really appreciated, and she was able to teach them in turn. They taught her how to make string from fibers gathered from various types of plants, something her tribe had not explained when she was little. Lexa quickly became accustomed to the daily routine and grew comfortable with her part in it.

Mornings were spent teasing Declan and Finn, though it was more of a free for all between the children, everyone brushing each other's hair, and eating at a table as a family. Liam, Maeve's father was there sometimes, but he was usually the first one up, and helping the other men of the village with whatever projects they had going on when he wasn't part of the hunting party. After that the children attended their morning lessons, and then were released for the day to enjoy the afternoon eating and playing before the older children assumed their duties to the village for a few hours. Then they were free to play and do whatever they liked until everyone came together at the end of the day to enjoy the day's catch, or whatever the hunting party brought home.

Perhaps Lexa was simply oblivious or didn't think too much into it, as Maeve had become her closest friend in the village, but some of the other kids treated her unfairly. Whether it was because she was an elf, or just different altogether, but one day as all the kids played together they finally decided to let it be known. Lexa and Maeve were playing jump rope with Declan and Finn, the boys swinging the rope back and forth as the girls skipped through back and forth giggling. Lexa always lasted the longest, and they all thought it was super impressive, but she didn't understand why. Some other kids, some boys and some girls, approached them as Maeve stumbled and stepped aside to watch Lexa continue. They took the rope from Maeve's brothers and intentionally swung them aggressively, hitting Lexa to the ground and laughing at her.

"Not as good as she thinks she is, is she?" one of the girls said.

"Why are you really here, elf?" one of the boys asked her as she sat up on the ground. "Your own people not want you around?"

"Shut up!" Maeve yelled at the boy and shoved him to the ground with both hands.

"Hey!" he cried out angrily.

"Why would you say something so cruel?" Maeve barked at the boy.

"Maeve..." the boy stammered. "I—"

"You will apologize to her right now Connor!"

"Why should he?" another boy accompanying him asked before glaring at Lexa.

Maeve glared at them, her face turning beat red. "Now! Or I'll tell Miss Barnes it's your lot that's been farting in her jars!" Lexa tried not to laugh aloud at Maeve's threat, but it worked. Their faces turned ghostly white, and the girls that had taken their side looked sick and cried out in horror and disgust.

Connor looked at Maeve as if he was begging for her to take back the threat, which only made the girl cross her arms and double down on it. He looked at Lexa, all the fight having fled his face and replaced with guilt, and lowered his head in shame. "I'm sorry, elf…"

Maeve cleared her throat and he snapped his head up at her, fear in his eyes. "I'm sorry Lexa, really."

Lexa got up, walked up to him smiling, and leaned in as if she were going to thank him and accept his apology. In one swift motion she raised her hands like claws and sneered at him, flashing her fangs, her eyes wide and growled fiercely. He screamed, his voice cracking, sounding more like a girl's cry, and Lexa, Maeve, and all the other kids started laughing. "Apology accepted, Connor." Lexa giggled.

"Shut up!" Connor ashamedly groaned to his friend, but then joined in on the laughter. "You too, Caden," Connor told his friend, nodding to Lexa, and Caden abruptly stopped laughing, causing everyone else to laugh some more.

"I'm sorry Lexa, really," Caden said. The others chimed in and they all played tag together for the rest of the day.

Later that evening after everyone had eaten, Lexa was running around with the other kids some more when something from the tree line stole her attention. She stopped and listened, her heightened senses tingling. She began wandering toward the trees and looked toward the tree line. The feeling she got was akin to the one that had woken her up the first time she found the large animal footprint way back when her and Jarik hadn't been together all that long. She had mixed feelings as she stared into the depths of the trees, the sun getting lower and lower with each passing minute. On the one hand, whatever was out there could be a threat to the village. She contemplated informing the men, so the hunting party might keep an eye out. On the other hand, she felt a sense of gratitude toward whatever left those footprints behind. She would not have found the village if not for following them after all.

"Hey," Maeve said, drawing Lexa from her thoughts. "Everything okay?"

"Yeah," Lexa answered her friend, deciding to let it go for the time being. "Thank you for earlier Maeve, for standing up for me like that."

"You don't need to thank me. What are friends for? Come on!" Maeve pulled her back toward the village.

As she followed along she looked over her shoulder toward the tree line once more. She'd find herself doing that a lot over the course of the next few months, half expecting for some giant animal to charge into the village, but that never happened, and neither did she ever spot whatever it was out there. Winter blossomed into spring and the snow melted, leaving behind more colors than Lexa had ever seen, as plants and flowers sprouted up everywhere. She'd grown accustomed to her new life, and was accepted by everyone, including all the children. She was one of them, and she'd never felt more at peace. She figured she'd eventually join the men hunting, and had leaned heavily into her role as a girl, fulfilling the feminine duties the village had come to expect from her. She never thought herself pretty before, but between the boys and the women, there was no shortage of compliments.

"What do you think of Caden?" Maeve asked her one evening as they talked in her bedroom. "I think he likes you."

"Likes me?" Lexa asked. "...but he doesn't say very much to me." She laughed. "I think he's afraid of me."

"Gee, I wonder why that is..." Maeve stuck her tongue out and laughed. "I think he's just nervous around you. Boys are like that sometimes when they like a girl. It's kinda weird... they're all about flexing their muscles and beating on each other, and never shut up most of the time, but when it comes to girls they forget how to talk!" The girls shared a laugh.

"What about you?" Lexa asked. "I think Connor has a thing for you, and he's cute, isn't he? I mean... for a human boy, right?"

Maeve squinted at Lexa as if trying to interpret her words differently. "Connor has had a thing for me since we were little. Like, *really* little, and I suppose he's cute, but he isn't the cutest kid in the village."

"Who do you think is the cutest kid in the village?" Lexa asked.

"Here," Maeve said as she dug under her bed for something. "I have a framed picture of them, somewhere." She fished under the bed for a moment and handed a frame to Lexa. "Oh, turn it around."

Lexa turned the frame around and took a peak. She saw a pretty, pale kid in the picture. It was a girl with purple eyes and white wavy hair, nearly invisible markings on her face, and watched as the girl's mouth curled into a smile in the framed mirror she held. Her cheeks began to flush as she lowered the mirror and shoved it into Maeve's lap. They shared another laugh and Lexa fought away the fluttering in her stomach.

Throughout the spring, Lexa would smell flowers for the first time, swim in a river for the first time and blow the other kids' minds as her elven runes would glow in the cold mountainous water. Lexa would lay under the stars with Maeve and the other kids sometimes, and tell them stories of the constellations she grew up learning among the snow elves. Other times it was just the two of them, and Lexa would tell Maeve about her ancestors, how they watched over her and the other snow elves from the ether among the stars, and how she was taught that elves had come to their world from another one out there somewhere. They'd watch shooting stars, and make up their own stories for their own constellations. Lexa's memories of Jarik and her people were slowly becoming less and less painful the longer she lived among the people... with Maeve. Her heart was happy, her life was full of laughter and joy, and she didn't think of her life before meeting Maeve all that often anymore.

Lexa had never been happier in her life. That all changed one day when Lexa and Maeve woke to villagers screaming. Lexa ran from the room and found Aeryn at the door. She turned to see Lexa beside her. "Oh, Gods." Her voice trembled with fear. "Stay back, Lexa. You and Maeve need to take the boys and hide!"

"What's going on?!" Lexa asked the woman. She rushed under her arm and looked outside, but Aeryn tried shoving her back inside.

"It isn't safe, child!" Aeryn snapped at her.

"I can protect you!" Lexa snapped back, and Maeve's mother was struck dumbfounded. Lexa looked out the door and what she saw made her blood run cold in her veins. A beast was storming through the village tearing people apart. The men that had remained behind when the hunting party left earlier that morning had already been slaughtered. Distant howls pierced the still morning, echoing from somewhere deep in the woods, and the beast stopped abruptly to return its own deafening howl before resuming its feral attack on the defenseless village. Lexa ran out the door from under Aeryn's arm and toward the beast.

"Lexa!" Maeve cried out after her.

The beast spun around, spotted, and charged at the elf. It stood on its hind legs and had a wolf-like face, a primal rage burning in its eyes. Lexa slid between its legs, digging her claw-like fingernails into its flesh as she did, and the beast roared in anger. It kicked Lexa away ferociously, the snow elf flying across the way and hitting another building hard, getting the wind knocked out of her. As she recovered she watched the beast turn back toward Maeve's home and advance in that direction.

"Hey!" Lexa roared as she got back on her feet and charged the monster. The beast turned to regard her once more and roared defiantly, racing back toward the snow elf. Lexa dove at it and slashed at it with her nails with reckless abandon, but it then it snatched her up in its beastly hands.

"Lexa, no!" Maeve ran out after her, and Lexa's heart sank when the beast turned and scooped her friend up in its maw and shook its head violently. Maeve went flying down the main avenue of the village, her garments pooling with blood as she lied unmoving upon the ground.

"Maeve!" Aeryn's blood curdling cry rang in Lexa's ears, but so too did it ring in the beast's ears. It seemed momentarily stunned as it held Lexa in one hand, its eyes blinking rapidly for a second. A second was all Lexa needed, however. She forced the shock of seeing her friend motionless in a pool of her own blood aside, and with all her strength she drove her fingers through the beast's chest, her nails leading the way. She felt its blood pouring down her arm as she wriggled her fingers inside its chest cavity, searching for its most vital organ. With a fierce growl, Lexa retracted her hand from its chest, her fingers clutching its still beating heart... until it wasn't. Lexa dropped from its loosened grasp, landing nimbly on her feet and watched the beast look down at her confused, all its rage having evaporated.

The beast dropped to its knees and fell over dead. The village went silent, and people found themselves in shock, staring at a little elven girl covered in the beast's blood, its heart between her fingers. Lexa's chest rose and fell as the adrenaline subsided, and her eyes fell upon her friend. "Maeve!" Aeryn cried out as she rushed over to her. "Oh Gods, please!" Lexa rushed over and joined Aeryn at Maeve's side. Aeryn was desperately checking for a pulse, for any sign of life when Maeve groaned. "Oh, thank the Gods!" she cried. "Lexa, help me get her inside! Get the door!"

Lexa dropped the beast's heart where she stood, having forgotten it was in her hands, and did as she was told. As she held the door open for Aeryn, she looked at the ravaged village that had become her home. Many were dead, and many more were injured, but the ones that hadn't suffered any injuries were already tending to their wounded. *How did this happen?* Lexa thought, and wondered if she could've prevented it.

Relief overwhelmed Lexa and Maeve's family as she came to. The girl was not too injured, and had only suffered some minor puncture wounds across the sides of her torso. They would heal though, and as Aeryn treated Maeve's wound, Lexa would assist the other villagers with their wounded. The hunting party, including Maeve's father, returned to the village empty handed, and missing a few men. They had run into similar beasts in the woods, and some of the men had been killed. He was relieved to find that his family was okay, and overjoyed Lexa had been with them when he learned of her bravery. She was hailed a hero, even if some of them had grown suspicious of her after seeing what she was capable of.

That evening, strangers wandered into their village. When the villagers gathered to meet their new guests, they were greeted by more than a dozen men, highly decorated and some more heavily armored than others. They were warriors of sorts, from far away by the looks of them too.

"Greetings!" one of the men said. "We have been hunting our prey for days, and my men are quite weary. When we spotted this village, I was hoping we would find hospitality, however..." The strangers looked around and took in the sight of dead bodies and injured villagers. With a gesture, the one who'd been talking had a few of his men investigating the area. "It seems you have had your own troubles recently."

"We would gladly break bread with you and your men if our hunt had been successful earlier, but we were attacked by monsters, and were forced to return empty handed," Liam announced to the strange warriors.

"These monsters..." the man said. "Can you describe them to me?"

"They were like monstrous wolves! Could walk on their hind legs. Incredibly strong, and vicious," one of the other men from the hunting party answered.

"Why? Were these beasts the prey you were after?" Liam asked.

"Over here, sir." One of the strangers that had been investigating the area called out. "It's as you said. One of them attacked these people. It's dead." The man leaned down to investigate the body further. "Missing its heart."

"Listen up!" Their leader called out. "I need everyone injured by the beasts lined up. These things are cursed, and we'll need to inspect the injuries to determine how to best treat them, or they will fester uncontrollably." The man announced and spat on the ground. "Wretched things."

"Who are you?" Liam asked since no one else had.

"Bone Collectors," the leader said as he tapped the crossbones insignia he wore as if it were obvious. Neither Liam nor the others seemed to recognize the name. "Your village is well hidden."

"Ignorance is bliss aye, Devon." One of the Bone Collectors laughed, but their leader, Devon, glared at him. "Erm, commander, sir," he corrected himself.

"We are protectors of the realm. Those beasts that attacked you have been our sworn enemies for decades! We specialize in hunting them and exterminating them... and treating the wounds they inflict upon the innocent, so gather up! Let's see!"

Aeryn was about to escort Maeve to the lineup of injured villagers, but Lexa stopped her with an upraised hand, shaking her head at the confused woman. A moment later the

Bone Collectors slaughtered all the injured in one fell swoop. Cries and horrified screams of grief and wailing filled the evening air. Aeryn gasped under her breath and stumbled backward into the home, her hand over her heart.

"Why?!" one of the village men screamed as he, Liam, and some others drew their weapons on the strangers, but they knew they were outmatched. If they attacked, they'd all perish.

"Those beasts were werewolves, and death is the only cure. You're welcome," Devon retorted.

"Werewolves?" a villager asked.

The Bone Collector commander rubbed his eyes incredulously. "You really have no idea how lucky you people have had it hidden away here," Devon said dismissively, thoroughly flabbergasted by their ignorance.

Lexa snuck outside, remaining behind the adults, and looked on in horror at the freshly murdered victims. She gasped in shock and took note of the men's faces, a lethal look coming over her. She knew she recognized the scent... these so-called Bone Collectors had murdered Jarik, and damn near killed her as well. She began shaking with rage, but she knew there was nothing she could do, so she remembered Jarik's training instead. She steadied her breaths, inhaling deeply, hold, and release... repeat. Her emerald eyes became purple once more as she continued watching between the men's legs.

"Very well!" Devon said. "Be grateful you'll all be safe now, and take care!" The Bone Collectors turned to leave the village, but then Devon paused. He turned around, deep in contemplation. "Who killed that werewolf there?" he asked. He studied each and every reaction, following a set of stray eyes behind the men's legs before someone began to speak up. "You there! Behind everyone. Come out here."

Lexa took one last deep inhale and exhale to calm her nerves before stepping out from behind the men's legs. Still covered in the blood of the werewolf, she stopped before the Bone Collectors as they looked her over. "Impressive!" Devon cooed. "You did that? All by yourself?" Lexa nodded a single nod. "An elf among humans... isn't that peculiar? You weren't injured?" Lexa shook her head once, left to right, and back. The Bone Collector studied her for a moment before turning his sights on Liam. "How long has this one resided here? A few months, I wager?"

"A few years, actually," Liam answered. "She was orphaned. Hunting party found her with her deceased parents a few winters back, and we took her in. You may go now, if that is all." Devon turned his sight back upon Lexa, a smug look on his face, and left with his men in tow.

Things would start calming down after a couple weeks, and the villagers forced themselves to carry on with their routines, but the lives lost would haunt them forever. Despite being hailed a hero to their people, some people's trust in Lexa waned after the strange confrontation with the foreign warriors, but Maeve and her family were steadfast in her defense. As far as they were concerned, Lexa didn't have to explain herself to anyone, not even them. Maeve's injuries were healing nicely, in no small part due to her mother's ointments and creams. She was determined to bring a lightheartedness to everyone around her, though Lexa couldn't shake an ominous feeling that had taken hold of her since the attack, despite her friend's best efforts.

One night as Lexa and Maeve were laying in the grass deep in conversation, the full moons rose into the night sky, Maeve's eyes rolled into the back of her head and her body began convulsing violently. "Maeve!" Lexa called out to her. "What's wrong? What's happening?"

Connor ran up to them when he heard Lexa's alarming inquiry. "Is she okay?"

"I don't know!" Lexa cried.

Connor got on his knees and started examining Maeve, but then her bones started snapping, twisting and turning. Her face began contorting. "What the hells!" Connor cried out. "What is this?"

Lexa's heart sank. This couldn't be happening. Maeve began screaming in agonizing pain, and Lexa remembered what that felt like. "No!" Lexa screamed. A crowd had now gathered around the girls, including her horrified parents, and no one knew what to do. Maeve was changing. Lexa wracked her brain desperately, trying to think of something she could do. Maeve's eyes rolled back around, and had changed colors.

Lexa began praying desperately to her ancestors in elfish, and then an idea came to her. She looked Maeve in the eyes and continued her prayers. She filled herself with memories of her people, traversing the endless tundra alongside the snow elves, hunting, and joining in elfish traditions, song and dance. She remembered her sole purpose growing up, and her need to be a warrior of her tribe. She filled herself with what it meant to be Snehóvškriátok. She reminded herself of the significance of her tattoos... how speaking the language made her feel, and never once broke eye contact with her friend.

Maeve's convulsing began to slow down, becoming less and less intense, and then her body relaxed in Lexa's arms. Maeve's bones slowly began repairing themselves as tears ran down the sides of her face. "Lexa... what... happened?" she asked softly. *It's working!* Lexa began crying, and smiling as she kept going. Her parents and her brothers were trembling and crying as well, and Connor pat Lexa on the shoulder and nodded his approval. "Some... thing's... wrong..." Maeve cried before erupting into another screaming fit. Her bones began snapping violently as her body threw her back and forth upon the ground, her face collapsing in on itself and extending outward into a maw.

"No!" Lexa cried. "It didn't work... Maeve! Come back to me!"

Then Maeve's transformation was complete. She grew silent and stopped convulsing. Lexa backed away slowly, and the others followed her lead. She waved them away and remained closest to her friend. Maeve leaped upon Lexa, slashing and biting at her. "Maeve!" Lexa cried. "It's me!" Lexa looked into Maeve's bright red eyes and saw no sign of her friend there. She knew how terrifying and confusing losing herself to her tiger had been, and that was with training and guidance... was this what she was? A were... tiger? What exactly did that even mean? "Stop!" Lexa roared at her friend, her eyes igniting with a green blaze, her words echoing between her voice and a growl. Maeve leaped from Lexa and ran toward the other villagers. "No!" Lexa cried as she chased after her friend. She watched helplessly as Maeve leaped upon Connor and slashed him to shreds, biting at his neck and whipping her head back and forth before taking off toward

Declan and Finn. She ran past the dying boy after Maeve.

Lexa changed into her tiger form as she chased after her friend, tremendously picking up speed upon shapeshifting. She caught up to Maeve just as she was about to tear her brothers apart and Lexa threw her arms around her. "Please..." Lexa begged, tears running from her tiger's eyes. "Please Maeve... come back... please, please, *please*..."

Maeve began roaring and shaking wildly in Lexa's arms, her maw snapping open and closed at her little brothers just feet away from her. She howled into the night for a split second, and then silence. Lexa snapped her neck with no other options before her, and held her friend in her arms as they both fell to the ground. They returned to their human and elf forms as they did, Lexa coddling the corpse of her best friend, a gut-wrenching pain stabbing her in the abdomen. She choked on her wailing as the air fled her lungs, and pulled Maeve in close, hugging her for her dear life... as if her tears and her hugs could bring her back. "I'm sorry... Maeve... please..." She heaved and choked on her sobs as she rocked back and forth with her. "Why!"

"She's one of them!" one of the villagers yelled.

"Did you see!?" another snapped.

"She's a monster!"

"Get her!"

"Wait!" She heard Liam try to defend her, but his conviction quickly faded, or the others merely drowned him out as they came for her.

Lexa looked up through the glaze in her eyes trembling, and would've let them kill her, but the tiger had other ideas. A bipedal borealis tiger fled into the woods... for how long she did not know, but she fled until the world faded into darkness. When she came to she was tied up and being dragged through the woods by the Bone Collectors. They were talking amongst themselves.

"—good idea Devon, using the werewolves to find the little bitch," one of them said, praising their commander.

"It's a shame about the commander though. I wish we didn't have to—" another started.

"Anders was a fool! He was weak!" Devon retorted angrily. "He wasn't willing to do what was necessary to get the job done. He didn't deserve his—"

Rage burned within Lexa as she tried tearing free of her restraints. "Let me go!" she screamed at them.

"—I knew that was you!" Devon sneered at her as he shuffled over to their little prisoner. "I mean, what were the odds? You killed all our hounds, and a lot of my men that night." He spat at her.

"Good!" Lexa screamed at him, and he smacked her across the face. "You killed my friends! I'll make you pay! I'll make you suffer!" Lexa growled, and a fist was the last thing she saw before her world went black again.

When she came to once more, some of the Bone Collectors were asleep, and some were on watch. A fire burned nearby, and she was tied up and leaning against a tree as if she were haphazardly thrown aside, half upside down where they'd left her. She coughed and grimaced as she tried to break free, but it was no use. Clouds of fog rolled through the forest as the fire burned low in the very early morning and everyone was asleep minus the one or two standing guard, when the forest grew eerily silent. Even the air seemed to go still, and the hairs on the back of Lexa's neck stood on end. A familiar feeling overcame her. She sucked in her breath as she heard the near silent approach of something large... her heart began to race, and all she could do was wait. The closer the entity got the more terrified she became as an unnatural and ominous wave of unease settled over the camp.

Men began screaming and gurgling as they were attacked and mutilated. Others drew their weapons, but Lexa couldn't see what was happening. She could hear the fighting, the screaming and the primal fear in the men's cries, but she had no idea what was happening. "Ancestors save me." Lexa wept with a shaky voice. She clenched her eyes shut as she listened to the nightmare unfolding around her. Then all was silent.

"There is no need to fear me, child," a deeply guttural, yet kind, voice said to her.

Lexa peaked out of one eye and gasped in astonishment. The largest bear she'd ever seen stood before her, and it had spoken to her! Patterns of scars ran across its bulbous face, but it made no move to do her any harm. "Have you been following me?" Lexa asked the bear.

"Indeed," the bear answered as he tore through Lexa's bindings. "Are you hurt?"

Lexa thought about the question for a moment, and then burst into tears. "I killed her!" she cried. "Why did I have to do that! It isn't fair! I killed her!"

The bear wrapped her in a giant hug, stroking her hair with its large paws. "I know, child..." he said. "Truly, a tragedy. I'm so sorry."

"Who... what... are you?" Lexa asked as she started to

calm down in the comforting embrace.

"My name is Baelezar," the bear answered. "And like you, I never want anything like that to happen ever again. I've seen what you're capable of. We can change the world, you and I. I know of a place where we'll be safe from these Bone Collectors, where all of us will be safe. We can help others like your friend, so that you will never have to do anything like that again. Will you join me, little one?"

A fierce fire burned inside Lexa, and she nodded, more determined than she'd ever been. "My name is Lexaldra." She corrected him. "Lead the way," and just like that, her purpose became clear. She knew she couldn't save everyone from Maeve's fate, but she'd be damned if she didn't try.

An Interview with Nathan Sykes

WHEN DID YOU START WRITING AND WHY?

I began writing in elementary school. At first, I wrote stories tailored after the ones I'd tell while playing with action figures and stuffed animals. When I was a little older, I began writing fanfiction stories after some of my favorite tv shows or video games such as *Digimon* and *Golden Sun*, respectively. I'd often draw my characters and creatures from my stories, and eventually I made friends who wanted to participate in both the drawing and writing. I was disappointed when those collaborations didn't pan out, but it wasn't long before I discovered roleplaying on A.O.L. Instant Messenger, where people collaborated and told stories together in the chat rooms. Somehow, I missed the transition from AIM to forums, but I've been using them since a friend brought them to my attention in 2011.

WHICH AUTHORS OR BOOKS OR MEDIA INFLUENCED YOU THE MOST AS A WRITER?

The first book I ever read was *The Transall Saga* by Gary Paulsen, and that book paved the way for all others. Off the top of my head, I'd say R.A. Salvatore's *Drizzt Do'Urden* books were highly influential in many ways. Laurell K. Hamilton's *Anita Blake Vampire Hunter* series is up there as well. Darren Shan's *Cirque du Freak* series is another, and of course *Lord of the Rings. Beast Wars Transformers, Digimon, Star Wars, Titan A. E., Final Fantasy, Legend of Dragoon,* and even the *Legend of Zelda* games were all influential as I developed as a writer.

WHICH AUTHORS OR BOOKS OR MEDIA HAD THE BIGGEST IMPACT ON YOU AS A PERSON?

By and large, the biggest impact on me as a person award goes to the animated series *Avatar the Last Airbender.* Nothing comes even remotely close for me. In my opinion, it is the closest thing to perfection a show has ever given us in terms of its writing and appeal. It's taught me many things. Respect for nature and spiritual woo-woo aside, the world building and character development are unmatched, and reset the standards for me. As a fantasy enthusiast, and fan of eastern cultures and religions, *Avatar* touched me to my core. Highly recommended. Anyone that is a fan of good writing and storytelling in general should absolutely give it a watch.

WHICH OF YOUR ORIGINAL TWELVE PROMPT STORIES ARE YOU MOST PLEASED WITH?

I am probably most pleased with 'Under the Sister Moons' as it is the origin story for one of my roleplay characters, but I am biased. If I had to choose another though, I'd have to go with 'The Beach' as it forced me out of my comfort zone, and even though it's unlike most things I write, I think it proved to me that my talents are broader than I knew. 'The Beach' is also a deeply personal piece of work to me, and was a means of closure, to a degree. It was also the only story directly inspired by real life people and events. So maybe proud is the right word for it.

WHICH OF YOUR ORIGINAL TWELVE PROMPT STORIES DID YOU FIND THE MOST DIFFICULT TO WRITE?

'Cargo.' With that story, I had built this whole world and idea in my head (that was honestly probably better fit for a roleplay or a novel), and to make things worse, January was a very rough month for my entire family. The combination of all these factors made fleshing out the story painstakingly difficult for me. I think at some point I just decided to phone the rest of it in and get it over with to have one less thing to worry about. It is a mess of a story, but the concept is there, and that's what excited me.

WHAT BOOK ON WRITING DO YOU RECOMMEND?

This may or may not come as a surprise to anyone that's read my work, we're all our own worst critic after all, but I have never once read a book on writing. I have listened to some podcasts on mistakes not to make when writing fantasy though. I took a creative writing class in high school once, and went through a poetry phase after that.

WHAT ADVICE WOULD YOU GIVE AN UNPUBLISHED WRITER?

Just write. You don't need to have a story in mind at all. Don't let the idea that whatever it is has to be perfect prevent you from writing. It doesn't need a beginning, middle, or end. Start with a scene you are most excited about. Find a writing contest in your area, or online, and make it a goal to participate. Also, if the idea of collaboration appeals to you in any way, give roleplaying online a shot. Just search for rp sites. I've made a lot of friends, and have written a lot of work I am very proud of doing that. Just write.

DO YOU HAVE A "DREAM PROJECT" AS A WRITER? WHAT WOULD IT BE?

I've always wanted to write a movie script for Gary Paulsen's *The Transall Saga*, but I have no experience writing scripts. I've thought about taking a course, but I'll likely pick up a book one of these days. I think even more than that though, a dream project of mine would be writing a novel, or series of novels, based on some of my roleplay characters and their worlds. I have a dream of following Tolkien's path, and seeing them on the big screen in either animation or live action someday. Or on a streaming service as a series. I'd also love to write for television.

YOUR STORIES WILL BE PUBLISHED IN A SET OF PROMPT COLLECTIONS WITH THE OTHER THIRD GENERATION AUTHORS BUT ALSO AS A COLLECTION OF JUST YOUR OWN WORK. DID YOU HAVE A CONSCIOUS THEME FOR YOUR COLLECTION?

I did not have a conscious theme in mind when I started, no. However, as the months went on I realized there was indeed a theme taking place. Every story, perhaps with the exception of one, at the very least hints at the existence of other realities, or higher dimensions, etc. Some of the stories throws it right in your face too, making that concept front and center. At some point I had the idea to use that to connect all the stories, as if they all existed in the same universe somehow, but I chose not to go that route. Although, I did connect some stories, even if in subtle ways.

WHO DO YOU WRITE FOR AND HOW DOES IT DRIVE YOU TO CREATE?

On the one hand, I write stories for my collaborators. A lot of my work wouldn't exist without them, and I look forward to expanding our characters and their stories. On the other hand, I write for me. I have so many concepts and ideas constantly flooding my mind, and it's very rewarding when I get to realize them and read it when I am done. There's a sense of accomplishment that comes with that. I'd be remiss though if I didn't mention the characters. As they often exist in my mind, almost with their own identities, they write themselves. There have been numerous times I thought a story would go one way, but the characters had other ideas, and I can't deny them the story they are telling. So, I write for them too. The drive to create is just something that has always been there, and writing is just an outlet for me. If I could draw, I'd be doing that as well.

OPTIMALLY, WE'RE ALWAYS GROWING AND IMPROVING AS AUTHORS. TALK ABOUT HOW YOU GREW OR CHANGED AS A WRITER OVER THE COURSE OF CREATING YOUR STORIES FOR *PROMPT: THE THIRD GENERATION*.

This is a hard one for me. I guess, writing to a deadline changed a lot for me. I was one of those people who suffered from needing everything I write to be perfect. So, often times I just wouldn't do it, because I knew nothing I wrote would suffice. Definitely not good enough to be published, and so it's always been something I did just for fun, for my friends and I. I can't tell you how many times I nearly backed out of this project, all those months leading up to the first prompt, because of that. I didn't believe anything I could possibly write for a publisher would ever be good enough to wrap up and tie a bow on, but getting published has always been a dream of mine as well. I had an opportunity, and I knew if I backed out, I'd never do it. I held my breath as the first month approached, read the prompt, and got to work. I'd say I grew as a writer by overcoming myself, and the limitations I've always placed in my own way, and learning that it doesn't have to be perfect, because nothing is perfect... except maybe *Avatar the Last Airbender.*

IMAGINE THE PERFECT COVER FOR YOUR PERSONAL COLLECTION. DESCRIBE IT... EVEN IF IT'S IMPOSSIBLE.

There's a scene in 'Under the Sister Moons' where the protagonist gets a glimpse of the cosmos, and all the intertwining realities and worlds, upon worlds. I'd pick that scene despite how abstract it sounds, bordered by mystical runes, each rune representing an aspect from each story, and maybe another layer to the realities depicted in the image.